ELLERY QUEEN'S EYES OF MYSTERY

ELLERY QUEEN'S EYES OF MYSTERY

Edited by
ELLERY QUEEN

THE DIAL PRESS

DAVIS PUBLICATIONS, INC.
380 Lexington Avenue
New York, New York 10017

COPYRIGHT NOTICES AND ACKNOWLEDGMENTS

Grateful acknowledgment is hereby made for permission to reprint the following:

The Last Answer by Hal Ellson; © 1962 by Davis Publications, Inc.; reprinted by permission of Scott Meredith Literary Agency, Inc.

The Gracious, Pleasant Life of Mrs. Afton by Patricia Highsmith; © 1962 by Patricia Highsmith; reprinted by permission of McIntosh & Otis, Inc.

Credit to Shakespeare by Julian Symons; © Julian Symons 1961; reprinted by permission of Curtis Brown, Ltd.

Blood Brothers by Christianna Brand; © 1965 by Christianna Brand; reprinted by permission of Brandt & Brandt Literary Agents, Inc.

The Opposite Number by Jacob Hay; © 1966 by Jacob Hay; reprinted by permission of Harold Matson Company, Inc.

The Beddoes Scheme by James Powell; © 1967 by James Powell; reprinted by permission of the author.

The Lithuanian Eraser Mystery by Jon L. Breen; © 1969 by Jon L. Breen; reprinted by permission of the author.

Wit's End by Michael Harrison; © 1970 by Michael Harrison; reprinted by permission of the author.

A Matter of Equine Ballistics by R. Bretnor; © 1971 by R. Bretnor; reprinted by permission of the author.

The Man Who Never Told a Lie by Isaac Asimov; © 1972 by Isaac Asimov; reprinted by permission of the author.

Over the Borderline by Jeff Sweet; © 1975 by Jeff Sweet; reprinted by permission of the author.

Whatever Happened to Barty Wilson? by Mary Braund; © 1974 by Mary Braund; reprinted by permission of McIntosh & Otis, Inc.

Mr. Strang Picks Up the Pieces by William Brittain; © 1975 by William Brittain; reprinted by permission of the author.

Dover Does Some Spadework by Joyce Porter; © 1976 by Joyce Porter; reprinted by permission of John Cushman Associates, Inc.

C As in Crime by Lawrence Treat; © 1967 by Davis Publications, Inc.; reprinted by permission of the author.

The Long Cry for Help by Hugh Pentecost; © 1975 by Hugh Pentecost; reprinted by permission of Brandt & Brandt Literary Agents, Inc.

The Adventure of the Three R's by Ellery Queen; copyright 1946, 1952 by Ellery Queen, renewed; reprinted by permission of the author.

The Tiger of the Mekong by MacLean O'Spelin; © 1975 by MacLean O'Spelin; reprinted by permission of the author.

Night Fear by Lika Van Ness; © 1976 by Lika Van Ness; reprinted by permission of the author.

The Tragedy at Brookbend Cottage by Ernest Bramah; reprinted by permission of the Estate of Ernest Bramah.

Blind Man's Bluff by Roy Vickers; copyright 1947 by The American Mercury, Inc., renewed; reprinted by permission of James Brown Associates, Inc.

CONTENTS

5 More of the "Best"

THE EYES OF MYSTERY

INTRODUCTION

Dear Reader:

Most devotees of fictional detection believe that the series of annual anthologies called BEST DETECTIVE STORIES OF THE YEAR began in 1946, under the editorship of David C. Cooke. In concept, this is not true. The series really began 15 years earlier, in 1931, when Carolyn Wells edited THE BEST AMERICAN MYSTERY STORIES OF THE YEAR: VOLUME ONE, distinguished by the inclusion of Dashiell Hammett's "The Farewell Murder."

Carolyn Wells's anthological experiment became an authentic series the next year, 1932, when she published THE BEST AMERICAN MYSTERY STORIES OF THE YEAR: VOLUME TWO, again including a story by Dashiell Hammett—"Death and Company."

Then the short-lived series stopped. Why Carolyn Wells decided not to continue we don't know. Perhaps she tired of annual "searches and seizures"; perhaps the reading, sifting, and decision-making had become too arduous. Perhaps the first two books did not sell well; in this period, the early Thirties, mystery-crime-detective anthologies were not popular in the United States—very few were published. True, they were quite popular in England, but not many copies crossed the Atlantic.

Fourteen years later David C. Cooke took up the 'tec torch, reviving the series under a change in title—to BEST DETECTIVE STORIES OF THE YEAR. He steered the sleuthian ship for 15 years (1946-1960), then passed the baton (really mixing our metaphors!) to Brett Halliday, whose 'tec tenure lasted only two years (1961-1962).

The publisher, in selecting a new editor, made the wisest of choices. In 1963 Anthony Boucher occupied the editorial chair and edited the series brilliantly for six years (1963-1968). His untimely death brought the series to a shocked halt—no annual volume appeared in 1969. Then the editorial helm was placed in the expert hands of Allen J. Hubin, who steered a steady criminological course for six years (1970-1975), maintaining the excellent traditions of the series.

Pressures of other duties and projects, especially Hubin's editing of the monumental THE BIBLIOGRAPHY OF CRIME FICTION, 1749-1975, forced him to give up his stewardship of the BEST, and in 1976 the editorial reins were picked up by Edward D. Hoch, who, for six years (1976-1981), carried on the noble work of Wells, Cooke, Halliday, Boucher, and Hubin, upholding the high standards of this important series, which, including its time lapses, has endured for 50 years.

It occurred to us that you would enjoy reading representative stories of the BEST. We decided to begin with the collection published in 1963, and to pick one story from each year (except 1969) through 1977. To have started earlier than 1963 would have involved greater difficulties in clearing the reprint rights and would probably have resulted in choosing stories that are perhaps dated for today's taste.

Here, then, in this anthology, we present the eyes of mystery (two stories, one about a blind detective, the other about a blind murderer), selections from the BEST (14 stories), and 5 other "Bests." They will give you many hours of excitement, suspense—and startling surprise.

ELLERY QUEEN

Hal Ellson

The Last Answer

The nightmare began at 12:30 one hot summer night when Strickland, who had to finish writing a report by morning, took the elevator in the nearly empty building to his office on the 13th floor ...

Downtown is a tomb after six o'clock. Come up from the subway at midnight and you can walk for blocks through the side streets and meet no one—not a single soul.

Broadway isn't much different—a little traffic, a few pedestrians, dark brooding buildings, with a light here and there where a cleaning woman is doing her chores.

Strickland stopped off at Carey's Bar. It was quiet there—a few office workers drinking. He ordered—all he wanted was a quick one, but a great deal of work waited for him at the office and the night was hot. So he had another, then a third before he finally stepped outside.

Immediately he was made aware of the buildings towering over Broadway, somber and silent, yet neither dead nor asleep; with a thousand shadowed eyes they kept watch over the street.

Strickland turned into a narrow side street, his shadow stretched before him enormously, his footsteps echoing. He came to the building where he worked, and entered. The lobby was empty, and the single elevator door was open.

He walked to it, expecting to be greeted by sleepy-eyed Pat. Instead, a new operator was there, standing stiffly at attention, at 12:30 on a hot night in an almost empty building.

"Floor, please?"

Strickland almost laughed, then caught himself. "Thirteen," he answered.

The door closed abruptly, and the car shot upward at full speed, while the new operator stood at attention, ramrod-straight. Another misplaced General, Strickland thought, and on a sweltering night like this.

The car halted at the thirteenth floor. The operator reached out to open the door, stopped his hand, and turned. His eyes were like two black stones, his face a pale mask.

"Well, aren't you going to open the door?" Strickland asked.

"A question, sir."

"Let's have it."

"Are you for freedom or for slavery?"

Strickland wanted to laugh, but the man was dead-serious, wait ing, impatience smoldering in his black eyes.

He's either drunk or crazy, Strickland decided, no longer amused by the situation he found himself in—alone, thirteen floors up in an elevator with this strange character. He stared back at the man, wondering which side he favored. To give the wrong answer might mean—

"I'm for freedom," Strickland answered.

"The correct answer," said the operator, abruptly opening the elevator door.

Strickland stepped out and went down the dim hall to his office. He was somewhat ruffled by the incident. I wonder what would have happened, he thought, if I hadn't given the right answer . . .

An hour later the elevator door opened on the thirteenth floor. Strickland heard it from his private office, then heard footsteps on the marble floor. He raised his head, wondering. It was too early for the night watchman to be passing through.

The office door opened and closed. Strickland turned in his swivel chair and waited. A shadow darkened the frosted glass of the door.

"Who's that?" Strickland asked.

The door swung open, and there stood the elevator man. "I hope you're not too busy," he said.

"I've a report to finish by morning, but what is it?"

"Another question, sir."

Strickland wanted to order the fellow out, but he restrained himself. Obviously this fool was drunk. He had to be, and it would be better to humor him. "All right, what's the question?"

"Are you for truth or for lies?"

"For truth," Strickland said quickly. "Now if you don't mind . . ."

"One moment, please."

"Yes?"

"You're quite sure you believe that?"

"Quite sure. Now will you please go."

The elevator man stood motionless, as if he hadn't heard, then turned to the door, opened it, and looked back. "I believe you," he said soberly.

"Thanks," Strickland answered. The door closed behind him. The report lay on his desk, but he didn't go back to it. Instead, he listened. Footsteps sounded in the hall. Finally the elevator door clanged shut.

Strickland reached for the phone to call the building superintendent. He wanted that stupid elevator operator off his back. He picked up the phone, then dropped it and smiled. After all, a complaint might cost the elevator man his job . . .

The night didn't cool off. At 3:00 A.M. not a breath of air stirred. Strickland pushed away the report, wiped his face, got up, and left his desk. The water cooler was in the big office. He'd gone to it half a dozen times already. Now as he filled another paper cup, he again heard footsteps in the hall.

The night watchman, he thought, and the front door opened, closed. Footsteps padded toward the receptionist's empty desk, passed it, and softened on deep carpet. Suddenly the elevator man stepped from behind a glass partition.

Strickland stood perfectly still, the paper cup forgotten in his hand. From the other end of the room he watched the elevator man go to the office he'd just left, pause in front of the door, then go in.

Only a few moments later the elevator man came out. Strickland still hadn't moved. His best chance was to remain quiet and perhaps the fellow would go away.

But the elevator man didn't go away. Stopping, he surveyed the big office, sweeping the empty desks with his eyes. Against the far wall he saw Strickland's shadow, then Strickland himself gaping at him and at the gun in the man's hand.

The elevator man smiled.

"So there you are," he said and started toward him.

Strickland tried to tell himself that this was some kind of joke, or nightmare. It certainly wasn't real. But the gun was, and obviously a madman was holding it. Everything came together now—the foolish questions, the queer face of the man, his fanatic eyes.

I've got to get that gun from him, Strickland told himself.

The elevator man grinned and aimed the gun at him. "All right, let's see how smart you are," he said. "You have another question to answer. Maybe this time you'll flunk it."

Strickland began to protest, but only to gain time. The night watchman should be here any minute.

"Shut up," said the elevator man. "Get ready to think, and you'd better have the right answer. Now, what are you for—love or hate? You've got ten seconds to give me the correct answer."

The correct answer was obvious—or was it with a madman rendering judgment? Strickland bit his under lip. The elevator man was counting the seconds.

"All right, time's up," he said, motioning with the gun.

"Love!" said Strickland, and the elevator man smiled at him.

"Very good," he said, lowering the gun. "I had an idea you'd slip this time, but you didn't. You're a very intelligent chap."

"So are you," Strickland answered quickly. "I'm sure you are, and that being the case, I know you'll listen to me."

"I'm listening."

"Look, if you hand me that gun, the whole matter will be forgotten. If you don't . . ."

"What then?"

"You'll find yourself in a lot of trouble. In another minute the night watchman will be here to clock in."

"The night watchman?" The elevator man smiled and shook his head. "I'm afraid you're mistaken."

"What do you mean?"

"He didn't pass the test."

"What test?"

"The same one you just passed. You see, I met him down below and he wasn't as smart as you. This happens to be his gun."

"You mean you killed the old man?"

"But what else? He was stupid. He couldn't answer the question correctly."

Strickland sucked in his breath, and then the phone rang in his office. He looked at the elevator operator. "I'd better answer, don't you think?" he said.

"I'll answer," the elevator operator said, aiming the gun at him again. "Come along."

They walked into the office and the elevator operator lifted the phone. "Hello," he said and listened for a few moments; then he cradled the instrument and smiled at Strickland. "A message for you. What's your name?"

"Strickland "

"Well, you're not to leave this office until you're informed to do so. You see, there's an insane man roaming the building. He's dangerous—a killer."

Strickland met the elevator operator's gaze. He saw the horrible grin on the man's face and shivered.

"Now, Mr. Strickland, what do you think?"

"Think?"

"Ah, you look confused. Perhaps you're frightened, but don't be. You're a very intelligent chap. Now one more question—the last question. Am I sane or insane? You have exactly ten seconds to answer correctly."

Patricia Highsmith

The Gracious, Pleasant Life of Mrs. Afton

"Dr. Bauer did not often find such pleasant people among his patients—but then Mrs. Afton had come to him last Monday in regard to her husband, not in regard to herself" ...

Prober: DR. FELIX BAUER

For Dr. Felix Bauer, the psychoanalyst, staring out the window of his ground-floor office on Lexington Avenue, the afternoon was a sluggish stream which had lost its current, or which might have been flowing either backward or forward. Traffic had thickened, but in the molten sunlight the cars only inched along behind red lights, their chromium twinkling as if with white heat. Dr. Bauer's office was air-conditioned, actually pleasantly cool; but something—his logic or his blood—told him it was hot, and the heat depressed him.

He glanced at his wristwatch. Miss Vavrica, who was scheduled for 3:30, was once more funking her appointment. He could see her now, wide-eyed in a movie theater probably, hypnotizing herself so as not to think of what she should be doing. There were things he could be doing in the empty minutes before his 4:15 patient, but he kept staring out the window.

What was it about New York, the doctor wondered, for all its speed and ambition, that deprived him of his initiative? He worked hard—he always had—but in America it was with a consciousness of working hard. It was not like living in Vienna or Paris, where he had been able to relax with wife and friends in the evenings, and then found energy for more work, more reading, until the early hours of the morning.

Suddenly he saw in his mind the image of Mrs. Afton, small, rather stout, but still pretty with a rare, radiant prettiness of middle-age—scented, he remembered, with a gardenia cologne. The image superimposed itself on the memory of the old European evenings.

Mrs. Afton was a very pleasant woman from the American South. She bore out what he had often heard about the American South—that it preserved a tradition of living in which there was time for meals and visits and conversation and, simply, for doing nothing. He had detected it in a few of Mrs. Afton's phrases that might not have been necessary but were gratifying to hear, in her quiet good manners—and good manners usually annoyed him—which her anxiety had not caused her to forget. Mrs. Afton reflected a way of life which, like an alchemy, made the world into quite another and more beautiful one whenever he was in her presence. Dr. Bauer did not often find such pleasant people among his patients—but then Mrs. Afton had come to him last Monday in regard to her husband, not in regard to herself.

His 4:15 patient, earnest Mr. Schriever, who got full value for every penny he paid, came and went without making a bobble on the afternoon's surface.

Alone again, Dr. Bauer passed a strong, neat hand over his brows, impatiently smoothed them, and made a final note about Mr. Schriever. The young man had talked off the top of his head again, hesitating, then rushing, and no question had been able to steer him into more promising paths.

It was such people as Mr. Schriever that one had to believe one could finally help. The first barrier was always tension—not the almost objective tension of war or of poverty that Dr. Bauer had found in Europe, but the American kind of tension which was different in each individual and which each individual seemed to clasp all the closer to himself when he came to a psychoanalyst to have it dissected out.

Mrs. Afton, he now recalled, had none of that tension. It was regrettable that a woman born for happiness, reared for it, should be bound so tightly to a man who had renounced it. And it was regrettable that Dr. Bauer could do nothing for her. Today, he had decided, he must tell her he could not help her.

At precisely 5:00, Dr. Bauer's foot found the buzzer under the blue carpet and pressed it twice. He glanced at the door, then got up and opened it. Mrs. Afton came in immediately, her step quick and buoyant for all her plumpness, her carefully waved, light-brown head held high.

"Good afternoon, Dr. Bauer." She loosened the blue chiffon scarf that did not quite match, yet blended with his carpet, and settled herself in the leather armchair. "It's so divinely cool here! I shall dread leaving today."

"Yes," he smiled. "Air-conditioning spoils one." Bent over his desk, he read through the notes he had jotted down on Monday:

Thomas Bainbridge Afton, 55. Gen. health good. Irritable. Anxiety about physical strength and training. In recent months, severe diet and exercise program. Room of hotel suite fitted with gym. equip. Exercises strenuously. Schizoid, sadist-masochist indics. Refuses treatment.

Specifically, Mrs. Afton had come to ask him how her husband might be persuaded, if not to stop his regimen, at least to temper it.

Dr. Bauer smiled at her uneasily across his desk. He should, he supposed, explain once more that he could not possibly treat someone through someone else. Mrs. Afton had pleaded with him to let her come for a second interview. And she was obviously so much more hopeful now that he found it hard to begin.

"How are things today?" he asked, as he always did.

"Very well." She hesitated. "I think I've told you almost everything there is to tell. Unless you've something to ask me." Then, as if realizing her intensity, she leaned back in her chair, blinked her blue eyes and smiled, and the smile seemed to say what she had actually said on Monday, "I know it's funny—a husband who flexes his arms in front of a mirror like a twelve-year-old boy admiring his muscles; but you can understand that when he trembles from exhaustion afterwards, I fear for his life."

With the same kind of smile and a nod of understanding, he supposed, if he should begin, "Since your husband refuses to come personally for treatment . . ." she would let herself be dismissed and leave his office with her burden of anxiety still within her. Mrs. Afton did not spill all her troubles out at once as so many middle-aged women of her type did, and she was too proud to admit such embarrassing facts as, for instance, that her husband had ever struck her. Dr. Bauer felt sure that he had.

"I suspect, of course," he began, "that your husband is rebuilding a damaged ego through his physical culture regime. His unconscious reasoning is that having failed in other things—his business, socially perhaps, losing the property in Kentucky that you told me about, not being as good a provider as he would like to be—he can compensate by being strong physically."

Mrs. Afton looked off and her eyes widened. Dr. Bauer had seen them widen before when he challenged her, when she tried to recollect something; and he had seen them narrow suddenly when something amused her, with a flirtatiousness of youth still sparkling through the curved brown lashes. Now the tilt of her head emphasized the wide cheekbones, the narrower forehead, the softly pointed chin—a motherly face, though she had no children.

Finally, very dubiously, she replied, "I suppose that might be logical."

"But you don't agree?"

"Not entirely." She lifted her head again. "I don't think my husband considers himself quite a failure. We still live very comfortably, you know."

"Yes, of course."

She looked at the electric clock whose second hand ate away silently at the precious forty-five minutes. Her knees parted a little as she leaned forward, and her calves, like an ornamental base, curved symmetrically down to her slender ankles that she kept close together. "You can't suggest *anything* that would help me to moderate his—his routine, Dr. Bauer?"

"There's not the remotest chance he might be persuaded to come and see me?"

"I'm afraid not. I told you how he felt about doctors. He says they can tinker with him once he's dead, but he's through with them for the rest of his life. Oh, I don't think I told you that he sold his body to a medical school." She smiled again, but he saw a twitch of shame or of anger in the smile. "He did that about six months ago. I thought you might be interested."

"Yes."

She went on with the least increase of importunity. "I do think if you could simply see him for a few moments—I mean, if he didn't know who you were—I'm sure you'd be able to learn so much more than I could ever tell you."

Dr. Bauer sighed. "You see, whatever I could tell you even then would be only guesswork. From you, or even from seeing your husband for a few moments, I cannot learn the facts that in the first place caused his obsession with athletics. I might advise you to help him build back what he has lost—his social contacts, his hobbies and so on. But I'm sure you have tried already."

Mrs. Afton conveyed with an uncertain nod that she had tried.

"And still, psychologically, that would be only correcting the surface," Dr. Bauer said, almost apologetically.

She said nothing. Her lips tightened at the corners, and she looked off at the four bright yellow echelons the venetian blinds made in a corner of the room. But despite the eagerness of her posture there was an air of hopelessness about her that made Dr. Bauer drop his eyes to the capped fountain pen that he kept rolling under one finger on his desk.

"Still, I'd be so grateful if you'd just *try* to see him, even if it's only across the lobby of our hotel. Then I'd feel that whatever you said about him was more—more definite."

Whatever I say *is* definite, he thought; then he abandoned his objection, his mind going on to what he must say next—that there was nothing left for her to do but go to a domestic relations court. The court would probably advise that her husband be taken away for treatment, and Mrs. Afton, he knew, would suffer a thousand times more than when he had suggested that her husband had been a failure. She still loved her husband, and divorce was not in her mind, she had said, or even a short separation. Not only did she still love him, she was proud of him, Dr. Bauer realized.

Then suddenly it occurred to him that seeing her husband, glimpsing him, might be the final gesture of courtesy he had been groping for. After he had seen him, he would feel that he had made the maximum effort it was possible for him to make.

"I can try," he said at last.

"Oh, thank you! I'm sure it will help—I know it will." She smiled and sat up taller. She shook her head at the cigarette that Dr. Bauer extended. "I'll tell you something else that happened," she said, and he felt her gratitude radiating toward him. "I was to see you at two thirty on Monday, you know; so to get away alone, I told Thomas I was to meet Mrs. Hatfield—my oldest friend at the hotel—at two thirty in Lord and Taylor's. Well, I was having lunch in the hotel dining room by myself at two o'clock, when Thomas came in unexpectedly. We never lunch together, because he goes to a salad bar on Madison Avenue. And there I was having lobster Newburgh, which Thomas thinks is the nearest thing to suicide, anyway. Lobster Newburgh is a specialty of the hotel on Mondays, and I always order it for lunch. Well, I'd just told Thomas I was to meet Mrs. Hatfield at two thirty, when Mrs. Hatfield herself came into the dining room. She's near-sighted and didn't see us, but my husband saw her as clearly as I did. She sat down at a table and ordered her lunch and obviously she was going to stay there an hour or more. Thomas just sat opposite me without a word, knowing I'd lied. He's like that sometimes. Then it all comes out at some other time when I'm least expecting it." She stopped, breathing quickly.

"And it came out—when?" Dr. Bauer prompted.

"Yesterday afternoon. He knew positively then that I'd gone to lunch with Mrs. Hatfield, because she came upstairs to fetch me. We had lunch at the Algonquin with a couple of our friends. When I came home at about three, Thomas was in a temper and accused me of having gone to see a picture both afternoons, though clearly there hadn't been time to go to a picture after lunch yesterday afternoon."

"He doesn't like you to go to films?"

She shook her head, laughing, a tolerant laugh that was almost gay. "The bad air, you know. He thinks all theaters should be torn down. Oh, dear, he is funny sometimes! And he thinks the pictures I like are the lowest form of entertainment. I like a good musical comedy now and then, I must say, and I go when I please."

Dr. Bauer was sure she did not. "And what else did he say?"

"Well, he didn't say much more, but he threw his gold watch down. It was such a petulant gesture for him, I could hardly believe my eyes."

She looked at him as if expecting some reaction, then opened her handbag, brought out a gold watch, and wrapped its chain once around her forefinger as if to display it to best advantage. As the watch turned, Dr. Bauer saw a monogram of interlocked initials on its back.

"It's the watch I gave him the first year we were married. I'm old-fashioned, I suppose, but I like a man to carry a big pocket watch. By a miracle, it's still running. I'm just taking it now to have a new crystal put in. I simply picked up the watch without saying anything to him, and he put on his coat and went out for his usual afternoon walk. He walks from three till five thirty every day, rain or shine, then comes home and showers—a cold shower—before we go out to dinner together, unless it's one of his evenings with Major Stearns. I told you Major Stearns was Thomas' best friend. They play pinochle or chess together several evenings a week. —Could you possibly see my husband this week, Dr. Bauer?"

"I think I can arrange it for Friday at noon, Mrs. Afton," he said. He worked at a clinic on Friday afternoons, and he could stop by

the hotel just before. "Shall I call you Friday morning? We'll make
our plans then. They're always better made as late as possible."

She got up when he did, smiling, erect. "All right. I'll expect your
call then. Good day, Dr. Bauer. I feel *ever* so much better. But I'm
afraid I've overstayed my time by two minutes."

He waved his hand protestingly, and held the door open for her.
In a moment she was gone—all but the scent of her cologne that
lingered faintly as he stood by his closed door, facing the dusk that
had come at the window . . .

When Dr. Bauer arrived at his office the next morning at 9:00,
Mrs. Afton had already called twice. She wanted him to call her
immediately, his secretary told him, and he meant to as soon as he
had hung up his hat; but his telephone buzzed first.

"Can you come this morning?" Mrs. Afton asked.

The tremor of fear in her voice alerted him. "I'm sure I can, Mrs.
Afton. What has happened?"

"He knows I've been seeing you about him. Seeing *someone*, I
mean. He accused me of it outright this morning, just after he came
back from his morning walk—as if he'd discovered it out of thin air.
He accused me of being disloyal to him and he packed his suitcases
and said he was leaving. He's out now—not with the suitcases,
they're still here, so I know he's just walking. He'll probably be back
by ten or so. Could you possibly come now?"

"Is he in violent temper? Has he struck you?"

"Oh, no! Nothing like that. But I know it's the end. I know it can't
go on after this."

Dr. Bauer calculated how many appointments he would have to
cancel. His 10:15 appointment, and possibly his 11:00. "Can you be
in the lobby at ten fifteen?"

"Oh, certainly, Dr. Bauer!"

He found it hard to concentrate during his 9:15 consultation, and
remembering Mrs. Afton's voice, he wished he had started off immediately for her hotel. Whatever the circumstances, Mrs. Afton
had engaged his services, and he was therefore responsible for her.

In a taxi at 10:03, he lighted a cigarette and sat motionless, unable
to look at the newspaper he had brought with him. Mid-morning of
a day in mid-June, he thought, and while he was borne passively
in a taxi that continually turned corners and met red lights, Mrs.
Thomas Bainbridge Afton was at the crisis of more than twenty-five
years of marriage.

And of what use would he be to her? To call for help in case of violence, and to utter the usual phrases of comfort, of advice, if her husband had come back and then gone away with his suitcases? It was the end of the gracious, pleasant life of Mrs. Afton, who without her husband would never be quite so happy again with her friends.

He could hear the remarks she had already made to them: "Thomas has his peculiarities . . . he has his little fads." And finally, after embarrassments, compromises, to herself: "He is impossible." Yet through pride or breeding or duty, she had maintained, along with her sense of humor, the look of being happily married. "Thomas is an ideal husband—*was* . . ."

A swerve of the taxi interrupted his thoughts. They had stopped in the middle of a block between Fifth and Sixth Avenues in the Forties, at a hotel smaller and shabbier than he had anticipated—a narrow, tucked-away building that he supposed was filled with middle-aged people like the Aftons, residents of decades or more.

Mrs. Afton walked quickly toward him across the black and white tile floor, and her tense face broke into a smile of welcome. She wiped a handkerchief across her palm and extended her hand. "How good of you, Dr. Bauer! He's come back and he's upstairs now. I thought I might introduce you as a friend of a friend of mine—of Mrs. Lanuxe of Charleston. I could say you've just stopped by for a moment before you have to catch a train."

"As you like." He followed her toward the elevator, relieved to find her in such good command of herself.

They entered a tiny, rattling elevator manned by an old man, and were silent as the elevator climbed slowly. Close to her now, Dr. Bauer could see the traces of gray in her light-brown hair, and could hear her too fast breathing. The handkerchief was tightly clenched in one hand.

"It's this way."

They went along a darkish corridor, down a couple of steps to a different level, and stopped at a tall door.

"I'm sure he's in his own room, but I always knock," she whispered. Then she opened the door. "This is the living room."

Dr. Bauer had unconsciously stuffed his newspaper into his jacket pocket so that his hands would be free. Now he found himself in an empty, rather depressing room containing hotel furniture, a few books, a brass chandelier that was a spray of former gas pipes, and an undersized black fireplace.

"He's in here," she said, going toward another door. "Thomas?" She opened the door cautiously.

There was no answer.

"He isn't in?" Dr. Bauer asked.

Mrs. Afton seemed embarrassed for a moment. "He must have stepped out again. But you can come in meanwhile and see what I've been talking to you about. This is his gymnasium, as he calls it."

Dr. Bauer entered a room about half the size of the living room, and much dimmer, since it had only one fire-escape window. It took him a moment to make out the odd shapes lying on the floor and hanging from the ceiling. There was a punching bag, a large cylindrical sandbag for tackling, an exercise horse with handgrips, and two basketballs on the floor. He picked up a boxing glove from the floor and the other came with it, fastened by its laces.

"And he has a machine for rowing. It's in the closet there," Mrs. Afton said.

"Can we have more light?"

"Oh, of course." She pulled a cord and a bare lightbulb came on at the ceiling. "Any other day, he'd be right here now. I'm so sorry. I'm sure he'll be back any minute."

The laces of the boxing gloves, Dr. Bauer saw, were crisp and white, threading all the eyelets, as if they had never been undone. Under the light now he saw that all the equipment looked brandnew. The exercise horse was a little dusty, but its leather bore no sign of wear. He frowned at the tan-colored sandbag only a few inches from his eyes. On the side nearest to him a diamond-shaped paper label was still pasted. Certainly none of the equipment had been used. It was such a surprise to him that at first he did not realize what it meant.

"And there's the mirror." She pointed to a tall mirror resting on the floor but quite upright against a wall. She chuckled. "He's eternally in front of that."

Dr. Bauer nodded. Despite her smile, he saw more anxiety in her face than on the afternoon of their first interview—an anxiety that made ugly, tortured ridges of her thin eyebrows. Her hands shook as she picked up a measuring tape and began to roll it neatly around two fingers, waiting trustfully for some comment from him.

"Perhaps I should wait in the lobby," Dr. Bauer murmured.

"All right. I'll call down and have you paged when he comes in.

He always uses the stairs. I suppose that's how we missed him when he went out."

The stairway was directly in front of Dr. Bauer when he went out into the hall. He took it somewhat dazedly. A slight blond man came up the stairs, seemed to eye him a moment before he passed, but Dr. Bauer was sure it could not be Mr. Afton.

He felt stunned, without knowing exactly what had stunned him. In the lobby he looked one way, then the other, and finally went to the desk that was half hidden under a different set of stairs.

"You have a Mrs. Afton registered here," he said, stating it more than asking.

The young man at the switchboard looked up from his newspaper. "Afton? No, sir."

"Mrs. Afton in Room Thirty-two."

"No, sir. No Afton here at all."

"Then who is it in Room Thirty-two?" At least he was sure of the room number.

The young man checked quickly with his list over the switchboard. "That's Miss Gorham's suite." And slowly, as he looked at Dr. Bauer, his face took on an amused smile.

"Miss Gorham? She's not married?" Dr. Bauer moistened his lips. "She lives by herself?"

"Yes, sir."

"Do you know the person I mean? A woman about fifty, somewhat plump, light-brown hair?"

He knew, he *knew*—but he had to make sure, doubly sure.

"Miss Gorham, yes—Miss Frances Gorham."

Dr. Bauer looked into the smiling eyes of the young man who knew Miss Gorham, and wondered what the clerk knew that he didn't. Many a time Mrs. Afton must have smiled at this young man, too, ingratiated herself as she had with him in his office.

"Thank you," he said. Then absently, "Nothing more."

He faced in the other direction, staring at nothing, setting his teeth until the sensation of reality's crumbling stopped and the world righted itself again and became hard, a little shabby like the hotel lobby ... until there was definitely no more Mrs. Afton.

He was walking toward the door when a compulsion to return to routine made him look at his wristwatch, made him realize he could be back for his 11:00 appointment after all, because it was not quite 10:40. He veered toward the coffin-like form of a telephone booth that was nearly hidden behind a large jar of palms. A shelf with telephone directories was at the side under a light, and some stubborn, some senseless curiosity prompted him to turn to the A's in the Manhattan directory.

There was only one Afton, and that was the trade name of some kind of shop.

He entered the booth and dialed his office number.

"Would you try to reach Mr. Schriever again," he told his secretary, "and ask him if he can still come at eleven. With my apologies for the changes. And when is Mrs. Afton's next appointment?"

"Just a moment. We have her tentatively scheduled for two thirty Monday."

"Would you change that please to an appointment for Miss Gorham?" he said distinctly. "Miss Frances Gorham for the same time?"

"Gorham? That's G-o-r-h-a-m?"

"Yes. I suppose so."

"That's a new patient, Dr. Bauer?"

"Yes," he said.

Julian Symons

Credit to Shakespeare

This first-night performance of "Hamlet" was notable for various reasons: one was the scandalous background of some of the cast; another was such stuff as Shakespeare never dreamed on . . .

Detective: FRANCIS QUARLES

"It won't do," said acidulous dramatic critic, Edgar Burin, to private detective, Francis Quarles. "The fact is that this young producer's too clever by half. You can't play about with a masterpiece like *Hamlet*."

Burin wrinkled his thin nose in distaste as the curtain rose on Act Five.

This *Hamlet* first night was notable because the production was by a young man still in his twenties named Jack Golding, who had already obtained a reputation for eccentric but ingenious work. It was also notable because of the casting. Golding had chosen for his Hamlet a star of light comedy named Giles Shoreham. His Laertes, John Farrimond, had been given his part on the strength of Golding's intuition, since Farrimond had played only one walk-on part in the West End.

Olivia Marston as the Queen and Roger Peters as the King were acknowledged Shakespearean actors, but their choice was remarkable in another sense. For the name of Olivia Marston, an impressive personality on the stage and a notorious one off it, had been linked by well-informed gossip with those of Peters, Farrimond, and even with Jack Golding himself.

Those were the rumors. What was certain was that Olivia, a tall handsome woman in her forties, had been married a few weeks ago to Giles Shoreham who was fifteen years her junior.

This agreeably scandalous background was known to most of the first-night audience, who watched eagerly for signs of tension among the leading players. So far, however, they had been disappointed of anything more exciting than a tendency on the part of Giles Shoreham to fluff his lines.

By Act Five the audience had settled to the view that this was, after all, only another performance of *Hamlet*, marked by abrupt changes of mood from scene to scene, and by the producer's insistence on stressing the relationship between Hamlet and the Queen.

So the curtain rose on Act Five. Golding had taken unusual liberties with the text, and Burin sucked in his breath with disapproval at the omission of the Second Gravedigger at the beginning of this scene. Giles Shoreham, slight and elegant, was playing now with eloquence and increased confidence.

Then came the funeral procession for Ophelia and Hamlet's struggle with Laertes in Ophelia's grave. Here one or two members of the audience sat forward, thinking they discovered an unusual air of reality as Shoreham and Farrimond struggled together, while Roger Peters, as the King, restrained them and Olivia Marston looked on.

Shoreham, Quarles thought, had gained impressiveness as the play went on. With Osric he was now splendidly ironical, and in the opening of the duel scene he seemed to dominate the stage for all his slightness of stature compared with Farrimond's height and breadth of shoulder.

This scene was played faster than usual, and Quarles vaguely noted cuts in the speeches before the duel began. There was Laertes choosing his poisoned foil; there was the poisoned cup brought in and placed on a side table. Then foils were flashing, Hamlet achieved a hit, took the cup to drink and put it down without doing so, with the speech, "I'll play this bout first; set it by a while."

Then another hit, and the Queen came over to wipe Hamlet's brow, picked up the cup, and drank. Laertes wounded Hamlet with his poisoned foil, and Hamlet snatched it from him and wounded Laertes. The Queen, with a cry, sank down as she was returning to the throne, and at once there was a bustle around her.

Osric and two attendants ran to her. The King moved upstage in her direction.

"How does the Queen?" Hamlet asked, and the King made the appropriate reply. "She swoons to see them bleed."

There was a pause.

Should not the Queen reply?

Quarles searched his memory while Burin grunted impatiently by his side.

Hamlet repeated, "How does the Queen?" and knelt down by her side.

The pause this time was longer.

Then Hamlet looked up, and on his face was an unforgettable expression of mingled anguish and irresolution. His lips moved, but he seemed unable to speak. When the words came they seemed almost ludicrous after the Shakespearean speech they had heard.

"A doctor," he cried. "Is there a doctor in the house?"

The other players looked at him in consternation. The curtain came down with a rush. Five minutes later, Roger Peters appeared before it and told the anxious audience that Miss Marston had met with a serious accident.

When Burin and Quarles came onto the stage, the players were standing together in small, silent groups. Only Giles Shoreham sat apart in his red court suit, head in hands.

A man bending over Olivia Marston straightened up and greeted Quarles, who recognized him as the well-known pathologist, Sir Charles Palquist.

"She's dead," Palquist said, and his face was grave. "She took cyanide, and there's no doubt she drank it from that cup. Somebody knocked the cup over and it's empty now, but the smell is still plain enough."

"Now I wonder who did that?" Quarles said. But his meditation on that point was checked by the arrival of his old friend, brisk, grizzled Inspector Leeds.

The Inspector had a wonderful capacity for marshaling facts. Like a dog snapping at the heels of so many sheep, he now extracted a story from each of the actors on the stage, while Quarles stood by and listened.

When the Inspector had finished, this was the result. The cup from which Olivia Marston had taken her fatal drink was filled with red wine and water. The cup had been standing ready in the wings for some time, and it would have been quite easy for anybody on the stage—or, indeed, anybody in the whole company—to drop poison into it unobserved.

As for what had happened on the stage, the duel scene had been played absolutely to the script up to the point where Peters, as the King, said, "She swoons to see them bleed." The Queen should then have replied to him, and her failure to do so was the reason for the very obvious pause that had occurred.

Shoreham, as Hamlet, then improvised by repeating his question, "How does the Queen?" and went on his knees to look at her, thinking that she felt unwell. But when he saw her face, half turned to the floor, suffused and contorted, he knew that something was seriously wrong. Shoreham was then faced with a terrible problem.

Clasping his hands nervously, white-faced, Shoreham said to the Inspector, "I could have got up and gone on as though nothing had happened—after all, in the play the Queen was dead—and within ten minutes the play would have been over. That way we should have completed the performance." Shoreham's large eyes looked pleadingly round at the other members of the cast. "But I couldn't do it. I couldn't leave her lying there—I just couldn't."

"Since the poor lady was dead, it didn't make any difference," said the Inspector in his nutmeg-grater voice. "Now, this lady became Mrs. Shoreham a few weeks ago, I believe? And she was, I imagine, a pretty wealthy woman?"

Giles Shoreham's head jerked up. "Do you mean to insinuate—?"

"I'm not insinuating, sir—I'm merely stating a fact."

Quarles coughed. "I think, Inspector, that there may be other motives at work here."

He took the Inspector aside and told him of the rumors that linked the names of Farrimond, Peters, and Golding with Olivia Marston. The Inspector's face lengthened as he listened.

"But that means any of the four might have had reason to kill her."

"If they felt passionately enough about her—yes. Which would you pick?"

The Inspector's glance passed from Farrimond, big and sulky, to the assured, dignified, gray-haired Peters and on to the young producer Jack Golding, who looked odd in his lounge suit and thick horn-rimmed spectacles among this collection of Elizabethans. "I'm hanged if I know."

"May I ask a few questions?" The Inspector assented. Quarles stepped forward. "A small point perhaps, gentlemen, but one I should like to clear up. The cup was found on its side with the liquid spilled out of it. Who knocked it over?"

There was silence.

With something threatening behind his urbanity Quarles said, "Very well. Let us have individual denials. Mr. Shoreham?"

Shoreham shook his head.

"Mr. Farrimond?"

"Didn't touch a thing."

"Mr. Peters?"

"No."

"Any of you other gentlemen who were on the stage? Or did anyone see it done?" There were murmurs of denial. "Most interesting. Miss Marston replaced the cup on the table and then some unknown agency knocked it on its side."

The Inspector was becoming impatient. "Can't see what you're getting at, Quarles. Do you mean she didn't drink out of it?"

Quarles shook his head. "Oh, no, she drank from it, poor woman. Mr. Shoreham, did you know that you had some rivals for your wife's affections? And did she ever hint that any one of them was particularly angry when she decided to marry you?"

A wintry suggestion of a smile crossed Shoreham's pale face. "She once said she'd treated everybody badly except me and that one of these days she'd get into trouble. I thought she was joking."

"Mr. Golding." The producer started. "I'm not a Shakespearean scholar, but I seem to have noticed more cuts in this *Hamlet* than are usually made."

"No," said Golding. The thickness of his spectacles effectively masked his expression. "*Hamlet* is very rarely played in full. I haven't made more cuts than usual, I've simply made different ones."

"In this particular scene, for instance," Quarles went on, "you've cut the passage early—where the King drinks and sends somebody across to Hamlet with the cup."

"That's right. It seems to me an unnecessary complication."

"What about the rest of the scene? Any cuts in that?"

"None at all. After what you saw we adhere to the standard printed version."

Quarles bent his whole great body forward and said emphatically, "Doesn't that suggest something to you, Mr. Golding? Remember that the cup was knocked over and emptied. Do you understand?"

On Golding's face there was suddenly amazed comprehension.

The Inspector had been listening with increasing irritation. "What's all this got to do with the murder? Why the devil was that cup emptied?"

"*Because the murderer thought he would have to drink from it.* Remember what happens after the Queen dies, crying that her drink was poisoned. Laertes tells Hamlet that he has been the victim of treachery. Hamlet stabs the King. And what happens *then*, Mr. Peters?"

Roger Peters, truly kingly in his robes, was smiling. "Hamlet puts the poisoned cup to the King's mouth and forces him to drink."

"Correct. In fact, Shoreham stopped the play before that point was reached. But the murderer couldn't be sure that Shoreham's instinct as an actor wouldn't impel him to go on and say nothing. And then what would have happened? The King would also have had to drink from the poisoned cup. You couldn't risk that, could you, Mr. Peters?"

Peters' hand was at his mouth. "No. You are a clever man, Mr. Quarles."

"So there was only one person who would have had any motive for knocking over that cup."

"Only one person. But you are a little late, Mr. Quarles. I had two capsules. I swallowed the second a few seconds ago. I don't think, anyway, that I would have wanted to live without Olivia."

Peters' body seemed to crumple suddenly. Farrimond caught him as he fell.

"Well," said Burin, the dramatic critic, afterward, "you had no evidence, Quarles, but that was a pretty piece of deduction."

"I was merely the interpreter," Quarles said mock-modestly. "The credit for spinning the plot and then unraveling it goes to someone much more famous."

"Who's that?"

"William Shakespeare."

Christianna Brand

Blood Brothers

*Inspector Cockrill said, "Well, well, so you're the famous Birds-
well twins! ... An almost mystic bond, I hear? ... In fact, you
might properly be called—blood brothers?" ...*

Detective: INSPECTOR COCKRILL

And devoted, I hear? ... David and Jonathan?" he said. "In
fact, you might properly be called," he said, with that glitter
in his eye, "blood brothers?"

Well, he can sneer, but it's true we was pally enough, Fred and
me, till Lydia came along. Shared the same digs in the
village—Birdswell's our village, if you know it?—Birdswell, in Kent.

Everyone in Birdswell knows us—even if they can't easily tell the
difference between us—and used to say how wonderful it was, us
two so alike, with our strong legs and big shoulders and curly red
hair, like a kid's; and what a beautiful understanding we always
had, what a bond of union. Well, people talk a lot of nonsense about
identical twins.

Lydia couldn't tell the difference between us either—seemingly.
Was that my fault? Fair enough, she was Fred's girl first—unless
you counted her husband, and to some extent you did have to count
him: six foot five, he is, and it isn't only because he's the blacksmith
that they call him Black Will.

But she switched to me of her own accord, didn't she?—even if I
wasn't too quick to disillusion her, the first time she started with
her carryings-on, mistaking me for Fred. "*I* can't help it if she fancies
me more than you, now," I said to Fred.

"You'll regret this, you two-timing, double-crossing skunk," said
Fred. He always did have a filthy temper, Fred did.

Well, I did regret it, and not so very long after. Fred and me shares
a car between us—a heavy, old, bashed-up, fourth-hand "family
model," but at least it goes. And one evening, when he'd slouched

off, ugly and moody as he was those days, to poach the river down by the Vicarage woods, I picked up Lydia and took her out in it, joyriding.

Not that there was much joy in it. We hadn't been out twenty minutes when, smooching around with Lydia, I suppose, and not paying enough attention to the road—well, I didn't see the kid until I'd hit him. Jogging along the grass verge the kid was, with his little can of blackberries, haring home as fast as his legs would go, a bit scared, I daresay, because the dark was catching up on him.

Well, the dark caught him up all right, poor little kid. I scrambled out and knelt down and turned him over; and got back again, quick. "He's gone," I said to Lydia, "and we'd best be gone too."

She made a lot of fuss, womanlike, but what was the point of it? If he wasn't dead now, he would be mighty soon, there wasn't any doubt of it, lying there with the can still clutched in his fat little hand and the blackberries spilt, and scattered all around him. I couldn't do nothing; if I could have, I daresay I'd have waited, but I couldn't. So what was the use of bringing trouble on myself, when the chances were that I could get clear away with it?

And I did get clear away with it. The road was hard and dry, the cars that followed and stopped must have obscured my tire marks, if there were any. They found half a footprint in the dried mud, where I'd bent over him; but it was just a cheap, common make of shoe, pretty new so that it had no particular marks to it; and a largish size, of course, but nothing out of the ordinary.

So no one knew I'd been on that road—everything Lydia did with us two was done in deep secret, because of Black Will. Will was doing time at the moment, for beating up a keeper who came on him, poaching (we all spent most of our evenings poaching). But he'd be back some day, Black Will would.

And Fred promised me an alibi when I told him about it, clutching at his arm, shaking a bit by this time, losing confidence because Lydia was threatening to turn nasty. "I'll say you was in the woods with me," he said.

And he did, too. They came to our door—"regulation police inquiries." But Lydia didn't dare tell, not really—I could see that in the light of day—and they had no other sort of reason to suspect me, especially. And nobody did—it could have been any stranger, speeding along the empty country roads.

Fred pretended to be reluctant to alibi me, cagey about saying where we was—because of the poaching. He managed it fine, sort of threw their interest halfway in a different direction. I thought it was decent of Fred, considering about me and Lydia. But brotherly love is a wonderful thing, isn't it?

Or is it? Because it hadn't been all for nothing. No sooner was I clear of that lot than he said to me, "Well, has she told you?"

"Told me what?" I said. "Who? Lydia?"

"Lydia," he said. "She's having a baby."

"Well, don't look at me," I said, and quick. "I've only been going with the girl a couple of weeks."

"And her husband hasn't been going with her at all," said Fred. "On account of he's been in prison for the past five months."

"For half killing a man," I said thoughtfully; and I looked Fred up and down. Fred and me are no weeds, like I said, but Black Will, he's halfway to a giant.

"And due out at the end of October," said Fred.

"Well, good luck to the two of you," I said. "It's nothing to do with me. I went with her for a couple of weeks, and now even that's over. She reckons I ought to have stopped and seen to the kid; she's given me the air."

"She'll give you more than the air," he said, "and me too, when Will comes home. When he knows about the baby he'll beat the rest out of her; and then God help you and me too."

"The baby could be Jimmy Green's," I said. "Or Bill Bray's. She's been out with them, too."

"That's her tales," he said, "to make you jealous. They're a sight too scared of Will to let Lydia make up to them. And so ought you and I have been too, if we'd had any sense." Only where Lydia was concerned, there never seemed to be time to have sense; and six months ago, Fred said, Black Will's return had seemed like a century away.

"So what are you going to do?" I said.

"What are *you* going to do?" he said. "A hit-and-run driver—you can get a long stretch for that."

Good old brotherly love!—Fred worrying about me, when after all I *had* pinched his girl. And him in such trouble himself.

We went out in the car where no one could hear us—our old landlady's pretty deaf and takes no interest at all in our comings and goings, but Fred wasn't taking no chances.

Because it was all Fred's idea; that I will say, and stick to it—it was all Fred's idea. Dead men tell no tales, said Fred; nor dead girls, neither. "If they find she's in the family way—it's like you said, she'd been going with half the men in the village. So once she was past talking, Will couldn't pin it on us two—not to be certain, he couldn't."

"Speak for yourself," I said.

"She'd be past talking about the hit-and-run, too," he said. "You say she's sore about that. She won't tell now, because it means admitting she was joy-riding with you; but once Black Will gets it out of her that she was—and he will, you can bet on it—then she'll tell about the accident too; it'll make her feel easier."

"So what do you suggest?" I said. "*I'm* not killing the girl, I can tell you that, flat."

"No," he said, "I'll do that. You've done one killing—that'll do for you. All I want from you now is an alibi."

"What, me alibi you?" I said. "No one'd believe it for a minute. One twin speaking up for another—the whole village would testify how 'close' we are."

But Fred had thought of all that too. If a straight alibi failed, he said, there were other ways of playing it. He had it all worked out—suspiciously well worked out, I should have thought; but he gave me no time for thinking. "It won't come to any alibi, our names probably won't even come into it—as you say, the baby could have been fathered by half the male population of Birdswell. But if it does—well, you alibi for me and I alibi for you. They'll know it was one of us, but they'll never know which one; and if they don't know which of us, they'll have to let both of us go."

"And Black Will?" I said. "When we've not only seduced his wife, but murdered her—which one of us will *he* let go?"

"Oh, well," he said, "we'd have to clear out if it got as far as that, start again somewhere else. But the chances are a hundred to one it'll never come to that. After all, no one suspected you of the hit-and-run affair, did they?"

He kept coming back to that, sort of nastily. I didn't forget that I'd done him wrong, pinching his girl. But that was his lever, really—while he kept reminding me, he could pretty well force me to go in with him. He was in trouble—but I was in trouble even deeper.

So we worked it out—we worked out everything to the last detail. This was Tuesday, and we'd do it Thursday night. I'd see nothing more of the girl; but he'd get her to go driving with him on the pretense of talking over the baby business. And he'd lead round to the accident, advising her to confess to the police it was me, and then drive past where it happened. And get her out of the car and show him just where the boy was lying. And then—well, then there'd be a second hit-and-run killing on that lonely spot. "*You* got away with it once," he kept saying. "Why not another?"

There was a kind of—well, justice, in it, I thought. After all, it was because she was threatening to tell about the hit-and-run that I was letting her be murdered.

"But what about clues?" I said. "Even I left a footprint."

He had worked that out too. He and I are the same size, of course, and most of our clothes are the same as one another's. Not for any silly reason like dressing identical, but simply because when he'd go along shopping, I'd go along too, and mostly we liked the same things; or he'd buy something and it'd be a success, so I'd buy the same, later.

We'd dress the same Thursday night, he said, because of the alibi; and we checked our stuff over—shoes, gray slacks, shirts, without jackets—this all happened in September.

Our blue poplins were in the wash—we'd worn them clean Sunday, and second-day Monday; so it would have to be the striped wool-and-nylon—a bit warm for this weather, if anyone remarked it, but we'd have to risk that, I said, we daren't ask the old woman to wash out our blue ones special. The last thing we wanted was to do anything out of the ordinary. That was what the police looked for—a break in routine. That was asking for it.

Our shoes were the same—same size, same make, bought together, with a rubber sole that had bars across it; but, like I said, new enough not to be worn down, or have any peculiarities. And everything else we'd wear would be identical—not only for the alibi, but in case of bits caught in the girl's fingernails or whatnot—you've only got to read the papers to know what they look for.

Not that he meant to get near enough for that. But she might not—well, she might not kick in at once, if you see what I mean; he might have to get out of the car and do something about it. And in case of scratches, he said, I'd better be prepared to get some scratches on my own hands too—we could say we'd been blackberrying or something.

"Blackberrying," I said. "That'd be bloody likely! We both detest blackberries—everybody knows it; or anyway, the old woman knows it, we never touch her blackberry pie."

I knew he'd only said it to remind me of the kid—him and his little can of blackberries, spilt all around him.

"Oh, well," he said, "say we got scratched pushing through the brambles down by the river. Do your poaching down by the bramble patch."

But she didn't scratch him. It was all a bit grim, I think; he couldn't be sure she was properly done in and he had to get out of the car and have a look and—well, go back and take a second run at her. But she didn't have the strength left to scratch him.

All the same, he looked pretty ghastly when finally we met in the moonlight, in the Vicarage woods. He didn't say anything, just stood there, staring at me with a sort of sick, white heaviness.

I couldn't exactly say anything either; it was worse than, talking it over, I'd thought it ever would be. I sort of—well, looked a question at him; and he gave me a weary kind of nod and glanced away towards the river. It was easier to talk about my angle, so I said, at last, "Well, I saw the Vicar."

"But did he see you?" he said. We'd agreed on the Reverend because he always walked across to the church of a Thursday evening; you'd be sure of passing him if you went at a certain time.

"Yes," I said. "He saw me. I gave a sort of grunt for 'good evening,' and he said, 'Going poaching?' and gave me a bit of a grin. You'd better remember that." He nodded again but he said nothing more; and more to ease the silence than anything else, I said, "Is the car all right? Not marked?"

"What does it matter if it is?" he said. "It's marked all over, no one could say what's old or what's new—you know that, from bashing the boy." As for bits of her clothing and—well, blood and all that, he'd had the idea of spreading a bit of plastic over the front of the car before he—well, did it. He produced the plastic folded in brown paper, and we wrapped the whole lot round a stone and sank it, then and there, in the river. There was blood on the plastic, all right. It gave me the shudders.

But next thing he said that I really had something to shudder at. "Anyway, *your* number's up, mate. She's shopped you."

"Shopped me?" I said. I stood and stared at him.

"Shopped you," he said. "She'd already sent off an anonymous note to the police. About the hit-and-run."

"How do you know?" I said. I couldn't believe it.

"She told me so," he said. "It was on her conscience, what you'd done."

Her conscience! Lydia's conscience! I started to laugh, a bit hysterical, I suppose, with the strain of it. He put his hand on my wrist and gave me a little shake.

"Steady lad," he said. "Don't lose your head. I'm looking after you." It wasn't like him to be so demonstrative, but there you are—it's like the poem says, when times are bad, there's no friend like a brother. "It's just a matter of slanting the alibi," he said.

Well, we'd worked that out, too. There'd always be a risk that they wouldn't accept a brother's alibi, that the two of us was together. The other time, about the accident, they'd had no special reason to suspect me, so they'd accepted that all right; but this time it might at any moment turn into a murder inquiry—and a murder inquiry into *us*, now that they knew about the hit-and-run.

But as Fred said—we had the alternative all ready.

I hadn't counted on its being Inspector Cockrill. When I realized it was him—come all the way over from Heronsford—I knew they meant business. And to be honest, it struck a bit of chill into the heart of me.

A little man he is, for a policeman, and near retiring age he must be—looks like a grandfather; but his eyes are as bright as a bird's and they seem to look right into you. He came into the old woman's best parlor and he had us brought in there, and he looked us up and down.

"Well, well," he said, "so you're the famous Birdswell twins! You certainly are identicals, aren't you?" And he gave us a look of a sort of fiendish glee, or so it seemed to me, and said, "And devoted, I hear? An almost mystic bond, I hear? David and Jonathan, Damon and Pythias, and all the rest of it? In fact," he said, "you might properly be called—blood brothers?"

We stood in front of him, silent. He said at last, "Well, which is which?—and no nonsense."

We told him—*and* no nonsense.

"So you're the one that killed the child?" he said to me. "And drove on, regardless."

"I never was near the child," I said. "I was in the woods that evening—poaching."

"Yours is the name stated in the anonymous letter."

"I don't know who wrote the letter," I said. "But no one can tell us apart, me and my brother."

"Even your fancy girl?" he said. "It appears it was she who wrote the letter."

"I don't know what you mean," I said, "by my fancy girl."

"Well, everyone else does," he said. "All the village knows she was playing you off, one against the other. And all the village has been grinning behind their hands, waiting for her husband's home-coming."

"But I tell you none of them can tell us apart," I said. "I was out poaching."

"That's a damn lie," said Fred, playing it the way we'd agreed upon. "That was me, poaching."

"One of you was poaching?" said Inspector Cockrill, very smooth, "And one of you was with the lady? And even the lady couldn't have said which was which?"

He said it sort of, well, suggestive. "I daresay she might," I said, "later on in the proceedings. But there couldn't have been any pro-ceedings that night—there wouldn't have been time because the accident happened."

"Why should she say so positively it was you, then?"

"I daresay she thought it was me," I said. "I daresay he told her so. She'd finished with him—it would be the only way he could get back at her."

"I see," said Inspector Cockrill. "How very ingenious!" I didn't know whether he meant how ingenious of Fred to have thought of it then, or of me to think of it now.

"Don't you listen to him, sir," said Fred. "He's a bloody liar. I wasn't with the girl that night. I tell you I was poaching."

"All right, you were poaching," said Inspector Cockrill. "Any wit-nesses?"

"Of course not. You don't go poaching with witnesses. I used to go with him," said Fred bitterly, gesturing with his head towards me, "but not since he pinched my girl, the bloody so-and-so."

"And last night?" said the Inspector softly. "When the girl was murdered?"

"Last night too," said Fred. "I was in the woods, poaching."

"You call *me* a liar!" I said. "It was me in the woods. The Vicar saw me going there."

"It was me the Vicar saw," said Fred. "I told him, Good evening, and he laughed and said, 'Going poaching?'"

"There!" said Inspector Cockrill to me, like a teacher patiently getting the truth from a difficult child. "How could he know *that?* Because the Vicar will surely confirm it."

"He knows it because I told him," I said. "I told him I'd been poaching and I hoped the Vicar hadn't realized where I was going."

"Very ingenious," said Inspector Cockrill again. "Very ingenious."

It seemed like he couldn't get over it all, sitting there, shaking his head at the wonder of it. But I knew he was playing for time. I knew that we'd foxed him.

And Fred knew too. He suggested, reasonably, "Why should you be so sure, sir, that the girl was murdered? Why not just a second hit-and-run?"

"A bit of a coincidence?" said Inspector Cockrill mildly. "Same thing in the same place and so soon after? And when on top of it, we find that the girl was threatening a certain person with exposure, about the first hit-and-run . . . " He left it in the air. He said to his sergeant, "Have you collected their clobber?"

"Yes, sir," said the sergeant. "Two pairs of shoes—" and he gave the Inspector a sort of nod, as if to say, Yes, they look as if they'll match very nicely—"and all the week's laundry."

"Including Monday's?" said Cockrill.

"Including Monday evening's, sir The old woman washes of a Monday morning. Anything they've worn after that—which includes two shirts to each, sir—is in two laundry baskets, one in each bed-room."

"Two baskets?" he says, looking more bright-eyed than ever. "That's a bit of luck. Their laundry's kept separate, is it?"

"Yes, it is," said Fred, though I don't know what call he had to butt in. "His in his room, mine in mine."

"And no chance of its getting mixed up?" said Inspector Cockrill. He fixed Fred with that beady eye of his.

Fred, of course, was maintaining the mutual-accusation arrangement we'd agreed upon. "Not a chance, sir," he said a bit too eagerly.

I wasn't going to be left out. I said, "Not the slightest."

"That's right, sir," says the sergeant. "The old lady confirms it."

"Good," said Cockrill. He gave a few orders and the sergeant went away. People were still buzzing about, up in our bedrooms. "I'm coming," the Inspector called up to someone at the head of the stairs. He turned back to us. "All right, Cain and Abel," he said. "I'll leave you to stew in it. But in a day or two, as the song says, 'I'll be seeing you.' And when I do, it'll be at short notice. So stick around if you know what's good for you."

"And if we don't?" I said. "You've got nothing against us. You can't charge us, so you've got no call to be giving us orders."

"Who's giving orders?" he said. "Just a little friendly advice. But before you ignore the advice take a good, hard, long look at your-

selves. You won't need any mirrors. And ask yourselves," he said,
giving us a good, hard, long look on his own account, from the soles
of our feet to the tops of our flaming red heads, "just how far you'd
get."

So that was that; and for the next two days, we "stewed in it."
David and Jonathan, Cain and Abel—like he'd said, blood brothers.

On the third day he sent for us, to Heronsford Police Station. They
shoved Fred into one little room and me in another. He talked to
Fred first, and I waited. All very chummy, cigs and cups of tea and
offers of bread and butter; but it was the waiting . . .

Long after I knew I couldn't stand one more minute of it, the
Inspector came in. I suppose they muttered some formalities, but I
don't remember. Fred and I might hate one another, and by this
time we did, well and truly, there's no denying it—but it was worse,
a thousand times worse, without him there. My head felt as though
it were filled with gray cottonwool, little, stuffy, warm clouds of it.

Inspector Cockrill sat down in front of me. He said, "Well, have
you come to your senses? Of course you killed her."

"If anyone killed her," I said, clinging to our patter, "it must have
been him."

"Your brother?" he said. "But why should your brother have killed
her?"

"Well," I said, "if the girl was having a baby—"

"A baby?" he said surprised, and his eyes got that bright, glittering
look in them. "But she wasn't."

"She wasn't?" I said. "She *wasn't?* But she'd told him—"

Or had she told him? Something like an icicle of light—ice-cold,
piercing, brilliant—thrust itself into the dark places of my cottonwool mind. I said, "The bloody, two-timing, double-crossing. . . !"

"*He* didn't seem," said the Inspector softly, "to expect her to have
been found pregnant."

So that was it! So *that* was it! So as to get me to agree to the
killing, to get me to help him with it . . . I ought to have been more
fly—why should Fred, of all people, be so much afraid of Black Will
as to go in for murder? Will's a dangerous man, but Fred's not exactly
a softie.

The icicle turned in my mind and twisted, probing with its light
rays into the cotton wooliness. Revenge! Cold, sullen, implacable
revenge on the two of us—because Lydia had come over to me,
because I had taken her away from him. Death for her—and I to be
the accomplice in her undoing, and in my own undoing.

I knew now who had sent the anonymous note about the hit-and-run accident—so easily to be "traced" (after she was dead) to Lydia.

But yet, he was still as deep in it as I was—even deeper had he but known it. I said, fighting my way up out of the darkness, "Even if she *had* been pregnant, it wouldn't have been my fault. I'd only been going with her a couple of weeks."

"That's what you say," Cockrill said.

"But all the village—"

"All the village knew there were goings-on, but nobody knew just where they went on, or how long. You must, all three, have been remarkably careful."

I tried another tack. "But if she wasn't pregnant, why should I have killed her?"

"You've just told me yourself that you thought she was," he said.

"Because he told me—my brother told me. Now, look, Inspector," I said, trying to think it out as I went along, trying to ram it home to him, "you say she wasn't having a baby? So why should I have thought she was? *She* wouldn't have told me, if she hadn't been. So it was he who told me—my own brother. But you say yourself, he knew it wasn't true. So why should he have told me?"

He looked at me, cold as ice, and he said, "That's easy. He wanted *you* to kill *her* for *him*."

He wanted *me* to kill her! I could have laughed. The thing was getting fantastic, getting out of hand; and yet at the same time I had a feeling that the fantasy was a hard, gripping, grim fantasy, that once it had its hold on me it would never shake loose. I stammered out, "Why should he have wanted her killed?"

"Because," he said, "she was threatening to tell that it was he who ran the child down, and left it to die." And the Inspector said, cold and bitter, "I have no wish to trap you. We know that it was your brother who killed the child—we have proof of it. And we know it was you who killed the girl—we have proof of that too. There's her blood on your cuff."

On my cuff. Where Fred had put his hand that night—taking my wrist in his grasp, giving me a brotherly little shake "to steady me." I remembered how I'd thought, even then, that it wasn't like him to be so demonstrative.

Putting his hand on my wrist—fresh from the blood-smeared plastic he'd put on the front of the car. Making such a point, later on, about there being no chance of our soiled shirts getting confused, one with the other's.

So there it is. I wonder if we'll be doing our time in the same prison, sharing the same cell, maybe?—we two being blood brothers.

Because he'll be doing time all right, as well as me. While I'm doing my time for *his* killing the girl, he'll be doing his time for *my* killing the child.

Well, that's all right with me. He'll be first out, I daresay. Is it murder to leave a kid to die? I suppose not; the actual knocking down would be accidental, after all, not planned. So Fred'll be out first, and Black Will will be there to meet him. By the time I get out, I daresay Will will be back "in" for what he done to Fred—so it looks like being a very long time away, my ever meeting Black Will, I mean.

But can you beat it?—Fred working it out so far ahead, leading up to it so patiently, so softly, so craftily? Planting the blood on my cuff—and then leading up to it so softly, so craftily. And all for revenge—revenge on his own twin brother! And him planning and expecting me to pay for it all, and him planning to go scot-free.

After all, what *I* did, was done in self-preservation—there was no venom in it against Fred. That night after the car accident, I mean, when, clutching his arm and begging him to help me, when just to be on the safe side I rubbed his sleeve with the juice of a blackberry.

"Q"

Jacob Hay

The Opposite Number

*You simply have to read this story to believe it; but we urge you
to keep tongue in cheek and one eye closed tight—you see, you
can't swallow with your tongue in cheek (try it), and one eye closed
is, after all, a long wink, a wink in suspension. . .*

E van Pulsifer never really thought of himself as being, in effect,
an Espionage specialist; rather, he considered himself an Intelligence analyst doing what was really a humdrum job in a smallish
cubicle, surrounded by scores of equally smallish cubicles occupied
by his colleagues of the C.I.A. At five o'clock each evening, unless
there was a flap on, he left his cubicle and drove quietly back to his
home in one of the suburbs overlooking the Potomac, just north of
Washington, and became simply another one of the residents with
some kind of job with the government. There, he rarely if ever
thought about Sundala.

Thus he was completely unprepared for the advent of Colonel
Noganami Falsaki.

Pulsifer's preoccupation with the emerging Republic of Sundala
was by way of being an accident of education. When the Republic
of Sundala adopted the obscure Sunda dialect as the nation's official
language, it developed that in all the Central Intelligence Agency
only Pulsifer could both read and speak it. He had been born in the
Sunda region, where his parents were missionaries of the Presby-
terian persuasion.

So Pulsifer became the Sundala specialist, which was a relatively
simple job since there wasn't much there to begin with. The Republic
occupied a small wedge of land on the west coast of Africa which
was notable chiefly for a particularly annoying variety of malaria
and had once been useful as a coaling station for the ships of the
Royal Navy. The inhabitants were largely Arabs and Indians, with
an admixture of Portuguese; the economy defied easy analysis, since
it appeared to be based almost entirely on the fortunes of the State-
owned Sundala Air-Africa Airline, into which the Republic had

poured nearly all the foreign aid it received in bounteous abundance from the United States, Soviet Russia, Communist China, the Arab League, and Luxembourg.

It was believed that certain powerful interests in Luxembourg were convinced that there were vast mineral deposits in the western highlands, although this could not be established until means were found to reach the western highlands. This could not be accomplished until and unless other means were found to pacify the Batungi of Hok, a powerful tribal leader who claimed to be the rightful ruler of Sundala as an honorary great-grandnephew of Queen Victoria. Otherwise, there just wasn't much to say about Sundala.

On occasion, Pulsifer had thought of asking to be transferred to another desk to handle the affairs of some more interesting country. This, on the other hand, would have meant gathering a large mass of new facts and a lot of assiduous study. As it was, he knew all the answers there were to know about Sundala. But it was undoubtedly a dead end, even for an Espionage specialist or an Intelligence analyst.

"All quiet in your part of the world, Pulsifer?" his Chief would ask, and invariably Pulsifer would have to reply that it was, indeed, all quiet. The Sundalans had never had it so good. The Batungi of Hok, although adamant in his claim, was a graduate of Cambridge University and preferred to advance his cause through the medium of the World Court, where his plea was docketed for the late 1970s.

So Pulsifer was not at all prepared for Colonel Falsaki's telephone call to his home that quiet spring evening.

"Yes, this is Pulsifer," he had replied to the quiet inquiry, spoken in an accent that blended British with something Pulsifer couldn't quite put his finger on.

"I believe," said the Colonel, having identified himself, "it will be to our mutual advantage to meet and chat."

"I'd be delighted," Pulsifer declared sincerely. "I take it you've just been assigned to your Embassy here." It was his business to know everyone on the Sundalan Embassy's staff, and he'd never heard of a man named Falsaki.

"In a manner of speaking, yes. Would you care to suggest a meeting place, sir?"

"Why not come on out here to my home in Potomac Heights?" Pulsifer said.

"I should prefer some more public establishment downtown," Falsaki answered, to Pulsifer's mild surprise. He didn't feel a bit like driving all the way into the center of Washington. But business was business. So they arranged to meet an hour later in the Men's Bar of the Mayflower Hotel.

Pulsifer had been seated in the bar for only a few minutes when the Colonel appeared, guided by the *maître d'* with whom Pulsifer had left his name. The Colonel was a tall youngish man with a light mahogany complexion and an expression that would undoubtedly have been amiable if it had not been slightly harassed. Although the evening was mild, he carried a heavy and much bestrapped trench coat over one arm, and in his hand he clutched a dark felt hat.

He sat down opposite Pulsifer, after the customary handshaking, and sighed with something like relief before ordering a double Scotch.

"Well now, what can I do for you, Colonel?" Pulsifer inquired pleasantly. Colonel Falsaki's eyes were sweeping the room, sharply examining faces.

"It is, rather, sir, a question of what we can do for each other," the Colonel replied gravely. "Let me lay my cards on the table, Mr. Pulsifer—or is it, perhaps, Major Pulsifer? Or Commander?"

"Just Mister. Garden-variety civil servant, I'm afraid."

"Oh?" The Colonel seemed a trifle disheartened, and then smiled knowingly. "Of course, sir. I should know your practice better. Military titles do not have the same value here as they do in my country. Nevertheless, Mr. Pulsifer, you are my Opposite Number and I, sir, am yours."

"My word," Pulsifer said, astonished. "I'm afraid I don't quite follow you, Colonel."

"It is quite simple, really. Your job is to keep an eye on Sundala. My job, therefore, is to keep an eye on you."

The Colonel looked at Pulsifer cheerfully for the first time, seeing before him a pleasant-looking young man with a crewcut and horn-rimmed glasses, wearing a neat gray suit and dark tie. And an expression of bafflement.

"Should you be telling me this?" Pulsifer asked dubiously. "I mean—well, it does seem somewhat irregular. And you seem to think we can help one another? How?"

"Cheers," the Colonel said, taking a deep gulp of the Scotch the waiter had just set before him. "For a month now, I have watched you, Mr. Pulsifer." Pulsifer started uneasily, and the Colonel held up a large calming hand. "Unexceptionable. Absolutely unexceptionable. Mr. Pulsifer, let me be brutally honest with you: you have bored me almost as much as Sundala must bore you."

He sighed, and continued, "To work at seven thirty each morning; back home at five each evening. A charming wife and two delightful children, just as I myself have left behind me in Sundala. Church every Sunday. Gardening in the evenings. Tennis on Saturday mornings. I myself prefer polo. But in sum, sir, you constitute no menace."

"Menace? You did say menace?"

"Nor, by the same token, do I constitute a menace to you, you see."

"I should hope not. In fact, I've always thought our relations with Sundala have been very close to ideal, although I'll admit that from time to time I've worried about the Batungi of Hok."

"A splendid chap, by the way. But that is precisely my point. Relations are indeed ideal. Which is not, Mr. Pulsifer, what you and I are getting paid for."

"We aren't?"

"My dear sir, how long has it been since you were summoned to the office of your superiors and commended for some feat of Intelligence analysis?"

"Well, as a matter of fact—" Pulsifer began hesitantly. "To be perfectly honest, never, although I did get a nice note from the Chief for tipping him off to the Luxembourg involvement."

"Pah!" Colonel Falsaki snapped a contemptuous finger. "It is even worse with me. Until two months ago I was a happy man, sir, commanding a regiment of the national army on the Hok frontier, playing polo against the Batungi's team in the demilitarized zone, enjoying my family—in a phrase, the good life. Then what? I am called to the capital, Teritza, by my uncle, the President. 'Here,' he says, 'read these,' and hands me the complete works of Ian Fleming. 'Sundala, too, shall have an Intelligence Service, and you shall be its Chief, my boy.' I could not refuse. 'Clearly, too, Washington will be your most important post. Go there as soon as you have finished reading, and let us know what your Opposite Number is up to.' "

"But how did you find out it was me?"

"I telephoned the Central Intelligence Agency and asked."

"Oh. That seems quite clear-cut and aboveboard."

"That, as I say, was over a month ago, shortly after my arrival. Since then, nothing. My uncle, the President, is becoming impatient. Almost daily I receive a coded telegram through our Embassy. Here, look—I have decoded his latest."

Colonel Falsaki handed Pulsifer a rumpled piece of paper.

"F," Pulsifer read, "INSIST YOU FORWARD SOONEST CIA PLOT OVER-THROW GOVERNMENT FAVOR OF BATUNGI OF HOK. LOVE, UNCLE THEO-DORE."

"But I assure you there is no plot," Pulsifer protested.

"Quite. I know that, and you know that. So, in fact, does my Uncle Theodore, the President of Sundala, and that is the trouble. If there is no plot, how can he go to the Russians and the Chinese for more foreign aid? How will Sundala Air-Africa be in a position to build a supersonic transport? Who will keep my splendid regiment equipped with machine guns?"

"I can see it would present problems. Our not having a plot, that is."

"Then, too, there is the question of my physical safety," Colonel Falsaki continued gloomily. "Not one attempt to run me down by automobile. Not one kidnaping and torture session."

"My dear Colonel, the C.I.A. simply doesn't go in for that sort of thing."

"I know." Glumly. Then, brightening, "But cannot you see, my dear sir, that this could be a two-way street?"

"Again, I don't quite follow you, Colonel."

"The Batungi of Hok," the Colonel replied triumphantly. "For you, he will acquire Chinese technicians and mysterious crates that could conceal purely defensive missiles. For me, he will receive air drops from planes flown by C.I.A. mercenaries from secret bases. For you, he will threaten to move into our neighboring country of Transu. For me, he will infiltrate operatives into our capital city of Teritza."

"Hmm," murmured Evan Pulsifer, his manner thoughtful. "Hmm," he murmured again.

He was thinking about Stanton, who had until just recently oc-cupied the cubicle adjacent to his own in the vast rabbit warren of a building in Virginia. And then Stanton had deduced the existence of a conspiracy to replace the legally constituted government of the Republic of Upper Volta with a military junta. Actually, this had turned out to be the annual mobilization of the Upper Voltan na-tional militia for summer exercises, but Stanton had, as a reward, been posted to the Embassy in Paris. Paris! Paris in the springtime! *Pari uk ubim wiktik dzang*, Pulsifer thought in the Sunda dialect he knew so well.

"Done," he said, holding out his hand. It was seized in a manly grip.

"And done," cried Colonel Falsaki. "And now you will please to kidnap me, sir. I will explain later. Simply walk quite closely behind me. It will look better thus." He smiled. "Your good wife will not object to a house guest for a few days, I trust."

"But what about your Embassy?" Pulsifer asked. "They're sure to go to the police."

"His Excellency, the Ambassador—another of my uncles—has also read the works of Mr. Ian Fleming. He knows well that in the submerged world of espionage, men vanish without reason. He will expect it of me, and it will look better when I return with word of the Batungi's evil plot."

Leaving the Men's Bar they walked to their cars. The Colonel's was a long low Italian sports car carrying diplomatic license plates. He surveyed it ruefully before getting in. "They would not sell me an ejection seat," he told Pulsifer. "I will follow you, sir."

And so they drove out to Potomac Heights to inaugurate The Sundalan Crisis.

Marge, Pulsifer's wife, was enchanted with Colonel Falsaki, whom Pulsifer introduced as a Ford Foundation fellow in Washington to study the Smithsonian Institution. Marge, being a good wife, asked no questions, having in mind that Pulsifer's last foreign guest had also been similarly introduced. It was, she had decided, probably a C.I.A. policy.

Pulsifer and the Colonel sat up until the small hours, developing their plots and counterplots.

The following morning the Colonel telephoned his other uncle, the Sundalan Ambassador. "Good morning, Uncle William," he began courteously. "I trust you are well. Splendid. Well, I thought I should let you know that I have been kidnaped but am being well treated. No, not to worry. It seems that the people who hold me captive want me out of the way for a few days. But I think I am on to something big."

The Colonel turned to Pulsifer. "That should set him to thinking," he added.

It was not until late that afternoon that Pulsifer was summoned to the office of Mr. Crabtree, the Chief of African Affairs (Emerging Nations Division).

"This morning report of yours," Mr. Crabtree began without preface, "I'm not sure I like the look of it, Pulsifer. What's a delegation of Chinese Boy Scouts doing in the Hok territory?"

"That's a good question, sir. If they really *are* Boy Scouts. My contact at the Sundalan embassy is checking into it."

"Really? I wasn't aware that it was our policy to make that sort of contact by our people in this office, Pulsifer. That's a job best done by our field operatives."

"I am aware of that, sir. However when the opportunity presented itself, I thought I might supplement the reports of our men in Sundala. The arrival of a group of visiting Boy Scouts in the Hok territory might escape their notice, but when my contact further advised me that these were *Chinese* Boy Scouts, I thought it wise to bring the matter to your attention."

"Hmm. Perhaps you're right, Pulsifer. In any case, I won't discourage you. Keep an eye on the situation, will you?"

Several days later, having fully worked out their individual programs, Colonel Falsaki and Pulsifer parted company, agreeing to keep in touch by telephone. The Colonel, employing one of Marge's paring knives, put a few artful slashes in his trench coat.

"Our men in Sundala are named Sullivan and Foster," Pulsifer advised. "Sullivan is posing as an importer of sewing machines; Foster's cover is that of the Ambassador's chauffeur. They're about due to be rotated home on leave before reassignment, so there's no harm whatsoever in your exposing them." He shook hands with the Colonel. "Lots of luck."

"Together, sir, we shall go far in our respective countries' Intelligence Services," replied the Colonel, much moved. "I will let you know immediately when my cousin, the Minister of Commerce, informs me that the large mysterious crates he is having made, in accord with the instructions I cabled him, are ready for shipment to the interior."

Four days later Pulsifer was enabled to report that an Albanian freighter had discharged a cargo marked FRAGILE—USE NO HOOKS in the harbor of Teritza. "The cargo consists of large crates, the contents of which are alleged to be farm machinery ordered by the Batungi of Hok."

"But the Albanians make no farm machinery," Mr. Crabtree protested to Pulsifer, summoned again to his Chief's office. "What's your thinking, Pulsifer?"

"Missiles, sir," Pulsifer replied simply.

That same afternoon, the United States Ambassador to the Republic of Sundala cabled that C.I.A. operatives Sullivan and Foster were being expelled as *persona non grata*.

"Something's up, Pulsifer," Crabtree said at the emergency session called that evening. "The Director here thinks you ought to go out yourself and have a look around." The Director nodded gravely.

"Of course, you'll need a cover," the Director observed.

"We've thought of that, sir," said Crabtree. "Pulsifer will go as a Fulbright Scholar with a grant to study the currents of the Quangaha River, which rises in the western highlands of Hok. No Caucasian has ever penetrated there before."

"Sounds dangerous," commented the Director.

"It is," replied Mr. Crabtree.

A month later Pulsifer neared the Quangaha River port of Nguli, the last outpost of what passed for civilization in that remote region. He had spent the previous three weeks in bed suffering from the customary bout of what are locally known as the Sunda Shakes. He was wretched, and the boat he had chartered was temperamental, its steam engine smoking horridly. The native captain, an Arab named Hussein, was much addicted to hashish and kept putting his ancient craft on mud banks. "Allah's will," he would explain to Pulsifer.

At the town dock, the *Houri*, as the steam launch was named, rammed several pilings before she finally berthed. Pulsifer emerged from his tiny, steamy cabin to find himself facing a familiar figure.

"Colonel Falsaki!" he cried. The splendid figure in the uniform of a General of the Army of the Republic of Sundala saluted smartly, and grinned with pleasure.

"My dear Mr. Pulsifer, welcome to the headquarters of the Third Frontier Corps, which I have the honor to command. We are, of course, on twenty-four hour alert—" he nodded at several sleeping sentries on the dock— "but there is always time for a leisurely dinner, is there not?"

Over the third of a series of increasingly powerful gin-and-tonics General Falsaki explained to Pulsifer that his present post was in the nature of a reward for his services to Sundala in uncovering the vile C.I.A. plot to make the Batungi of Hok ruler of the nation.

"Not only a promotion, but the chance to return here to the frontier to defend my country," the General added as a house boy, bearing a fourth round of drinks, padded down the broad verandah of his elegantly furnished, air-conditioned bungalow. "I really had no taste for Intelligence work, you know."

"That's all very well for you, General," Pulsifer said, his tone unhappy, "but what about me? What about *my* crisis?"

"There is that," General Falsaki agreed thoughtfully.

"And what about this river I'm supposed to study? I've got to keep up appearances, you know."

"My dear Mr. Pulsifer, for a few Sundalan pounds Captain Hussein will falsify his log—assuming he bothers to keep one. You do not look at all well as it is. No, you will remain here as my guest for a time, and we will discuss the matter of the Batungi of Hok."

"Did somebody mention my name?" asked a new voice, and a towering, impeccably tailored figure appeared from the deepening afternoon shadows. "My dear Noganami, you must introduce me to your guest," the voice continued in a crisp Cantabridgian accent.

"My dear Claude, what a pleasant surprise! I hadn't expected you so early. Is Sylvia with you?"

"She's opening a new branch of the Hok Women's Volunteer Friendly Services up-country, but sends her regrets," replied the Batungi, inserting a monocle in his eye.

"Mr. Pulsifer, the Hereditary Batungi of Hok, my cousin Claude Fitzhugh-Mgallah," the General performed the introductions. "Mr. Pulsifer is with the Central Intelligence Agency."

"Delighted," said the Batungi.

"Yes," said Pulsifer, bemused.

"You play polo, Mr. Pulsifer?" the Batungi inquired courteously.

"Claude is a nine-goal player," General Falsaki said proudly.

"Oh," Pulsifer replied. "That's nice."

He was, he felt, either sloshed or down again with another siege of the Sunda Shakes. A fifth gin-and-tonic appeared on the small table beside his chair.

"Mr. Pulsifer has a problem," the General said. "He is investigating The Sundalan Crisis."

"Which one?" asked the Batungi.

"Your Chinese missiles, my dear chap. Your oriental advisors and technical missions. Frontier forays by armed bands of Hok guerrillas. That sort of thing."

"Thank you," said the Batungi, accepting a drink from the silent house boy. "Cheers, all," he added, easing himself into a chair. "Well, if you don't mind a suggestion from a comparative stranger, my dear Pulsifer, I should build it up a bit more. There's this matter of a loan for the new high dam on the Quangaha—do my people no end of good, you know—with American aid funds. As a gesture of good will it would go far to placate me in my blood feud with the present regime. Also, a pitched battle might help."

"Isn't that going a bit far?" Pulsifer asked anxiously.

"Not if we all use blanks," General Falsaki explained, "as we always do. Can't have our chaps hurt, you understand."

"What about this coming Friday?" the Batungi suggested. "Right after the polo match?"

"Excellent," agreed the General in Command of the Third Frontier Corps. "And now, gentlemen, shall we go in to dinner?"

Two days later the Director of the Central Intelligence Agency summoned Mr. Crabtree to his elegantly appointed office. "What's this from the Embassy in Sundala?" he asked brusquely. "Things hotting up there, eh?"

"We've just decoded Pulsifer's own report, sir. It looks like war. Limited, naturally, but war all the same."

"Has he any ideas?"

"Friday—tomorrow—is when he thinks things will blow up. Hok troops are reported mobilized on the frontier," Mr. Crabtree reported, his manner grave.

"Any suggestions?"

"Pulsifer seems to feel that the proposed high dam on the Quangaha River might help stabilize the country's economy, and since it will also irrigate a lot of the Hok territory, it might calm down the Batungi."

"Sounds reasonable. You know, Crabtree, it's just possible that we've underestimated Pulsifer in the past. What's his present status? Intelligence analyst, eh? That young man would do very well as a Chief of Mission, if you asked me."

"Quite possibly, sir. Will you see the Secretary of State on the Quangaha high dam allocation, sir? A hundred million should see the foundations laid, at least."

"Let's make it five hundred," replied the Director. "Never look cheap, Crabtree."

It was Pulsifer's stirring report of the Battle of Nguli which prompted approval, the following Monday, of a $650,000,000 allocation to the Republic of Sundala. Government troops, Pulsifer cabled, had been driven back with heavy losses but had rallied under the inspired leadership of their commander, General N. Falsaki, to push the invading Hok legions back across the hotly disputed frontier. Casualties had been light on the Hok side of the combat, but the Batungi had nonetheless agreed to negotiate rather than continue hostilities.

"I am most optimistic that, acting as mediator, I can get both contestants together on a settlement," Pulsifer's cable concluded. He had written it Friday evening after consultation with his host and the Batungi. By this time he had quite recovered from the Sunda Shakes.

"Amazing chap," said the Director, back in Washington, after the Western Highlands Truce and Watershed Agreement had been formally signed in Teritza a week before. His eye fell on a dispatch just in from Paris, and he frowned. "I wonder how he'd do with a really rough assignment, Crabtree."

"We can but try, sir," responded his loyal aide

At the airport in Teritza some days later, Field Marshal Falsaki shook Pulsifer's hand.

"We shall miss you, my dear Pulsifer," he said sincerely, his brown eyes moist.

"Given a bit more time, we should have made you into quite a passable polo player," added the Batungi of Hok. "So much of it's in the forearm, you know."

And Pulsifer entered the cabin of the Sundala Air-Africa jetliner, much touched by the thoughtfulness of his two friends. In his lapel was the rosette of the Order for Civilian Merit of the Republic of Sundala, Second Class, with Oak Leaves.

Two weeks later, after the briefest of home leaves, Pulsifer and his wife, Marge, took over the commodious apartment recently vacated by the C.I.A.'s Chief of Mission for Paris. It overlooked the Boulevard Haussmann.

Life was good, Pulsifer thought as he sipped a brandy on his balcony.

The Sundalan Crisis had taught him much, indeed, and on his newly increased salary, Marge would be able to afford at least one Paris gown. Quite possibly, two.

Thus he was quite prepared for the telephone call when it finally came.

"M'sieur Pulsifer?" the voice at the other end of the line inquired politely. "This is Colonel Pierre Saint-Luc Marie du Joinville speaking. You have heard of me?"

"Yes," said Pulsifer calmly. "You are my Opposite Number?"

"*Exactement*, M'sieur."

There was, Pulsifer felt as the quiet voice continued in his ear, no reason, really, why he should not end up as the Director. A man's ambitions should be limited only by his abilities.

"I think," he said slowly, "it would be well, Colonel, if we laid our cards on the table, *n'est-ce-pas?*"

James Powell

The Beddoes Scheme

Mr. Powell's light-hearted but deeply satirical novelets are not quite like anything else being written today, in the mystery field or out; and the character of Acting Sergeant Maynard Bullock of the Royal Canadian Mounted Police (they always get their man) is one of the freshest detective creations in many a moon . . .
The Beddoes Scheme, we warn you, is big, BIG, BIG, *BIG!!!*

Detective: SERGEANT MAYNARD BULLOCK (R.C.M.P.)

My first night in the gatehouse had been unsettling. Sometime after midnight the storm woke me. As I lay there in the strange bed, listening to the rain and to the old house creaking like a shoe, a flash of lightning illuminated the window and I saw an ungodly face peering in at me. Its eyes were wide, the mouth was slightly open and the head lolling to one side as though in a noose. Lightning again. Then the window was empty.

Up on the hill a lonely square of light hung in the castle tower. Mr. Beddoes, whoever he was, was working late. Resolving to pull down the shades the next night, I rolled over and went back to sleep.

When I awoke again, the storm had moved out to sea. Whispering voices were coming up the road from the shore. As they passed my window someone stumbled. His curse was in a Romance language, probably Rumanian or Romansh, the only two I wouldn't have recognized.

I went to the window in time to see five dark shapes following the pale egg of a flashlight on the ground. They passed through the gate and up toward the castle. Mr. Beddoes' friends spoke foreign languages

As I prepared breakfast I could see the castle from the kitchen window. It seemed smaller by half in the daylight: the ramparts were lower, the square tower about which rooks had circled in the moonlight was more massive than high . . . Duff Castle, mentioned in Holinshed.

In the late 1880's when old Garth McTaggart sold his Halifax distillery (McTaggart's Regular, McTaggart's Pride, and Tears of McTaggart Select) to the Montreal whiskey interests, he bought Duff Castle which had loomed over his impoverished boyhood in Scotland. Its stones had been the cargo of the *Great Eastern* on her maiden crossing. Duff Castle, transported and rebuilt near the tiny fishing village of Robbie's Cove, had become McTaggart's Folly, now a Cape Breton landmark for almost a century.

Lowney's old car turned the corner and went through the gate, breaking my thread of thought. The cardboard in the windshield read ROYAL MAIL. The evening before at the Watford railway station it had read TAXI.

It was from Lowney that I first learned the castle had been rented. When the McTaggart property finally went to the county for back taxes, the land beyond the wall including the gatehouse had been sold off. But Duff Castle itself had found no buyers. The county had managed to rent it once before—in the Thirties to a Hollywood company shooting exteriors for a movie entitled *Son of Macbeth*. And now to Mr. Beddoes.

I had decided to begin each day with a walk along the beach for exercise. But there wasn't any beach. Beyond the coarse grass was a shelf of dark, pooled rock. Picking my way over the wet surface, I didn't see the girl until she spoke. "Hi," she said. "That's English for hello. I'm afraid I don't speak Latvian if you're a Lat or something." She was sitting on a rock close to the water—a very pretty girl in an authentic-looking slicker.

"I thought I'd have the sea to myself," I said.

She smiled. "You must have arrived with the batch last night. I didn't see you at dinner."

"I'm staying at the Campbells'—the gatehouse," I said.

She blushed. "I'm sorry. I thought you were one of my father's friends. I'm Amy Beddoes."

"I'm Charles Simpson," I said. But I was pleased by her mistake. At the Watford station, when I had asked Lowney to take me to the gatehouse rather than to McTaggart's Folly, he had nodded sourly. "I spotted you not being a friend of Mr. Beddoes right off," he had said, an estimation clearly not in my favor.

"I really envy you," said Amy Beddoes. "If I owned a castle I'd live in the gatehouse and make the gatekeeper live in the castle."

"That wouldn't be too practical," I said and was about to explain why, when she shrugged.

"The view from the outside is the best," she said. "Father says he's going to live here forever. But I'm only out for the summers. I'm a senior at a college in New Haven, where the trains come from."

I told her I was an Assistant Professor of classics at Brock College on the Niagara peninsula. Dr. Campbell, my department head, hadn't been able to use his Cape Breton summer home this year, so he had offered it to me. I was here to turn six years of research into a doctoral thesis: *The Influence of Etruscan Fertility Rites on Latin Poetry to 30 B.C.* When I had talked a bit about my work, Amy Beddoes said, "I'm surprised I took you for one of my father's friends. You're not the type at all."

"What does your father do?" I asked.

Amy Beddoes didn't reply. Instead she closed her eyes and threw back her head. "Listen." I heard the sea. "It's just like one of those shells you hold up to your ear," she said. Then she got to her feet. "I'd better be getting back. I play gin rummy with my mother in the mornings to keep her mind off how long it takes the sun to rise above the yardarm."

Have I said that Amy Beddoes was very pretty? Have I said that as we parted at the gate she said, "Tomorrow we'll talk some more about you"? I had to pull myself together before I could sit down at the desk and start to work. When I did, I had the distinct impression that some of my notes were not in the order I had set them out the night before. But I decided to let that pass. I worked through the rest of the morning and afternoon.

About three o'clock a black Rolls-Royce went silently through the gate. There was a solitary figure in the rear seat. An hour later, when the car returned, there were three men in the back. Apparently Mr. Beddoes had met two of his friends at the railway station.

By late afternoon my mind had started to wander. I was staring out the window and thinking about Amy Beddoes when suddenly something moved in the trees on the other side of the road. I blinked. It was gone. Then a red shape flitted from behind the trunk of one tree to another, then after a moment to another, and so on until it had disappeared from view.

I threw down my pen in exasperation. Something curious was

obviously going on: a tortured face at the window, foreign voices on the road at night, a mysterious tenant in the castle whose friends were not like me—and now something red and furtive flashing among the trees. If it hadn't been for Amy Beddoes I think I would have packed up and gone back to Brock College where I could work in peace.

That night the gatehouse was plagued with noises. I was going around pulling down the shades to ward off faces in the night when I noticed a light blinking far out at sea. It was answered by a light on the wharf. A code, apparently. I shook my head and went to bed.

In the middle of the night I was awakened by a loud crash and shout from the kitchen. I rushed in, my curses at the ready. A low moan came from the closet that led up to the attic. Opening the door I found myself looking down on a large red-faced man in the scarlet tunic, blue riding breeches, white lanyard, and wide-brimmed hat of the Royal Canadian Mounted Police.

"All right," he said patiently, "who moved the ladder?"

Before dinner I had used it to replace the light bulb in the hall.

He shook his head sadly, got up, straightened his tunic which had bunched up under the armpits, and ran a thumbnail through his trim mustache. "You must be—Simpson," he said, consulting his notebook.

"Yes, I'm Mr. Simpson," I said, looking him up and down. "Con-stable—?"

"Acting Sergeant Maynard Bullock," he said, placing three fingers significantly on the bare sleeve of his tunic. He moved past me to the refrigerator.

"Would you mind telling me what's going on?" I asked.

Bullock paused with the refrigerator door open. "I wish I knew, Simpson. I really wish I knew," he said. He took two eggs and began to scramble them. "I keep a record of all I take," he said. "When I leave I'll give you a voucher redeemable at any post office. And there'll be a little form I'd like you to sign saying I left the kitchen tidy."

Dabbing a dollop of jam on his toast he added, "Have you ever tried that marmalade that comes in those little stone jars? No? Good old Mavis, my wife, always keeps a jar in the house. It's my only vice. Well, let's go into the living room and talk this thing out."

We sat facing each other. Bullock balanced the plate on his knees and ate heartily for a few minutes. Then he said, "First off, Simpson, I'm going to have to swear you to secrecy."

I told him I didn't want to be sworn to secrecy. "I just want you to get out of here so I can get some work done."

"That might prove inconvenient," said Bullock, "though not impossible. I once lived for an entire week in the dead of winter concealed in an old hollow tree to capture the celebrated Jean-Loup Batoche who was smuggling in American cigarettes along the Champlain Trail. The very next day after I got into the tree, I might add, Batoche snowshoed by, 5000 filter cigarettes and all."

Bullock set his empty plate on the floor and brushed the crumbs from his tunic. "So you see, Simpson, I could leave. But what—"

"Wait a minute," I said. "You said you stayed in that tree for a week."

Bullock smiled sourly and pulled a large curved pipe from his pocket.

"As it happened," he said, "when Batoche came by I discovered that my arms were wedged in at my sides and I couldn't get out. Three days later when he came by with a second load I had worked my handcuffs out of my pocket and my right hand up to a hole in the trunk. I decided to try a bluff. I called him over. He was a very surprised smuggler, let me tell you. Explaining who I was, I ordered him to hold his wrist up to the hole. Well, as he himself pointed out, it was blowing up a blizzard. So he chatted amiably for a while, pressed several packs of cigarettes on me, and left. The local RCMP barracks received an anonymous phone call three days later telling them where I was."

Bullock puffed thoughtfully for a bit. Then he leaned forward with his elbows on his knees and the pipe wrapped in his large fists. "For the sake of argument," he said, "let's assume you've been sworn to secrecy." He nodded toward my notes and manuscript. "I've checked you out, Simpson, and you seem on the level. I need your cooperation. I want to use this house as my base of operations."

"I don't understand," I said.

"By godfrey, Simpson," said Bullock, waving toward the castle, "you and I know something fishy's going on up there. What about those deliveries of electronic equipment in boxes marked Dog Food? Why are the African drums around Lake Chad beating out Beddoes' name? And what about those submarines of Panamanian registry slipping people ashore here and taking them away at night? We could nail your Mr. Beddoes on that last business alone. But that's

nickel-and-dime stuff. What's behind it all? Smuggling? Counter-
feiting? Espionage? *Some* kind of monkeyshines, we know that."

Bullock opened his notebook. "Listen to this: Jacob Henderson
Beddoes, born 1910; worked way through Harvard as a professional
boxer . . . Ever hear of Gentleman Jake Beddoes, the heavyweight
contender in the early Thirties?"

When I shook my head Bullock continued his reading. "Joined the
Klein and Dawes Advertising Agency in 1935, which became Beddoes and Klein in 1938. Battlefield commission in Sicily in 1943.
Congressional Medal of Honor the following year: *His command
destroyed and though wounded himself, Captain Beddoes, armed
only with a portable bullhorn, did induce four crack Panzer units to
surrender.*" Bullock looked up. "You've heard of the Manhattan Project?"

"The atomic bomb," I said.

Bullock nodded. "But have you ever heard of the Beddoes Project?
It was top secret. All we know is that the atomic bomb got there
first." He returned to his notebook. "In 1945 he founded the Beddoes
Agency. By 1949 all the major advertising agencies had merged
under him to form the Beddoes Group. Then about four years ago
there was a scandal of some sort. The Beddoes Group dissolved almost overnight and Beddoes himself dropped from sight." Bullock
snapped the notebook shut.

"Take a look at this," he said and pulled a large photograph out
of his tunic. "I took it from the attic." The photograph showed a
terrace in front of Duff Castle. The shadows were those of a few
minutes before sunset. Twelve men with after-dinner cigars were
standing at a respectful distance watching a thirteenth, a tall man
with a large impressive head topped with gray hair turning white
at the temples. He was feeding some large black birds on the lawn.

"There's your Beddoes," said Bullock. "But have you ever seen
birds like that before?"

"Rooks," I said. The night of my arrival I had asked Lowney what
they were. "They came with the castle," Lowney had said sullenly
as he took my bags from the trunk of his car. "There's a legend
around here about those rooks." Lowney had closed his eyes and
recited: "As long as there are rooks at McTaggart's Folly, Robbie's
Cove will ne'er go on Daylight Saving Time."

"Notice anything strange about Beddoes and those birds?" asked
Bullock.

"He seems to be talking to them."

"That's only half of it," said Bullock. "But a detective sees the other half, the important half." He tapped the photograph with his finger. "Those birds are *listening.*"

I looked again. Bullock was right.

"And who are these other people?" he said. "The one on the end there is Hakkim Raschid, the mystery man of the Middle East. Saint or sinner? Interpol would like to know. The one with the pipe is Sir Harley Smith-Watkins, the nuclear physicist. The one in the leather shorts is Emerich Schnitzler, whose grandfather founded Schnitzler S.A., the chemical complex. Neither side can use a whiff of poison gas without paying royalties to Schnitzler S.A. This one, the grandson, is a medical missionary in a South Seas leper colony and an author of bawdy limericks. In the blue overalls we have Hao Yang Cheng, the Red Chinese ideologist. Beside him in the leggings is either the Dean of Newbury Cathedral, C. of E., or the R. C. Cardinal, Archbishop of Graetz, Austria. This one is Joseph Makembwa, the Bantu philosopher and humanitarian, known popularly as the Heart of Darkest Africa. The double-breasted suit is Avo Montenegro, the Croat novelist. The one in the dhoti is Rabindranath Sudraka, celebrated guru and contract bridge champion. Next we have Wallingford Riggs, the baby food magnate. And next to him Massimo Scarlatini, the motion picture producer. This one here is Dr. Toshiya Katasuru, Nobel Prize winner in oceanography. And finally, M. I. Scriabin, the Soviet commentator and guest panelist. Find the common thread linking these people and the rest of Beddoes' strange friends and we've unraveled our enigma!"

"*Your* enigma," I said, getting to my feet. "Suit yourself about staying. As for me, I'm going to bed."

"Sleep well," said Bullock. "I'm going to sit up for a while and see if I can sort this thing out. You know, Simpson, I've spent the last five years guarding the flowerbeds in front of the Parliament Buildings in Ottawa. Then out of the blue I'm assigned to this investigation. Talk is that the Minister of Justice himself asked for me by name." Bullock bowed his head modestly. "I think they've got their eye on me."

The next morning down on the rocks I tried to ask Amy about her father but she shook her head. "We're supposed to talk about you," she insisted.

I've often suspected that I'm a bit of a stick-in-the-mud. But as I began to speak, the depths of my ordinariness appalled me. To my surprise, however, Amy was a contented, almost eager listener. In fact, for the next week we talked every morning about me, about my humdrum life at Brock College, about the security of tenure that would be mine with the thesis accepted, and even about the thesis itself.

For some strange reason she liked to hear me talk about the thesis. Once, when I had outlined a chapter, she said dreamily, "Boy, there's no chance of that making the best-seller list." Another time she seemed anxious to assure herself that apart from scholarship my study of Etruscan fertility rites was of no practical value.

"The Etruscans are extinct, if that's what you mean," I said.

So my days began to take on a regular pattern. I would meet Amy on the shore. Then I would work while Bullock, deep in thought, paced up and down the living room puffing on his pipe. Except for excursions "to take a look-see for footprints, et cetera," Bullock stuck close to the gatehouse. "We don't want to tip our hand too soon," he would say with a wink.

Whenever the Rolls-Royce or Lowney's taxi passed, taking visitors to and from the railway station, Bullock would crouch by the window, his ballpoint pen would go click-click and he would write down the license number and the exact time. Once he staggered back from the window and said, "My old eyes must be playing tricks on me, Simpson. I could have sworn one of the men in that car was our own Deputy Minister of External Affairs."

Each night, between watching the after-dinner strollers through field glasses and the signal from the offshore submarine, Bullock phoned Ottawa. "Acting Sergeant Bullock here . . . No, no *new* developments. However, I . . . Check . . . Check . . . But I—" Each time an invisible hand slapped Bullock's face and I knew he had been hung up on.

Once when he caught me watching, Bullock shouted into the dead receiver, "Yeah? Well, why don't you go soak your head?" and slammed down the phone. " 'Are you asleep at the switch out there, Bullock?' " he mimicked for my benefit. " 'Don't forget to touch home base, Bullock.' 'Where's your expense account in triplicate, Bullock?' By godfrey, Simpson, the man in the front line needs a little of the milk of human kindness, not all this badgering and red tape. Well, if Beddoes' business is as big as I think it is, it could mean a desk job for yours truly with one of those stuffed buffalo heads on the wall and my own telephone. By godfrey, I'd make the other fellows hop."

He thought about that for a minute. Then he said, "Say, I could go for a game of cribbage to sharpen the old wits."

"I think I'll turn in," I said.

One overcast afternoon with Bullock off somewhere in the trees having a "look-see," the Rolls-Royce glided through the gate and was gone. Soon after the rain began.

An hour later it was coming down in sheets. Suddenly there was a pounding on the front door. I opened it to find myself face to face with the apparition in the window the night of my arrival. The eyes were wide. The mouth hung open. The head lolled to one side as though in a noose. Only the chauffeur's cap with the water dripping from the visor was new. The mouth moved but the sounds were guttural and unintelligible. The man raised a fist to the side of his head in a menacing way. When I stepped back, he brushed past me to the telephone.

"I'm afraid Hogan is a bit hard to understand at first, Mr. Simpson." Beddoes himself, large and imposing, was standing in the rain on the doorstep. "I'm your neighbor, Jake Beddoes," he said, offering me a firm handshake. He stood patiently in the rain until I recovered myself and invited him in. "I'm afraid we've gotten ourselves stuck in the pothole," he said. "Hogan refuses to let me walk up to the castle in all this rain. He gets quite excited if I don't let him baby me."

While he spoke Beddoes was appraising me openly. All at once I had the impression he approved of what he saw. Only then did he smile. "Rather than wait in the car, I thought I'd take this chance to introduce myself," he said.

We came into the living room where I put a match to the wood in the fireplace. However, it was not the fire but Beddoes, at ease and courtly, who was the room's center. Hogan came in, said something, and took up a place behind Beddoes' chair. "Have you met Mr. Lowney, the reeve of Robbie's Cove?" said Beddoes. "He'll be coming by for us in a few minutes."

We talked a bit about the weather. Then Beddoes said, "Do you mind my asking what brings you to these parts, Mr. Simpson?" I mentioned my thesis and his face brightened. With questions revealing more than a layman's knowledge of my field he drew me into a description of my work.

"Well," said Beddoes finally, "if you're looking for peace and quiet, this is the place. The television station in Sydney doesn't broadcast this far and back in the Thirties when the government thought up radio-license fees the only radio in Robbie's Cove was taken out to sea and dropped overboard right in the middle of the Major Bowes Amateur Hour." Hogan said something. "That's right," said Beddoes. "Old Mrs. Mears has a wind-up Victrola and some Sir Harry Lauder records. Hogan is our expert on what's going on in the area. Yes, you might say that we're living in the quiet eye of the communications hurricane. A fitting retreat for a retired advertising man, don't you think?"

"Somehow you're not my idea of an advertising man," I said. "To be honest, I've always agreed with my colleagues in the English Department that advertising is a gigantic insult to human intelligence."

Hogan had started forward angrily at my words, but Beddoes waved him back. "I admire your frankness, Mr. Simpson," he said. "Well, tell your colleagues they are right."

Beddoes smiled sadly. "How strange that sounds coming from me! You know, Mr. Simpson, I can recall my first big advertising account as though it were only yesterday. The Royal Shoe people were marketing a new brogan. I called it Foot Prince—*Foot Prince—The Shoe Fit for a King*. Under that name it sold beyond all expectations. I was delighted. You see, Young Jake Beddoes told himself that if today he could persuade people to buy shoes, perhaps tomorrow he would hit upon that certain slogan or bright box that would charm people into leaving all the Brand-X fears, hatreds, and anxieties on the shelf and take instead the giant-size package of Peace and Brotherhood. That was his dream, Mr. Simpson—to find that bright box. Was that really so wrong?"

"I think it sounds like a very worthwhile idea," I said.

Beddoes had risen at the sound of a car stopping outside. He considered my last remark. "Yes, I believe you do," he said. He shook my hand. "Perhaps you'll have dinner with us one of these evenings. Our hospitality is a bit overextended at the moment. But the next five or six days will see the end of that. How does a week from tonight sound?"

I said that would be fine.

Lowney was standing with Hogan at the door. He looked me over suspiciously. "Is this man giving you any trouble, Mr. Beddoes?" he asked.

Beddoes laughed out loud. "No. Of course not, Mr. Lowney."

Later that evening as Bullock stood in his underwear ironing the brim of his rain-warped hat, he said, "You can fall for that casual visit stuff if you like, Simpson. I say he suspects something. Maybe it's time to make my move."

The next morning Bullock propped a shaving mirror on the fireplace mantel and began carefully to smear his face and behind his ears with the end of a burnt cork. "One of the tricks of the trade," he said as he worked. Then I watched from the window as, red-coated and black-faced, Bullock slipped through the gate.

Have I said that Amy was sometimes perplexing? For example, when I mentioned my meeting with her father, adding that he struck me as a fine person, she said, "Oh, he's certainly that." But then she pulled at a clasp on her slicker and said sadly, "I guess you were bound to meet him sooner or later."

But if I found her sometimes perplexing, there was no mistaking her interest in me. Indirectly, and as far as honesty would permit, I began to draw an agreeable picture of the life of an Assistant Professor's wife at Brock College.

As for Bullock, he returned each night to eat and make his phone report to Ottawa. "That Hogan keeps the pantry under lock and key," he said over scrambled eggs. "And I need my little snacks. I find it hard to think without something sticking to the old ribs. But I think I've got the whole business figured out. In three words: sweepstake tickets—an international sweepstake-ticket ring."

Another night as he combed the kitchen for a fresh cork to burn, he looked at me solemnly and said, "Try this one on for size, Simpson: suppose Beddoes is one of those mad scientists about to unleash an electronic monster of his own creation on an unsuspecting world." With that he said, "Sleep well, Simpson," and slipped outside and back up to the castle.

Over the next few days there was a flurry of activity at the castle as the last of the visitors departed. The night before I was to have dinner with Beddoes, Bullock, who had just brushed the crumbs off his tunic and lit his pipe, exclaimed, "By godfrey, E. J. Canby!" He looked at me triumphantly. "Simpson, like the little man who wasn't there I've seen a lot these last few days and heard an earful, though most of it in languages I couldn't understand. However, one name kept recurring: E. J. Canby. Does that ring a bell?"

I shook my head.

"About four years ago the body of E. J. Canby, the most powerful man in Wall Street, was found washed up on a beach near New York City. The verdict was accidental death by drowning. I knew I had heard the name before, but it only just came back to me. Something about the case stuck in my craw at the time. Why, I asked myself, should the drowned body of a financial tycoon be wearing a bicycle clip on one trouser leg? Simpson, I have reason to suspect that Beddoes was responsible for the death of E. J. Canby."

"I'm sure there's some perfectly natural explanation," I said.

As I walked through the gate and up the road for the first time, the setting sun glinted in the windows of Duff Castle and the rooks circled the tower. A shelf of dark clouds sat on the horizon behind the walls, waiting to move out to sea. I had imagined that the stones of the castle would be numbered, marked by the Scot dismantlers to guide the rebuilders, that the castle would stand against the sky like a giant painting-by-numbers project. Of course it did not. Nor was there a massive, animal-head knocker on the door or even a trumpet hanging by a chain. Below a card holder that said BEDDOES was an electric bell.

I was shown into the great hall under Hogan's distrustful eye. It was a paneled and beamed room with an immense fireplace and a thick-banistered staircase leading up to a gallery.

A trim, blonde woman in her forties with a tired but not unpleasant face rose unsteadily as I entered and raised a Martini glass in my direction.

When she had poured me a drink and refilled her own she said, "My daughter speaks very highly of you, Mr. Simpson."

"I'm afraid meeting me may be something of a disappointment," I said.

"I hope so," she said. "I suppose you find that strange. Well, Amy has told me about the two of you and if you want my blessing I give it to you. You see, I don't want Amy to make my mistake. I don't want her to marry the alternative to the atomic bomb."

"You mean the Beddoes Project?" I asked.

She nodded. "The idea was simple enough. Parachute Jake into the garden of Emperor Hirohito's summer palace. The Emperor would be watching the cherry blossoms and composing haiku. Jake would float down and talk to him. My husband's Japanese is fluent. The Emperor would announce Japan's unconditional surrender and apply for membership in the United Nations."

Mrs. Beddoes took a drink from her glass. "Mr. Simpson," she said in a half whisper, "what I'm trying to say in a roundabout way is that if you love my daughter you must take her away from here before it's too late. It was bad enough before, but now there is a terrible goodness about this place."

"Well, I see you've met my better half, Mr. Simpson." It was Beddoes, speaking through a smile as he came down the staircase.

"Your wife was just telling me about the Beddoes Project," I said.

Beddoes took a sip of the Martini his wife handed him. "That was a long time ago," he said. "But it was no hare-brained operation, believe me," he said. "My team had gone over it detail by detail. I remember I had just made my fifteenth practice jump onto a patio belonging to a real estate man near Albuquerque when we received word that the Manhattan Project people"—he fluttered a disparaging hand—"and their bomb had won out."

"More people were killed by the bomb than the world knows, Mr. Simpson," said Beddoes. "Let me tell you a story about that. Our last conversation may have left you with too flattering an impression of the man now standing before you."

Mrs. Beddoes poured herself another drink.

"It was five years ago next August 17, as I remember well," Beddoes went on. "We still had the place on Long Island. There were guests out for the week-end. A good crowd, and among them a dozen quiet men who, I may say without fear of contradiction, controlled America's finances and vast communications structure—bankers, corporation presidents, the king of a newspaper and newsmagazine empire, heads of the major radio and television networks, a book club president, and an advertising man second only to myself. There were also a number of relatively younger men—vice-presidents, editors, junior partners—in related fields. I had brought them all together for a purpose of my own.

"Early in the evening I led the conversation around to a familiar subject—the relative merits of Wall Street versus Madison Avenue. With everyone a bit in their cups the discussion became quite animated. 'Well,' I said, 'why not decide the whole question on the playing field?' They thought I meant Indian wrestling. 'No, no,' I said, 'I have just had a brainstorm. Polocycle, gentlemen. Polocycle, the game of the future.'

"A dozen tricycles and croquet mallets were brought in. I had picked them up a few days before for a local orphanage. The twelve quiet men took up the idea at once, amused by the prospect of seeing their juniors make fools of themselves. Wall Street and Madison Avenue shouted challenges at each other. The younger men were less enthusiastic. I believe it was the crash helmets, six black and six white, that carried the day.

"The lawn in front of the house was flat and large enough for our purposes before it fell in terraces to the Sound. We marked off a field, sixty feet from goal to goal. During the warm-up, knees were everywhere, but with the help of two stiff stirrup cups the kinks worked themselves out. An Undersecretary of the Navy acted as referee. The toss went to Madison Avenue. The clash of mallets. Some fine passing. Furious pedaling on the breakaways. Up and down the field.

"As I recall, Wall Street beat off a last-minute, hell-for-leather charge to win three games out of five. There was great joy in the Wall Street camp and several new board members were named on the spot.

"As you might imagine, the Wall Street seniors laid it on their Madison Avenue colleagues unmercifully—the dissolute character of uptown life, the value of *mens sana in corpore sano*, the clear eye, the level head.

"Finally, smarting under all this abuse, a network president who, at sixty-five, prided himself on his flat stomach, shouted the challenge I knew would come. The crowd fell silent. Then, as their juniors looked on with awe, the twelve quiet men, uneasy but determined, donned the crash helmets and took their respective places on the tricycles.

"I watched with amusement as the unseemly spectacle began anew. I felt great power, Mr. Simpson—I was controlling those who themselves controlled so much.

"Then abruptly came a rush on the Wall Street goal. The ball went out of bounds and E. J. Canby, former head of the World Bank, now Chairman of the Board of the Barlow Trust, faded back to recover."

At the mention of Canby's name I heard a faint click-click. Bullock and his ballpoint pen were hiding somewhere in the shadows.

Beddoes paid no attention and continued. "But as Canby faded back he passed too close to the terrace and before our eyes his tricycle plunged down the incline out of control.

"He struggled for mastery of his little machine but when he hit the next level, going faster, his feet slipped from the pedals and he careened down the next slope with ever-increasing speed. We all stood there thunder-struck. Yet somehow as I watched that helpless, terrorized man with his portly bottom enveloping the little leather tricycle seat, I thought of the World Bank and the Barlow Trust and I laughed. It was an ugly laugh and it rang in the silence.

"Canby heard me for as he hit the final slope that ended in a ten-foot drop to the swift currents of the Sound, he shouted, 'Damn you, Beddoes!' Then the tip of his cigar arced brightly down into the darkness and he was gone.

"It is no small thing to be cursed by the Chairman of the Board of the Barlow Trust, Mr. Simpson. Of course no one held me responsible—an unfortunate accident, they said. But the word was out: Jake Beddoes is insincere. And overnight all doors were closed to me."

Beddoes stopped.

Amy, looking very pretty—it was the first time I had seen her without the slicker—had joined us and was watching me. Just then Hogan announced that dinner was ready.

The meal began in silence. I was waiting for Beddoes to speak again and trying to locate Bullock's hiding place. Amy sat quietly at her place, while Mrs. Beddoes had brought another cocktail to the table and was working away at it with great deliberation. Bullock's pen went click-click when, past the soup and well into the roast, Beddoes began again as though thinking out loud.

"How did Jake Beddoes come to find himself at the height of his power laughing as E. J. Canby rode a tricycle to oblivion? Where was he now, that idealistic young man who had dreamed of a bright box to purvey Justice and Brotherhood? I'll tell you: when the Beddoes Project lost out to the equations of the atomic scientists, Beddoes had turned imperceptibly sour. He and E. J. Canby were as much victims of the bomb as the people of Hiroshima and Nagasaki. It just took the radiation a little longer.

"Was it all over then for the young man's dream? No. That couldn't be true. Young Jake Beddoes and his bright box had to have another chance.

"Why? Here's one reason why."

Beddoes pointed to Hogan who was silently hobbling around the table with a napkined basket of rolls. "What do you see, Mr. Simpson? The babbling wreckage of a man. Well, it wasn't always so. Hogan was once my good right arm, loyal to me in all things, privy to all my dreams, a Yale man and a fine person in his own right. For me he drove himself too close to the edge and when all we had built up collapsed, something inside Hogan snapped and he became what you now see. In part it was for his sake and for many others like him that I knew I must try again. Isn't that right, Hogan? We're trying again. And it will work. By god, it will work!"

Hogan's eyes lit up excitedly. Beddoes' words seemed to pluck at nerves all over his body. A roll fell from his basket. I thought he was going to fall to his trembling knees and kiss Beddoes' hand.

Beddoes patted him on the arm. "Good man. Good man."

At that moment I saw a scarlet sleeve come out from under the table, snatch up the roll, and disappear again.

Beddoes returned to me. "But the task before me was a difficult one, Mr. Simpson. Abstractions are not marketable. Peace and Brotherhood, just the bare bones of them, won't sell. You need a peg to hang them on—that bright box.

"Well, I thought and I thought and gradually an idea began to take shape in my mind. I pondered it, found it good, and set it down on paper. I sent what I had written to certain friends of broad and varied influence whom I had met in my world travels. Their response was overwhelmingly favorable.

"I set out immediately on an extended journey, traveling as a certain George Muncie, import-export, for secrecy had to be the heart of our endeavor. I visited the capitals of Europe. In Berlin I slipped behind the Iron Curtain, visited Eastern Europe, Russia, China, emerging in Hong Kong. Through the Far East. Australia. Throughout Latin America. Everywhere there were clandestine meetings with my special people. From these meetings and my original outline we developed what I called simply The Scheme. But they wanted a name. I suggested we call it the E. J. Canby Memorial Scheme. But they said no. No, they said, let's call it the Beddoes Scheme. And so we did.

"The past two years have been spent here in this quiet castle, working out the details in close cooperation with my friends."

Hogan appeared with the coffee.

"Well, enough of the Beddoes Scheme for now," said Beddoes, as we rose and adjourned to the chairs around the fireplace. "But afterward I have some things I'd like to show you." Then Beddoes added in a low voice, "By the way, if you run into Acting Sergeant Bullock in the hall, as I'm sure you will, please pretend you don't see him. I'm afraid he thinks burnt cork makes him invisible. I gather it means a lot to him."

Following coffee, Beddoes asked his wife and Amy to excuse us and I accompanied him upstairs. We walked along the gallery and into a hallway and suddenly came upon Bullock hurrying from the other direction. He flattened himself against the wall in what little shadow there was and squeezed his eyes shut. We had to turn to avoid bumping into him. I followed Beddoes up a spiral staircase.

Beddoes unlocked his study and showed me in. One half of the room was filled with television control panels, cameras, and equipment. Four easels draped with green felt stood against the wall.

"What would you say, Mr. Simpson, if I told you that we have found the bright box that can draw all men together in universal solidarity and banish guilt and fear?"

"I'd say you really have something," I said.

Beddoes looked away and said, "But suppose I told you that the bright box is a person?"

Before I could answer he had crossed to the first easel. "This is Phase One of the Beddoes Scheme," he said. "Of course, what you are about to see is only a small part of one aspect of Phase One." He removed the cloth.

There was a stack of posters on the easel. The uppermost was a drawing of a tall heroic figure in gray overalls reaching up and touching the moon, while behind him, all eyes on his face, stood a worker holding a large monkey wrench, a farmer with a spike of wheat, a secretary with a pad and pencil, and other representative figures. "The inevitability of history moves the Russian people toward the moon," said Beddoes, translating the Cyrillic legend.

The next poster showed an American dentist with one of those round reflectors on his head. The caption said, "Some plain talk to Moms and Dads about tooth decay."

The last poster showed an Arab in a burnoose letting a handful of sand pour through his finger as he pointed over his shoulder at the Aswan Dam. "Tomorrow the Garden of Allah," translated Beddoes.

The three posters had a certain compelling quality that held my eye. But I couldn't see the point. Beddoes watched me silently. I was about to shake my head when it came to me. I flipped back through the posters. In each of them, from the man touching the moon to the Arab, the face was Beddoes' face.

"Yes," he said shyly, "it's me. I am also the face of Amerigo Vespucci on the forty-lire commemorative stamp and Hans Christian Andersen on the new Danish ten-kroner note. In a certain Latin American republic a larger-than-life-size statue of Garcia Morales, the Father of His Country, was recently unveiled and that too is me.

"Yes, Jake Beddoes is the bright box I had been looking for. Initially, you see, we had to make Jake Beddoes' face familiar and give it a positive association. Along with these posters there were also walk-on parts in films and television dramas, scenes shot in the course of my trip with a story built around them: I was the man whose hand Lenin is shaking so warmly at the Finland Station; I was the celebrated brain surgeon who saves the hero for his life of great music; I was the kindly judge whose 'Case dismissed' saves a woman's life.

"And as we made the face familiar, so the voice. I speak most languages fluently. Our friends in the various regimes, civil services, and networks introduced what we called 'The Thought for the Day' into their programming. Beddoes speaks for half a minute without being identified. And we used these same spots for piped music, the kind you hear in department stores, bars, and elevators. The music stops. A voice speaks out of nowhere. What do I say? A thousand things, Mr. Simpson. I like people. I like the human condition and I'm not ashamed of it.

"This initial phase lasted for a year. Then it was time to make Jake Beddoes known by name. Phase Two."

The first poster on the second easel showed Beddoes in a double-breasted suit seated at a Louis XIV desk with a tapestry of knights and unicorns at his back. The pose and the lighting were arranged so as to accentuate his nose. "Jake Beddoes says: We must share the glory of France with the world," translated Beddoes.

In the next he wore a pearly-king outfit, a cockney grin, and held up two fingers to form a V. "Jake Beddoes says: There'll always be an England."

The next poster was a drawing much like the man touching the moon except that the figures were Chinese and it was an oriental Beddoes in blue overalls who held aloft what looked like a metal loaf of bread. "Jake Beddoes says: The People's Republic can achieve its pig-iron quota," translated Beddoes.

The last one showed Beddoes in a fire ranger's hat. "Jake Beddoes says: Please! Only *you* can prevent forest fires."

Beddoes tapped the second set of posters. "In many a totalitarian country," he said, "Youth for Beddoes Groups risk imprisonment or death putting up posters like these in the night.

"Meanwhile a hidden radio transmitter in the Urals is beaming Radio Free Beddoes through the Communist world, while picket ships off Zanzibar, Cape Hatteras, and the mouth of the Orinoco transmit The Voice of Beddoes, music in good taste for your listening pleasure, and on the hour, a fifteen-minute prerecorded 'Coffee-Break with Beddoes.' I tell bureaucrats to be human beings, children to be obedient, old people to be patient. Perhaps I just tell them to boil their drinking water or fasten their seat belts. What's important is that they hear a voice that really cares and understands.

"The past month has been our Phase Three," continued Beddoes, as he uncovered the third easel. The top poster showed an African native squatting on his haunches. "Jocomo Kavubu likes Jake Beddoes," said Beddoes, translating the caption. "You might call this the testimonial stage. The subjects here are all national types but their endorsements are nonetheless real. I spent time with all of them, talking, listening, getting acquainted. 'Stay here, Beddoes,' Jocomo said when I had to leave, 'and you and I will sit together and watch the rest of the world go by.' But I couldn't stay, Mr Simpson, though I was sorely tempted.

"And here you have Jan Marttens, a retired barge captain in Rotterdam. He likes Jake Beddoes. And so does Mrs. Doris Weams here, Iowa mother of five.

"Along with these posters we have a number of novelty items—bumper stickers, Beddoes buttons, balloons and kits." Beddoes laughed. "Here, you might get a kick out of this." He opened a drawer and tossed a red felt beanie on the desk. It had *I like Beddoes* stitched in gold script across the front. On each side was the plastic replica of a human ear. "Mine," smiled Beddoes, touching his ears. "One of our friends on the West Coast got the idea and had a few dozen made up. I thanked him for the thought but said I wasn't sure it was exactly the kind of thing we were trying to do.

"By Phase Three, as you might imagine, certain people had started wondering what was going on—heads of secret police who weren't sleeping too well, newspaper editors with the smell of a story in their nostrils, politicians chewing cigars over strange signals from the grassroots. I gather most of them suspect it's some kind of advertising stunt, but they can't figure out the product." Beddoes looked at me and smiled. "Perhaps you can't either, Mr. Simpson "

I shook my head.

"World solidarity, Mr. Simpson. All peoples united by one thing—they all like Jake Beddoes. When that happens, then all their fears of each other will go out the window and with the fears, half the political, economic, and psychological problems of our planet.

"And what about the other half of their fears? That is our ace in the hole—Phase Four." Beddoes unveiled the final easel. The single poster was a large close-up of Beddoes' face. Strong, relaxed, thoughtful. The eyes ready to smile, the mouth to speak many things to many people. Underneath was the simple caption: "Jake Beddoes likes you."

"First we get rid of the fear," said Beddoes. "Now we get rid of the guilt. Jake Beddoes likes them. Once we get that message across, then the little man everywhere will rise up and march side by side with his neighbor toward a future free of ideology, venal compromise, antagonisms of class, race, or creed, a future where all his reverses will be insignificant because they cannot dull the one essential truth—that he likes Beddoes and that Beddoes likes him. Phase Four goes into operation tomorrow.

"Well, there you are, Mr. Simpson. The Beddoes Scheme. What do you think?"

"It's a big idea, sir—really big," I said. "And it just might work."

"It *will* work, Mr. Simpson. It *will* work," said Beddoes. "And next week from a hidden launching site near Lake Chad we put up our first communications satellite into orbit—Beddsat. Every evening from then on I will come up here after dinner, sit at that desk, and in a broadcast seen live around the world I will talk to them all. 'An Hour with Beddoes.' We will broadcast from here because this is the home I have sworn never to leave. No, personal power and glory aren't what I'm after. Jake Beddoes, the person, is dead. In his place is the bright box. You know, this may sound blasphemous, Mr. Simpson, but just as in simpler times gods became men to make men better, perhaps it's time for one man to give his fellow men hope by assuming a little bit of the Divinity in their eyes. Just a little bit." He measured it out between a thumb and index finger.

Distant thunder intruded into the room. Beddoes looked at his watch. "I'm afraid the ladies will be wondering what happened to us."

He was about to turn off the light when I crossed to the desk. "Would you mind if I kept this, sir?" I said, picking up one of the beanies.

Beddoes laughed. "As a kind of souvenir of our little talk? Go right ahead, Simpson."

"Mother decided to turn in," said Amy. "With the decanter, if you're thinking of a nightcap."

I said I'd better be getting back. As Beddoes shook my hand he invited me to lunch the next day. "We can talk some more," he said. Watching him go back upstairs I felt guilty because I knew he was going up to his study where, alone and well into the night, he would ponder over another Hour with Beddoes.

Though I protested that the storm was about to break, Amy insisted on walking me back to the gatehouse.

The wind was in the trees as we walked down the driveway. Every few seconds lightning made the horizon glow as the thunder came closer.

Finally Amy said, "I expect he told you everything."

"It's big, Amy—I had no idea how really big! And here's the beautiful part—it will work."

"Oh, it may work, it really may," she said. "But what about us? What about all the humdrum, dull routine of the Assistant Professor of classics and his wife?"

"How's that going to be changed?" I asked.

"But it's already changed," she said. "Just look at yourself. You're all worked up. It's a side of you I've never seen before."

Bullock was eating scrambled eggs in the living room. When he saw Amy he said, "Oh, hello there," and threw me a wink. "I was in the neighborhood and thought I'd drop in." I introduced him as an old friend and asked Amy to make a pot of coffee.

When she had gone into the kitchen, Bullock said, "That was using the old noggin, Simpson. I'm just about to call Ottawa and nip Beddoes in the bud."

"I don't think you understand," I said.

"Don't tell me. Let me guess," said Bullock smugly. "What I overheard tonight tied all the pieces of our puzzle together." Bullock went to the phone and began to dial.

"But it's Peace and Brotherhood."

"So I understand," said Bullock. "But on whose terms?" Then he spoke crisply into the telephone. "Acting Sergeant Bullock here. I'm ready to close the case. I have reason to believe that the entire castle is an immense Doomsday machine, an immense atomic bomb

... Listen, this is far from a laughing matter. The way I see it, this Beddoes fellow has his finger on the button and unless we agree to his fiendish terms of World Peace and Brotherhood he'll blow our poor tired planet to smithereens. The way I see it we ... but ... Check ... Check ..." An invisible hand slapped Bullock's face. He stared at the dead receiver in disbelief and collapsed into a chair. "They're dropping the whole investigation," he said in an astonished voice. "Apparently Beddoes has friends in high places. Even in Ottawa." Bullock put his face in his hands. "Our poor tired planet," he moaned.

"But the Beddoes Scheme isn't what you think," I said. I described my conversation with Beddoes in the tower room and what I had seen there. He seemed to take heart at my words for when I had finished Bullock peered at me through his fingers.

"No Doomsday machine? No fiendish terms?" he said.

"Beddoes is a great man, Bullock," I said. "I like Beddoes"—I pulled the beanie out of my pocket—"and he likes me."

"Say," said Bullock, admiring the beanie, "that's nifty. You know, I came here with a job to do. But just between you, me, and the lamppost, I've rather come to like the man myself."

Amy set down the coffee tray heavily when she saw the beanie.

"Well, why not?" I said. "Amy, your father is a great man. I don't think you appreciate all he's trying to accomplish. Well, I do and I'm behind him all the way."

I waved the beanie in front of her. "I want you to know I'm not ashamed of this," I shouted and with only a moment's hesitation I popped the beanie on my head.

At that instant a brilliant flash of lightning overexposed the trees and a detonation of thunder rattled the casements. We rushed to the window. Duff Castle was bathed in an eerie light. The lightning came again as we watched. A heavy crack of light struck the castle tower. The tower wavered like a boxer throwing off a punch. The lightning struck again, a shorter, more deliberate stroke. The tower trembled, turned slightly, and then McTaggart's Folly collapsed in ruins.

"By godfrey!" said Bullock.

The morning light was tracing out the smoking timbers and broken walls when Lowney and the men from Robbie's Cove found Beddoes beneath the rubble, his face noble in death. Across his body lay the faithful Hogan. Dead in her bed, Mrs. Beddoes wore a smile of final peace, the decanter at her side.

As the pickup truck carried the bodies down the hill I said to Amy, "The rooks are gone. I guess that means Daylight Saving Time for Robbie's Cove."

Bullock nodded, puffing grimly on his pipe. Then he turned and looked at me. "Those are the ears of a good man," he said.

"Thank you," I said before I realized he meant the plastic replicas of Beddoes' ears on the beanie still on my head.

"Ears are the windows of the soul," said Bullock. "Your criminal ears are shifty, with cunning little twists and whorls. But these stand right out and say, 'Hi there. I am an honest man.' If I'd had my eyes peeled I might have heard what Beddoes' ears had to say."

"Don't blame yourself," I said. "Suppose this had been January. He'd probably have been wearing earmuffs."

Bullock thought for a moment, then nodded. "A good point, Simpson," he said. "A very good point."

Jon L. Breen

The Lithuanian Eraser Mystery

Mr. Breen gives the full parody treatment to Ellery Queen, having fun and playing games (as EQ often does) with the "dying message" clue ..

Detective: E. LARRY CUNE

The theatrical season of 1968 began in a disconcerting manner. E. Larry Cune went to a play. For E. Larry was an unabashed sentimentalist who loved to return to the scenes of his past detectival triumphs.

Witness, for example, his periodic visits to the small town of Wyattsville, the New England village that had the highest per-capita murder rate of any incorporated community in the world, including even St. Mary Mead, England. Since murder seemed to follow E. Larry, he had taken on the aspect of a Jonah, or so some thought; but the police department of Wyattsville was never sorry to see him since they had a 100% record of solutions to their homicides, a record also unmatched by any community anywhere in the world.

But this is not a tale of Wyattsville, disappointing as that may be to the many Wyattsville fans everywhere; it is the story of E. Larry's return to the old and revered Greek Theatre (the one on Broadway, not the one in Hollywood), the scene of his first great triumph, the solution of the vicious murder of Mr. Anagopolous, an asthmatic but otherwise inoffensive member of the audience—a case known to the world as *The Greek Coughin' Mystery*.

That was many years ago, in 1929, when E. Larry had been in his early thirties, and his father, Inspector Richard Cune, had been the elderly and respected birdlike bulldog of Centre Street. Now almost forty years had slipped by, wars had come and gone, skirts had lowered again and risen again, *pince-nez* and Duesenbergs had gone out of style, science had advanced and humanity deteriorated. Now, in 1968, E. Larry was in his late thirties, and his father, Inspector Richard Cune, was the elderly and respected birdlike bulldog of Centre Street, having survived one serious bout with retirement.

Nostalgically, E. Larry surveyed the huge playhouse from his orchestra seat. He and a full house of first-nighters were waiting to see the premiere of Orson Coward's new musical comedy, *Gold,* a one-man tour de force with book, music, and lyrics by Orson Coward, who had also produced and directed. He had also planned to star as the show's youthful hero, but advancing years and a spreading waistline had led him to retire as a performer, for this production at least. The new show was a musical version of Frank Norris' turn-of-the-century novel, *McTeague.* Many scoffers doubted that this grim naturalistic story of greed and tragedy would make suitable musical comedy material, but after all hadn't Orson Coward made musical success of Theodore Dreiser's *An American Tragedy* and John Steinbeck's *The Grapes of Wrath?* (It's not true, however, that he paid two million dollars for the theatrical rights to *How To Avoid Probate.*)

Shaking hands with the famed writer-director-producer-composer prior to the curtain, E. Larry was conscious of an edginess in Orson Coward's manner, something he had never seen there in the many years he had known Orson Coward, dating back to the thirties when the then-boy wonder could have played teen-aged heroes with ease. Thus, tonight's nervousness could hardly be ascribed to opening-night jitters.

As they parted, E. Larry to return to his seat and Orson Coward to return backstage, the great man (Orson Coward, not E. Larry) said, "The show must go on, you know."

Must go on.

In spite of what?

Had that been fear in Orson Coward's demeanor?

What had he to fear?

E. Larry, of course, realized that his very presence at any function put the fear of sudden death in all those around him. He hadn't attended a play, sports event, or party in years without having to solve a murder at some time during the festivities, perhaps because so many potential murderers (and, in fact, their victims) leaped at the opportunity to match wits with him. But why was Orson Coward so sure he'd be tonight's victim? This would bear watching.

The curtain rose.

E. Larry had seen from his program that the first musical number was to be an ensemble titled "Be a Friend to Your Dentist." So he was surprised to see the show's ingenue, Pat Alison, come onto the stage and immediately begin to sing "Never Been Kissed," a sentimental ballad that was scheduled to close the first act.

"E. Larry, that's not right," squealed Nora Redcap, his companion of the evening.

"I know," said E. Larry. And as he watched the lovely young Pat Alison sing the words of the haunting melody, he thought he noticed an expression of puzzlement on her face, as though this change in the program were a surprise to her too.

Apparently the script had been rewritten sufficiently so that the opening number seemed naturally placed. Although several actors were somewhat unsure of their lines, the story progressed well enough until the time came for the second song. It proved to be "Alone in My Solitude," sung by the show's star, Van Washington, portraying the young dentist McTeague.

"E. Larry," Nora implored him, "that song isn't supposed to come until the second act! And it doesn't make sense to have two pensive ballads in a row. I don't understand this at all."

"Nor do I," said E. Larry pensively.

Van Washington was in good voice, but his face also betrayed a lack of understanding.

For some reason Orson Coward had changed the order of the musical numbers, E. Larry told himself.

Why? What did it mean?

Closing the initial scene, Washington appeared again, lustily singing the show's biggest potential hit, "I Know the Score Now."

"E. Larry," Nora almost screamed, "that's supposed to be the finale!"

"You're right, Nora," E. Larry said.

"He's ruining the show, E. Larry."

Orson Coward ruining a show? A man with his sense of showmanship, with his dedication to the theater? E. Larry told himself it could not be. Somehow, subtly, Orson Coward must be improving the show.

After the first three, the songs came in their proper order and the actors seemed more at ease, as though playing the show as rehearsed. By the curtain of Act One the enthralled audience had almost forgotten the curious early events of the evening.

During intermission a man E. Larry recognized as Hugh Vivyan, a backer of the show and long-time friend of Orson Coward, rushed up to E. Larry's aisle seat, saying breathlessly, "Mr. Cune, you must come backstage at once! Orson Coward has been murdered!"

Grieved but scarcely surprised, E. Larry followed the distraught "angel." He found Orson Coward's body lying in a hallway off the dressing rooms. The writer-director-producer-composer had been murdered by a heavy blow to the head, obviously the work of a blunt instrument. A volume entitled *The Complete Wit of Orson Coward*, found near the body, appeared to be the weapon.

Standing over the body were Pat Alison, the ingenue; Van Washington, the star; Millicent Grady, the wardrobe lady; Alfie Tanager, the stage manager; Flossy Blore, a Broadway showgirl romantically linked with Orson Coward; and Victor Towne, the assistant producer.

Washington was saying, "This is a calamity, Towne! What a loss to show business!"

Victor Towne nodded gravely. Flossy Blore wept quietly into her crocodile bag. Millicent Grady's beady eyes darted back and forth. Alfie Tanager looked truculent. Pat Alison looked ingenuous.

"Mr. Cune, who could possibly have done this terrible thing?" Towne asked.

"I don't know, Mr. Towne. Yet. But I know this: Orson Coward expected to be murdered tonight. He left me a clue to his murderer's identity."

"A clue?" said Pat Alison. "How?"

"By his rearrangement of the musical numbers in the show," E. Larry reasoned.

"So that's it!" exclaimed Van Washington. "We couldn't understand why he did that. Five minutes before curtain he handed each of us a revised script."

"Each of us" included 89 principals and 203 singers and dancers, most of whom were now milling around behind the great Greek Theatre curtain, since there was not enough room to join the suspects in the hallway.

"Mr. Tanager," E. Larry told the stage manager, "check with the unions and see if one of your men can call Centre Street. Have him ask for Inspector Cune, the birdlike bulldog. I expect to have this case wrapped up before Dad gets here, though."

"Mr. Cune," said Vivyan, the backer, "why didn't Orson say something if he expected to be murdered? Why did he simply allow it to happen, do nothing to prevent it?"

"When he saw me in the audience," E. Larry admitted sadly, "he knew there was no hope; he was doomed. Showman that he was, he knew his role now was to leave me a dying message, or a predying one in this case, to help me deduce the murderer."

"Can't you solve a murder without a dying message?"

"Yes, but it usually takes me a whole novel to do it. I should wrap up this one in a few thousand words."

"I hope so," Van Washington said fervently. "The curtain for Act Two is already overdue."

"Yes, indeed," said E. Larry. "So let's get on with this at once." Suddenly E. Larry's keen silvery eyes spotted something on the floor near the body. He stooped to pick it up. "Ah, just what I've been looking for!"

"What's that, Mr. Cune?" Towne asked.

"A rubber eraser." He turned it over. On the less worn side was clearly stamped: MADE IN LITHUANIA.

"Is that a clue, Mr. Cune?" Pat Alison asked.

"We shall see, Miss Alison," E. Larry replied, slipping the eraser into his pocket. "Now to the message: what do those three songs in sequence mean?

'Never Been Kissed'
'Alone in My Solitude'
'I Know the Score Now'

How do they apply to the people here? I seriously doubt that any of you has never been kissed. One or more may be lonely, but that seems tenuous as a clue. Was anyone here ever an athlete, amateur or professional?"

"I played football in college," Vivyan admitted. "Second string all-American."

"Are you lonely?"

"Well, I guess so—but no lonelier than the average Broadway show backer."

"Have you ever been kissed?"

"Really, Mr. Cune, is this necessary?"

"Have you ever been kissed?"

"Yes, frequently. I've been married four times."

"All right, Mr. Vivyan. No need to get excited. Let's take a different approach. The letters of the first words of each of these songs—do they spell anything?"

"N-A-I," said Nora Redcap, who had joined the group backstage. "I don't see any meaning in that, E. Larry."

"Try the last letters."

"D-E-W. That could mean something. But what?"

"Early morning, I suppose. How about spelling it backward?"

"W-E-D."

"And the first letters?" exclaimed E. Larry, triumph rising in his voice.

"I-A-N."

E. Larry whirled to face the other ladies present. "Has any of you ever been married to a man named Ian?"

"No, no Ian," Flossy Blore said. Pat Alison and Millicent Grady shook their heads.

E. Larry struck his forehead with the heel of his hand. "Who is this Ian? Whom did he wed? If we can find a woman who has been married to a man named Ian, we'll have the killer!"

The assembly seemed impressed. E. Larry was in the fervor of creative ratiocination that his intimates knew so well.

"Imagine Orson telling us so much," Van Washington marveled, "simply by changing the order of the numbers."

Suddenly E. Larry stopped in his tracks.

"Numbers. Numbers. Of course! I'm an idiot, a moron, a gibbering imbecile. I should have seen it at once. How could I have been so blind? Numbers!"

"Numbers, E. Larry?" A small birdlike man had appeared on the scene.

"You're just in time, Dad. I've cracked the case."

"It's just like 1929 all over again!" said Inspector Cune, beaming.

Hugh Vivyan appeared thunderstruck at the remark. "My God! I must call my broker at once!"

Inspector Cune, his face mirroring puzzlement, watched the backer's retreating back. "Why's he in such a hurry, son? Is he the killer?"

"No, let him go, Dad, he's not the culprit. Mr. Tanager, I'm going to address the audience. Open the curtain. The rest of you come out, too, and we'll wrap this thing up the way Orson Coward would have wanted."

CHALLENGE TO THE READER: *Who killed Orson Coward? And how did E. Larry know? What was the meaning of Orson Coward's pre-*

dying message? All the clues are now in your possession, so match wits with E. Larry Cune.

The stage manager shrugged resignedly and signaled for the great Greek Theatre curtain to open, to the surprise of hundreds of extras. E. Larry then walked onto the stage, raising his hands for silence, and the others filed quietly out behind him, even the star Van Washington content in this instance to play a supporting role.

"Ladies and gentlemen, I regret to announce that there has been an unfortunate occurrence—"

Immediately men with black bags began making their way to the aisles all over the massive playhouse.

"No, we don't need a doctor. I must tell you that Orson Coward is dead." A startled roar from the audience. "Murdered." This came as an anticlimax, since most of them had already recognized the famous E. Larry Cune.

"Fortunately, Mr. Coward left behind a clue to his murderer's identity. You may have noticed that the first three musical numbers in tonight's performance were not in the order indicated on your program. This was devised by Mr. Orson Coward to tell me who he *knew* was planning to kill him.

"Note the titles of the three numbers, ladies and gentlemen:
'Never Been Kissed'
'Alone in My Solitude'
'I Know the Score Now'
What does each of these suggest?

"Each suggests a number," E. Larry italicized. "For instance—sweet *sixteen* and never been kissed."

The crowd gasped at the revelation.

"Now, what number does 'Alone in My Solitude' suggest?"

"One!" shouted a voice from the balcony.

"Right! And the third title, 'I Know the Score Now'?"

Silence.

"Score, score!" E. Larry insisted.

"Twenty!" Inspector Cune exclaimed.

"Exactly, dad," said a proud son. "Twenty. Now examine the three numbers—16, 1, 20. What do they tell us?"

Silence.

"It's a simple code. *The numbers represent the letters of the alphabet.* A equals 1, B equals 2, C equals 3, and so on. Thus the sixteenth letter is—"

Suddenly Pat Alison was running across the stage, but her flight was interrupted when she became trapped in the hammy hands and beefy arms of Sergeant Healy.

The audience was on its feet giving E. Larry Cune a standing ovation in recognition of the long established fact that he, like Orson Coward, was a great showman.

As the tumult subsided, Inspector Cune said, "But, E. Larry, will we have a strong enough case to stand up in court?"

"I don't know, Dad. Thank God I'm not the District Attorney."

"I must tell you something," said Millicent Grady, the wardrobe lady. "I'm her mother; Orson Coward, my ex-husband, was her father. She hated him for keeping me on in such a menial position, but I really liked it for I still loved him. And I can reveal now that she was once married to Ian Fellmer, the spy-story writer."

"Now I know we have a case that'll stand up in court," said Inspector Cune with birdlike satisfaction.

"I'm relieved, Dad. I hate to have my cases end in messy suicides." E. Larry did not know at the time that Hugh Vivyan had just leaped nine stories to the sidewalk below from his broker's office on Wall Street.

"I have just one question, Mr. Cune," said Victor Towne, the assistant producer. "What did the Lithuanian eraser have to do with the case?"

"Not a thing really. But doesn't it make a marvelous title?"

Michael Harrison

Wit's End

Meet the Tarvish brothers—detective Iain Tarvish and school-master Andrew—in a tale admittedly of the Intellectual School, a tale of pure reasoning and deducing, with a few "points of interest" that surely would have appealed creatively to G. K. Chesterton, and which, we are sure, would have struck John Dickson Carr and Agatha Christie as prime creative material. . .

Detective: IAIN TARVISH

One can be funny just once too often—but even had he had the warning, Jenkins would not, could not, have heeded it. He had been what they call "a born wag"—he looked like a wag, spoke like a wag, thought like a wag. Nor was he a snobbish kind of wag—simple jests were as attractive to him as the more complex, the more subtle. Even at 40 he could still be tempted to pull a chair back as someone was about to sit down. His image of himself was "The Life and Soul of the Party." If any of his innumerable victims had ever learned why he died, there isn't one of them who wouldn't have murmured, "Served him damn well right!" He was that sort of wag—a very common type. What was not so common about him was the mode of his dying. He died—literally—joking.

Henry Jenkins was the self-appointed Honorary Secretary of the South Norwood and Penge Numismatic Society. He really did know something about coins; and the man on whom he was calling wished that the information Jenkins was bringing could have been got without the necessity of hearing it from Jenkins' all-too-jocular lips.

Ralph Hudson had met Jenkins through a letter that the former had written to the Secretary of the Royal Numismatic Society, asking for information on an apparently uncatalogued coin. The Secretary had replied to Hudson, advising the inquirer to communicate with Mr. Henry Jenkins, who had submitted a short paper to the Society on this very coin.

Hudson had written to Jenkins and Jenkins had replied—his waggishness, oddly enough, never infected his rather pompous letter-writing style; so he gave no warning of his excruciating facetiousness to the very different Hudson. The men met, and Hudson spent an awkward hour, listening to a scholarly talk on the *hapax legomenon* coin that Jenkins had found in a junk shop in Brighton—scholarly talk broken with unseemly jests and asides which belonged (in spirit, if not in text) to the dubious wit of last century's music halls.

Still, Jenkins, the other man admitted, knew his subject; and now Jenkins was on his way to Hudson's comfortable flat in St. James's, bringing the only known example of an unsuspected Algerian gold coin, of the period when Lundy Island was occupied by troops of the Dey of Algiers—the only known example, that is, until Hudson's gold piece had turned up . . .

Jenkins, entering the well-appointed entrance hall of Holbein Court, was aware of a strong surge of jealousy. This was a bit fancy, he reflected, for a man trying to get free information. Carpeted hall, polished brass everywhere, flunkeys in livery creeping out of doorways—a bit different from South Norwood!

Jenkins hadn't taken to Hudson when the two first met in the library of the Royal Numismatic Society; now Jenkins found himself actively disliking the man who lived in a style so superior to Jenkins' own!

As the elevator—carpeted of course!—opened silently to let Jenkins out on the fifth floor, Jenkins' jealousy and dislike of Hudson had grown to an active animosity. Even a rough-and-tumble Army psychologist would have had no trouble in explaining why Jenkins now behaved as he did.

He walked along the corridor to Apartment 507—shoulders back, feet pounding the foam-backed Wilton. He had become Chief Detective Inspector Henry Jenkins, C.I.D., for this little bit of play-acting—and when he reached the door of 507 he did not ring the bell but bashed his prominent knuckles against the white-enameled panel of the door.

His voice rang out loud and clear. There was a grin on his face. His eyes were shining with the malice of the born practical joker.

"Open up there!" he shouted. "Police!"

It was the last thing he said.

The man behind the door acted almost too quickly for thought. He flung the door open, saw a tall figure in dark clothes, a bowler on his head, and emptied the magazine of the Beretta .38 into Jenkins' back. The force of the bullets pounded the body into the still-closed door outside which Jenkins had been standing, though none of the bullets penetrated the door.

You might have expected the killer to have bolted for the fire-escape stairs which led to a flat roof. But it was a killer who could think. He *never* did what people would have expected him to do.

Hudson was a schoolmaster, with private means. He could afford either to do no work or to work where his inclination led him. He was now Assistant English Master at Bradlands, the well-known school in Sussex. He was talking, in the Masters' Common Room, with a newcomer, Ardley, the product of a very different environment.

"What brought this to mind," Hudson was saying, "was young Ferris' putting up his hand to ask what 'at one's wits' end' meant. I was just going to tell him when it occurred to me that my shining example of what a 'wit's end' could be was hardly the sort of thing to discuss in class. So I went on with what I was saying. But, this odd business having come to mind, I couldn't get it out of my head."

Ardley said, "You say you heard this man Jenkins shout, 'Open up there! Police!'—and then you heard a fusillade of shots. You didn't know it was Jenkins?"

"Well, that's funny, but I did. Jenkins had a curious way of breathing—through his nose and very loudly. I was expecting him; I heard the lift come up to my floor, heard someone get out. Then I heard heavy feet pounding along the corridor—somehow they sounded like Jenkins' feet—and through my open transom I distinctly heard that highly distinctive breathing. No, frankly, I was never in any doubt that it was Jenkins."

"Even when there was that pounding at your door, and someone shouted, 'Open up there! Police!'"

"Well, again yes. Don't forget that I'd already made the acquaintance not only of Mr. Jenkins but also—if I may so put it—of Mr. Jenkins' character as well. It seemed to me exactly the sort of silly way in which Jenkins might choose to announce himself. He was that sort of chap, you know.

"But, in a room just across the corridor, there was this criminal on the run. He didn't expect *Jenkins*—he expected the *police*. He heard Jenkins sing out; he opened the door, saw someone—might have been a plainclothesman—and let fly. This chap was on the *qui vive* and armed—ready to shoot—when Jenkins turned up with just the cue this other chap needed to go into action. The 'wit's end' in its perfect manifestation. Poor Jenkins! That was his last joke."

"If you knew it was Jenkins, didn't the shooting surprise you?"

"Not really. Shook me. Very nearly shattered me. But no, it really didn't surprise me. I wonder if I can make you understand what happened? Jenkins arrives—I *know* it's Jenkins; I can *hear* it's Jenkins. And Jenkins, on the dot, is standing outside my door. But, instead of doing the *expected* thing—yes, expected even from Jenkins—he calls out in that damfool way of his that he's the police. As it happened, he didn't frighten me. But he *did* frighten the man hiding in the flat across the corridor."

"You say even the shots didn't surprise you?"

"That's so. Look: Jenkins had announced himself, jokingly, as the police. He had, however fatuously, set the scene for a police atmosphere, if I may so put it. Somehow the shooting seemed *in keeping.* It's not easy to explain now how I felt about it—everything happened so quickly. But I can assure you that surprise was the last emotion I experienced. More than that: I *knew* what had happened. And why not? I realized that somebody with hair-trigger nerves had reacted—unthinkingly, instinctively, violently—with a hair-trigger gun. I remember thinking: 'God, he's quick!' And I knew I had to think even faster."

"You stayed put?"

"Not exactly. I didn't move, of course, but my not moving wasn't the important part. The important part was my *listening.*"

"Listening?"

"To hear what he'd do. I couldn't look out until I was certain the killer had gone—so I had to listen hard to make sure that he wasn't out there waiting for me. And that's when I found myself thinking once more, 'God, this man is quick!' "

"Why did you think that again?"

"Because a man who didn't think so quick would have shot and bolted—perhaps up the fire escape to the roof—they're flat roofs, and he would have had a good chance of getting away. But he was a far quicker thinker than his swift reaction to the supposed appearance of the police might have led me to think. He was a quick enough thinker to be able *to pause and choose the best way out*—and that calls for very quick thinking, indeed.

"You see, he had to make sure that he wasn't leaving a witness behind. That was me—if there was a me."

"How do you mean?"

"Jenkins had called at a certain door, shouting loudly that he was the police. The only reason the killer shot the supposed police-man—poor old Jenkins—was that the killer believed the policeman to be after him. The reasoning—swift as it was—went like this: 'This copper's got the wrong door. In a few moments he'll realize his error and start getting near *me*.'

"So—again in a flash of double-quick thinking—he decides to eliminate the supposed copper before the copper comes face-to-face with him. He does this, knows that the copper must be dead—and now has to decide what to do before the sound of the shots brings up a mob of far-too-inquisitive people.

"But our killer, you must remember, isn't quite his own master. He has just shot a man outside a door behind which he has every right to assume that an innocent, God-fearing, law-abiding man is now terrorized.

"Then our killer begins to wonder why this man doesn't come out. Perhaps there's no one in the flat? But if there is someone, *why* doesn't he come out?"

"He'd risk being shot—as Jenkins was shot."

"True. But it's far more instinctive to fling open a door in such circumstances. The killer wonders why this man—if there *is* a man—didn't fling open the door. Now, why is the killer so interested in whether or not there *is* anyone in the flat?"

"Because, if the killer leaves the room he's in, chances are the man in the flat—if there's a man in the flat—will see him and remember what he looks like."

"Yes. That's what I thought, too. And, of course, it's true enough. But, as I stood on the other side of the door, and wondered what *I* was going to do, I realized that there was a much more important reason why he should want to know whether or not there was anyone in my flat.

"Suppose there was someone inside, and suppose that someone could be persuaded to open up. What better place for the killer to hide? In fact, of all the places to which the murderer might have flown after the killing, this was surely the best of all. Now, what do you suppose I was thinking all this time?

"I was wondering what to do, of course. I could just stay where I was, and let him go away. Or if he tried to get in I could always shoot the bolt. It seemed to me, though, that it would be better if he believed that I *was* there."

"What did you do?"

"I shot the bolt. Loudly. Then I yelled, 'Don't try to come in.'"

"Why did you do that?"

"Because, as I stood behind the door, trying to decide what to do, I remembered something. I remembered that, if he were looking out—and I had to assume he was—*he could see me.*"

"Could *see* you? Through your closed door?"

"They have transom lights in Holbein Court, and the backs are painted with some dark color. They hang from an upper set of hinges, and you fix them where you wish by a sort of ratchet device. As the back of the transom is painted, the glass front set at an angle of forty-five degrees, reflects quite a lot of the corridor. It was as simple as that—my man must have been able to see me standing in my foyer, behind my door. He *knew* there was someone in my flat. No point in my keeping up the pretense any longer. I just told him, bolted my door, and wished him to blazes."

"Do you know anything about him?" Ardley asked.

"Well, probably young. Certainly agile. Look at the way he leaped onto the settee in the corridor!"

"Why did he do that?"

"I'm surprised, as you teach Science, that you don't realize what a transom at an angle of forty-five degrees would show. In my foyer I would be invisible from the corridor floor; jump up a couple of feet onto the settee, and the man would be able to see the foyer of my flat reflected in my transom window."

"That's right," said Ardley. "But it doesn't take much agility to climb up onto a settee."

"He *leaped* up. I was listening. They know the size of his shoes, of course—but it's size eleven, and how many millions of men wear size eleven! I wear size eleven myself."

"How do they know the size?" Ardley asked.

"Because of the indentations of his soles on the leather of the settee."

"They don't seem to know too much about him," Ardley mused.

"They may not know what he looks like, but they have a pretty shrewd idea of what he'll do."

"As, for instance?"

"As, for instance," said Hudson calmly, "he'll make it his job to get very close to me. Why? Because of one small doubt in his mind.

He knows that he saw me in the transom window. What he doesn't know is how much I saw of *him*."

"Well, how much *did* you see?"

"Not his face, if that's what you mean. He had clapped a handkerchief over his face—I told you that he was a quick thinker. I told you how I warned him to clear out. He leaped down from the settee and must have got away over the roof, they think. But, just as he was leaving, he heard a slight noise, and glanced back to see my transom window rising—I was pushing it up with a hooked rod supplied for that purpose. He assumed that I had pushed it up to look through it—but I had no chair, and so I couldn't get up to look through."

"Then why were you raising the window?"

Hudson tut-tutted, half smiling. "Ardley, you really astonish me! Elementary Optics. The angle of incidence is equal to the angle of reflection. I was trying to see something more than the man's face. I couldn't see through a handkerchief. I wondered, if I lifted the window to give myself a better view of the corridor, what I *could* see."

"You were risking a bullet."

"I have been risking a bullet ever since," said Hudson, looking over Ardley's shoulder at the tall thick-set man who was talking to Brown-Johnson, the Math master. The tall man, catching Hudson's eye, got up and sauntered over.

"Well, go on—what did you see?"

"Brass buttons and white gloves," said Hudson, challenging Ardley to ask why. "Why did the buttons tell me anything?"

"You mean he was a soldier?"

"No, my dear fellow, he was in livery. It explained how he'd got into the building. His white gloves explained why he left no fingerprints, and his livery, how he got away so quickly. I said that he must have got away over the roof, but it would hardly have mattered had he gone down in the lift. Who would challenge a servant in livery in Holbein Court. Oh, Tarvish, how do you do? Take a pew—I don't think you know Ardley, one of our new masters? We were just talking about that mysterious shooting outside my flat. I was telling Ardley what I saw through the transom window—reflected, of course. I saw this man in livery open the door of the fire escape and go through.

"It *is* a fire-escape door, of course, but it simply leads to a back stairway, where it's just as easy to go down as to go up. So, though the police *think* he got away over the roof, they haven't any proof that this was so."

The newcomer, Tarvish, now asked, "Well, if he didn't get away over the roof, and if he elected to go downstairs instead, how *did* he go downstairs?"

It was Ardley who replied. "A man who goes downstairs is a man who goes downstairs. What you mean is: 'How did a murderer go downstairs?' But who knew he was a murderer? To anyone but Hudson, he would have been just an ordinary human being; a liveried porter. Why shouldn't he have gone downstairs? Who was to stop him? Who was to know him?"

"That's true," Hudson agreed.

"And there's another thing," said Ardley. "Hudson's told us that he was impressed by the man's nerve—by his remaining so cool. Well, if he was as cool as all that, he wouldn't have batted an eyelid just walking down the stairs or even going in the lift."

"Anyway," said Tarvish, with the air of one wishing to end an argument, "do you think this murderer may come back—to get to you, Hudson?"

"It could well be, I'm afraid," said Hudson. "I imagine he won't be happy until he's suppressed my evidence—permanently."

"Let's hope he's too busy elsewhere. By the way, Hudson, you've got young Selby more hours than I have. Don't you think it's time he went to the hospital and had his adenoids out?"

"Adenoids? I hadn't noticed," said Hudson.

"I'm surprised you haven't noticed that awful open-mouthed snuffling of his."

"I can't say that I have," said Hudson, trying hard to recall any peculiarities of young Selby's breathing.

Andrew Tarvish, English Master at Redlands—and so Hudson's senior—sat with his brother, Detective Inspector Iain Tarvish, in the latter's cozy little flat at the wrong end of Kensington.

Andrew Tarvish was saying, "I take it that you haven't found the man who shot that coin collector—what was his name? Ah, yes, Jenkins—who was calling on a colleague of mine, Mr. Ralph Hudson."

"Good lord, Andy! I never realized that Hudson was a colleague of yours. In which way?"

"Actually, he's my junior—my assistant master. That doesn't make for the best blood between us, I can assure you."

"Why?"

"More money than I. Less economic need to work than I. Better varsity, better bred—at least, as the English regard these matters. I'm telling you this because I want to explain that Hudson's dislike for me and my dislike for Hudson have nothing—absolutely nothing—to do with what I'm about to ask."

"And what are you about to ask, Andy?" Inspector Tarvish asked, refilling the two glasses.

"Exactly what you are hunting for in the man who shot Jenkins."

"I thought this was something to do with Hudson, your colleague?"

"First things first, Iain. Cheers, by the way." They drank solemnly, Scots-fashion. "But what—or whom—are you chasing?"

Iain Tarvish shook his head, staring moodily into his glass. "Nobody, really. There are one or two bad boys with the itchy finger, the nerve, and the knowledge that you can't be hanged for murder in England any more, to make them chance gunning someone down on the impulse. We know their names—but we haven't yet found one who fits the bill."

"The man you're hunting has been well described to me by Hudson—quite a full psychological picture," said Andy.

"I've heard it," said his brother, with a tolerant smile.

"He was telling it again last night, in the Masters' Common Room He'd about come to the end when I joined in."

"Word-perfect by now, I suppose?"

Andy shook his head. "Not quite. Not *quite.*"

"Oh?"

"I've been thinking," said Andy. "I've heard the tale from Hudson a half dozen times, perhaps more. And—well, Iain, it was only tonight that a very *odd* thing struck me: you—and the whole police of Great Britain—are searching for a man. You don't know what this man looks like. You have a few vital statistics, as they call them—"

"Very few."

"But suppose you had ten times as much—but all from the same source of information?"

"I —good God!"

"Exactly. The man you're seeking is young, active, about six foot tall, wears number eleven shoes, last seen wearing the chocolate livery with gold facings of the management of Holbein Court. Dark hair. Features unknown. In fact, Iain, you're not seeking a known face; you're trying to fit a known psychology to a pattern of behavior. But who presented you with this pattern of behavior?"

Iain Tarvish took a deep swig of his whiskey and shook his head.

"I see what you mean. But you don't like this chap Hudson? Would—"

"I don't like him. I told you so. But would my dislike influence my reasoning? I don't think so. Still . . . why not try the reasoning first?"

"Go ahead then," said Iain. "If you're thinking what I *think* you're thinking, what about the motive? A small-town coin collector coming up to talk with a fellow collector—no, Andy, it's not likely to convince the Public Prosecutor, even if we made out a good psychological case."

"You've been so busy hunting the killer of Mr. Henry Jenkins that you haven't bothered to ask what Mr. Jenkins was calling on my colleague Hudson about. Do you know?"

"They were going to discuss a coin."

"Ah, yes, Iain—'a coin'! There speaks the voice of ignorance. 'A coin.' But there are coins and coins, Iain. And some coins are worth a lot of money, my dear brother! As I get it, Jenkins was bringing a rare coin to show to Hudson, and Hudson was going to compare it with his.

"Jenkins had one, Hudson had one. But what you don't realize is that Jenkins had a coin which was *unique*. And then Hudson came across another; and that took away the peculiar value from the first. The first was no longer unique."

"No," said Inspector Tarvish thoughtfully, "but the quality of uniqueness can attach itself to the second—or the third—or the three-thousand-and-thirty-third—provided someone gets rid of all the others."

"True. So, if one's concerned with the *uniqueness* of a coin, Hudson had as much interest in *his* as Jenkins had in *his*—if you get my meaning?"

"Yes. I wondered about *cui bono*. But how—assuming you're right—could Hudson bank on Jenkins' saying 'Open up! It's the police!'—or whatever the words were?"

"My dear Iain! Who *said* that Jenkins ever uttered such words?"

"But—oh, I see."

"Yes. You're thinking in a disastrous *circularity*, if I may coin a word. You're arguing like this: If Jenkins didn't say 'Open up! It's the police!' the lurking bandit wouldn't have shot him. If the lurking bandit did shoot him, then Jenkins *must* have said, 'Open up! It's the police!' But there are two things wrong with your reasoning. First, you've no proof that there *was* a lurking bandit—"

"All right, granted. And the second?"

"It's not important whether or not Jenkins actually did say 'Open up! It's the police!' What is important is that it should be accepted all round that Jenkins *could* have said those words. You have interviewed several people who knew Jenkins. I suggest that they all agreed that Jenkins—the incorrigible practical joker—could have said something like that. Yes—but this is what matters: whatever Jenkins said, or even if he'd said nothing at all, *he'd still have been shot!*"

"My dear brother," said the Inspector, "I see well what you mean—that Hudson shot Jenkins. I know what your answer will be—but, *why?*"

"I'll drive you mad by answering you indirectly."

"Very well, then: answer me indirectly."

"Have you inquired into Hudson's private means?"

"No. But I understand he's a wealthy man."

"Because he lives in Holbein Court? Well, I suggest you make a few inquiries."

"Let's anticipate that the inquiries reveal facts damaging to Hudson. What next?"

"Have you had a word with someone at Glendining's or Sotheby's or Christie's or Parke-Bernet? Or had a word with the editor of *Coins* or of *Coin Collecting* or *The Numismatist?*"

"No. What should I have had a word with these people about?"

"A gold moidore, minted in Portugal in 1610 for the Dey of Algiers, for use in Algerian-occupied Lundy Island. You look surprised, but it's a fact that this small island, only a few miles from the English coast, and situated right smack in the middle of the Bristol Channel, was actually occupied by the Dey of Algiers—at any rate up to about 1625, in the reign of Charles I. This is the coin that Mr. Hudson has—or so he says."

"What does 'so he says' mean?"

"Just that. Mr. Hudson claims he has a mint gold moidore of the Lundy Island issue, dated 1610—or, to be precise, Year of the Hegira 988 or 989. I was interested enough to make inquiries about its value. You'd be surprised what the experts think it would fetch at auction. Guess how much."

"A lot of money? A thousand? Two thousand?"

"*Fifty* thousand. Perhaps even double that."

"Good Godfrey! Fifty *thousand!* Who'd be mug enough to pay that for a *coin?*"

"Plenty. Don't forget that though the existence of such a coin has been suspected for years, no such coin had ever been recorded until the late Mr. Jenkins revealed its existence a few months ago."

"So," said Iain Tarvish slowly. "Hudson did it? How?"

"You'd have got it in one if you hadn't accepted Hudson's *very* detailed story."

"Because it was so detailed?"

"Perhaps. But no matter. Hudson's clever. He thinks quickly, he's ruthless, he's—well, he's got all it takes to achieve the perfect murder except . . . luck.

"A pity, really. For he used one superbly clever element in his plot: he made sure that your inquiries would back up his story. That was *really* clever! And so simple, after all!"

"How so?"

"Well, he knew that you—or any other copper—would investigate. Tactfully—or otherwise—you'd get around to this odd tale of Jenkins' saying, 'Open up! It's the police!' You'd be *thinking* that you were asking whether or not Jenkins had said just this; but the person whom you were asking would think you meant, not did Jenkins actually say the words, *but could he have said the words?* And everyone who knew Jenkins would say, 'Yes—typical of Jenkins!' You forgot that Hudson had met him, too."

"Well, what did Hudson actually do?" Iain asked, a little quiet now, as he always was when his brother solved his cases for him.

"He summoned Jenkins to London by letting Jenkins believe that his rare coin wasn't the unique item he'd thought it. Put yourself in Jenkins' place. Fifty to a hundred thousand if the coin's unique—perhaps a tenth of that if people learn there are more than one of them around. Just think what Jenkins must have felt—"

"Like murder," said Inspector Tarvish.

"Ah!"

"Good Godstone in Surrey! Do you mean to say that *Jenkins* is the murderer, and not Hudson, after all?"

Andy Tarvish smiled, and reached for his glass. He took a long swallow of the good Scotch before he answered, "Not quite. But first I want you to think of the small corridor between the two flats—the only two flats on the fifth floor at Holbein Court. Lift door—one of those solid, opaque jobs—at one end. Only access to the outer world through which a stranger could have come: the fire exit. Two flats—one occupied by Hudson, the other empty."

"But how did he get a passkey to open it?"

Andy laughed. *"No one opened the flat—for no one was in it.* Don't you see? It's so simple! How Hudson's heart must have leaped when he heard that fool Jenkins rap smartly on the door, with the tailor-made sort of practical joke that Hudson must have prayed for. 'Open up! It's the police!' It's so much easier telling a good story if you can stick to the facts. Liar as he is—and a practised one, too—Hudson must have felt grateful that, in the matter of what he heard Jenkins say, he wouldn't have to invent anything.

"Very well, then. Jenkins raps on the door with his damn-fool police-officer stuff. And Hudson—as he rightly told us—doesn't open the door. And, again as he told us, his transom is open. All that Hudson says—his hand on the catch, to be able to swing the door back instantly—is probably: 'Looking for Mr. Hudson? Opposite door, please!' He probably disguised his voice—but it wouldn't have mattered if he hadn't. No one thinks in such circumstances. He must have opened his door just as Jenkins swung around to face the opposite door—and it was then that Hudson shot him—*in the back*.

"Now, listen carefully, Iain. I know you're the copper—but I don't like Hudson, and I've spent a bit of time working this thing out. It was this business of *the shot in his back* which has been the biggest red herring in the whole case. In the *back?* But what do we mean by 'in the back'? All Hudson had to do, after Jenkins had fallen, was to swing him round by the legs—thus 'proving' that Jenkins had been shot from the open door of the untenanted flat—exactly as Hudson's detailed story has testified."

Iain nodded, deep in thought. "So Jenkins was shot from Hudson's flat—by Hudson himself. And all he had to do was to swing the body round—damn, we could have seen that the pile of the carpet had been scuffed—"

"No. That would have been explained by the dying man's contortions. Of course, Hudson had to do one other thing."

"Yes?"

"He had to find the Algerian moidore that Jenkins had brought with him. But that was safe enough—you can see by the lights above the lift door where the lift is. It would have given Hudson plenty of warning. In any case, he would only have been rushing to Jenkins' help . . . But no one came as he was rifling his victim of the gold moidore. Indeed, there was even time to add an artistic piece of evidence—to jump up on the leather settee in the corridor to show us that the 'murderer' wore size eleven shoes."

"Yes, he would have had to take the coin from Jenkins, so as to make sure that his own wouldn't be reduced in value."

Andy laughed. "*His own? My poor Iain, you are* slow this evening! There is—there was—no other coin. Hudson never had an Algerian gold moidore of 1610. He wanted Jenkins'—and was prepared to commit murder to get it."

"But how on earth do we pin the murder on him?"

"Well, we never found a moidore on Jenkins, did we? It was assumed either that the presumed murderer had taken it, or that Jenkins had come without it. Hudson can't possibly have *two*—he'd have to account for the second one. Frankly, I'd let him put it up for auction, and then stop the sale on the grounds that there is a 'mark' on it which shows that it was the coin that belonged to Jenkins."

"Andy! We couldn't!"

"You'll have to—if you want to convict Hudson."

However, after the police had made their discreet inquiries, and had discovered that Mr. Hudson's financial affairs were indeed in grave disorder, that it was Hudson who had approached Jenkins, and that the sale of Jenkins' moidore would stave off a seemingly inevitable bankruptcy—when all this had been established, Inspector Iain Tarvish obtained consent to adopt his brother's plan.

The moidore was duly put up for auction by Hudson and the police stepped in—with a courteous request that the item be withdrawn.

Then an Inspector—not Andy's brother—called on Mr. Hudson. He asked a lot of questions in a disconcertingly roundabout way. But his questions all boiled down to this: "Mr. Hudson, sir, you have entered a gold coin at Glendining's next auction sale—a very valuable coin, I believe. Well, sir, the trouble's this—and we'll be very glad if you'll help us out. You see, Mr. Jenkins' gold coin—"

"Mr. Jenkins' gold coin? Which coin was that?"

"Why, the coin he wrote up in the *Numismatic Journal*, sir."

"I see. Very well. This coin, then, what about it?"

"Well, sir, it's a bit difficult, but there's a mark on the coin you've offered to Glendining's which looks—I only say *looks*, sir—the dead spit of one that Mr. Jenkins put on his."

"I see. And the suggestion is that the coin I'm offering may, in fact, be Mr. Jenkins'—which, of course, couldn't—or shouldn't—be in my possession. Is that it, Inspector?"

"More or less, sir."

"I think we can take it that means rather 'more' than 'less.' Can you describe this mark, Inspector?"

"It's done very small, sir. I've got a drawing of it here. As I said, it's very small—you can only see it with a high-powered magnifying glass, sir. But it's plain enough: H.J."

"Could it stand for Henry Jenkins? I believe his name *was* Henry."

"Yes, sir, it was," said the Inspector, deadpan in the cause of duty.

"Then I wonder what's happened to mine?" Hudson mused aloud.

"Yours, sir? Yours is at Glendining's! Yours, sir, is the one that we had to remove from the sale, because we thought it might have been the property of the late Mr. Jenkins."

"*Might* have been? My dear sir, if it's got H.J. scratched on it, it almost certainly *is* Mr. Jenkins'!"

"But—"

"You see, Inspector, *mine* never had anything scratched on it. I can assure you that I very carefully examine any coin which ever comes into my possession. But, happily, there is a proof of that. Just to make sure that I had found a genuine—and exceptionally rare—Algerian Lundy moidore—I had some photographs taken. First, though, I asked the photographer to examine the actual coin under a magnifying glass, and—after he had taken the photographs—to sign them on the back. And date them, of course."

He went to a small safe, spun the knob of the combination-lock, and took out a manila envelope. "Here are the photographs. You will see that no such mark as you describe was on the coin I handed to Glendining's for sale. This is *most* disturbing! If there has been a mixup, if Glendining's have somehow got hold of poor Jenkins' moidore, and lost mine... But how *could* they? They are such a first-rate firm."

"There was no mark on the coin, of course?" Andy asked.

"Of course not! We wouldn't have dared tamper with evidence like that! We don't hang them anyway, these days," said Iain Tarvish, "and I suppose I ought to say that a clever so-and-so like that almost deserves to get away with it. All the same—"

"But how did you get over the story that there were scratches—the letters H.J.—on the coin?"

"Well, fortunately, the man we sent round to see Hudson hadn't a photograph, only a supposed sketch of the marks. So it wasn't that difficult to concoct a story that there had been a mixup, and that it wasn't the Algerian moidore which had been marked, but some other coin. What made it easy for Hudson to accept the lame explanation was that he knew quite well what we were trying to do, and why we had to back off. Do you think he might have rumbled that it was you who gave us the tip?"

Andy grinned, somewhat ruefully.

"I'll say! Of course, he had the coin photographed as soon after the murder as he could. But did he rumble me? Well, yes. He came to me a day or two ago, and said, 'Oh, by the way, Tarvish, I forgot to mention that when you were out one day I needed to have something of mine photographed—it was that gold moidore, actually—and I found that we hadn't a camera. The fool of a photographer had come without one. So I took the liberty of borrowing yours. I did use my own film, of course, but I hope you don't mind my having borrowed your camera?"

"What did you think of that?"

"I remembered how he'd praised the intelligence of this imaginary murderer of his. And I couldn't help thinking that he was even cleverer than that. Did you see what the coin fetched, by the way?"

"I did, Andy. Don't rub it in! . . . Of course, as we have no evidence against him he is legally as innocent as a newborn babe. By the way, did it ever occur to you that he might *be* innocent?"

"No, never," said Andy coolly. "*You* may have no evidence—but *I* have. He tells his story in a different way now. There used to be a quite dramatic bit about how he heard, through the open transom, the noise of Jenkins' loud and highly individual breathing. He's dropped that bit now—after I asked him, in the Masters' Common Room one night, what he was going to do about the adenoids which were causing young Selby's snuffles. He mumbled something, I remember, about not having noticed."

"You mean that he couldn't hear Selby's snuffles, and so couldn't have heard Jenkins' breathing, as he said?"

"Not quite. Actually, Selby doesn't snuffle. But a man with hearing as good as Hudson claimed for himself would have been *sure* of that.

"No, he's guilty all right. Too bad he was so much cleverer than all of us, Iain!"

R. Bretnor

A Matter of Equine Ballistics

"A Matter of Equine Ballistics." is a novelet of medieval mood and trappings set in the England of today—a fascinatingly anachronistic tale of the reenactment of the Battle of Woads, complete with catapults, ballistae, and trebuchet, to say nothing of the most unusual murder weapon in the history of fictional (and factual) crime—guaranteed unique! Talk about blunt instruments! . . .

Detective: ALASTAIR ALEXANDROVITCH TIMUROFF

If Alastair Drummond of Skrye had not escaped from the Tower in 1654 and taken service in Muscovy under the Czar Alexei Mihailovitch to fight the Polonian and the Turk, more than three centuries later his descendant, Alastair Alexandrovitch Timuroff, would probably not have been a dealer in antique arms. Nor would he have been in the north of England trying to buy the great Lessingham Collection when the curious case of the horse Hinchpeth came to public notice. Nor would he ever have been, among his many brief careers, an officer in the cavalry of the Argentine Republic. In short, given all these *ifs,* the violent and tragic death of Sir Cedric Substance would have remained unsolved—or, even worse, might have been "solved" erroneously.

Timuroff was the guest of Major Mark Drummond-Mowbrey, M.C., Chief Constable of Hallamshire and a distant relation. Like the Russian Fanshawes, the Timuroffs had always maintained their British connections, sending their eldest sons at least to be educated at Edinburgh or Oxford, and sometimes bringing brides back to Russia, until the Revolution tumbled everything down. The Chief Constable had, indeed, known Timuroff since boyhood. Besides, he had been a close friend of old Lessingham's, and he collected Scottish flintlock pistols, in which the Lessingham Collection was particularly strong. He was being very helpful to Timuroff.

They were having breakfast on the loggia when the news reached them. It was a splendid midsummer day; you could look down on the valley from the village of Upper Tiptilton at one end to Lower Tiptilton at the other, with the squat town of Frognall just showing its dull factory roofs in the mid-distance, and the absurd parapet of Parmenter's Folly rearing up out of the trees halfway to Lower Tiptilton. Timuroff and his host had been arguing, in a friendly way, about horses, Timuroff maintaining that all horses were incredibly and incorrigibly stupid, and Drummond-Mowbrey asserting with fervor that they were the best friends a cavalryman like himself ever had.

"In fact, Tim," he suggested, "after lunch let's ride down to the battle together. I'd imagine my boots and breeches still fit you—"

"The *battle?*" Timuroff interrupted.

"Didn't I tell you? The reenactment of the Battle of Woads—Wars of the Roses, I think. They're going to lay siege to the Folly, storm it, and burn the place down. It's been condemned anyhow, to make way for something dull and socialistic. Pilfer and Crombie and Substance and their crowd have their siege engines down there all ready to go. They brought them in yesterday, behind tractors, with half the Tiptilton youth dressed up in medieval costumes. It's for sweet charity's sake, naturally—the tourists are expected to leave behind hundreds of pounds."

Timuroff is a hard compact man—so much so that he usually looks a bit smaller than his five foot eleven. His forehead has a touch of the Tartar about it, which seems strange over eyes and a jaw straight from the Hebrides. The scar on his left cheek—the result, as he puts it quite truthfully, of a car accident in Montevideo—runs from the trim corner of his greying moustache to his cheekbone. He groaned, but his groan, as always, sounded implausible.

"Must we go?" he complained. "All collectors are crazy, but these let's-go-back-to-the-past, let's-build-siege-engines people are the maddest of all. Why would anyone want to spend twice the price of a Rolls-Royce on an enormous catapult or ballista?"

"They're useful," replied the Chief Constable. "You can bundle up enemy ambassadors and send them back over the walls with your compliments."

"Well, if you'll promise me *that* as part of the program I'll even ride one of your nags," Timuroff said.

"You can take that lovely tall mare that Mary's been riding." Drummond-Mowbrey was obviously pleased. "You can prance up and down watching the carnage, like Napoleon in one of those David paintings—" He broke off. A car had just screamed its brakes at the front of the house. "Now who can *that* be?"

Car doors banged; voices were heard; and presently a mountainous man in a black suit and bowler hat came round the corner of the house.

"Oh, my God!" muttered Drummond-Mowbrey.

"Who is he?" asked Timuroff.

"He's Police Superintendent Hesiod Plumley. He is a bird of ill omen. Whenever anything really dreadful happens, he rushes to tell me in person; then he accuses me falsely of meddling too much in procedural matters. And he always declaims as if he were reading Blair's *The Grave* at a funeral. Well—" He rose; the bird of ill omen was now within earshot. "Good morning, Plumley. Is anything wrong?"

The Superintendent advanced in an ominous silence. Six feet away he came to a halt, his dewlaps quivering. *"Wrong,* sir?" he boomed dismally. "You may well ask what is wrong. Murder's been done, sir. If I may say so, murder most foul! The first murder we've had hereabouts"—he opened his notebook—"since July the Twelfth, Nineteen Thirty-Seven."

"An interesting datum," said the Chief Constable, "but who has been murdered?"

"Sir Cedric Substance, sir."

"How? Who did it? Out with it, Plumley!" Drummond-Mowbrey was visibly shocked by the news.

"How? Well, I suppose one might say he was shot, sir. In a manner of speaking, that is."

"How the devil can one be shot in a manner of speaking?"

"Ah, sir! You see, he wasn't shot ordinarily. He was shot with a *horse.*"

The Chief Constable sat down, speechless; and Timuroff stepped into the breach. "I've heard of people being shot *on* a horse," he observed. "I've heard of people being shot *from* a horse; it kicked over a gun at the stables. But, Mr. Plumley, how does one shoot a man *with* a horse?"

Mr. Plumley regarded him with disfavor. "The late Sir Cedric Substance"—he consulted his notebook again—"was shot to death with a horse named Hinchpeth, the property of Mr. Randolph Pilfer of Tiptilton Manor, Lower Tiptilton, near Frognall, et cetera."

"Good God, of *course!*" Timuroff exclaimed. "Hugh, has Pilfer or one of his lunatic friends built a trebuchet lately?"

The Superintendent ignored him. "The horse Hinchpeth," he intoned, "was propelled through the air from and by an obsolete engine of war, also the property of the aforesaid Mr. Randolph Pilfer, at the hands of a person or persons unknown."

"Trebuchet?" said the Chief Constable. "Is that the kind with about a thirty-foot arm and a few tons of stones in a bucket to make it take off? If that's it, then Pilfer did build one. He was pleased as Punch. Went around bragging how he'd scored off Substance, who had only a catapult."

"The horse Hinchpeth," Mr. Plumley went on, "was impelled through the air for a distance of thirty-eight yards, over the moat, and struck the deceased at the foot of the tower known as Parmenter's Folly, where he was walking or standing."

"Rather good shooting," remarked Timuroff.

"Death, I am happy to say, was instantaneous. The very considerable mass of the horse Hinchpeth fractured the skull of the victim. The report of the autopsy surgeon will doubtless reveal other grave injuries. If I may say so, sir"—Mr. Plumley nodded with vast satisfaction—"murder is an unhappy business."

The Chief Constable sighed. "It is indeed, Plumley. Substance was no friend of mine, but he's always been part of the landscape. I feel sorry for Cecily—she was fond of the pompous old ass." He shook his head sadly. "Well, I suppose an investigation is called for. We'll drive down to the Folly and join you there."

The Superintendent began to turn red. "That will not be necessary, *Major,*" he declared. "I have already investigated the affair. The poor broken body"—his voice fell funereally—"has been taken away. The next of kin have been notified. *If* I may say so, sir, these matters are far, far better left to the professional police, whose training and background qualify them to make an accurate assessment."

Drummond-Mowbrey betrayed irritation. "Plumley, are you an expert on horses?"

The Superintendent made it clear that he was not.

"*I* am, Plumley. So is Mr. Timuroff here. You will have two former cavalrymen to assist you. Our training and background qualify us especially to solve all problems concerning them."

"Besides," Timuroff added, "I, Alastair Alexandrovitch Timuroff, am the world's foremost authority on the ballistics of the horse. My knowledge will be of inestimable value to you."

The Superintendent opened his notebook. He asked Timuroff to spell his name. "Well," he said, "that's as may be, but I regret to inform you, gentlemen, that we of the police already know the identity of the murderer, and that as soon as a warrant is issued I shall take him into custody."

"Who the deuce is it?" demanded the Major.

"Mr. Randolph Pilfer," said Plumley. "If I may say so, sir, the jaws of justice are about to close on him."

Whatever comment Drummond-Mowbrey might have made was cut off by a housemaid, who informed them that Miss Cecily Substance had phoned, in tears, to ask whether he was driving down to the Folly, and whether she could ride with him. He said yes, of course.

As they got into the car, Timuroff tried to cheer him. "You know, Mark," he declared, "I'm beginning to be interested in this murder of yours. In San Francisco I'll dine out for a month on the horse Hinchpeth and your man Plumley. And I'll probably really become the greatest authority on equine ballistics. I'll write papers for the Arms and Armour Society. You know, *The Horse's Flight from Engine to Target* and *How Properly to Truss the Dead Horse for Firing.* That sort of thing. Of course, it may turn out not to have been a murder after all."

"What do you mean?"

"Perhaps," said Timuroff, "it was an accident. Maybe they just didn't know the thing was loaded."

"Tim, shut up. I didn't like Substance, but I do like his niece. Besides, Randolph's a friend of mine, even if he is crazy. I just wish there was more I could do, but I really don't like to interfere with Plumley's handling of things."

"I'm sorry, Mark." Timuroff was sincerely contrite. "But the whole business does seem a little far out, doesn't it? Who on earth would name a horse Hinchpeth?"

"He was named after a butler," replied Drummond-Mowbrey, "of whom the family were particularly fond. The man died, I believe, and they named the horse after him. It was a lumpy fat thing, as old as the hills, and a great pet of the children's. Used to follow them everywhere hoping for sugar."

"Hinchpeth seems an odd name even for a butler."

"Oh, *his* name really was Inchpeth. He was a bit loose with his aitches, you see."

"I see," murmured Timuroff.

"Funny things, names. If it weren't for names, probably there'd have been no ill will between Randolph and poor Substance. Of course, it was all on Substance's side. Randolph just tried to laugh off the whole thing—at least, in the beginning. It was only later that he got really irritated. You see, Cecily and Ronnie Pilfer—he's Randolph's son—have been wanting to get married for three years now, but Substance was dead set against it. You know his firm, Worth and Substance?"

Timuroff, long a reader of *Country Life,* had indeed seen the name. However, he had merely ticked it off as a specimen of the curious nomenclature of British estate agents, which includes such well-known samples as Giddy & Giddy, Sanctuary & Son, and Ralph Pay, Lord, & Ransom.

"Well, Substance got the notion that Ronnie was really trying to weasel his way into the firm which would then, in due course, become Worth, Substance & Pilfer, or even worse, Pilfer, Worth & Substance—which I admit might not have inspired confidence in the customers. Of course, there wasn't the least danger of it. Ronnie's much too decent, and besides he's a naval architect on the way up. But it kept Substance awake nights. Finally he went to Randolph and suggested, in all seriousness, that he change the name from Pilfer to Paillefer, which would have the added advantage of sounding aristocratically Norman. Randolph was pretty rude to him, I'm afraid, in an earthy Anglo-Saxon sort of way."

"And then came the trebuchet?"

"Not right away. But Substance kept pushing the silly Paillefer idea, and making unpleasant remarks, and finally Randolph had the huge thing put together. Substance was awfully annoyed; he used to wander around muttering and mumbling about it until even Cecily began to think he was slipping a cog. Well, I thought I'd just fill you in on the background, but let's say no more about it right now—she'll be waiting for us there at the gatehouse." He pointed at a chimneyed roof directly ahead.

Cecily Substance stepped out into the road as he put on the brakes. She wore a tweed jacket and jodhpurs, but Timuroff could see that she had forgotten all about riding. She said a few words to a gnarled old man walking with her, then came on alone. Timuroff opened the door, got out, and gave her the front seat, a gesture she acknowledged abstractedly. She was a very tall, very dark blonde with a delightful complexion, beautifully feminine but somehow not truly beautiful. Nor were her tearstains responsible; the imperfection was more subtle. It was only after they had exchanged a few words that Timuroff detected what was wrong. Miss Substance's nose, and not only her nose but her personality, reminded him gently but inescapably of the great Duke of Wellington.

They got under way again, Drummond-Mowbrey clucking avuncular advice, Timuroff putting in that well-bred minimum required of any concerned and courteous stranger, and Cecily Substance assuring both of them that, thank you, she was now going to be perfectly all right. It had been a great shock, of course, especially when that wretched policeman Plumley—she dabbed her eyes—asked all those silly questions about secret enemies. But somehow it—well, she'd not been surprised, because Uncle Cedric had been terribly angry when he stalked out after supper. When he hadn't returned by morning, she just *knew* something terrible had happened—

Timuroff and the Major exchanged glances.

"B-but it was such a dreadful thing to d-do!" she sobbed indignantly. "I can't imagine how anyone could do that to a horse. Why, *everybody* loved Hinchpeth. Only Uncle Cedric thought he was a nuisance; he used to swear like anything when Hinchpeth followed him, you know, for sugar. I hope the poor beast was a-already dead when—when—"

"I'm sure he was, Cecily dear." The Major reached across and patted her. "Otherwise they couldn't very well have, well, *loaded* him."

Timuroff, considering the unusual moral values revealed in this conversation, said nothing.

"At least," declared Miss Substance in a firmer voice, "we won't have to wait very long. That Plumley promised me he'd have the wicked criminal fettered—those were his very words—by noon today." She noticed the unhappy look on the Major's face. "You don't think he'll fail us, do you? If he doesn't catch him it'll be simply terrible!"

Drummond-Mowbrey groaned audibly. "My God, Cissie, didn't he tell you whom he's planning to arrest? He's getting out a warrant for Randolph!"

Miss Substance sat bolt upright. The hint of Wellington was suddenly stronger than before. "He's stark, raving mad!" she cried out. "He's addled. He—he's a kook! It's unthinkable—why, Hinchie was one of the family! Besides, if Randolph's arrested it'll just spoil *every-thing!*"

"Not between you and Ronnie, surely?"

"Of course not! I mean *today*. We'll have to cancel the whole thing—the battle, and knocking down the Folly. We'll have to give back all their money, and if we try again later on, then nobody will come no matter how much we advertise. Look there! Just look at that!"

The twisting road had finally made up its mind and was meandering along the military crest that overlooked Parmenter's Folly and the Battlefield of Woads. Now the cupped green slopes around the moat were clearly visible. So were the combatants-to-be, a scattering of the upper-middle classes dressed as knights and noblemen, and any number of the yokelry got up as men-at-arms, churls, and varlets.

In their midst crouched the grim engines of approaching war: three great catapults, two ballistae, and, conspicuous among them not only because of its vast size but because it obviously had been fired, Mr. Randolph Pilfer's trebuchet, its mighty arm straight up in the air. Around the edges, gathering thick and fast, were the first-comers of the crowd, with their wives, in-laws, dogs, and noisy children, in numbers far beyond all expectation.

"Cecily," exclaimed Drummond-Mowbrey, "surely you aren't expecting a public entertainment—not after what's happened!"

Miss Substance looked him in the eye; then she looked Timuroff in the eye for good measure. "The show," she said decisively, "must go on. It is what Uncle Cedric would have wished. His death was tragic." She sobbed again momentarily. "It was certainly a bit premature. But wasn't it just the sort of death he would have chosen? Better than lingering in a nursing home, I'd say. Besides, it's the first time something like this has happened in the family—at least, since the Crusades. And anyway it's really what brought half these people here—they heard it on the wireless this morning."

The inconsistencies of the female mind, like those of certain French military firearms, had always fascinated Timuroff. Shuddering slightly at the thought of what Miss Substance might be like when she eventually became a dowager, he asked why the arrest of Mr. Pilfer would cause the cancellation of festivities.

"Because," replied Cecily Substance, "*he's* the MC, the Commander-in-Chief, the Grand Panjandrum. Right now, so far as all these people are concerned, Uncle Cedric's death is just a mystery;

it makes things more dramatic, don't you see? But if they put the nippers on old Randolph, then it becomes Murder and everything will be impossible." She turned back to Drummond-Mowbrey. "You're the Chief Constable—you'll have to make him stop, that awful Plumley man, I mean."

The Chief Constable's face was flushed. "My dear child, I don't like him either, but he's a conscientious policeman trying to do his duty. The course of justice—"

"Pooh!" said Miss Substance. "Well, if you're afraid of him then I suppose we'll simply have to *find* whoever really did it. Probably it was someone like those Puggett brothers, somebody really stupid. It shouldn't be too difficult to find the culprit. You'll have at least two hours to do it in."

The Major groaned again. "The Puggett brothers," he told Timuroff, "are deaf-mutes. They are illiterate. They can perform simple tasks when patiently instructed with graphic gestures, but it would be almost impossible to interrogate them."

"Uncle Cedric used to hire them to work his catapult," Miss Substance said. "I wonder if he himself wasn't planning to shoot somebody else with Hinchpeth, and they misunderstood?"

The car was now picking its way through towards the area of the engines, which the police, much in evidence, had cordoned off. More and more of the folk they passed were girded for the fray, armed and costumed so diversely that any uninformed observer might reasonably have supposed the Battle of Woads to have lasted at least from that of Hastings to Culloden Moor. One of Plumley's minions passed them through, and they halted finally on the meadow behind the line of engines, where gay pavilions with bright fluttering pennants had been set up in preparation for the tournament which would precede the battle.

Beside the drawbridge, close under the wall and with two legs in the air, lay a dead horse. They spied it simultaneously as they left the car, but only Cecily Substance commented on the sad sight. "You know," she said, "since poor Hinchpeth's already copped it, is there any reason why we can't use him over again? Over the walls, you know. He'd be quite a dramatic climax, wouldn't he?"

Luckily, Drummond-Mowbrey did not hear this suggestion. He had been summoned to the aid of two elderly ladies from the R.S.P.C.A., concerned about the possible fate of four live percherons due to be ridden in the tourney.

In front of the pavilions had been placed a platform heraldically adorned. On it were benches fanning out from a splendid elevated throne, and on the throne, broad and apple-cheeked, sat Mr. Randolph Pilfer. He wore a furred robe of some magnificence, which Timuroff correctly guessed to have been designed for the role of Boris Godunoff, and on his head reposed a kingly crown. Pages bearing such symbols of his sovereignty as sword and sceptre stood at either hand, and he himself, in the midst of his busy entourage, was trying valiantly to cope with all the cares of state, summoning and dismissing, deciding weighty issues, reproving the unworthy. He was perspiring freely, for the presence of Superintendent Hesiod Plumley in the immediate background was contributing nothing to the brave panoply of medieval war.

The Superintendent stood with two grim companions, and his expression, though still quite suitable for churchyard wear, was now indubitably that of one who, hungrily awaiting the arrival of a warrant, is certain that his hunger will soon be satisfied.

"If it flaps its big black wings, watch out!" announced Cecily Substance in a penetrating voice. "That means it's going to flip over and peck poor Hinchie's eyes out."

"Good morning, Miss." Stiffly, Plumley ignored her remarks. "I am happy to report that the ends of justice have been properly served. We have gathered much new evidence—incontrovertible evidence, if I may say so, Miss."

"They've probably already been pecked out." Miss Substance cocked her head appraisingly. "The creature looks revoltingly well fed."

Plumley regarded her reproachfully. "We of the police," he told her, "are used to obloquy. If I may say so, Miss, sticks and stones may break my bones, but aspersions—even unpleasant ornithological aspersions—can do me no real injury." He favored them with an appalling grin. "Nor can they undermine the evidence we have. We have a note, found in the victim's pocket, asking him to meet Mr. Pilfer by the engines at eleven o'clock—and we have two eyewitnesses.

"Last night, at a few minutes past eleven, the Puggett brothers, Sam and Ludlow, aged twenty-nine and thirty-four respectively, of Tilton Undertree, saw the suspect, Mr. Randolph Pilfer, work the trigger mechanism of his traybooshay, causing it to fire, thereby bringing about the dreadful death of Sir Cedric Substance, whom they had previously observed crossing the drawbridge which, I regret to say, he was fated never to cross again."

"Poppycock!" said Sir Cedric's next of kin. "Pure, shameless, drivelling idiocy. And we're going to prove it."

She had made no effort to modulate her tones; and now a young man, who had detached himself from the group around the throne, quickened his pace and came to her. He was of middle height, with what would ordinarily have been an open cheerful countenance; his scarlet surcoat, over chain mail, sported three golden griffins, and he carried a two-handed sword. He clanked ominously as he walked, glared even more ominously at Superintendent Plumley, and seemed completely lost in the glories of the past.

After chivalrous platitudes had been exchanged, Miss Substance introduced him as Ronald Pilfer, and Timuroff gained his immediate favor by complimenting him learnedly upon his arms. But he was not to be distracted long. Suddenly he gripped his sword, bared his teeth, and demanded loudly, "Fair maiden, has yonder knave, yon ill-bred varlet, dared to molest you? Only tell me and I shall split him to the chine! Or perhaps even a little further."

Superintendent Plumley puffed, spread his wattles, and reminded him that British Law forbade cleaving to or beyond the chine, and all other forms of violence to all persons civil or military—except, of course, occasionally in the performance of their duties. "Indeed, if I may say so, gentlemen, it even forbids—though perhaps not explicitly—shooting people to death with horses. As we shall see. Oh, yes *indeed*—as we shall soon see! And may I also add that—as I'm sure our Chief Constable here will testify—we of the police are no molesters of young ladies! Our characters are constantly subjected to the severest scrutiny."

"What a strange interpretation!" remarked the unrelenting Miss Substance. "We of the police must have a horribly dirty mind."

"*Cecily!*" The Chief Constable had rejoined them just in time to overhear the last of this exchange. He was properly horrified. "Cecily, that was an *outrageous* thing to say! Plumley, I'm sure Miss Substance will apolo—"

He was too late. The Superintendent, turning with a wounded-walrus roar, was bellowing orders at his underlings, sending them off to thwart thieves, pounce on pickpockets, and (with special emphasis) manacle molesters.

Finally the Chief Constable indicated that they might as well resume their march. "Well," he said unhappily, "there go our chances of any cooperation from that quarter. Cecily, don't you realize what a pickle poor Randolph's already in?"

Ronnie Pilfer retorted hotly that Plumley was a base-born clod who was plotting to commit *lese-majeste* by seizing the person of the king. Drummond-Mowbrey argued that, while it was hard to take Superintendent Plumley seriously because the man was such a bloody mountebank, his powers were very real and very, *very* serious.

Timuroff, who was beginning to suspect what made the Superintendent tick, asked if anyone would mind if he wandered off and rejoined them in the royal presence in ten or fifteen minutes? Then he dropped quietly back and made his way to where Mr. Plumley stood wrapped in gloom, anger, and high purpose. Coming up behind him, Timuroff sighed heavily by way of introduction.

Plumley turned. "What do *you* want?" he growled suspiciously.

"What?" replied Timuroff, all innocence. "Why, I want nothing, except perhaps to understand the ways of man. What I have heard today distresses me. You, Superintendent Plumley, are a policeman. You may not understand. But we who've seen the world across the footlights of a stage, who've worn the sock and buskin—ah!" He sighed even more deeply than before. "We know only too well that 'All the world's a stage, and all the men and women merely players.' We watch them as they strut and fret, all unaware, that the final curtain, Death, awaits us all."

Plumley's jaw dropped. "You think I do not understand?" he cried.

"Only too well indeed, if I may say so, sir! Oh, that's the pity of it." Abruptly, suspicion raised its head again. "Do you mean to tell me that you have played *professionally?*"

"I played Mercutio from Belfast to Bologna," lied Timuroff. "I have been Sir Lucius O'Trigger in Los Angeles, Faust in Ottawa, and Othello in more towns than I can name. Yes, and for one too-brief season I was Tamburlaine, because Tamerlane, or Timur, is supposed to have been my ancestor; Sir Tancred would allow no one else to play the part. I was triumphant! The stage was my career; since boyhood I had dreamed of nothing else. But it was not to be. Vile critics brought me down. I fled into the army of a foreign land."

Timuroff was proud of his two speeches, which he had tried to make as Plumleyesque as possible; and now he witnessed their complete success. The Superintendent had at long last found a kindred soul; it was his turn to sigh, abysmally.

"I too have had the same experience, Mr. Time-you're-off. I have aspired. I have been cast down. 'Of comfort no man speak: Let's talk of graves, of worms and epitaphs; make dust our paper and with rainy eyes Write sorrow on the bosom of the earth.'

"I was to the theatre born. My fond father, unhappily no more, headed a repertory company, Plumley's Players. As a babe in arms I made my first appearances in such productions as *The Scarlet Letter*. As a mere child I was Moth and Mustardseed, for often we presented scenes from *A Midsummer-Night's Dream*, Father having been universally proclaimed the greatest Bottom of them all. Nor shall I soon forget the vast applause which greeted my success as Peter Pan at Brighton. Oh, how I wish the great Sir Tancred Solomon had seen *me* then!" His voice broke. "B-but no! 'Twas not to be. Poor Father died. I was apprenticed to an undertaker, I know not why. My talent, all unknown, shrivelled, died."

"Oh, surely not!" Timuroff patted him on the back consolingly. "Surely, Superintendent, you have been able to employ your skills and your theatrical perceptions as well in your profession as I in mine?"

Plumley's gloom did not lift, but it did seem to thin a little round the edges. He admitted that his dramatic background had given him a distinct advantage, sometimes earning him the plaudits both of his superiors and the press. He lowered himself to a convenient hummock—

" 'For God's sake, let us sit upon the ground/And tell sad stories of the death of kings—' "

Obediently, Timuroff sat upon the ground beside him.

" 'How some have been deposed; some slain in war; Some haunted by the ghosts they have deposed; Some poisoned by their wives;some sleeping killed—' "

"Some shot to death with horses," thought Timuroff.

" *'All murdered!'* " intoned the Superintendent. "And, if I may say so, sir, that king we're looking at"—he gestured at Randolph Pilfer on his throne—"will also meet his fate, his just and dismal fate. Had Hesiod Plumley never trod the boards, he might have gotten off scot-free. Had I not mastered the arts of wordless pantomime, the terrible truth could not have been extracted from the dull minds of those two hulking boors, both deaf and dumb since birth. Not only did they witness the firing of the traybooshay, but earlier they observed Mr. Pilfer leading the horse Hinchpeth by a rope."

"Incredible!" exclaimed Timuroff. "You got all this with gestures?"

"With gestures *and* expressions, if I may say so, sir. For instance, when I conveyed the picture of that awesome instrument hurling death at poor Sir Cedric, my features had to mirror its intent even while my body limned the functioning of its mechanism. Then, in return, I had to be alert to each emotion that displayed itself upon their brutish faces. You, Mr. Time-you're-off, as an accomplished thespian, might have been able to do much the same—had you, of course, had my years of rigorous training and experience in the police."

Timuroff protested modestly that he did not deserve this compliment. Then, having obtained the information he was after, he listened politely to a few more minutes of theatrical reminiscence, declared that his confidence in British justice had been restored, and broke off the conversation with genuine regret.

All was not calm around the throne when Timuroff returned to pay his delayed *devoirs.* Miss Substance, looking more than ever like the eve of Waterloo, made a remark under her breath about people who gave aid and comfort to the enemy; and Drummond-Mowbrey, as nervous as the rest, introduced him first to His Majesty, then for a second time to Ronnie Pilfer, then to a lean Dame Marigold who was excited because she could find no one fitted to command the brave defenders of the Folly and deliver a final speech of defiance from its doomed battlements, and finally to a Mr. Robertson, the local veterinarian.

Miss Substance resumed her interrupted exhortation angrily. "What's the matter with the lot of you?" she demanded. "At any moment our vulture's going to swoop down, and all you do is moan and run around in circles. Why aren't *we* out trying to get new evidence?"

"My dear Cecily," protested Drummond-Mowbrey, "I'm sure we're all aware of what's at stake. But, just as Plumley says, we're not professional policemen, and time's running out, and—well, I admit I don't know which way to turn."

"My God, can't any of you think of *anything* to do?"

There was a despairing silence, punctuated by throat clearings and the shuffling of feet. Timuroff waited till he was certain that there would be no more positive reaction. Then he said politely, "I have thought of several things to do."

Miss Substance sneered, but king and court set up an instant clamor, snatching at the unknown straw held out to them.

Timuroff held up a hand for silence. "First," he said, "we may well need more time. Therefore let's start by having the crown prince change costumes with the king. In a pinch, Ronnie will be able to run faster than his father." He smiled. "Isn't it lucky for the criminal classes that the British police aren't allowed to carry guns?"

Agreement was immediate and virtually unanimous. Only Drummond-Mowbrey protested weakly that, after all, he was Chief Constable, and wouldn't they be, well, obstructing justice?

"Then," Timuroff went on, "we'll need a Polaroid. And a notepad of some sort. And I should like a photo of Sir Cedric. You see, I'm going to finish questioning the Puggetts. I'm not sure that Superintendent Plumley got all the information they possess."

The camera was almost immediately forthcoming, and Timuroff quickly took recognizable pictures of Randolph Pilfer, of the defunct Hinchpeth, and of the trebuchet. Cecily Substance—though she expressed serious doubts about his sanity—produced a likeness of her uncle from her purse. Timuroff was now ready. "Hugh," he suggested, "why don't you stay up here so that Plumley won't realize what we're doing? Miss Substance, I'd like to have you come with me. You know the country people hereabouts and I do not."

Prince Ronald held his peace. Miss Substance, declaring that she would go with anyone if it would help to save the day, attached herself to Timuroff. King Randolph said, "Mr. Timuroff, if you can stop this ludicrous arrest, I—all of us—shall be forever in your debt."

"All I'll require," said Timuroff, "is gleaners' privileges."

"What?"

"A fine medieval custom, Your Majesty. We dealers in old arms descend upon a battlefield and gather all the weapons of the slain. And of the badly wounded too, of course—though that can sometimes get a little stickier."

He bowed. Miss Substance curtseyed. Escorted by a page they took their leave.

The Puggett brothers were not hard to find. The page discovered them behind a catapult, drinking bottled beer; and Timuroff's conclusion, at first glance, was that they were not as stupid as everyone believed. They were big, clumsy men, raw-boned, with huge hands, feet, and ears. But the expression in their little eyes was one of cunning—low cunning possibly, but cunning nonetheless—and their deaf-and-dumbness had not prevented them from being *au courant* with the winds of fashion.

Their clothing and adornments—from filthy moccasins and skin-tight sackcloth trousers past gaudy plastic vegetables on strings to floppy hats and Farmer Giles beards—were mod, as mod was being

interpreted by a musical ensemble called The Living Twitch. Timuroff decided that he had done wisely to fill his pockets with shil-
lings and half-crowns; he very obviously began to transfer a few of
them from one hand to the other.

The Puggetts' first reaction was unfavourable. Ludlow drove an
elbow into Sam's brisket and pointed angrily. Sam made a rude
gesture indicating, at the least, that they preferred to remain alone.
Then both recognized Miss Substance and, simultaneously, the legal
tender Timuroff was juggling. At once, cunning and a coarse *bon-
homie* replaced cunning and hostility on their faces. Ludlow drove
his elbow into Sam again and pointed at the beer, and Sam hospit-
ably offered two bottles, one of which Timuroff graciously accepted.

After that the interview proceeded at the rate, roughly, of one
coin per question. Timuroff learned almost immediately that the
Puggetts were not quite illiterate, for they could read and write the
numerals and their own names. He found out, too, that they disliked
Superintendent Plumley, who had paid them not a penny. And he
discovered that Ludlow, especially, had a primitive talent with the
pencil, snatching it at the first opportunity and producing a series
of sketches which made everything he had witnessed the night before
completely clear.

There were, of course, minor hitches. Ludlow insisted on stimu-
lating Sam's memory with his elbow, and Sam occasionally replied
in kind. However, a proffered coin always prevented actual fratri-
cide. Finally, when nothing more was to be learned, Ludlow offered
beer again, which this time Timuroff refused politely, and Miss
Substance responded with a pound note, which was accepted instantly. They parted on the best of terms.

Timuroff was pleased. Not only had he succeeded in his purpose,
but he had converted Sir Cedric's heiress into a friend and ally.

"Well!" she declared, eyes flashing. "*That* settles Mr. Plumley's
hash! I can hardly wait to see his beak drop open when we tell him.
He'll probably regurgitate"—she shuddered slightly—"you know,
hair, bones, all that sort of thing, the way owls do."

"A fascinating prospect," said Timuroff. "But hadn't we best wait?
He hasn't any chance of getting a conviction, but *he* still doesn't
know it—and in his present mood we can't convince him in time to
stop him making the arrest—not without good hard evidence to back
us up. So let's not even tell His Majesty the King; let's just say
things are looking up, and that we're hopeful."

"I daresay you're right, but you deserve *some* credit. The way you got through to those Puggetts was simply wonderful."

"It was just that I knew more about my audience than Mr. Plumley did, Cecily—and that I'm not half as stagestruck."

Then, while they walked the remaining distance to the royal seat, Timuroff discussed more pleasant matters, praising Ronald Pilfer's great two-handed sword, and asking casually whether it was an old family heirloom with which its owner couldn't bear to part.

The group about the king was still milling uncertainly, disconcerted by the change in his identity; and Timuroff took advantage of this to march up demanding instant action, the utmost haste, and no questions asked. He was ably and penetratingly seconded by Cecily Substance, who quelled the faltering hesitations of the Chief Constable.

"Mark," Timuroff said, "if you and I and Mr. Pilfer here, and of course Mr. Robertson, start right away, perhaps we can check out Hinchpeth's remains and the Folly too before Plumley descends on us. We'll leave the impostor"—he smiled at Ronnie Pilfer—"to delude the Plumleyan eye. Cecily can stay with him to speed him on his way when the great hour arrives. Now let's get cracking."

The Chief Constable bade farewell to Dame Marigold, who was still frantically trying to recruit a Guardian of the Keep; the true King issued a few last-minute orders; Mr. Robertson began to hum *The Flowers of the Forest* dolefully; and as inconspicuously as possible, they strolled towards the drawbridge.

"Mr. Pilfer," asked Timuroff, as they pushed through the thickening crowd, "you were observed last night firing off your trebuchet. This is part of Superintendent Plumley's web of evidence. Did you fire it?"

"Just before I went home I did. Some fool had left the arm drawn back and ready. Even though there was nothing in it, I didn't want it to go off and hurt anyone."

"Is it easy to draw back?"

Mr. Pilfer blushed. "Easier than they used to be. I have a geared-down engine in it. Otherwise it'd be too much work, and churls and varlets come pretty high these days."

"By the way, how do you load it?"

"We use a forklift when we're practice-shooting, but today we'll have the soldiery push stones up ramps."

"Are you aware that you were also seen leading the horse Hinchpeth towards the trebuchet?"

"Must've been those miserable Puggetts, though how they got the message through I can't imagine. I found the beast tied to a wagon back of the pavilions. I supposed some kid had ridden him down bareback—they do that sort of thing. It was much too late by then to take him home again, so I moved him down by the trebuchet where there's grass, and I had a rope there long enough to let him graze. I suppose that crazy Plumley thinks I slaughtered him and hoisted him up into the basket?"

"I'm afraid so," replied Timuroff. He refrained from mentioning that, to those who did not build ancient siege engines, the idea of those who did shooting each other with dead horses might not seem at all farfetched. "The Superintendent believes that he has established motive, opportunity, and means—the three classic requirements. Besides, he has enough contributory evidence to justify arresting you—unless we can demolish the evidence, of course. There's that note you wrote to the deceased, for instance."

"My God, that was day before yesterday. I asked Substance to meet me at eleven in the *morning*—yesterday morning."

They had by then crossed the moat and were surveying Hinchpeth, whom a man-at-arms was guarding from a ring of open-mouthed small boys. Robertson, the vet, was the first to comment. "If I hadna been told he was a horse," he stated solemnly, "I believe I would have taken the creature for a hinny, which, as you weel know, is a mule the other way around, but wor-r-rthless."

"I see your point," said Timuroff, "but doesn't that neck betray a touch of dinosaur somewhere in his ancestry? I can think of nothing else that might account for it."

Mr. Pilfer, aggrievedly, pointed out that, while Hinchpeth might indeed have been a compendium of the worst points of horses, he had possessed a spirit of rare gentleness and beauty. "And believe me," he added ferociously, "whoever killed him is going to pay for it!"

In death Hinchpeth was an unlovely sight. He was a very fat horse, with very thin, very uneven extremities. His scruffy coat was of a mottled mud-color. His lips had curled back from long yellow teeth which betrayed immense old age, and his stiffened limbs, all badly damaged, pointed in a variety of directions. While Mr. Robertson and Drummond-Mowbrey knelt to examine him more closely, Timuroff devoted his attention to the surrounding territory. After a few minutes he turned back to them. "Mr. Robertson," he asked, "can you say whether Hinchpeth was alive or dead when he hit the ground?"

The veterinarian replied judiciously that it was a little difficult to say positively without an autopsy, but that confidentially and just between themselves, aye, the horse had been alive. "Or at least," he added, "as alive as it probably has been during the past twelve years. But, och! what's the difference? The injuries would have killed two teams of perfectly sound horses."

"Yes," said Timuroff, "and considering the nature of these injuries and the animal's long flight through the air, isn't it strange that he appears to have landed, squashed Sir Cedric, and remained pretty much *in situ?* Look—" He pointed to the shrubbery between Hinchpeth and, scarcely fifteen feet away, the Folly's wall. "He doesn't seem to have ricochetted at all."

"I never thought about that," said Drummond-Mowbrey, "but is the trebuchet a high-angle-of-fire weapon? Could he have fallen practically straight down?"

"Hardly. Anything fired from a trebuchet is lobbed. The angle's fairly high, but not much higher than a horse taking a tall fence steeplechasing—and look how far they can roll after a fast fall. I told you I was the world's foremost authority on the ballistics of the hor—"

He stopped abruptly. A tumult of shouts, police whistles, piercing screams, and running feet had burst out in the crowd.

"What's that?" cried Mr. Pilfer.

"Quick!" snapped Timuroff. "Let's get inside the Folly. Plumley's trying to serve his warrant. Mr. Robertson, if Superintendent Plumley comes this way, please delay him as long as possible. We've only minutes to find whatever we're looking for."

"Ah, weel," Mr. Robertson replied, "if I canna see where you are going, certainly I canna tell the man where you have gone." And as Timuroff hustled the other two away, he turned back to his examination. In the crowd the royal raiment appeared and disappeared as young Pilfer sought to outdistance his pursuers.

"What the devil do you expect to find in here?" protested the Chief Constable a little irritably as they passed through the sally port.

"Who knows?" said Timuroff. "The good investigator must try everything."

The front aspect of Parmenter's Folly made it appear a great, square, lowering keep. Once inside, however, one saw that it was indeed only one-and-a-quarter sides of such an edifice, the quarter, off at one end, crumbling into deliberately contrived ruin, the rest achieving a similar effect through long neglect.

"Not much stone in it," commented Drummond-Mowbrey. "Just enough for looks. Most of it's lath and plaster."

"Can we get up to those two turrets over the sally port?" asked Timuroff.

"We can," Pilfer answered. "We've kept the place locked up, but I have keys even though Substance owned it—more evidence, I suppose Plumley'd say." He fished in the scarlet surcoat's anachronistic pocket. "Here they are, two to the downstairs doors leading to the ramps and two more to the turret chambers—His and Hers, we used to call them. On moonlit nights Parmenter's wife—her name was Guinevere or Isabeau or something like that—would come out through that long embrasure in her turret, right over where poor Hinchpeth's now lying, and stand on a little iron balcony they had there. She always wore a filmy Burne-Jones sort of nightie, with her long hair streaming down over her shoulders. Then he'd sing to her from a gondola on the moat, twanging his lute. As she was awfully overweight, and as he always sang lilting love songs in Middle Scots, the effect must've been quite memorable."

As he talked, Mr. Pilfer unlocked one of the doors, admitting them to a dark and cobwebbed corridor. "After she died, when he'd become pretty well crippled by arthritis, he pulled the stairs clean out and had these ramps put in, so that a couple of stout village lads could push his wheel-chair up into her bower—not out of sentiment, you understand, but so he could sit in the embrasure and take pot-shots at this and that with his old Genoese crossbow. He was a vile shot and never hit a thing, which was lucky because a couple of times towards the end he tried to wing one of the local peasants. He was a bit of a nut, really."

"Did he build siege engines?" Timuroff asked mildly.

"Not a bit of it," replied Mr. Pilfer. "He was just one of those silly mid-Victorian romantics—no scientific spirit whatsoever."

They made their way up a long ramp and down another corridor, and, with the King beginning to puff slightly, repeated the process two more times. Finally they stood before the portal of the bower. Mr. Pilfer again produced his keys. The door creaked open. And—

"There," cried Timuroff triumphantly, "is our evidence! Randolph Pilfer was not the murderer of Sir Cedric Substance!"

"I'll be damned!" exclaimed Drummond-Mowbrey.

"Wh-why—why, this is incredible!" Randolph Pilfer gasped. "Perhaps now we'll find out who really killed him."

"There's no time for that now," said Timuroff. "I'll take a look around, then Mark and I can show poor Plumley the error of his ways. You'd best wait here; the sight of you at this point would just infuriate him."

Quickly he examined the floor of the empty room, with its souvenirs of spiders, bats, owls, and rodents. From it he picked up a few shreds of scarlet paper. "I'll take these along to help persuade him," he announced. "But we'll leave the real evidence right here; it'll be more impressive. Come on, Mark, let's go."

From the drawbridge they saw that the Pretender had been taken into custody. Three of Plumley's men had dragged him back to the royal platform to prevent his rescue by a threatening crowd of ardent royalists. Superintendent Plumley, majestic in his wrath, was lecturing all and sundry on the impropriety and peril of defying British Law.

"Mark," said Timuroff, coming to a halt, "I wonder if you'd mind my handling this? I think I may be able to bring him round without blood being spilt."

"You're handling things quite nicely, it seems to me." Drummond-Mowbrey smiled wryly. "If you were a British subject, I'd resign and recommend you for my job."

Timuroff took his notepad from his pocket:

Dear Friend and Fellow Player (he wrote),

I send this message in great haste and secretly, for the wrong people must not know of it.

Shocking new evidence has been discovered which changes the whole case, and I strongly urge you—indeed, for the sake of your talent and career, I beg you!—to do nothing before I have a chance to tell you of it. At the moment, after much persuasion on my part, the Chief Constable is, I think, amenable. Come to the trebuchet immediately.

Faithfully,
Alastair Timuroff

"That ought to do it," he remarked, folding the document and whistling to a lad of eight or ten. "Here's a shilling for you, son. Take this note to that big man over there, the angry, purple one. It won't matter who sees you, but act as if you're trying not to be seen. Catch on?"

The boy dashed off yelping excitedly. They saw him vanish in the crowd, reappear on the platform, then sneak his way very obviously to Plumley's side; they observed the Superintendent read the paper, hesitate, crumple it into his pocket, and then, with a word or two to his subordinate, depart.

As they took off for the rendezvous, Dame Marigold, more agitated than ever, buttonholed the Chief Constable, demanding that a true Guardian of the Keep be found for her immediately.

"Madame," interjected Timuroff firmly, "I can assure you that Major Drummond-Mowbrey and I shall soon have just the right man for your purpose."

They met a troubled Plumley by the trebuchet. "You were wise to heed my warning, Superintendent. No, do not say a word!" Timuroff held a conspiratorial finger to his lips. "Come with us! We wish to show you everything."

He led the way across the drawbridge once again. He spent several minutes pointing out the technicalities of Hinchpeth's impact and injuries. Then he led Plumley through the sally port and up into the tower.

When they descended shortly afterwards, in the company of the erstwhile accused, it was obvious that the Superintendent, if not a broken man, was at least bent badly out of shape. His face was pallid. His jowls had lost their buoyancy. He walked as though he carried the weight of a dead horse on his shoulders. But for all that he did not shirk his duty. Heavily, followed by Timuroff, the Chief Constable, and the restored King, he mounted to the platform. So tragically did he hold his hand up to command attention that instantly all were still.

"A terrible error has been made," he announced sepulchrally, "an error for which we of the police apologize and which we infinitely regret. New evidence has, if I may say so, come to light. It has not yet revealed precisely how the late Sir Cedric Substance met his death, nor at whose hands, but it has shown beyond doubt—" Here Plumley choked and, for a moment, had rather heavy going. "It has shown beyond any doubt whatsoever that Mr. Randolph Pilfer is completely innocent. All charges against him have been dropped."

"Long live the King!" shouted nobles, knights, and commoners. "God save good King Randolph!"

Miss Substance, having embraced the Crown Prince (who was promising everyone high wassail in the Great Hall come sundown)

shouted out, "Long live Mr. Timuroff!" But no one else took up the
cry.

"I'm glad somebody appreciates me," Timuroff said to the Chief
Constable. "I'm sure Plumley doesn't, or he'd be telling them the
truth, the whole truth, and nothing but. He knows how the late Sir
Cedric Substance met his death as well as you and I know."

"Probably he's waiting until the show is over. Anyhow, here he
comes, poor devil. Looks a bit flattened out, doesn't he?"

"Well, we'll soon fix that." Timuroff moved off to intercept the
Superintendent. "The curtain has not fallen for our hero. . . . Dame
Marigold!" he called. "Dame Marigold? Ah, there you are. Here's
someone you simply have to meet—"

The day went off famously, and many of its happenings, much
embellished, were woven into the tapestries of local folklore and
local history. Wearing Miss Substance's favor, Sir Ronald acquitted
himself honorably in the tourney, prevailing over a number of op-
ponents until he was unhorsed abruptly by a grizzled knight who
happened to be a retired rough-riding sergeant-major of the Blues.
Before the jousts there had been minor combats between the common
folk, who cheerfully bruised each other with wooden swords, quar-
terstaves, and dummy battleaxes. There had been shooting at the
popinjay and at the mark. There had even been a lovely fist fight
between the Puggett brothers, who had set to over their last bottle.
The crowd was in a fine medieval mood.

During the lull before the battle and the siege, the gnarled old
man who had been with Miss Substance at the gatehouse appeared
leading three horses, one of hers and two of Drummond-Mowbrey's
—apparently someone had been in touch with him by nonmedieval
telephone. Close on his heels came a boy carrying two pairs of the
Chief Constable's boots and breeches, into one set of which Timuroff
was reluctantly persuaded. There was nothing for it but to watch
the battle from a convenient grassy knoll, where the lovely tall mare
snorted, danced, pranced, and caracolled, and drew everyone's attention as Timuroff, bowing to social pressure, put her through her
paces.

The attackers, of course, were triumphant; the defenders beat a
disorderly retreat across the drawbridge; the wounded screamed and
writhed realistically enough to satisfy every schoolboy in the audience; and Miss Substance, her nostrils flaring, surveyed the field

as though, with Boney's armies hastening back to France, she were regarding the Torres Vedras Lines.

Then it was announced that the last desperate assault upon the keep would soon begin, and, as trumpets blared, a defiant, solitary figure appeared in Mrs. Parmenter's embrasure. Superintendent Plumley wore a leather jerkin, a cuirassier's breast-plate, a Cromwellian lobster-tail helmet, and great jack-boots. Held in his right hand was a huge halberd; and while the awe-struck crowd momentarily held its breath, he launched into the first mighty stanzas of *Horatius at the Bridge*. It was a magnificent performance, which earned him a highly favorable review from the dramatic critic of a Dublin paper who happened to be drinking his way through rural England; and when he asked who would stand at his right hand and keep the bridge with him it was all his constables could do to restrain the volunteers.

However, Plumley was not able to turn the course of reconstructed history. At the critical moment someone—Timuroff suspected Cecily Substance, who had ridden down to inspect the troops manning the engines—caused the trebuchet to fire prematurely, and the horse Hinchpeth was sent sailing through the air to crash against the turret, rebound, break off a tree branch, and strike again almost at the moat's edge. Actually, *vis-a-vis* the Superintendent, Hinchpeth hit about twenty feet low at eight o'clock. But he hit effectively.

The horse's flight was taken for a signal, and instantly catapults and ballistae discharged their fearsome stones and giant shafts. Horatius, who had been about to plunge into the Tiber, disappeared. The crowd went wild. And the besiegers, massed round their battering ram, surged forward uncontrollably. Fortunately, perhaps, the Greek Fire which was supposed to have been catapulted into the Folly a little later on fell short into the moat and fizzled out; and the Fire Brigade were able to do the incendiary bit more safely and tidily with gasoline.

It was a great day for almost everyone, including Timuroff. Old Mrs. Lessingham had admired his horsemanship, and the purchase of the Lessingham Collection was practically assured. Ronnie Pilfer, prodded by Cecily into gratitude for his father's timely rescue, had remembered that his sword, by no means an heirloom, had been purchased by a cousin at a country auction in 1947, and had presented it to the rescuer. Even the tall mare had shown herself to be so responsive and amiable an animal that Timuroff privately apologized to her for his general estimate of equine intelligence.

After Ronnie had been persuaded that Cecily's bereavement was not a time really suited to high wassail, they drove back together to a quiet dinner, Timuroff and Drummond-Mowbrey in the front seat, the two Pilfers flanking Miss Substance in the rear. As soon as they were clear of the dispersing visitors, Cecily's fiancé leaned forward. "Mr. Timuroff," he asked, "who on earth *did* kill Uncle Cedric?"

"Nobody killed him," Miss Substance said. "He—" She dried a solitary tear. "He committed suicide."

"He *what?*" exclaimed both the Pilfers simultaneously.

"It's really very simple," said Timuroff. "I think there's no doubt whatever that Sir Cedric's mind had come unhinged, and that in his distorted world Mr. Randolph Pilfer was the enemy. What gave him the idea of engineering his own death and blaming it on you we'll never know, but having you convicted by your own horse and your own trebuchet must have seemed a specially sweet revenge."

The Pilfers and Miss Substance murmured pityingly.

"At any rate, he counted on your motive, your instrument, your opportunity, and the fact that there'd be witnesses to testify to this and that, all in an atmosphere sufficiently—shall we say, eccentric?—to make an otherwise improbable occurrence believable. Yesterday evening he must have led Hinchpeth down to the battlefield himself. He had equipped himself with several lumps of sugar, and with two enormous firecrackers with long fuses. I imagine he also had a flashlight."

"He always had a little pocket torch—to keep the goblins off, he used to say," put in Miss Substance.

"He probably went back and forth several times getting things ready, and it must've been on one of those occasions that the Puggetts saw him. He found Hinchpeth again where Mr. Pilfer had tied him, and led him over to the Folly. Tugging at the halter, and using sugar when that didn't work, he got him all the way to the top storey and into my lady's bower. He lit his fuses—I daresay he'd timed it all carefully earlier in the day—quickly locked the door, and hurried down again. The firecrackers went off—*BANG! BANG!*—and Hinchpeth, terrorized, leaped through the only exit. And that was that. Actually, it was a rather clever plan. If no one but the Superintendent had been involved, it might have succeeded."

"I still don't understand how you managed to convince Plumley so decisively," said Ronnie Pilfer. "Surely it wasn't just the paper from those—what did you call them?—firecrackers."

"Oh, no. That would have been too easy to explain away. The evidence we showed him was much more conclusive. When your father saw it, up there in the turret room, he was too upset to realize its true significance. But it proved conclusively that Hinchpeth had been there and that he'd leaped from the embrasure, and Plumley saw at once that that meant suicide.

"Sir Cedric made two errors. The first was in not foreseeing that some horsy people might get in on the investigation. That was bad enough, but the second was disastrous." Timuroff smiled. "Knowing little or nothing about horses, he neglected to watch *both* ends of Hinchpeth instead of just the one he was leading."

Isaac Asimov

The Man Who Never Told a Lie

At this session of the Black Widowers the guest, brought by artist Mario Gonzalo, gives the club a problem in pure logic. Mr. John Sand seemed to be the only possible culprit; yet he denied guilt, and as everyone knew (and the reader can take this as gospel), Mr. Sand always told the truth, the whole truth, and nothing but the truth . . .

Detectives: THE BLACK WIDOWERS

When Roger Halsted made his appearance at the head of the stairs on the day of the monthly meeting of the Black Widowers, the only others yet present were Avalon, the patent-attorney, and Rubin, the writer. They greeted him with jubilation.

Emmanuel Rubin said, "Well, you've finally managed to stir yourself up to the point of meeting your old friends, have you?" He trotted over and held out both his hands, his straggly beard stretching to match his grin. "Where've you been the last two meetings?"

"Hello, Roger," said Geoffrey Avalon, smiling from his stiff height.

Halsted shucked his coat. "Damned cold outside. Henry, bring—"

Henry, the only waiter the Black Widowers ever had or ever would have, already had the drink waiting. "I'm glad to see you again, sir."

Halsted took it with a nod of thanks. "Twice running something came up—Say, you know what I've decided to do?"

"Give up mathematics and make an honest living?" asked Rubin.

Halsted sighed. "Teaching math at a junior high school is as honest a living as one can find. That's why it pays so little."

"In that case," said Avalon, swirling his drink gently, "why is free-lance writing so dishonest a racket?"

"Free-lance writing is *not* dishonest," said free-lance Rubin, rising to the bait at once.

"What have you decided to do, Roger?" asked Avalon.

"It's this project I've dreamed up," said Halsted. His forehead rose white and high, showing no signs of the hairline that had been there perhaps ten years ago, though the hair was still copious enough around the sides and in the back. "I'm going to rewrite the *Iliad* and the *Odyssey* in limericks, one for each of the forty-eight books they contain."

Avalon nodded. "Any of it written?"

"I've got the first book of the *Iliad* taken care of. It goes like this:
"Agamemnon, the top-ranking Greek,
To Achilles in anger did speak.
They argued a lot,
Then Achilles grew hot,
And went stamping away in a pique."

"Not bad," said Avalon. "In fact, quite good. It gets across the essence of the first book in full. Of course, the proper name of the hero of the *Iliad* is Achilleus, with the 'ch' sound as in—"

"That would throw off the meter," said Halsted.

"Besides," said Rubin, "everyone would think the 'u' was a typographical error and that's all they'd see in the limerick."

Mario Gonzalo, the artist, came racing up the stairs. He was host for this session and he said, "Anyone else here?"

"Nobody here but us old folks," said Avalon.

"My guest is on his way up. Real interesting guy. Henry will like him because he never tells a lie."

Henry lifted an eyebrow as he produced Mario's drink.

"Don't tell me you're bringing the ghost of George Washington!" said Halsted.

"Roger! A pleasure to see you again. —By the way, Jim Drake won't be here with us today. He sent back the card saying there was some family shindig he had to attend. The guest I'm bringing is a fellow named Sand—John Sand. I've known him on and off for years. Real crazy guy. Horse race buff who never tells a lie. I've heard him *not* telling lies. It's about the only virtue he has." And Gonzalo winked.

Avalon nodded. "Good for those who can. As one grows older, however—"

"And I think it will be an interesting session," added Gonzalo hurriedly, visibly avoiding one of Avalon's long-winded confidences. "I was telling him about the Black Widowers Club and how the last two times we had mysteries on our hands—"

"Mysteries?" said Halsted, with sudden interest.

Gonzalo said, "You're a member of the club in good standing, so we can tell you. But get Henry to do it. He was a principal both times."

"Henry?" Halsted looked over his shoulder in mild surprise. "Are they getting you involved in their idiocies?"

"I assure you, Mr. Halsted, I tried not to be," said Henry.

"Tried not to be!" exclaimed Rubin. "Listen, Henry was the Sherlock of the session last time. He—"

"The point is," said Avalon, "that you may have talked too much, Mario. What did you tell your friend about us?"

"What do you mean, talked too much? I'm not Manny Rubin, you know. I carefully told Sand that we were priests at the confessional, one and all, as far as anything in this room is concerned, and he said he wished he were a member because he has a difficulty that's been driving him wild, and I said he could come the next time because it was my turn to be host and he could be my guest and—here he is!"

A slim man, his neck swathed in a thick scarf, was mounting the stairs. The slimness was emphasized when he took off his coat. Under the scarf his tie gleamed blood-red and seemed to lend color to a thin and pallid face. He was thirtyish.

"John Sand," said Mario, introducing him all round in a pageant that was interrupted by Thomas Trumbull's heavy tread on the steps and the code expert's loud cry of "Henry, a Scotch and soda for a dying man!"

Rubin said, "Tom, you could be here early if only you'd relax and stop trying so hard to be late."

"The later I come," said Trumbull, "the less I have to hear of your stupid remarks. Ever think of that?" Then he was introduced too, and they all sat down.

Since the menu for that meeting had been so incautiously planned as to begin with artichokes, Rubin launched into a dissertation on the preparation of the only proper sauce. Then, when Trumbull said disgustedly that the only proper preparation for artichokes involved a large garbage can, Rubin said, "Sure, *if* you don't have exactly the right sauce."

Sand ate uneasily and left at least one-third of his excellent steak untouched. Halsted, who had a tendency to plumpness, eyed the remains enviously. His own plate was the first one to be cleaned. Only a scraped bone and some fat were left.

Sand seemed to grow aware of Halsted's eyes and said, "Frankly, I'm too worried to have much appetite. Would you care for the rest of my steak?"

"Me? No, thank you," said Halsted glumly.

Sand smiled. "May I be frank?"

"Of course. If you've been listening to the conversation around the table, you'll realize frankness is the order of the day."

"Good, because I would be anyway. It's my—fetish. You're lying, Mr. Halsted. Of course you want the rest of my steak, and you'd eat it, too, if you thought no one would notice. That's perfectly obvious, but social convention requires you to lie. You don't want to seem greedy and you don't want to seem to ignore the elements of hygiene by eating something possibly contaminated by the saliva of a stranger."

Halsted frowned. "And what if the situation were reversed?"

"And I was hungry for more steak?"

"Yes."

"Well, I might not want to eat yours for hygienic reasons, but I would admit I wanted it. Almost all lying is the result of a desire for self-protection or out of respect for social conventions. To me, however, a lie is rarely a useful defense and I am not at all interested in social conventions."

Rubin said, "Actually, a lie *is* a useful defense if it is a thoroughgoing one. The trouble with most lies is that they don't go far enough."

"Been reading *Mein Kampf* lately?" said Gonzalo.

Rubin's eyebrows went up. "You think *Hitler* was the first to use the technique of the big lie? You can go back to Napoleon III; you can go back to Julius Caesar. Have you read his *Commentaries?*"

Henry was bringing the baba au rhum and pouring the coffee delicately when Avalon said, "Let's get to our honored guest."

Gonzalo said, "As host and chairman of this session I'm going to cancel the grilling. Our guest has a problem and I direct him to favor us with its details." He was drawing a quick caricature of Sand on the back of the menu card, with a thin sad face accentuated into the face of a distorted bloodhound.

Sand cleared his throat. "I understand everything said in this room is in the strictest confidence. But—"

Trumbull followed Sand's glance, then growled. "Don't worry about Henry. He is the best of us all. If you want to doubt someone's discretion, doubt someone else."

"Thank you, sir," murmured Henry, setting up the brandy glasses on the sideboard.

Sand said, "The trouble, gentlemen, is that I am suspected of a crime."

"What kind of crime?" demanded Trumbull. It was his duty, ordinarily, to grill the guests, and the look in his eye was that of a person who had no intention of missing his opportunity.

"Theft," said Sand. "There is a sum of money and a wad of negotiable bonds missing from a safe in my company. I'm one of those who knows the combination, and I've had a chance to open the safe unobserved. I also have a motive—I've had bad luck at the races and needed cash urgently. So it doesn't look good for me."

Gonzalo said eagerly, "But he didn't do it. That's the point. He didn't do it."

Avalon twirled the half drink he was not going to finish and said, "I think in the interest of coherence we ought to allow Mr. Sand to tell his story."

"Yes," said Trumbull, "how do *you* know he didn't do it, Mario?"

"That's the whole point, damn it. He *says* he didn't do it," replied Gonzalo, "and if he says so, that's good enough for me. Maybe not for a court, but it's good enough for anyone who knows him. I've heard him admit enough rotten things that other people wouldn't—"

"Suppose I ask him myself, okay?" said Trumbull. "*Did* you take the stuff, Mr. Sand?"

Sand paused. His blue eyes flicked from face to face, then he said, "Gentlemen, I am telling the absolute truth. I did not take the cash or the bonds."

Halsted passed his hand upward over his forehead, as though trying to clear away doubts.

"Mr. Sand," he said, "you seem to have a position of some trust. You can get into a safe with negotiable assets in it. Yet you play the horses."

"Lots of people do."

"And lose."

"I didn't quite plan it that way."

"But don't you risk losing your job?"

"My advantage, sir, is that I am employed by my uncle, who is aware of my weakness, but who also knows I don't lie. He knew I had the means and the opportunity to steal, and he knew I had debts. He also knew I had recently paid off my gambling debts. I told him so. Yet the circumstantial evidence against me looked bad.

But then he asked me directly if I was responsible for the loss and I told him exactly what I told you: I did not take the cash or the bonds. Since he knows me well, he believes me."

"How were you able to pay off your gambling debts?" said Avalon.

"Because a long shot came through. That happens, too, sometimes. It happened shortly before the theft was discovered and I paid off the bookies."

"But then you didn't have a motive," said Gonzalo.

"I can't say that. The theft might have been committed as long as two weeks before its discovery. No one looked in that particular drawer in the safe for that period of time—except the thief, of course. It could be argued that after I took the cash and bonds, the horse came through and made the theft unnecessary—too late."

"It might also be argued," said Halsted, "that you took the money in order to place a large bet on the horse."

"The bet wasn't that large, and I had other sources. But, yes, it could also be argued that way."

Trumbull broke in, "But if you still have your job, as I suppose you do, and if your uncle isn't prosecuting you, as I assume he isn't— Has he notified the police at all?"

"No, he can absorb the loss and he feels the police will only try to pin it on me. He knows that what I have told him is true."

"Then what's the problem, for God's sake?"

"There's simply no one else who could have done it. My uncle can't think of any other way of accounting for the theft. Nor, for that matter, can I. And as long as he can't see any alternative, there will always be a residuum of uneasiness, of suspicion, in his mind. He will always keep his eye on me. He will always be reluctant to trust me. I'll keep my job, but I'll never be promoted; and I may be made uncomfortable enough to be forced to resign. If I do, I can't count on a wholehearted recommendation, and from an uncle, a half-hearted one would be ruinous."

Rubin was frowning. "So you came here, Mr. Sand, because Gonzalo said we solve mysteries. You want us to tell you who really took the stuff."

Sand shrugged. "Maybe not. I don't even know if I can give you enough information. It's not as though you're detectives who can go to the scene of the crime and make inquiries. If you could just tell me how it *might* have been done—even if it's far-fetched, that would help. If I could go to my uncle and say, 'Uncle, it might have been done this way, mightn't it?' Even if he couldn't be sure, even if he couldn't ever get the money and bonds back, it would at least spread the suspicion. He wouldn't have the eternal nagging thought that I was the *only possible* thief."

"Well," said Avalon, "we can try to be logical, I suppose. How about the other people who work with you and your uncle? Would any of them need money badly?"

Sand shook his head. "Enough to risk the possible consequences of being caught? I don't know. One of them might be in debt, or one might be paying blackmail, or one might be greedy, or just had the opportunity and acted on impulse. If I were a detective I could go about asking questions, or I could track down documents, or whatever it is they do. As it is—"

"Of course," said Avalon, "we can't do that either. —Now you say you had both means and opportunity. Did anyone else have them?"

"At least three people could have got into the safe more easily than I and got away with it more easily, but not one of them knew the combination, and the safe wasn't broken into; that's certain. There are two people besides my uncle and myself who know the combination, but one has been hospitalized over the entire period in question and the other is such an old and reliable member of the firm that to suspect him seems unthinkable."

"Aha," said Mario Gonzalo, "there's our man right there."

"You've been reading too many Agatha Christies," said Rubin. "The fact of the matter is that in almost every crime on record, the most suspicious person turns out to be the criminal."

"That's beside the point," said Halsted, "and too dull besides. What we have here is a pure exercise in logic. Let's have Mr. Sand tell us everything he knows about every member of the firm, and we can all try to see if there's any way in which we can work out motive, means, and opportunity for some other person."

"Oh, hell," said Trumbull, "who says it has to be *one* person? So someone's in a hospital. Big deal. The telephone exists. He phones the combination to a confederate."

"All right, all right," said Halsted hastily, "we're bound to think up all sorts of possibilities and some may be more plausible than others. After we've thrashed them out, Mr. Sand can choose the most plausible and tell it to his uncle."

"May I speak, sir?" Henry spoke so quickly, and at a sound level so much higher than his usual murmur, that everyone turned to face him.

Henry said, this time softly, "Although I'm not a Black Widower—"

"Not so," said Rubin. "You *know* you're a Black Widower. In fact, you're the only one who's never missed a single meeting."

"Then may I point out, gentlemen, that if Mr. Sand carries your conclusion, whatever it may be, to his uncle, he will be carrying the proceedings of this meeting beyond the walls of this room."

There was an uncomfortable silence. Halsted said, "In the interest of saving an innocent person's reputation, surely—"

Henry shook his head gently. "But it would be at the cost of spreading suspicion to one or more other people, who might also be innocent."

Avalon said, "Henry's got something there. We seem to be stymied."

"Unless," said Henry, "we can come to a definite conclusion that will satisfy the club and will not involve the outside world."

"What do you have in mind, Henry?" asked Trumbull.

"If I may explain—I was, as Mr. Gonzalo said before dinner, interested to meet someone who never tells a lie."

"Now come, Henry," said Rubin, "you're pathologically honest yourself. You know you are. That's been established more than once."

"That may be so," said Henry, "but I *do* tell lies."

"Do you doubt Sand? Do you think he's lying?" said Rubin.

"I assure you—" began Sand, almost in anguish.

"No," said Henry, "I believe that every word Mr. Sand has said is true. He didn't take the money or the bonds. He is the logical one at whom suspicion points. His career may be ruined. His career, on the other hand, may not be ruined if some reasonable alternative explanation can be found, even if that does not actually lead to a solution. And, since he can think of no reasonable alternative himself, he wants us to help find one for him. I am convinced, gentlemen, that all this is true."

Sand nodded. "Well, thank you."

"And yet," said Henry, "what is truth? For instance, Mr. Trumbull, I think that your habit of perpetually arriving late with a cry of 'Scotch and soda for a dying man' is rude, unnecessary, and, worse yet, has grown boring. I suspect others here feel the same."

Trumbull flushed, but Henry went on firmly, "Yet if, under ordinary circumstances, I were asked whether I disapproved of it, I would say I did not. Strictly speaking, that would be a lie, but I like you for other reasons, Mr. Trumbull, that far outweigh this verbal trick of yours; so telling the strict truth, which would imply a dislike for you, would end up being a greater lie. Therefore I lie to express a truth—my liking for you."

Trumbull muttered, "I'm not sure I like your way of liking, Henry."

Henry said, "Or consider Mr. Halsted's limerick on the first book of the *Iliad*. Mr. Avalon quite rightly said that Achilleus is the correct name of the hero, or even Akhilleus with a 'k,' I suppose, to suggest the correct sound. But then Mr. Rubin pointed out that the truth would seem like a typographical error and spoil the effect of the limerick. Again, literal truth creates a problem.

"Mr. Sand said that all lies arise out of a desire for self-protection or out of respect for social conventions. But we cannot always ignore self-protection and social conventions. If we cannot lie, we must make the truth lie for us."

Gonzalo said, "You're not making sense, Henry."

"I think I am, Mr. Gonzalo. Few people listen to exact words, and many a literal truth tells a lie by implication. Who should know that better than a person who always tells the literal truth?"

Sand's pale cheeks were less pale, or his red tie was reflecting more color upward. He said, "What the hell are you implying?"

"I would like to ask you just one question, Mr. Sand? If the members of the club are willing, of course."

"I don't care if they are or not," said Sand, glowering at Henry. "If you take that tone I might not choose to answer."

"You may not have to," said Henry. "The point is that each time you deny having committed the crime, you deny it in precisely the same words. I couldn't help but notice since I made up my mind to listen to your exact words as soon as I heard that you never lied. Each time, you said, 'I did not take the cash or the bonds.' "

"And that is perfectly true," said Sand loudly.

"I'm sure it is, or you wouldn't have said so," said Henry. "Now this is the question I would like to ask you. Did you, by any chance, take the cash *and* the bonds?"

There was a short silence. Then Sand rose and said, "I'll get my coat now. Goodbye. I remind you all that nothing said here can be repeated outside."

When Sand was gone, Trumbull said, "Well, I'll be damned."

To which Henry replied, "Perhaps not, Mr. Trumbull. Don't despair."

Jeff Sweet

Over the Borderline

Mrs. Sutherland had a confession to make to the police, but Lieutenant Foley had to let her tell the story in her own way ...

66 "D on't you see? He had to be stopped."

"Stopped, Mrs. Sutherland? Stopped from doing what?"

"If I hadn't acted she would have died. He would have killed her."

"Who, Mrs. Sutherland? Who would he have killed?"

"You're looking at me like you don't believe me, Lieutenant Foley. You think I'm just a batty old lady, don't you? An old lady who's lost her marbles."

"No, I don't. Really, I don't."

"Like crazy Mrs. Jessup who's always calling the police or the F.B.I. about enemy agents hiding under her bed. I'm right, aren't I? That's what you think."

"I swear, Mrs. Sutherland, I don't think that at all."

"Then why don't you believe me?"

"Well, I'll tell you, Mrs. Sutherland, it isn't that I don't believe you. It's just that I—well, I guess I really don't *understand*. I mean, I don't have the full picture."

"I've tried to answer all your questions, Lieutenant."

"Yes, and I appreciate that, Mrs. Sutherland. But still—"

"What?"

"Look, I have an idea. Why don't you tell me about it again, from start to finish? I promise you I won't interrupt."

"From start to finish? Yes, maybe that would be best, and I suppose the best place to start would be with Cora and Jim. Cora and Jim Franklin. Such a nice couple. They remind me of the late Mr. Sutherland and myself when we were young. A very nice couple, the Franklins. Of course, they have their problems. More than their share. She was pregnant when they got married, you know. That's not always the best way to start a marriage, especially since the baby wasn't Jim's. That awful Harrington Furth."

"Uh, Mrs. Sutherland—"

"Lieutenant, you promised you wouldn't interrupt."

"I know, Mrs. Sutherland, but I'm afraid I'm a little lost. Who is Harrington Furth?"

"Lieutenant, if you will hold your horses I'll get to that, I promise you. All in good time. But you mustn't interrupt."

"Yes, Mrs. Sutherland."

"Where was I?"

"Harrington Furth."

"Oh, yes, Harrington. A very rich, very irresponsible young man. His father is the president of Furth Electronics, you know—a very distinguished man. But Harrington, I'm afraid, doesn't take after his father. Or should I say Harrington *didn't* take after his father? Oh, well, you understand my meaning, I'm sure. It must have been very hard on old Mrs. Furth, having a son like Harrington. Always racing around in his fancy cars, always getting into trouble. And his father always coming to the rescue. I swear, if it had been me, I would have let that young man stew in his own juice! It might have taught him a sense of responsibility. And the way he drank!

"Anyway, there was poor Cora. She hadn't married Jim yet, you know. Jim was going with the Stanton girl then—the one with the big false eyelashes and all the teeth. What Jim saw in her I don't know. But like I say, there was poor Cora. Her mother had just died on the operating table and Cora was all alone. She was scared and vulnerable. And that awful Harrington saw this and—well, he took advantage of the situation, and when he'd gotten what he wanted he left Cora flat. Not too long after she found out she was pregnant."

"You mean with Furth's child?"

"That's what I said, didn't I? Really, Lieutenant, you must learn to listen. Anyway, around this time the Stanton girl left Jim and took up with young Harrington, which in my opinion served them both right. Meanwhile, Jim was desperate, almost suicidal, and then, one day, in came Cora. Did I tell you Jim was an obstetrician?"

"No."

"Well, he was, and all the girls on the staff at the hospital thought he was the handsomest doctor around. But he didn't pay any attention to them. And then, as I said, in came Cora and he told her she was pregnant and she just stood there, very bravely, fighting back the tears. But, of course, it wasn't any use. Before you could blink an eye she was in his arms, crying like a little girl. And he was holding her so tenderly. It was love from that first moment, I could tell. I could tell right off because it was just like that when Mr.

Sutherland and I met. Except I wasn't pregnant and Mr. Sutherland wasn't an obstetrician.

"What I'm talking about is the way you—well, you know in your heart when someone's just right for you. You don't think about it, you just *know*. That's the way it was with Mr. Sutherland and me. And that's the way it was with Cora and Jim.

"I'll never forget the day Jim proposed. She was in her eighth month then and he'd been seeing a lot of her. 'Marry me,' he said. 'No,' she said, 'I couldn't do that to you. I couldn't make you part of my shame,' she said. I remember how difficult it was for me to keep from shouting out to her, 'Don't be a fool, Cora! He loves you! Don't give up this chance for happiness!'

"But I needn't have worried because that's just what he said to her himself. 'I love you,' he said. 'You give my life purpose. If you don't say yes, I don't know what I'll do.' To make a long story short, she did say yes and they were married soon after. He even delivered the baby."

"Mrs. Sutherland, what nas this got to do with—"

"Lieutenant, please!"

"Sorry, Mrs. Sutherland."

"As I said, they were married and were so happy, and the baby didn't look a bit like Harrington. But I could tell they weren't over the worst of it. I knew in my bones that tragedy was going to strike, but for the longest time I didn't know how.

"To tell you the truth, I was having an awful time sleeping. I finally had to go to Dr. Sumroy and get a prescription for sleeping pills. I'd never used them before because I've heard so many stories of old people accidentally taking an overdose. And not just old people. Young people, too. It's supposed to be especially bad if you take them when you've been drinking, though in my case that was no problem. But I was having so much trouble sleeping because of all my worrying about Cora and Jim that I just *knew* something tragic was going to happen even though I didn't know what.

"Then, suddenly, it came to me. I can't tell you how it came to me because I honestly don't know how to explain such things. Call it woman's intuition, if you like, but I knew what was going to happen. *Harrington was going to kill Cora in an automobile accident!* It was inevitable. He'd just bought a new sports car—one of those fancy foreign things that makes a lot of noise, and it was common knowledge he was speeding recklessly all over town. So you see, it was logical.

"Of course, I couldn't let it happen. I remember how heartbroken I was when Mr. Sutherland died in an accident, only he wasn't killed by a foreign car. I was so miserable, I nearly died. So what was I supposed to do? I knew what would happen if something weren't done, and I couldn't just sit quiet and *let* it happen. I had to do something. But what?

"Then, today, an amazing coincidence brought me the answer. I came into the city to shop on Fifth Avenue for my nephew's birthday, and I stopped into a restaurant on Forty-Seventh Street. Not too far away from Radio City and Rockefeller Center, you know the area? And who was in the restaurant but young Harrington!

"I went up to him, and I said, 'Mr. Furth?' He smiled. I'll say that for him, he had a nice smile. 'Mr. Furth,' I said, 'I want to talk to you.' He stood up, a little woozy from all the liquor he'd been drinking, and offered me a seat, which I accepted. 'Mr. Furth,' I said, 'I'm going to speak plain. I know what's going to happen.' 'What's going to happen?' he said, still smiling. 'I know you're going to kill Cora Franklin with that fancy foreign car,' I answered.

" 'How did you find out?' he asked, obviously surprised. 'Never you mind how I found out,' I said. 'What I'm saying is so, isn't it? You're going to kill her with your sports car, aren't you?'

" 'Yes,' he said, 'that's so.'

"He admitted it! With a smile! There wasn't a trace of regret anywhere on his devilish face. He actually seemed happy about it! I knew I was in the presence of great evil.

"He excused himself and went to the men's room. I suddenly knew what I had to do. I opened my handbag and took out the sleeping pills I had got from Dr. Sumroy, and I dropped something like two dozen of them into his coffee. I left, waited until I was sure it was all over, then came here to turn myself in. And that, Lieutenant, is my confession."

"I see."

"Do you believe me?"

"Yes, I believe you, Mrs. Sutherland."

"One thing you have to know—I did this for them, Lieutenant. For Jim and Cora and the baby. You have to realize that it was the only way. You do understand, don't you?"

"Yes, Mrs. Sutherland, I think I do."

A few minutes later, after Mrs. Sutherland had been led away, Lieutenant Foley turned to Sergeant Warren, who was standing a few feet away. "Well, that settles that," he said.

"Lieutenant, maybe I'm some kind of an idiot," said the sergeant, "but I don't see that it settles anything. Her story about the overdose in Maxwell's coffee jibes, and she matches the waiter's description, but I'll be damned if I can figure out why she kept calling Taylor Maxwell by the name Harrington Furth."

"Sergeant, Taylor Maxwell was an actor."

"I still don't get it, sir."

"I've just been looking at his résumé. For the past few years he's been a regular on an afternoon TV soap opera called *The Will To Live*," explained the lieutenant. "The name of the character he played was Harrington Furth."

Mary Braund

Whatever Happened to Barty Wilson?

Mary Braund gives us a glimpse of American TV, but this time from an entirely different—and novel—view . . .

Barty Wilson became a celebrity in a rather unusual way—not a superstar, not really a star, but certainly a celebrity; and it all had a curious effect on his jealous, mean-spirited wife . . .

Harriet Wilson's husband, Barty, was an actor. You know the name, of course. Even if you are not familiar with the name, you will remember the face. Small, thin, sunken cheeks, deep-set eyes, haggard expression. Barty Wilson is—or was—a character actor, and had been reasonably successful in films and lately on television, playing the role of a henpecked husband in a popular TV series, never quite getting star billing, but making a good living for himself and Harriet. The role fitted him like a glove, because that was the role he played in real life.

Harriet Wilson—Harriet Ellsworthy, that is (stage name)—is, rather was, an actress. Permanently "at liberty," you might say. No one but Harriet can remember the last part she played. Actually, it was in a commercial extolling the virtues of a wonder detergent. Harriet took the part of a mother of eight children who found that this particular detergent was the only one that could get her family's wash clean—they were an extraordinarily dirty family—and that was a role Harriet could play without even rehearsing.

Harriet was a big woman, 160 pounds, with thick arms and a dominating expression. She could easily have been a mother of eight children, continually throwing piles of dirty clothes in a washing machine, and maybe that was one reason she was so unkind to poor old Barty. Because they never had any children. She was always telling him how she would have been a famous actress if only she hadn't thrown herself away on a small-bit actor like Barty, eating her way through boxes of chocolates and second helpings of French fries as she complained.

Not that Harriet had always looked like that. When she and Barty were first married, she had weighed a lot less than he did, a slender little thing with a winsome expression that hid a heart of steel, and in those days Barty had admittedly been on the scraggy side. Lean and rangy, his agent had called him, but the studios in Hollywood are full of actors who are lean and rangy, knocking hopefully on their agents' doors. The sunken cheeks and haggard look had come later as the years of marriage with Harriet had grated on, and with the look had come success. However, Barty had spent the early days of his working life serving in hamburger joints and washing up in high-class restaurants.

Harriet had been fairly successful in those days, getting small parts in B films, playing the part of the maid or the receptionist, and all the time haranguing Barty for his failure to make the big time. But Barty was a persistent man, and as Harriet's winsome expression had changed to reveal the disappointment beneath and Barty had got to look more and more like the downtrodden little man, so their roles had changed and it was Barty who got the parts and Harriet who knocked on the agents' doors.

The break came when Barty was given a bit part in the film "High Noon at Black Rock." You remember it, of course. It was a great success, getting the star an Oscar, and some of the gloss rubbed off onto Barty. There came a series of similar parts and then one day a new quiz game started on television, and Barty's agent insisted that Barty audition for it. "Stars and Their Future." A silly program, really, but for some reason it caught the popular imagination and Barty revealed a fine dry wit, honed by years of Harriet's company. Everyone loved him—everyone, that is, except Harriet.

"What sort of thing is that for an actor to be doing?" she had demanded after they had sat through the first telecast of the new quiz show.

"Let's face it, Harriet. It's good money and we need the money," Barty answered, downing his third martini and watching himself with satisfaction.

"But you're not acting," she persisted. "You're just playing." She took a breath. "You're just playing yourself."

"Nothing wrong with that, is there?" Barty retorted. "Lucky to be getting paid for being oneself, I'd say."

Harriet gobbled another chocolate. "Well, if that's what they want, a scrunched-up little man who's no good as an actor, I suppose you're right." She watched malevolently as Barty made his mild little jokes, and she did not laugh with the studio audience.

"It will never last," she predicted that first night.

However, the months went by and the show continued. When the network took it off for a short time, the public demanded its return. Barty began to get fan mail and Harriet went to a health spa. She lost fifteen pounds, then went back to see her agent. He spread his hands hopelessly.

"You know how it is these days, Harriet. They want someone with a bit of, well, sex appeal. Experience doesn't count for anything any more."

"Sam," she said. "When I used to come to you years ago, you said they didn't want young things, they wanted someone who knew the craft."

"You know how it is, Harriet. Times change. Believe me, I'll let you know just as soon as anything turns up."

"Yeah, Sam, I know. Don't call me, I'll call you."

As time went on, Barty became quite a celebrity around the country. He was invited to talk to women's clubs, he got several parts in films and TV specials, and became a favorite on late-night talk shows. He was not a star exactly, but he became a household name.

You would have thought Harriet would be pleased to have a regular paycheck coming in, to move from the apartment in downtown Los Angeles with no air conditioning to the ranch house out in the hills with a swimming pool and a trip once to New York and once to Honolulu. But she could not forgive Barty for having made his name that way.

"I don't understand it," she said. "You've no talent, that's obvious. Now I know the business. Why is it that I'm sitting at home while you're out there with the masses adoring you. It's not as though you are even good-looking."

"Some people think I'm not too bad," Barty said, on one of the few evenings he was home.

"And what does that mean, I'd like to know?" Harriet had a trick of raising her eyebrows in an arch manner that was particularly infuriating.

Barty grinned over his martini. "Like to know, Harriet? We've been married a long time, you and me, and there are still things you don't know about me."

So Harriet decided to find out. She could hardly believe that anyone would find poor old Barty the least bit attractive, but she'd already been proved wrong about the TV show and she found she was just as wrong about Barty's attractiveness to the opposite sex. After all, Barty was making a good income these days, so there was money to throw around, and eventually she tracked it down to where he was throwing it.

There was an assistant studio manager, a little blonde girl, fluffy and not too bright in Harriet's estimation, but it seemed she and Barty had been seen around in some of the smarter spots in L.A. The girl had a certain winsome expression that struck a chord in Harriet's mind and she was sure it was striking a chord in Barty's.

When she totted up the out-of-town trips he had been taking and the late nights he had been keeping, she was ready to tackle him. She hadn't been through the thin times to see it all go out the window on some little blonde with not too much between her ears.

It was one of those hot sticky nights in Southern California when she came to grips with Barty. He was inclined to shrug the whole thing off. "After all, Harriet, you and I haven't exactly been a loving couple for the past few years, have we? I can't see why you are making a fuss now."

He refilled his glass again, for about the fifth time during the argument.

"You're just a dirty little lecher. No good as an actor, never made it as a father, and now it turns out you're no good as a husband." She was infuriated beyond reason.

"Oh, come on, Harriet. You'll get something out of it. I'll give you this house."

"So that you can marry that dumb blonde? And leave me stranded? After I've thrown away my career looking after you? Why, who knows what I could have been if I hadn't devoted myself to building you up into what you are today?"

One thing about Barty, he had a sense of humor. He started to laugh, choking on his drink, and the sight of Barty laughing under the stars on the warm California night was more than Harriet could take. She gave him an almighty shove and he fell backward, drink still in hand, into the swimming pool.

The pool was there mainly for show. Barty couldn't swim, and though Harriet was really quite a strong swimmer, she didn't care to do too much exercise these days. So she stood at the side of the pool and watched Barty floundering in the water, going under and coming up two or three times until he disappeared under and stayed there. His martini glass was still clutched in his hand, and it was doubtful if he ever knew what happened to him.

Harriet did wonder about his will—if he had had time to change it or even to make one; but as she stood and thought about it, it was too late and Barty Wilson was gone forever, off the silver screen, off the flickering TV sets, out of Harriet's life, and out of the fluffy blonde's life, too.

As it turned out, Barty had never made a will, so everything went automatically to Harriet. It was quite a considerable amount. Harriet had to acknowledge that Barty had done better for himself than she had ever imagined. There was the house, bought and paid for, a sizable amount stashed away in the bank and some very good investments that Barty must have made with the help of professional advice. Yes, she was very well pleased with Barty, now that he was dead and gone, no longer interrupting her career, no longer making her trail around town tracking down his love affairs. Good old Barty!

It suited Harriet to stay on in the house—it was cool up there in the hills, and all the time the place was appreciating in value. Somehow, though, it seemed—well, empty in the days after Barty's sad "accident." The sprinklers ran on the lawn and the blinds were pulled down against the fierce California summer. The house was dim and hushed. Harriet could hear her own feet thudding on the thick wall-to-wall carpets as she padded backward and forward from one room to another, clearing Barty's things out of the closets, planning the trips she would take—Las Vegas maybe, or Palm Springs, or anywhere with a breath of life.

She switched the TV on for a bit of company, not to watch it so much as to have the sound of another voice in the house. Maybe, after all, the house was too big for her alone, maybe she should take a look at one of those condominiums that lined the beach. They were expensive, but she had enough money to do what she liked.

She was gathering together an armful of Barty's clothes to take down to the second-hand store where you got a percentage of the sales price, when she suddenly stopped dead in her tracks, whirling around to look at the TV. She couldn't believe her ears or her eyes.

There on the screen in "Stars and Their Future," cracking his little jokes, was Barty, for all the world as though he was still around and not lying in his grave this past month.

Harriet was incensed. What execrable taste these television people had, showing the program like that, not even mentioning that poor old Barty had passed on. What about the millions of people around the country who must be grieving over Barty, never mind her own feelings? She broke out in a gentle sweat and switched the TV off abruptly, then just as quickly switched it back on again. She found herself sitting in the chair, her arms full of Barty's suits, watching bemused as the camera flickered onto his face, then away, then back again. She was not listening to what was being said, just watching the expression on his face, looking for a hint that perhaps he knew what was going to happen to him.

"Macabre nonsense," she muttered to herself as the program ended with the usual string of commercials. The house settled in around her again.

After a few days the place began to get on her nerves. If only someone would call up, or come and visit; but Harriet had never had any real friends. Such friends as they had had been Barty's. She began to feel quite sorry for herself and on an impulse she called her sister Margaret who lived in the wilds of Kansas and whom she hadn't seen for years. She and Margaret had never been close, not even as children, and on an even more sudden impulse she found herself inviting Margaret to come and stay.

"Harriet," her sister's voice said at the other end of the line, "I'd love to, but you know how it is with me. I can't afford a ticket to Los Angeles. In any case, I couldn't leave the children." Margaret had been divorced for years and her children were now teen-agers. It had been a struggle for her to make ends meet these past few years. "But otherwise it would be a treat to come and see you again, Harriet, and talk over old times."

Harriet didn't believe that for a minute, but her desire for company was too strong. "I'll pay for your ticket," she said.

"What about the children, though?"

Harriet groaned. "All right, I'll pay for them, too."

So they came, filling her house with noisy teen-age laughter, splashing in the pool, treading wet feet and dripping bodies across her nice carpet, drinking gallons of pop and eating their way through mountains of hot dogs and hamburgers, potato chips and cookies. Harriet began to see the virtue of never having had a family.

Margaret sat back in the comfortable chairs and endlessly compared Harriet's life with her own and insisted they take in all the sights of L.A. They made a trip to Disneyland and bus tours around Hollywood and it all cost Harriet a heap of money.

Margaret also deemed it a mark of respect to the children's uncle by marriage that they should sit through every showing of "Stars and Their Future" and as that was the only time Margaret was completely silent, Harriet began to welcome the respite. She had forgotten that anyone could talk so much about so little.

It was also Margaret who pointed out to Harriet that a downtown movie theater was showing one of Barty's old films—a second feature, of course—and insisted that Harriet and the kids should go along and see it. "After all, Harriet, he's famous now, being dead and all that." Which didn't exactly please Harriet, but she went nonetheless and found herself quite comfortable in the theater, the popcorn passing between the kids as Barty played the part of the manager of a seedy hotel, screwing his eyes up against the smoke of a persistent cigarette in the old familiar way.

"Lovely, isn't it?" said Margaret as they emerged from the movie house, "being able to see Barty again like that, just as though he was in the world with you still. Must be a great comfort to you, Harriet."

Harriet snorted, but half-heartedly. There *was* something oddly comforting about the sight of Barty walking and talking his way around the screen, his scraggy old face looming up above her head. Who would ever have thought she would be glad to see that face again?

The summer vacation came to an end and the kids had to get back to school in Kansas. With relief Harriet took them all to the airport, and was glad to have the house to herself once more without the bother of fixing those endless meals for the ravening horde.

In fact, it was a chore to fix meals at all—she had somehow lost her appetite for food. It was easier to snack on crackers and cheese, washing them down with the neat vodka that she had begun to like, and though it was peaceful without Margaret's continual chatter and the inane giggling of the children, the house was very empty once again. She ate less and less and drank more. The pounds began to drop away from Harriet.

She found she was waiting each week for "Stars and Their Future," at a loss to know what to do with herself at the program's end. Then she discovered that "High Noon at Black Rock" was playing at one of the drive-in movies out in the sticks, so she drove out there one Monday evening, sitting alone in her car, waiting for the five minutes of Barty's appearance. She went back every night for the rest of the week.

It was with a feeling akin to despair that, tuning in for the usual episode of "Stars and Their Future," she found Barty's seat on the panel filled by a stranger. She phoned the local station indignantly, without giving her name. "Oh, yes, ma'am," the bored voice said, "all the prerecorded programs with Barty Wilson have been used up now. We won't be seeing him again."

For the first time Harriet could remember, she found herself shedding a few tears.

"That's it," she said to herself. "I must pull myself together." She packed a bag and drove off across the desert to Las Vegas. "A bit of the bright life, that's what I need." She talked to herself quite frequently these days.

She meant to play the tables and it was quite by accident that she discovered one of the theaters off the main drag showing a rerun of yet another of Barty's old movies, this one where he had a better part, on the screen much of the time; and so, instead of wasting her money gambling, she spent most of each day in the movie theater.

At the end of each day she went back to the hotel with her bottle of vodka. When the end of the week came, and the show changed, she got in her car and drove off to Palm Springs. She had lost the urge for the gambling tables and the lavish floor shows.

She checked into a motel in Palm Springs and there she found they were still showing the old episodes of "Stars and Their Future." She stayed for six weeks, until that too came to an end and Barty's chair was filled by the stranger.

Back in the house on the hill in L.A. she sat for a week, wondering what to do next, and then the phone rang. It was an event for the phone to ring. Of all people it was her almost-forgotten agent, Sam.

"Harriet," he said, "I've got just the part for you. Tailor-made. Get yourself down to my office as fast as you can. It's your big chance, baby. When the specifications came in, I just knew you were the right person. The lean years are over, Harriet."

There was no denying she was excited, but somehow not as excited as she should have been. Sam wouldn't tell her what the part was, except that it was on a new TV series, and though she tried to project herself back into the world of the bright lights and action, it had been too long. She had been alone for all those months since Barty died, with not enough people to talk to, with nobody to work her tongue on.

She searched through her closets for the right thing to wear, but nothing seemed to fit any more; all her clothes hung loosely on her. She dawdled with the idea of going out to buy something new, but she felt comfortable in her old clothes and by scrunching in her belt and arranging the folds around her lean hips so that the dress was no longer spread out over her once ample waist, she felt she would pass. Time enough to get new clothes after she got the part.

Sam's face fell when she walked into his office. He looked her up and down, distress all over his fat face. "Harriet," he said despairingly, "what's happened to you?"

Sam's question was merely rhetorical. She knew what had happened to her. "What do you mean, Sam?"

He groaned. "You've gotten so thin," he said. "They want a beefy middle-aged woman to play the dominating mother figure. Look at you. Last time I saw you, you were perfect for the part."

There was a full-length mirror in Sam's office, tucked away between the filing cabinets. Harriet stood in front of it and really looked at herself for the first time in months. She seemed taller, definitely skinny, her old clothes bedraggled on her, her cheeks thin and sunken, with great dark rings under her eyes, eyes that were dark and solemn. She looked and looked and then began to laugh, the laughter choking her.

"Sam," she said at last, "don't you see a resemblance?"

Sam was sucking on a fresh cigar, riffling through the papers on his desk.

"Resemblance? To what?"

"Why," said Harriet, "I look like Barty." And she laughed some more.

Sam was not amused. "I'll let you know," he said.

Somehow Harriet did not mind too much. Somewhere along the line her ambition had died. Without Barty to nag, life didn't seem the same. Without him to harass, to get fat for, to grumble over, to complain to, it just didn't seem worthwhile. The money stayed in the bank, the house on the hill deteriorated, the grass grew high, the parts never came in, the phone never rang.

Harriet found a detective agency that expressed no surprise at her strange request. They were to search the local papers, nationwide, and find out which movie theaters or TV stations were showing old Barty Wilson films. Harriet traveled the country, spending a week here and a week there in one-horse towns where the local theaters or the TV stations were showing old movies that Barty had made five, ten years before, her bottle of vodka always with her, the swimming pool back in L.A. growing algae.

The end came in Green Bay, Wisconsin. It was a bitter night, 15° below, and after the sparse audience had filed out, the ushers found

Harriet, hunched in her seat, empty vodka bottle on the floor beside her, face gray and sunken, already cold to the touch, her eyes wide-open and fixed where the screen had been. Tattered curtains, twenty years old, swished over the yawning space.

"Who is she?" someone asked, thumbing through her purse.

"God only knows." The manager of the theater shrugged. "And who cares? Just get her out of here quick. These old Barty Wilson movies are getting to be quite a cult these days. We don't want any old drunk, fan or no fan, queering the pitch."

W i l l i a m   B r i t t a i n

Mr. Strang Picks Up the Pieces

In which Mr. Leonard Strang, the gnome-like science teacher at Aldershot High School, investigates a jewelry-store robbery. There was only one possible suspect—one of Mr. Strang's pupils. Though the facts seemed to prove that no one else could have possibly committed the crime, Mr. Strang could not shake his conviction that the boy was innocent . . .

Detective: LEONARD STRANG

It was Mr. Strang's free period. The little old science teacher was at the demonstration table in his classroom, preparing a chemistry experiment and wishing he could grow another pair of arms. If he held the Erlenmeyer flask in place on the ringstand with his left hand, he could insert the rubber stopper with his right. But that meant more than a yard of glass tubing would be projecting horizontally with no support whatever. Flexing his gnarled fingers, he glared at the laboratory equipment on the table before him. Then he tucked the tubing into his armpit, gripped the flask awkwardly, and giving a perfect imitation of a man wrestling with a transparent octopus, he brought it toward the dangling stopper.

At that point there was a knock on the classroom door.

"Oh, Mastigophora!" muttered the teacher, laying down the apparatus with a clatter. He walked stiffly to the door and opened it.

The muscular young giant who entered the room wore a conservative gray suit and gripped a briefcase in one hand. He extended his other hand and smiled. "Good morning, sir."

"How are you?" said the teacher, a bit less testily. "And who are you? I'm rather busy now—"

"They told me in the office that I could come right up. I thought you'd remember me."

"You know, now that you mention it, you do look familiar. But

152

over the years I've had several thousand students in my classes here at Aldershot."

"Do you recall the time about ten years ago when somebody in your biology class dyed all the guinea pigs and hamsters bright green?"

"Of course I do. I could never prove it, but I always suspected a lad named—" As Mr. Strang's memory leaped back through his years at Aldershot High School, a grin spread across his face. "Kempel," he murmured. "Brewster Kempel. Welcome back, Bruiser."

Brewster Kempel, known throughout his high school years as "Bruiser," gripped Mr. Strang's arm with a huge paw that in earlier days had hurled footballs and paper wads with equally devastating accuracy. The diminutive teacher had often itched to tan young Kempel's britches. But Kempel's infectious grin and outgoing personality made it impossible not to like him.

"By the way, did you ever get the green dye off those animals?"

"I did. At the cost of a good deal of elbow grease. Can I assume this is a confession?"

"Yes, sir. But I'll have to remind you that the statute of limitations has run out on that one."

"Umm. I take it then that you followed through on your plan to become a lawyer."

"That's right. Passed my bar exams just a couple of months ago. Matter of fact, the law is why I'm here."

"Oh?" Leonard Strang's eyebrows shot up in the direction of his receding hairline. "Have I become involved in something illegal?"

"Not as far as I know," grinned Kempel. "But I could use a statement from you."

"What kind of statement?"

"Well, I'm with the county public defender's office. Our job is to assist people who can't afford a lawyer. Right now I'm on a case that—well, it looks pretty open-and-shut. Of course, my client insists he's innocent. Anyway, I thought if I could get one or two people to testify to his good character, it might help him when his trial comes up."

"I'd be glad to help if I can," said the teacher. "Who's the client?"

"Clifford Whitley."

"I see." Mr. Strang pursed his lips and stared at the floor. "So that's why he's been out of school the last couple of days. I've got to be honest, Bruiser. I don't know how well I'd serve as a character witness for him."

"Tell me something, Mr. Strang," said Kempel in a flat voice. "Are you shying away from this because Cliff's black?"

The teacher reacted as if he'd been slapped. His eyes flashed as he looked at the younger man, and when he spoke his voice was little more than a whisper.

"I think perhaps you'd better leave, Brewster," he said. "If you don't know me better than that last remark would indicate, I doubt that we have anything more to say to each other."

Kempel nervously shifted his weight from one foot to the other, like a small boy caught cheating on an exam. "Look, Mr. Strang, I'm sorry. I don't know of anybody who didn't get a square deal in your classes. But this is my first real case and I want to do as well as I can by Cliff. I just—well, spoke out of turn, I guess. But why won't you go to bat for him? He's a good student, isn't he?"

The teacher nodded. "His tests and homework are quite satisfactory. But he's also extremely militant. That's understandable, up to a point. But he can become violent at anything he considers an insult. The slightest remark can set him off, and when that happens there's no reasoning with him. Now if he's hurt somebody during one of those tantrums of his, he's got to take what's coming to him. What's right is right, regardless of skin color."

Kempel stared curiously at Mr. Strang. "Who said anything about Clifford hurting somebody?"

"If he needs a lawyer, I naturally assumed—"

A smile crossed the young man's face. "Clifford Whitley's charged with burglary, pure and simple. Smash-and-grab out of a store window. Nobody hurt, nobody even threatened. And Cliff didn't put up any resistance when he was arrested."

Kempel jammed his hands into his pockets and rocked back on his heels. "It's improper to jump to conclusions. You taught me that, Mr. Strang."

"A hit, Bruiser, a direct hit. I stand properly rebuked." Mr. Strang sat down at his desk. "Of course, under the circumstances, I'll do everything I can to help. But I find it hard to believe that Clifford is guilty. He might break a few heads over a chance remark, but I don't think he'd ever steal. He has too much pride for that."

"Mr. Strang, you don't even know the facts of the case."

"And you, Bruiser, don't know Clifford Whitley the way *I* do. Now before we get to my statement, I want to hear just what did happen."

"But there isn't time—"

"Of course there's time. The next period doesn't start for fifteen minutes. Sit down there, please."

Mr. Strang pointed imperiously at a chair, and Kempel slumped into it with a sigh. From his briefcase he took a yellow legal pad and began thumbing through its pages.

"It happened Tuesday evening. About seven o'clock. Bainbridge's Jewelry Store, down in the village. Do you know where it is?"

"Of course," said the teacher. "It's in that section called Peacham Lane, the area they advertise as 'a little bit of olde London towne.' Pseudo-Nineteenth Century architecture, narrow cobblestone streets, and so forth."

"That's the place. The way Louis Bainbridge tells it, he and his clerk Jerome Osborn spent about an hour after he'd closed the store working on inventory. Finally Bainbridge told Osborn to go home. Maybe five minutes after he'd left, Bainbridge was in the back room when he heard a loud crash in the front of the store, and at the same time his burglar alarm began bonging away. He came out to see what was going on."

"And what was going on?" asked the teacher.

"The display window in the front of the store was smashed. And Clifford Whitley was running off down Peacham Lane toward Main Street."

"A couple of questions, if you don't mind," said Mr. Strang. "First of all, I've always understood that most jewelry stores have some kind of special glass in their display windows. Devilishly hard to break. What about that?"

"The place was originally set up to be a boutique," said Kempel. "When the guy who was supposed to move in broke his lease, Bainbridge took it over. He was always going to put in one of those special windows, but he never got around to it. So he settled for installing that metal tape around all the windows and wiring it into an alarm system. He thought it would be safe enough for a while."

"Umm. I see." Mr. Strang took out his briar pipe and blew into the stem. "Another thing. At seven o'clock it must have been quite dark in Peacham Lane, even considering the lighted shop windows. How can Bainbridge be so sure Clifford Whitley was the boy running away?"

"Easy," grinned Kempel. "It seems one of the local cops, a man named Joe Bell, drives his patrol car up Peacham Lane every evening at just about seven for a look around. He heard the burglar alarm and spotted Cliff right away. Bell didn't have any trouble catching him. Cliff practically ran right into the front end of the police car. Before he had time to turn and go the other way, Bell was all over him. Cliff insisted he was just out for a walk and got scared when the window broke, but—" The lawyer shrugged.

Mr. Strang sucked absently at the empty pipe. "And I assume there was something missing from the window display at Bainbridge's. Otherwise the most you'd have on Cliff is malicious mischief."

"Right. A couple of detectives were sent over and had Bainbridge sort through the stuff in the window. There were all kinds of things in there from men's watches to gold keychains to who-knows-what. Plus a lot of broken glass. Bainbridge and the detectives went over the whole shebang. Finally it was discovered there were three engagement rings missing. Rather good stones in all of them. Worth close to four thousand bucks altogether."

"And the rings, of course, were found on Clifford."

"No," said Kempel. "He was clean when they searched him. And he insists that he doesn't know a thing about the rings. But Sergeant Roberts figures he must have tossed them away somewhere when he saw the police car."

"Wait a minute," interrupted the teacher. "That wouldn't be Paul Roberts, would it?"

"Yes, that's the one. He's the detective in charge of the case. Why, do you know him?"

"Yes, quite well, Bruiser. He should be able to help us cut a lot of red tape once we begin looking into this."

Kempel was puzzled. "Looking into what, Mr. Strang? All I want from you is to be a character witness for Cliff."

"Bruiser, from what you've told me so far, this case doesn't strike me as being open-and-shut. A window is broken and a scared boy runs away. Nothing criminal there."

"But, Mr. Strang, Cliff was the only one near the window when it was broken. It had to be him."

"Who says so?" asked Mr. Strang. "According to what you told me, Bainbridge was in the rear of his store when the window was broken."

"Two separate eyewitnesses, that's who says so," replied Kempel.

"Oh." The pipe between Mr. Strang's teeth drooped. "And who are these witnesses?"

Kempel flipped through the pages of the legal pad. "The first is Milton Gage, who owns a haberdashery right across the street from

Bainbridge's. Gage was working on a window display of his own. When he heard the glass break he looked up from a jacket he was fitting on a dummy. There, on the other side of the street, was the smashed window and Clifford Whitley running away."

"And the other witness?"

"Jerome Osborn, Bainbridge's clerk. He must have seen almost the exact same thing Gage did. You see, he was standing right outside Gage's store, in front of Gage's window, reading his paper. Since he'd worked late, he'd phoned for a taxi and was waiting for it to pick him up."

"Let me get this straight," said the teacher. "Both men were on the street directly opposite the jewelry store. Is that right?"

"That's it. In a perfect position to see what happened."

"Yes, but if what you tell me is true, neither one of them actually saw Clifford break the window."

"Of course they did!" cried Kempel. "I just got finished telling you that—"

"You told me," said Mr. Strang in a most professorial manner, "that at the instant of the crash, Gage was involved in dressing a dummy in his own window and Osborn was reading his paper. Neither man saw the alleged crime itself. Just the aftermath—the broken window and Cliff running away."

"Mr. Strang, be reasonable," said Kempel. "Okay, technically you're correct. But the fact is, *there was nobody else* in Peacham Lane at that time. How could the window have been broken if Cliff didn't do it?"

"Have you considered the possibility of a projectile of some kind?" asked the teacher. "Fired or thrown from some vantage point?"

Before Kempel could reply, there was the sound of a bell in the hallway outside, followed by hundreds of shuffling feet. The period was over.

Mr. Strang got up and stuffed his pipe into his pocket.

"My chemistry class wouldn't be the best place to continue our discussion, Bruiser," he said. "Tell Sergeant Roberts we'll be calling on him tomorrow—about four."

By 4:10 the following afternoon, Detective Sergeant Paul Roberts had a few thousand well-chosen words he felt like using on Brewster Kempel and Mr. Strang; but with a reluctant bow to the squad's public relations, he limited himself to just one.

"No."

"But, Paul," said the teacher, "we just wanted a few moments to discuss—"

"No."

"If only you'd—" Kempel began.

"No." Roberts shook his head, annoyed. "Kempel, I thought we had a deal. You'd advise young Whitley to plead guilty and we'd go as easy on him as we could. Now you want me to help you get Whitley off. I'm not out to railroad anybody, but in this case the prosecution has all the marbles. You've got nothing at all on your side. So why make trouble?"

"I no longer think it's that clear-cut," said Kempel. "Mr. Strang and I talked on our way over here. And he was pretty convincing."

"Yeah, he usually is," grumbled Roberts. "Okay, Mr. Strang, we can put Clifford Whitley right next to that window the exact moment it was broken. Two eyewitnesses across the street saw him there. Now you mentioned to Kempel the possibility of some kind of an object being thrown at the glass from a distance. Out of the question, and you know it. A bullet would have made a single small hole in the glass. And any object big enough to smash the whole window would have been lying around somewhere.

"We went over the display case behind the window with a fine-tooth comb when Bainbridge was checking what was missing. But there was nothing. And don't give me any of this jazz about some kind of sonic beam, either. We considered that possibility—for about fifteen seconds. Setting up a rig like that would cost more than this whole caper was worth."

"Paul," said the teacher. "If the glass was broken from the inside—"

Roberts shook his head. "Except for a couple of small hunks on the sidewalk, all the glass fell *into* the display case. The window had to have been hit from outside. And Whitley was the only one who could have done it. The only one. Period."

"But there are still a few things that aren't explained, Paul," said Mr. Strang.

"Yeah? Like what?"

"Well, for example, why did Cliff pick up the engagement rings rather than a watch or a keychain or something more in keeping with a boy's interests?"

"I dunno. Maybe he just took the first things he laid his hands on. Anyway, the rings were a lot more valuable than any of the other stuff."

"Another thing," Kempel cut in. "Cliff's a fairly sharp boy. Why try a stunt like this at the one time during the day when a police car could be expected to come by?"

"He didn't know about it, that's why," growled Roberts in annoyance. "Who do you know who checks patrol-car routes?"

"Perhaps," said the teacher. "Although if I were contemplating a crime, I'd take the trouble to find out about them."

"This wasn't planned ahead of time, Mr. Strang. Whitley saw a chance and took it. That's all."

"I see. But about those two men across the street—Gage and Osborn. They both heard the crash and immediately looked up. How long would that take? A fraction of a second?"

"I guess so," said Roberts, his patience beginning to wear thin.

"Then how could Clifford Whitley possibly have had time to reach into the window after he'd broken it and grab anything?"

There was a long moment of silence. Then Roberts slouched lower in his chair and pointed a finger at Kempel. "That last question—that's your case, is it?"

The lawyer nodded.

"Well, lemme tell you something. Time is relative. Maybe Gage and Osborn looked up right away and maybe they didn't. Maybe they were confused about where the sound came from and spent a couple of seconds looking up and down the street. I can't tell you that. But if that's the best you can come up with, take my advice and plead young Whitley guilty. It'll be easier on him."

Fifteen minutes later Brewster Kempel and Mr. Strang were riding back toward the teacher's roominghouse. "Sergeant Roberts is right, you know," said the lawyer glumly. "With what we've got right now, Cliff hasn't got a chance."

"That's why we're going to my place," said Mr. Strang. "You and I are going to spend the evening figuring out what really happened on Peacham Lane."

Mrs. Mackey, the teacher's landlady, seemed to sense the seriousness of the situation. Usually as garrulous as a stuck phonograph record, she served supper to the two men in Mr. Strang's room without a word.

By eight o'clock the floor of the tiny room was littered with scraps of paper, each covered with a diagram of Peacham Lane. Arrows and dotted lines were slashed across them, indicating the possible movements of Clifford Whitley, Bainbridge, Osborn, and Gage at the time of the burglary.

By 8:30 both men had to admit they were getting nowhere. Devices as varied as boomerangs, gigantic yo-yos, and trained monkeys had all been considered and discarded. The broken window and the theft of the jewelry remained a mystery.

Unless, of course, Clifford Whitley was indeed guilty. Reluctantly Mr. Strang admitted to himself that it seemed the only logical answer.

At nine o'clock there was a soft knock at the door of the room. "It's me, Mr. Strang," said Mrs. Mackey through the closed door, her voice like a breeze from off the Lakes of Killarney. "I thought ye might like some coffee."

Mr. Strang took the tray and thanked his landlady. Closing the door with a hip, he offered one cup to Kempel. "There's sugar and cream if you want it," said the teacher. Kempel took a large spoonful of sugar from the bowl as Mr. Strang went back to his small desk.

"Any new theories?" asked Mr. Strang, sipping from his cup. "Because if not, I'd suggest we close down Kempel and Strang, Private Investigators, forthwith. I guess I had Clifford Whitley wrong. Much as I hate to admit it, he has to be guilty. It's the only answer possible."

"Pfoo!" cried a guttural voice behind him.

"I beg your pardon, Bruiser?"

"Ugh!" gasped the lawyer. "It's this coffee."

"Mine tastes all right," said Mr. Strang.

"That's because you take it black. Mine's full of—of salt."

"Why, it can't—" The teacher stopped, then nodded knowingly. "Yes, it can, too. Mrs. Mackey keeps her cans of salt and sugar next to each other on the bottom shelf in the kitchen. Sometimes she's not too careful which can she picks up. Just last week she made a similar mistake and served a candied beef stew that had my taste buds begging for mercy. Wait here and I'll go down and get you some—"

His voice broke off suddenly. For a moment his mouth was just a small round opening between nose and chin. And then a grin spread across the old teacher's face.

"That's it, you know," he said to Kempel.

"What's it?" asked the lawyer, heading for the bathroom to rinse the salt from his mouth.

"The way it was done. The broken window. Oh, what prime idiots we've both been! It wasn't that the thing was too complicated. On the contrary, it was too simple."

"What are you mumbling about, Mr. Strang?"

"About Clifford Whitley. I didn't think I could be that wrong about him. He didn't steal anything. He's taking the hobo's blame, or whatever you call it."

"A bum rap?" suggested Kempel.

"Yes, that's it."

"How do you figure?"

"No time now, Bruiser. Look, here's what I want you to do. Get in touch with Paul Roberts. Call him at home if he's not at the squad room." Mr. Strang began scribbling words on the back of one of the diagrams. "Give him this."

"And where'll you be, Mr. Strang?"

"Down on Peacham Lane. Where else?"

Peacham Lane was deserted when Mr. Strang got there. Three streetlamps, designed to look like old-fashioned gaslights, were all that illuminated its length. Fortunately one was directly across the street from the boarded-up window of the Bainbridge Jewelry Store.

Mr. Strang shivered, only partly because of the cold. The atmosphere of the place was effective, he had to admit that. He half expected Bill Sykes, Abel Magwich, or some other sinister Dickensian character to move out of the deep shadows.

He found what he was looking for at the curb directly in front of Bainbridge's. His gloved hands fumbled for several minutes, but finally was ready to leave. As he got stiffly to his feet, he heard the grinding rumble of a distinctly modern garbage truck headed in his direction.

When he arrived at Paul Roberts' house, the detective and Kempel were waiting for him. "Can you cut this short, Mr. Strang?" asked the detective. "The news is coming on the tube, and I don't want to miss it."

"As short as you like, Paul," was the answer. "I just want to show you a couple of things and ask if you'll arrange a meeting of everyone involved in this case. Tomorrow after school, if that's possible."

"Sounds crazy, but I think I can arrange it if you've got something really important. What did you want to show me?"

"These." The teacher extended his hands toward the detective. . .

The little interrogation room in the precinct house seemed jammed almost to overflowing by the time Mr. Strang got there. In one corner

Brewster Kempel was murmuring something to Clifford Whitley and patting the shoulder of the scowling youngster reassuringly Opposite them, Louis Bainbridge and Jerome Osborn were whispering excitedly, waving their arms in broad gestures. At the table in the center of the room Milton Gage was explaining to Paul Roberts the problems of having to close his store in the middle of the day.

As Mr. Strang entered, Roberts got to his feet. "Glad you got here," said the detective. "I didn't know how much longer I could hold 'em without somebody threatening to walk out. I hope you can make good on what you told me last night. I sent a couple of men out, but they haven't phoned in yet."

"Hey, Mr. Strang!" called out Clifford. "You the dude what's gonna spring me? Man, I sure hope so. This cat what they got for my lawyer ain't been much good so far."

"If you keep talking that way, I may just let them keep you here," replied the teacher. "Your street vernacular is like something from a bad movie."

"I'm sorry, man—uh—Mr. Strang."

"Well, I'm sorry you called this ridiculous meeting," snapped Bainbridge. "I've got a store to run. And it's going to be twice as hard attracting customers with my display window gone. Let's get on with this."

"Very well," said the teacher. Then, carefully, he removed his glasses and polished them on his necktie. That finished, he waved them about in his right hand, at the same time inserting his left into a jacket pocket.

"Problem," he began. "How does one break a window and remove some of the most expensive jewelry behind it in the twinkling of an eye without anyone observing the actual theft?"

"But we did see—" Gage began.

"No, sir, you did not. All parties involved heard a crash and then saw Clifford running off down the street. The actual theft of the jewels was never seen."

"So what?" said Osborn. "Did the diamond rings jump out of that broken window by themselves? This young man had to be the one who stole them. There's no other way anybody could have got at them."

"Oh, but that isn't quite true." Mr. Strang turned to Bainbridge. "Is it?" he asked.

"Well, I don't see how else—" Bainbridge began.

"Oh, come now. All those watches and things didn't leap into place through the solid back wall of the display case. How do you arrange the display in your window, Mr. Bainbridge?"

"The back of the case opens up inside the store," was the reply. "That's how we get things in there."

"Exactly. And that's the way they were taken out, too."

"Hey, wait a minute." Bainbridge was on his feet, his face a fiery red. "I was inside the store, remember? And I'd have seen anybody who—"

"Of course you would. Assuming the jewelry had been stolen at the time the window was broken. But of course that wasn't the case. The rings, in fact, had been taken earlier that day. With the number of objects in that window a few missing items wouldn't be noticed, except on close examination."

"You know," said Bainbridge, "I don't like the way this conversation is going."

"Neither do I," chimed in Osborn. "Are you saying that Mr. Bainbridge stole his own stuff? For the insurance or something?"

"Of course not," said the teacher.

"Then what—"

"Mr. Bainbridge couldn't have taken it. Because you did, Mr. Osborn."

Osborn rushed to the table where Roberts was sitting and began shouting at the detective. Roberts took it for almost a minute. Finally he rose, towering over the smaller man, and grasped him by one arm. The detective half led, half carried him back to his chair.

"Let Mr. Strang have his say," murmured the detective softly. "Then, if he's wrong, we can all sit around and tell him he's got rocks in his head. Go on, Mr. Strang."

"Very well. Mr. Osborn here removed the rings during the day—very probably while you were out to lunch, Mr. Bainbridge. He just put them in his pocket, I'd imagine. However, he knew that eventually they'd be missed. So he'd developed a little plan to make the missing jewelry look like a simple burglary. All he had to do was break a window. Simple as that."

"Yeah, and that's where your half-baked theory falls apart," snapped Osborn, stabbing a finger in the teacher's direction. "When that window was broken I was standing on the other side of the street. I was right outside the window where Milt here was working. Couldn't have been more than a couple of feet from him."

"That's true, Mr. Strang," said Gage. "Of course I was busy dressing the dummy, but I'm sure I'd have seen Jerry run across the street and back. When the window shattered, I looked up almost immediately."

"Oh, Mr. Osborn didn't run across the street," Mr. Strang replied calmly. "He remained right there in front of your store, Mr. Gage."

"Then how could I have broken the window?" Osborn demanded.

"It was easy. You threw something at it."

Osborn stalked over to the detective again. "I'm telling you, Roberts, this—this schoolteacher is the one who should be locked up. You were on the scene. You and Mr. Bainbridge examined the window. How could I have—"

"Mr. Gage," interrupted Mr. Strang, "just before you heard the glass break, Osborn was standing right outside your window. And he was doing what?"

"Why, reading his newspaper."

"A newspaper which had to have been bought earlier in the day," said the teacher, "because all the stores were closed on Peacham Lane by the time he got out of work."

"Yeah, yeah," said Osborn. "I got the paper at lunchtime. I always do that. So what?"

"But you also purchased something else on your lunch break, didn't you? Something you had wrapped up in that newspaper when you left the store. And then waited in front of Mr. Gage's haberdashery, knowing he'd furnish you with a perfect alibi.

"At last you spotted Clifford coming towards you on the opposite side of the street. The perfect person to complete your plan. Who'd believe him, no matter how often he denied any knowledge of what had happened? Finally he passed the window. And that's when you took the object from inside your newspaper and hurled it across Peacham Lane so that it crashed through the window of the jewelry store opposite you.

"Mr. Gage didn't see that quick movement of your arm because he was involved in his work. And the Lane is so narrow you could hardly have missed. Clifford was startled and ran away. That's when Officer Bell picked him up."

"Wait a minute, wait a minute," said Bainbridge. "Jerry's been working for me almost a year now. I'm not going to believe he took those rings unless you can do better than that, Mr. Strang. I mean, what *kind* of thing could he have thrown across the alley *that nobody could find?*"

"I didn't figure it out until yesterday," replied the teacher. "It was when my landlady made a mistake and used salt for sugar. Those two look so much alike that—well, it's almost impossible by just looking at them to tell them apart."

"But what's that got to do with Jerry throwing something?"

Mr. Strang reached into a pocket and took out a small piece of paper. "I made a few phone calls during my lunch period today. One of them paid off. I have here a sales slip from the Aldershot Hardware Store. The clerk is ready to swear that Mr. Osborn made the purchase written on it."

"What purchase?" Bainbridge demanded.

"One pane of extra-thick glass twelve inches square."

"Glass? But—"

"Don't you see? Osborn kept the glass inside the newspaper. Then, at the proper moment, as Cliff passed the window, he scaled it across the narrow street in much the same manner that children fling those toys shaped like plastic discs. The glass struck the window and shattered it. At the same time the piece Osborn had purchased broke, either by hitting the window or by falling to the street. Just a few bits of extra glass that nobody would notice—something to pick up and put in the trash. Who'd go to the trouble of reconstructing a whole window, just to show there were some pieces of glass left over? Especially when there was a ready-made suspect."

"Y'know," said Bainbridge skeptically, "all this sounds very fine, Mr. Strang. But it's just a theory. No proof."

"There's proof, Mr. Bainbridge," said Roberts. "Last night Mr. Strang went back to Peacham Lane. He was lucky. You had a trash can full of broken glass set out on the curb, but the collection truck hadn't gone by yet. He found two pieces of glass. Two special pieces."

"Yeah? Why special?"

"Because one of 'em's only about two-thirds as thick as the other. It doesn't matter which is which. The fact is, there were *two kinds* of glass in that mess where your window was. But the window itself was just one solid piece. So the second kind of glass had to come from somewhere."

Before Bainbridge could put his next question, a uniformed officer came to the door of the interrogation room and motioned Roberts outside. As he left, Osborn turned to the teacher, a smirk on his face.

"Maybe you think you're going to hang this on me," he sneered. "But I bought that glass to fix one of my fish tanks. Yeah, I keep fish as a hobby. Anybody in my apartment building will tell you that. So where's your fancy theory now, Mr. Schoolteacher?"

Before Mr. Strang could reply, Roberts was at the door again. He looked at Kempel with a smile. "You and Cliff can go any time you want," he said. "But I think, Mr. Osborn, that you and I had better have a little talk."

"Me? Why?" asked Osborn.

"Because on the strength of the difference in those two pieces of glass that Mr. Strang found, I got a judge to issue a warrant to search your apartment. My men have been over there since shortly after you left the place. They found the stolen rings hidden in the gravel at the bottom of one of your fish tanks."

J o y c e   P o r t e r

D o v e r   D o e s   S o m e
S p a d e w o r k

S. S. Van Dine's Philo Vance was once described as the fictional detective one loved to hate. It might be said that Joyce Porter's Chief Inspector Wilfred Dover is the fictional detective one hates to love. The snarling, scowling, glaring, growling, grumbling, grunting, groaning, sneering, scoffing man from Scotland Yard may be a sloppy sleuth (clothingwise) and an invidious investigator (personalitywise), but as a detective he's, no question about it, one of a kind and no one else would dare create another! . . .

Detective: CHIEF INSPECTOR DOVER

"You're supposed to be a detective, aren't you?"

Chief Inspector Dover—unwashed, unshaved, still in his dressing gown and more than half asleep—stared sullenly across the kitchen table at his wife. The great man was not feeling at his best. "I'm on leave," he pointed out resentfully as he spooned a half pound of sugar into his tea. "Supposed to be having a rest."

"All right for some," muttered Mrs. Dover crossly. She slapped down a plate of bacon, eggs, tomatoes, mushrooms, sausages, and fried bread in front of her husband.

Dover had been sitting with his knife and fork at the ready but now he poked disconsolately among the goodies. "No kidney?"

"You want it with jam on, you do!"

Dover responded to this disappointment with a grunt. "Besides," he said a few minutes later when he was wiping the egg yolk off his chin with the back of his hand, "I'm Murder Squad. You can't expect me to go messing around with piddling things like somebody nicking your garden tools. Ring up the local coppers if something's gone missing."

"And a fine fool I'd look, wouldn't I?" Mrs. Dover sat down and poured out her own cup of tea. "My husband a Chief Inspector at Scotland Yard and me phoning the local police station for help! And I told you, Wilf—nobody stole anything. They just broke in."

Dover considerately remembered his wife's oft-reiterated injunctions and licked the knife clean of marmalade before sticking it in the butter. Well, it didn't do to push the old girl too far. "It's like asking Picasso to decorate the back bedroom for you, you see," he explained amid a spray of toast crumbs. "And if there's nothing actually missing. . ."

"Two can play at that game, you know." Mrs. Dover sounded ominously like a woman who had got all four aces up her sleeve.

A frown of sudden anxiety creased Dover's hitherto untroubled brow. "Whadderyemean?" he asked nervously.

Mrs. Dover ignored the question. "Have another piece of toast," she invited with grim humor. "Help yourself. Enjoy your breakfast. Make the most of it while it's here!"

"Oh, 'strewth!" groaned Dover, knowing only too well what was coming.

Mrs. Dover patted her hair into place. "If you can't do a bit of something for me, Wilf," she said with feigned reasonableness, "you may wake up one of these fine days and find that I can't do something for you. Like standing over a hot stove all the live-long day!"

"But that's your job," protested Dover. "Wives are supposed to look after their husbands' comfort. It's the law!"

But Mrs. Dover wasn't listening. "I wasn't brought up just to be your head cook and bottle washer," she claimed dreamily. "My parents had better things in mind for me than finishing up as your unpaid skivvy. Why"—she soared off misty-eyed into the realms of pure fantasy—"I might have been a concert pianist or a lady judge or a TV personality, if I hadn't met you."

"And pigs might fly," sniggered Dover, being careful to restrict his comment to the range of his own ears. "Well," he said aloud and making the promise, perhaps a mite too glibly, "I'll have a look at the shed for you. Later on. When the sun's had a chance to take the chill off things a bit."

Mrs. Dover was too battle-scarred a veteran of matrimony to be caught like that.

"Suit yourself, Wilf," she said equably. "Your lunch will be ready and waiting for you . . . just as soon as you come up with the answer." She began to gather up the dirty crockery. "And not before," she added thoughtfully . . .

"So that," snarled Dover, "is what I'm doing here! Since you were so gracious as to ask!"

Detective Sergeant MacGregor could only stand and stare. Almost any comment, he felt, was going to be open to misinterpretation.

But even a tactful silence gave no guarantee of immunity from Dover's quivering indignation.

"Cat got your tongue now, laddie?"

MacGregor suppressed a sigh. He didn't usually come calling when his boss was on leave, having more than enough of the old fool when they were at work in the normal way; but he needed a countersignature for his Expenses Claim Form and, since most of the money had been dispensed on Dover's behalf, it was only fitting that his uncouth signature should grace the document.

So when, at eleven o'clock, the sergeant had called at the Dovers' semidetached suburban residence, he had been quite prepared to find that His Nibs was still, on a cold and foggy December morning, abed. What he had not expected was Mrs. Dover's tightlipped announcement that her better half was to be found in the tool shed at the bottom of the garden. It had seemed a highly improbable state of affairs but, as MacGregor was now seeing for himself, it was true.

Dover, arrayed as for a funeral in his shabby black overcoat and his even shabbier bowler hat, was sunk dejectedly in a deck chair. He glared up at his sergeant. "Well, don't just stand there like a stick of Blackpool rock, you moron! Come inside and shut that damn door!"

Even with the door closed the tool shed was hardly a cosy spot, and MacGregor was gratified to notice that Dover's nose was already turning quite a pronounced blue. "Er—what exactly is the trouble, sir? Mrs. Dover wasn't actually very clear about why you were out here."

Dover cut the cackle with the ruthlessness of desperation. "She's got this idea in her stupid head that somebody bust their way into this shed during the past week and borrowed a spade. Silly cow!"

"I see," said MacGregor politely.

"I doubt it," sniffed Dover. "Seeing as how you're not married."

"A stolen spade, eh, sir?" For the first time MacGregor turned his attention to his surroundings and discovered to his amazement that he was standing in the middle of a vast collection of implements which, if hygiene and perfect order were anything to go by, wouldn't have looked out of place in a hospital operating theater. As MacGregor's gaze ran along the serried ranks of apparently brandnew tools he wondered what on earth they were used for. Surely not for the care and maintenance of that miserable strip of barren, cat-infested clay which lay outside between the shed and the house? Good heavens, they must have bought the things wholesale!

The walls were covered with hoes and rakes and forks and spades and trowels, all hung on special hooks and racks. A couple of shelves groaned under a load of secateurs, garden shears, seed trays, and a set of flower pots arranged in descending order of size, while the floor was almost totally occupied by wheelbarrows, watering cans, and a well-oiled cylinder lawn mower. MacGregor only tore his mind away from his inventory of sacks of peat and fertilizer when he realized that the oracle had said something. "I beg your pardon, sir?"

"I said it wasn't stolen," snapped Dover. "It was only borrowed." The lack of comprehension on MacGregor's face appeared to infuriate the Chief Inspector. "That one, you idiot!"

MacGregor followed the direction of Dover's thumb which was indicating the larger of two stainless-steel spades. He leaned forward to examine the mirror-like blade more closely. "Er—how does Mrs. Dover know it was—er—borrowed, sir?"

Dover blew wearily down his nose. "Why don't you use your bloomin' eyes?" he asked. "Look at it all!" He flapped a cold-looking hand at the tools on the wall. "They're all hanging on their own hooks, aren't they? Right! Well, every bloody Tuesday morning without fail Mrs. Dover comes down here and turns 'em all round. Get it? Regular as ruddy clockwork. One week all these spades and trowels and things have got their backs facing the wall and then, the next week, they've got the backs of their blades facing out to the middle of the shed. Follow me?"

"I understand perfectly, thank you, sir," said MacGregor stiffly.

Dover scowled. "Then you're lucky," he growled, "because it's more than I do. She reckons it evens out the wear, you know. Silly cow! Anyhow!"—he heaved himself up in his deck chair again and jerked his thumb at the spade—"that thing is hanging the wrong way round. Savvy? So that means somebody moved it and that means, since this shed is kept locked up tighter than the Bank of England, that somebody must have broken in to do it."

He sank back and the deck chair groaned and creaked in under-standable protest. "Mrs. Dover's developed into a very nervous sort of woman over the years."

MacGregor's agile mind had already solved the problem. "But, if

you'll forgive me saying so, sir, the spade *isn't* the wrong way round."
He moved across to the appropriate wall so as to be able to dem-
onstrate his thesis in a way that even a muttonhead like Dover could
understand. "All the tools are currently hanging with their backs
turned towards the shed wall, aren't they? With the prongs and
the—er—sharp edges pointing outward towards us. Right? Well, the
spade in question is hanging on the wall in just the same way as all
the other tools, isn't it? So, it's *not* hanging the wrong way round,
unless of course"—he ventured on a rather patronizing little chuckle—"Mrs. Dover has got a special routine for that particular spade."
Dover didn't bother opening his eyes. It would be a bad day, he
reflected, when he couldn't outsmart young MacGregor with both
hands tied behind his back. "She killed a spider with it last week,"
he explained sleepily. "When she was in doing a security check. God
knows what a spider was doing in this place, apart from starving
to death, but there it was. On the floor. Mrs. Dover's allergic to
spiders, so she grabbed that spade and flattened the brute."
"I see, sir," said MacGregor who had not, hitherto, suspected that
Mrs. Dover was a woman of violence.
"Then," said Dover, pulling his overcoat collar up closer round his
ears, "the spade had to be washed, didn't it? And disinfected, too,
I shouldn't wonder." He tried to rub some warmth back into his
frozen fingers. "Well, nobody in their right senses, it seems, would
dream of hanging a newly washed spade with its back up against
a shed wall. In case of rust. So Mrs. Dover broke the habit of a
lifetime and replaced the spade the wrong way round so that the air
could circulate freely about it."
"I see," said MacGregor for the second time in as many minutes.
"Our mysterious borrower, when he returned the spade, then un-
derstandably hung it back on its hook in the same way that all the
other implements were hung—with their backs to the wall. Yes"—he
nodded his head—"a perfectly natural mistake to make."
" 'Strewth, don't you start!"
"Sir?"
Dover wriggled impatiently in his deck chair. "Talking as though
this joker really exists. He damn well doesn't!"
"Then how do you explain the fact that the spade is hanging the
wrong way round, sir?"
"I don't!" howled Dover. "I wouldn't be sitting here freezing to
death if I could, would I, dumbbell?"
There was a moment's pause after this outburst. By rights

MacGregor should have emulated Mrs. Dover's way of dealing with pests by seizing hold of the nearest sufficiently heavy instrument and laying Dover's skull open with it; but the Metropolitan Police do too good a job on their young recruits. MacGregor swallowed all his finer impulses and concentrated hard on trying to be a detective. "Are there any signs of breaking in, sir?"

There was a surly grunt from the deck chair. "Search me!"

MacGregor crossed the shed and opened the door to examine the large padlock which had been left hooked carelessly in the staple. It looked as though it had recently been ravaged by some sharp-toothed carnivore.

Dover had got up to stretch his legs. He squinted over MacGregor's shoulder. "I had a job getting the damn thing open."

Oh, well, it wasn't the first time that Dover had ridden roughshod over what might have been a vital clue, and it wouldn't be the last. Just for the hell of it, MacGregor gave Dame Fortune's wheel a half-hearted whirl. "I suppose you didn't happen to notice when you unlocked the padlock, sir, if—"

Dover was not the man to waste time nurturing slender hopes. "No," he said, "I didn't."

MacGregor closed the door. "Well, presumably our chappie knows how to pick a lock. That's some sort of lead."

"Garn," scoffed Dover, "they learn that with their mother's milk these days." He began to waddle back to his deck chair. "Got any smokes on you, laddie?" he asked. "I'm dying for a puff."

MacGregor often used to bewail the fact that he couldn't include all the cigarettes he provided for Dover on his swindle sheet but, as usual, he handed his packet over with a fairly good grace. He waited patiently until Dover's clumsy fingers had extracted a crumpled coffin nail and then gave him a light.

"Fetch us one of those plant pots," ordered Dover. "A little one."

A look of horror flashed across MacGregor's face. A plant pot? Surely Dover wasn't actually going to—

"For an ashtray, you bloody fool!" snarled Dover. "Mrs. Dover'll do her nut if she finds we've made a mess all over her floor."

MacGregor felt quite weak with the relief. "I've been thinking, sir," he said.

"The age of miracles is not yet past," snickered Dover.

MacGregor turned the other cheek with a practised hand. "We can deduce quite a bit about our Mr. Borrower."

"Such as what?" Dover leered up suspiciously at his sergeant.

MacGregor ticked the points off on well-manicured fingers. "The spade must have been purloined for some illicit purpose." He saw from the vacant look on Dover's face that he'd better watch his language. "If the fellow just wanted a spade for digging potatoes or what-have-you, sir, he'd have just asked for it, wouldn't he? Taking a spade without permission and picking a padlock to get at it must add up to some criminal activity being concerned, don't you agree, sir?"

Dover nodded cautiously, unwilling to commit himself too far at this stage. "You reckon he nicked the spade to dig something up?" he asked, eyes bulging greedily. "Like buried treasure?"

"I was thinking more along the lines of him wanting to hide something, actually, sir. By concealing it in the ground. He returned the spade to the shed, you see. Surely, if he was merely digging up buried treasure, he wouldn't have gone to the trouble of putting the spade back carefully in its place?"

"*Burying* buried treasure?" Dover, dribbling ash down the front of his overcoat, tried this idea on for size.

"Or a dead body, sir," said MacGregor. "That strikes me as a more likely explanation."

Dover's heavy jowls settled sullenly over where his shirt collar would have been if he'd been wearing one. For a member (however unwanted) of Scotland Yard's Murder Squad, dead bodies were in his mind inextricably connected with work, and work always tended to bring Dover out in a cold sweat. He tried to concentrate on an occupation more to his taste: nit-picking. "How do you know it's a 'he'?" he demanded truculently. "It could just as well be a woman."

MacGregor was so anxious to display his superior powers of reasoning and deduction that he, perhaps, showed insufficient regard for Dover's slower wits. "Oh, I doubt that, sir! I don't know whether you've noticed, but Mrs. Dover had two spades hanging on the wall. The one that was 'borrowed' and a smaller one which is called, I believe, a border spade. You see? Now, surely if our intruder were a woman, she would have taken the lighter, more manageable border spade?"

Dover's initial scowl of fury was gradually replaced by a rather constipated expression, a sure indication that his thought processes were beginning to swing into action.

MacGregor waited anxiously.

"A *young* man!" said Dover at last.

"Sir?"

"You'd hardly find an old-age pensioner nipping over garden fences and picking locks and digging bloomin' great holes big enough to take a dead body, would you? 'Strewth, what you know about the real world, laddie, wouldn't cover a pinhead. We've had a frost out here for weeks! The ground's as hard as iron."

MacGregor's unabashed astonishment at this feat of unsolicited reasoning was not exactly flattering, but Dover, the bit now firmly between his National Health teeth, didn't appear to notice.

"And I'll tell you something else, laddie," he went on, "if our joker borrowed my missus's spade to bury a dead body with, I'll lay you a pound to a penny that it's his wife!"

MacGregor perched himself gingerly on the edge of a wheelbarrow, having first inspected and then passed it for cleanliness. Mrs. Dover certainly ran a tight garden shed. There was another deck chair stacked tidily in a corner but, since it was still in its plastic wrapper, MacGregor didn't feel he could really make use of it.

Having settled himself as comfortably as he could, MacGregor gave his full attention to putting the damper on Dover's enthusiasm. "Oh, steady on, sir," he advised.

"Steady on—nothing!" Dover had his fixations and he wasn't going to have any pipsqueak of a sergeant talking him out of them. In Dover's book, wives were always killed by their husbands. This was a simple rule of thumb which had more than a little basis in fact and saved a great deal of trouble all round—except for the odd innocent husband, of course, but no system is perfect. "A strapping young man with a dead body to get rid of, nicking a neighbor's spade. Use your brains, laddie, who else could it be except his wife?"

MacGregor retaliated by taking a leaf out of Dover's book and, instead of dealing with the main issue, quibbled over a minor detail. "A *neighbor's* spade, sir? I don't think we can go quite as far as—"

Dover went over his sergeant's objection like a steamroller over a cream puff. "Well, he didn't bloomin' well come over by Tube from Balham, did he, you nitwit? Twice? Once to get the bloody spade and once to put it back? Of course he comes from somewhere round here. He wouldn't have known about our tool shed otherwise, would he?"

Without really thinking about it, MacGregor had pulled his notebook out. He looked up from an invitingly blank page that was just aching to be written on. "Actually, sir, I have been wondering why anybody would pick on this particular tool shed to break into in the first place."

Dover had no doubts. "Spite!" he said.

"There must be dozens of garden sheds round here, sir. Why choose this one?"

Dover belched with touching lack of inhibition. His exile was playing havoc with his insides. "Could be pure ruddy chance," he grunted.

"He had to prize open a good-quality padlock to get in here, sir. There must be plenty of sheds that aren't even locked."

Dover turned a lacklustre eye on his sergeant. "All right, Mr. Clever Boots, so what's the answer?"

"It's because Mrs. Dover's tools are all kept so spotlessly clean, sir, and in such immaculate order. I'm sure our unwelcome visitor thought he'd be able to take the spade and return it without it ever being noticed that it had so much as been touched. You see, if the shed were dirty and dusty and untidy and covered, say, with cobwebs, it would be virtually impossible to borrow a tool and put it back without disturbing something. Do you follow me, sir? He'd be bound to leave a trail of clues behind him. But here"—MacGregor swept an admiring hand round the shed—"our chap had every reason to believe that, as long as he cleaned the spade and replaced it neatly on the wall with all the others, no suspicions would ever be aroused."

"He was reckoning without my old woman," said Dover with a kind of gloomy pride. "Like a bloodhound. More so, if anything." He shook off his reminiscent mood. "Anyhow, what you're saying just goes to show for sure that this joker is living somewhere round here. That's how he knows this is the cleanest garden shed in the country." He broke off to stare disgustedly around him. "She got all this lot with trading stamps, you know. It's taken her years and years. Never asks me if there's anything *I* want, mind you," he mused resentfully, "though they've definitely got long woolly underpants because I've seen 'em in the damn catalogue."

"I agree our chap probably does live near here, sir," said MacGregor, who'd only been debating the point just to keep his end up. "It's hard to see how he could have known about the tool shed or the tools otherwise. On the other hand, he must be something of a newcomer."

Dover snapped his fat fingers for another cigarette and used the time it took to furnish him with one in trying to puzzle out what MacGregor was getting at. He was forced to concede defeat. "Regular little Sherlock Holmes, aren't you?" he sneered.

Privately, MacGregor thought he was a jolly sight smarter than this supposed paragon, but he wasn't fool enough to confide such an opinion to Dover. "Our Mr. Borrower would hardly have come breaking into this particular tool shed, sir, if he'd known that you were a policeman. A Chief Inspector from New Scotland Yard, in fact."

Dover, almost invisible in a cloud of tobacco smoke, mulled this over. He was rather taken with the idea that all the barons of the underworld might be going in fear and trepidation of him. "He might be potty," he observed generously. "Otherwise he'd know he couldn't hope to pull the wool over the eyes of a highly trained observer like me."

Another thought struck him and he flopped back in his deck chair, suffering from shock. " 'Strewth," he gasped, "it's only a couple of hours since I first heard about this crime, and look at me now! I've solved it, near as damn it! All we've got to do is find a young, newly married villain who's recently moved into the district. And I'll lay odds he's living in that new block of flats they've built just across the way. They've got the dregs of society in that place.

"So, all we've got to do now is get onto the local cop shop and tell 'em to send a posse of coppers round to make a few inquiries. Soon as they find somebody who fits the bill, all they've got to do is ask him to produce his wife. If he can't—well, Bob's your uncle, eh? And that," added Dover, seeing that MacGregor was dying to interrupt and being determined to thwart him, "is why he had to borrow a spade in the first place! Because people who live in flats don't have gardens, and if they don't have gardens they don't have gardening tools, either!"

MacGregor put his notebook away and stood up. "Oh, I don't think our man is living in a flat, do you, sir?"

Dover's eye immediately became glassy with suspicion, resentment, and chronic dyspepsia. "Why not?"

"He'd have nowhere to bury the body, sir."

Dover's scowl grew muddier. "He could have shoved it in somebody else's garden, couldn't he?" he asked, reasonably enough.

MacGregor shook his head. "Far too risky, sir. Digging a hole big enough to inter a body would take an hour or more, I should think. Now, it would be bad enough undertaking a job like that in one's own garden, but in somebody else's—" MacGregor pursed his lips in a silent whistle and shook his head again. "No, I doubt it, sir, I really do. I think we must take it, as a working hypothesis, that—"

"He could have planted her in the garden of an empty house," said

Dover doggedly and, as a gesture of defiance against society, dropped his cigarette end into the empty watering can.

"Well, I suppose it's a possibility, sir," said MacGregor with a sigh, "and I agree that we ought to bear it in mind. The thing is, though, that you're hardly in the depths of the country out here, are you? I mean—well, everywhere round here does tend to be a bit visible, doesn't it?"

There are plenty of suburban mortgage holders who would have taken deep umbrage at such a damaging assessment of their property, but Dover was not cursed with that kind of pride. He simply reacted by nodding his head in sincere agreement. "Too right, laddie!" he rumbled.

"There's another point that's been puzzling me, sir," MacGregor said. "Why did our chap go to all this trouble to *borrow* a spade? The way he broke into this shed may carry all the hallmarks of a professional job, but he was still running a terrible risk. Anybody might have seen him and blown the whistle on him."

"He'd do it after dark," said Dover, "and, besides, you don't go in for murder if you aren't prepared to chance your arm a bit. And what choice did he have? With a dead body on his hands and no spade? He could hardly start digging his hole with a knife and fork."

"He could have bought a spade, sir."

"Eh?"

"He could have bought a spade," repeated MacGregor, quite prepared for the look of horror that flashed across Dover's pasty face. The Chief Inspector regarded the actual purchasing of anything as a desperate step, only to be contemplated when all the avenues of begging, borrowing, and stealing had been exhaustively explored. "It wouldn't have cost all that much, sir, and it would have been a much less hazardous operation."

Dover wrinkled up his nose. "The shops were shut?" he suggested. "Or he didn't have any money?"

"A professional villain, sir? That doesn't sound very likely, does it? And if he's going to nick something, why not nick the money? A handful of cash wouldn't be as compromising, if something went wrong, as Mrs. Dover's stainless-steel spade would be."

Dover shivered and shoved his hands as deep as they would go in his overcoat pockets. The shed wasn't built for sitting in and there was a howling gale blowing under the door. The sooner he got out of this dump and back into the warmth and comfort of his own home, the better. "That's why he didn't buy a spade!"

"Sir?"

"Put yourself in the murderer's shoes, laddie. You've just knocked your missus off and you're proposing to get rid of the body by burying it in a hole. Sooner or later people are going to come around asking questions. Well, I'd have said the last thing you wanted was a bloomin' spade standing there and shouting the odds. No, borrowing the spade and putting it back again shows our chap has a bit of class about him. He's somebody who can see further than the end of his nose. An opponent," added Dover with a smirk, "worthy of my steel. Well"—he raised a pair of motheaten eyebrows at his sergeant—"what are you waiting for? Christmas?"

Dover sighed heavily and dramatically. "It's no wonder you've never made Inspector," he sneered. "You're as thick as two planks. Look, laddie, what's a detective got to do if he wants to be everybody's little white-haired boy, eh?"

MacGregor wondered what on earth they were supposed to be talking about now. "Well, I don't quite know, sir," he said uncertainly. "Er—solve his cases?"

" 'Strewth!" snarled Dover, giving vent to his opinion with unwonted energy. "Look, you know what they're like, all Commissioners and Commanders and what-have-you. They're forever yakking about a good detective being the one who goes out and finds his own cases, aren't they?"

"Oh, I see what you mean, sir."

"Well, look at me!"

"Sir?"

"I'm on leave, aren't I?" asked Dover, warming gleefully to the task of blowing his own trumpet. "But I don't go around sitting with my ruddy feet up! On the contrary, from the very faintest of hints—the sort any other jack would have brushed aside as not worth his attention—I've uncovered a dastardly murder that nobody else even knows has been committed."

Too late MacGregor saw the danger signals. "But, sir—"

"But, nothing!" snapped Dover. "With the information I'm giving 'em, the local police'll have our laddie under lock and key before you can say Sir Robert Peel!"

"But we can't go to the local police, sir," said MacGregor, breaking out in a sweat at the mere idea. "After all, we've only been theorizing."

Dover's face split into an evil grin. "Of course *we* are not going to the local police, laddie," he promised soothingly. "Just you!" There

was a brief interval while the old fool laughed himself nearly sick.
"Ask for Detective Superintendent Andy Andrews and mention my
name—clearly! Tell him what we've come up with so far—that we're
after a young, agile newlywed villain who's just moved into a house
in this area. A specialist in picking locks."

"Oh, sir!" wailed MacGregor.

"There can't be all that many jokers knocking around who'd fit
that bill," Dover went on. "And, if there are, Andrews will soon spot
our chap because he'll be the one with a newly turned patch of soil
in his garden and no wife."

"You're not serious, sir?"

"Never been more serious in my life," growled Dover. "And I've
just thought of something else. If they're newcomers to the district,
that's why nobody's reported the wife missing. She won't have had
time to establish a routine yet or have made any close friends. Her
husband will be able to give any rubbishy explanation for her absence." He realized that MacGregor was still standing there. "What's
got into you, laddie? You're usually so damn keen they could use
you for mustard!"

"It's just that I don't feel we're quite ready, sir."

But Dover wasn't having any argument about it. He cut ruthlessly
through his sergeant's feeble protests. "And stick to old Andrews
like a limpet, see? Don't move from his side till you've got the handcuffs on our chummie—I don't want Andrews stealing my thunder.
I've solved this case and I'm going to get the glory for it. Well"—he
glared up at a very shrinking violet—"what are you waiting for
now? A Number Nine bus?"

MacGregor answered out of a bone-dry throat. "No, sir."

"Leave us your cigarettes," said Dover, not the man to get his
priorities mixed. "You'll not be having time to smoke."

Reluctantly MacGregor handed over his pack of cigarettes and
even found a spare packet of matches. When, however, he'd got his
hand on the door handle he paused. "Er—you're staying here, sir?"

In all the excitement Dover had not overlooked his own personal
predicament. "Call in at the house on your way out and tell Mrs.
Dover that I've solved the problem of her bloody spade and that
you're off to arrest the bloke for murder. I'll give you five minutes'
start, so she's got time to digest the good news, and then I'll follow
you. And I don't mind telling you, laddie"—he surveyed the scene
of his exile with a marked lack of enthusiasm—"I'll be glad to get
back to my own armchair by the fire." He waggled his head in mild

bewilderment. "Do you know, she's never let me come in here on my own before. Funny, isn't it?"

Long before the allotted five minutes was up, however, Dover was infuriated to discover that Sergeant MacGregor was coming back down the garden path at the double. Extricating himself from his deck chair, he dragged the door open and voiced his feelings in a penetrating bellow. "That damn woman! Is she never satisfied?"

MacGregor glanced around nervously, although the silent, unseen watchers weren't his neighbors and he really didn't care what they thought about the Dovers. "It's not that, actually, sir."

"Then what is it, *actually?*" roared Dover, mimicking his sergeant's minor public-school accent.

"It's a message from Mrs. Dover, sir."

Dover knew when he was being softened up for the breaking of bad news. "Spit it out, laddie," he said bleakly.

MacGregor grinned foolishly out of sheer embarrassment. "It's just that she's remembered she turned the spade round herself, sir. Mrs. Dover, I mean. It had quite slipped her mind, she says, but she popped down to the shed before she went to church on Sunday morning to count how many tie-on labels she'd got and the spade being hung the wrong way round got on her nerves, she says. And since she reckoned it must have dried off after being washed, she—"

"You can spare me the details," said Dover as all his dreams of fame and glory crumbled to dust and ashes in his mouth.

"Mrs. Dover was going to come down and tell you herself, sir, when she'd finished washing the leaves of the aspidistras."

Dover seemed indifferent to such graciousness. "You didn't get in touch with Superintendent Andrews, did you?"

MacGregor shook his head. "There didn't seem much point, sir. As it was Mrs. Dover who changed the spade back to its proper position, well"—he shrugged—"that did rather seem to be that. Nobody broke into the shed to borrow the spade and, if nobody borrowed the spade, that means there was no dead body to be buried. And if there's no dead body to be buried, that means that we haven't got a wife murderer and—"

But Dover had switched off. He had many faults, but crying over spilt milk wasn't one of them. He was already lumbering out through the shed door, his thoughts turning to the future. He tossed a final question back over his shoulder.

"Did she say what she was giving me for my dinner?"

Lawrence Treat

C As in Crime

The way Inspector Mitch Taylor of the Homicide Squad got himself hooked into murder cases was one for the books. Here he was ordering some window shades for his wife Amy—just minding his own business, you might say—and the next thing he knew he was in the doghouse with Amy and involved in a homicide case with the victim clasping some artificial flowers to her bosom, for Pete's sake . . . another brisk and breezy procedural yarn from Mr. Police Procedural himself . . .

Detectives: HOMICIDE SQUAD

After lunch Inspector Mitch Taylor, Homicide, had this summons to serve. It had something to do with a stolen car racket that he hadn't even worked on, so there was no particular hurry. About all it amounted to was, the Lieutenant wanted to keep him busy. Which was okay with Mitch.

Before he started out, he went across the street and had a cup of coffee at the Greek's, where you usually ran into some of the boys that worked down the hall, in the Records Room or the Bureau of Motor Vehicles or one of the other departments. Most of the time you picked up a little of this and a little of that, but nobody was around this afternoon and all Mitch learned was that it was going to rain and it wasn't going to rain. Still, there are always two sides to everything, or at least that's what they tell you, so how can you argue about the weather?

Because Mitch had nothing better to do than stall around for a while, he fished inside his pockets to see what was there. What he dug up was that measurement he'd made for the new window shades that Amy wanted.

He'd forgotten all about them, what with Joey getting sick last week and they almost had to call in the doctor. The kid was all right now, but as far as the window shades went, Mitch wasn't even sure where he was supposed to buy them. So he went over to the pay phone to consult with Amy.

He put his dime in and gave his badge number, which meant he'd get his ten cents back at the end of the month. Mitch called Amy at least once a day, usually on somebody else's phone, on account it looked funny at headquarters when you called your own house too often. And while you could always cook up a good reason to explain it, the Accounting Department was just cheap enough to refuse to shell out. You had to pretty much watch your step.

The way it worked out, though, Amy wasn't even home, and Mitch got his dime back and sat down for a while. After thinking it over he decided to buy the window shades from the big mail-order house, which had its main offices in the same direction he was going.

He had car Number Four, his regular one, and he headed uptown. Naturally, he tended to his own business first—the summons could wait—and for once he had no trouble parking. He reported to the despatcher and said he was leaving his car for a few minutes—he needed a Men's Room. That covered him for fifteen minutes or so, and he went into the mail order place and looked around before going to the catalogue desk. It was at the rear with a bunch of offices behind it, and he walked up to the counter. There was nobody there at first, but then this dame showed up and asked him what he wanted, and he told her.

She had big soft eyes, like a spaniel's, but otherwise she wasn't much; he'd have passed her in a crowd seven days a week. While she was checking up on the shades for him he noticed this Miss America type come out of one of the offices back there, and then he noticed the big good-looking guy who acted as if he ran the place. Meanwhile, this spaniel-eyed female found the dope on the window shades and got set to write out the order. When she asked him his name and he told her, it seemed she knew all about him.

"Oh, Mr. Taylor," she said, perking up. "You're the detective, aren't you?"

Mostly, Mitch just did his job, with no fuss and no putting on the dog, but this was something new. Here he was practically famous—dames he had no idea who they were, they knew all about him because they'd probably seen his name in the paper. So he nodded and said, "That's right, I'm with Homicide." He ran his hand through his wiry hair, and he let his eyes kind of nail her down.

"Mr. Taylor," she said, "I know who you are and I need help. I'm afraid something's going to happen—please help me—you can!"

Any cop who took on a private investigation without putting it through channels ought to have his head examined, and Mitch had sense enough to duck. "Better tell the precinct about it," he said. "They'll take care of it."

"No, this is different. Only you—"

She broke off suddenly, and Mitch turned around. The way it happens sometimes, a lot of people had come in at the same time. They crowded around the catalogue desk and they all wanted service and wanted it right away. The big good-looking guy sent Miss America to the desk and then took care of one of the customers himself. Anyhow, with people lined up like that, this spaniel-eyed dame got down to business and filled out the order for the window shades. And while she was doing it, Mitch asked her how come she knew about him.

She answered without looking up. "I know your wife," she said, and that ended Mitch's dream of being a celebrity. "Amy talks about you so much. She thinks you're just wonderful."

"She's pretty wonderful herself," Mitch said, and felt embarrassed. So with the gal's personal problem and all, he was glad to get out of the place.

He served the summons and then he cooked up something wrong with the car and brought it to the garage. By the time they decided the car was okay, it was almost five o'clock. Since it was a dull day, he got off early and went home.

He didn't mention this friend of Amy's until around the end of dinner. According to Amy her name was Natalie Freehan and she'd gotten divorced because her husband was a lush, and she was down in the dumps about it and he was getting deeper and deeper in the bottle and couldn't Mitch do something?

He sort of laughed it off, and then he told Amy what this Natalie dame had said—that something was going to happen and she was scared. Like Mitch said, it was probably some trouble about her husband, this Freehan. Only Amy nearly jumped out of her skin.

"You mean Natalie asked you to help her and you didn't do anything? Oh, Mitchell!"

"What could I do?" he asked. "My hands are tied until she tells me what she wants me for."

"Well, you might phone her now," Amy said. "Because a drunk like her husband—he can be dangerous."

So Mitch called, only there was no answer. Amy was sure something had happened, and Mitch was sure nothing had. He even looked up the movie ads to try and show Amy which one this Natalie could have gone to. After that, he and Amy talked about movies and made up their minds which ones they ought to see, and Amy seemed to stop worrying.

Mitch didn't think about Natalie any more, and why should he? He had plenty of other things on his mind, like who won the ball game he'd bet two bits on and whether to follow up on what that stool pigeon had said about the hijacked liquor, and so on. And in the morning he had to investigate an assault in a downtown restaurant. Some chef had crowned one of his helpers with an iron pot and the guy was in the hospital. The chef claimed this helper had thrown a ladle at him, but it turned out all the helper had done was put too much salt in the stew, so what else could the chef do except crown him? Anyhow, Mitch asked some routine questions and got some statements, and then he came out of the restaurant and reported back to the despatcher. And what the despatcher told Mitch knocked him for a loop.

It seemed there was a homicide and the victim was Natalie Freehan, and she'd been carved up. When Mitch heard the name, the first thing that struck him was how Amy was going to take the news. But the next thing was, she might wonder if Mitch couldn't have prevented it. So he had to show he couldn't have done anything about it, regardless. Or better yet, if her husband hadn't killed her, maybe it was a burglar or something, and then Mitch would really be off the hook.

The Freehan dame's apartment was only a couple of blocks from where she worked, and Mitch was one of the last cops to get there. He had to push his way into the living room in order to report to Lieutenant Decker, Chief of Homicide. Decker was a tall guy with gray hair, and he was handling the Homicide Squad and the precinct detectives and the big brass and the Commissioner all in one breath. The body had already been taken away, and the Medical Examiner had done his stuff and decided that Natalie had been killed the day before sometime between three and seven.

This news didn't sit so good with Mitch, because he'd gotten around to phoning her a little too late. If he'd followed up on her while he was still in the mail order office, a lot of things might not have happened.

Still, there was no sense aggravating himself about it, so he asked Charlie Small to give him the dope. Charlie said they hadn't made much progress yet.

"A neighbor of hers—he's clean, though—he noticed a key sticking in the lock of her front door this morning, so he opened it up. The dead dame was lying on the rug, her hands crossed over her breasts and she was holding onto some artificial flowers."

"Somebody put 'em there?" Mitch asked.

Charlie couldn't answer a straight question with a straight answer. "What do you think?" he said. "That she got up after she was killed and picked herself some funeral flowers?"

Mitch frowned and stared at the bloodstains on the rug. "Knife wounds?" he said.

"Strangled her first, and then used a kitchen knife," Charlie said. "Looks like he really meant it, huh?"

"Don't ask me," Mitch said. "Ask him." Which shut Charlie up nicely, so Mitch went to the Lieutenant and gave him his private, inside information. How Amy had known Natalie, and how Mitch had seen her yesterday afternoon and she'd been scared, and how her husband was a lush. In the middle of telling, Mitch stopped short.

"Those flowers," he said. "What did they look like? What kind?"

"Forget-me-nots," Decker said, and that made it easy.

The wife who'd been threatened by an ex-husband who was a lush, the key left in the lock, the threats she was scared of and the sentimental flowers that only a drunken killer would pick—what more could you want? Except where'd he get the flowers from? And what had he been threatening her about?

Well, there was no point in complicating matters until you had to. Meantime, the Lieutenant sent Mitch and Charlie Small to get hold of this George Freehan and bring him in. His address was easy to track down. He was living in a third-rate hotel, and Mitch and Charlie just knocked on the door and told him they wanted him at headquarters, that they had a few questions he might answer.

He was a small puffy guy up to his ears in booze, and he acted like he'd been expecting the police any minute. He went along without even asking what for. They practically floated him out of his room and poured him into the elevator and then decanted him into the patrol car. He was talking most of the time, except you could hardly understand what he was quacking about.

Mitch figured it would take most of the day to sober him up, and it wasn't a bad guess, at that. All Freehan was good for that afternoon was, he could hold up one finger at a time and let them ink it and roll it on a piece of paper, to get his prints. And when his

middle finger matched one of the bloody ones on the scene of the
crime, the case seemed clinched. Still, you had to wait for the guy
to sober up, otherwise you were just asking for trouble later on, in
court.

What with one thing and another, Mitch was pretty busy, but he
managed to be at headquarters when Amy came out of the office
after seeing the Lieutenant.

"How'd it go?" Mitch asked.

Her lips quivered and her eyes were kind of watery, and all she
could say was, "Oh, Mitchell!" Which was the same as saying it was
all his fault, that he could have saved this Natalie dame, only he
hadn't even bothered.

"Look," he said. "Somebody threatened her, and she had a complaint. If I took it myself, without going through channels, I'd get
in trouble. We just don't work that way—you know that."

"But all she wanted was some advice about her husband," Amy
said.

"I phoned her, didn't I?" Mitch said.

"She was dead by then," Amy said, and she put her arms around
Mitch and hung on tight. It did her good, for some reason, and when
she stepped back she almost looked like she always did, smart, full
of life, somebody real special.

"I know it wasn't your fault," she said, smiling. "Of course not."
But what she meant was, she blamed Mitch for the whole business,
only she wasn't going to push it. And while Mitch knew she'd try
her damnedest to forget it, he was pretty sure it would stick in her
mind and bug her for a long time.

He took her as far as the bus stop, then went back to headquarters.
What it came down to was, if Mitch could show that Natalie had
still been alive when he'd phoned, or if he could show she'd been
killed for some reason that had nothing to do with what she'd wanted
to tell him at the mail order desk, then he'd be squared away with
Amy. So he asked the Lieutenant if he could go up to Natalie's place
and poke around, and Decker said sure, go ahead, he'd been about
to tell Mitch to try and find out what he could about those flowers.
So Mitch went.

He started off with the super and got nowhere. Then he tried the
cleaner's next door, with the same result, and then he went to the
corner newsstand and the drug store and the bakery, and ended up
with blanks all around. So he went back to the mail order place,
only it was six o'clock by the time he got there and the offices were

closed. And that made it a full day's work plus, so he went home for the night. After dinner he and Amy took in a movie.

Next morning, the first thing Mitch did was to go up to the mail order place and see this Miss America, whose name was Brenda Blake, and ask her about Natalie. Mitch's angle was, his wife had been a friend of Natalie's and so had Brenda, so maybe she could tell him things she'd hold out from any other cop.

"You knew who she was scared of," Mitch said. He kept looking at this Brenda in all the wrong places, or maybe they were all the right places. Anyhow, he kept looking, and she knew it. "Somebody was breathing down her neck," he said, "and she told you all about it. So who was it?"

"She was scared?" Brenda asked, innocent-like.

"Look, Miss Blake, you want me to draw you a diagram?"

She gave him a look like he was judging her for Miss Universe and she wanted to know did he take bribes, which Mitch made like he was willing to, and then some. So he said it again. "Who was she scared of?"

What with the deep breath this Brenda took, Mitch waited for her dress to pop. When it didn't, Mitch got back to business. "I'm just a cop," he said, "and I'm asking something simple. Who was it?"

She let her eyelashes flip around a little, which was supposed to push up his pulse rate. Then she answered slowly. "I wasn't really a friend of hers. What makes you think I was?"

"You worked here together, the two of you. You probably spelled each other whenever you wanted a coffee break. Sure, you were friends."

"You don't know anything about it," Brenda said, starting to fuss. "She didn't do anything for me, I always got the dirty end. If there was a mistake, it was always my fault. If one of us had to work late or on a holiday, I had to do it. Do you call that being a friend?"

"So that's why you had this grudge against her," Mitch said, figuring if he needled Brenda he might get somewhere. "You were both out after the boss, and she landed him."

"Grudge?" Brenda said, like she didn't know the word. "On account of the boss? Why would I bother with a tinhorn like him? What would I want *him* for?"

Mitch saw he'd gone off course on that one, so he dropped it fast. "Okay," he said. "But who was she scared of, then?"

"I don't know," Brenda said. "And the man from the publicity department told me not to say anything that would involve the main office, and *he* can do things for a girl." She smiled and tried the deep-breath business again. "So why don't you talk to the man from the cleaning store? Natalie was always complaining about him. Why don't you go there, instead of annoying me?"

"Sure," Mitch said. "What's his name?"

"Hugo. And I'm telling you—if she was afraid of anybody, it was him."

With a lead like that a good homicide man couldn't miss, and Mitch didn't. He went back to the cleaning establishment and found this Hugo Tuttle, who stood six-three without shoes on and who had a funny twist to his mouth that always made him look like he was smiling down at you. Mitch kind of poured it on—why this Tuttle hadn't admitted being sweet on Natalie, or being in her apartment yesterday.

The apartment business was strictly a flyer, but Mitch got away with it. After five minutes or so the guy was begging Mitch to believe that all he'd done at Natalie's was open the door and look in and then beat it. He'd been there around five, yes. He'd come for a dress that she'd wanted cleaned. He knew the dress—it was the one that had the artificial flowers on it. He'd cleaned it before and she always cut the flowers off before he picked up the dress. She'd been clasping the flowers to her bosom (that was Tuttle's word), and she'd been dead.

No, he hadn't touched the flowers, he hadn't touched anything. He was sorry he'd looked in, maybe he shouldn't have, but the key was in the lock and so he opened the door. He'd almost keeled over at what he saw, but he'd been afraid to call the police because they might accuse him of killing her.

Why was he afraid the police would accuse him? It took Mitch only a few minutes to learn that Hugo had a real yen for this Natalie, but that she didn't go for cleaners. He'd been sore at the way she'd turned him down, and he'd threatened her, yes. But he hadn't really meant anything—Mitch *had* to believe him.

Mitch didn't, so he called the despatcher and asked for help in bringing in a suspect, and down at headquarters he told Decker what Tuttle had said. The Lieutenant took the news like he'd been expecting it all along.

"I'll talk to him," he said. "The only trouble is, Freehan's ready to confess."

Seeing as how confessions weren't what they used to be, and maybe never had been, Mitch didn't even blink.

"Think Freehan did it?" he said.

"Well," Decker said, "he admits going to the apartment around six or so, admits he was drunk and that he went there for a showdown. He wanted his wife back, but he doesn't remember what he said or did, except he claims he loved her and therefore couldn't have killed her, although he does remember putting the flowers in her hands and that she was lying stretched out on the carpet when he did it. Brother—save me from drunks!"

"He sober now?" Mitch asked.

"What's left of him is," Decker said. "But you go on a binge like he did and half of you gets boiled out."

"Yeah," Mitch said. "So it isn't exactly a confession."

"No. And you'd better see what else you can dig up on Tuttle."

Mitch dug and came up with a big zero, but while he was asking around, the lab matched up Tuttle's prints. That proved that he'd done a little more than open the door and just take a look, but it didn't exactly prove he'd committed a homicide.

That was about as far as they got in the next couple of days. The Homicide Squad were chasing leads till they were blue in the face, and Mitch missed dinner two nights in a row, and what for? Somebody said Natalie had come home early the day she'd been killed. Somebody else said they thought a girl friend had come to see her, but they couldn't describe her. Three anonymous tips named three different killers, and all three had 24-carat alibis.

What it came down to was there were two suspects, and the pair of them had motive and opportunity both, so which one of them should you pick? Ordinarily the answer to that wouldn't have bothered Mitch much. All that usually bothered him was drawing his paycheck and getting home in time for his favorite six o'clock news program.

But this time, with Amy thinking Mitch could have saved Natalie, the case was riding him. He was on edge and he kept thinking how if he could show that Tuttle had knifed her, and would have knifed her no matter what Mitch might have done, then Amy would lose that funny look of hers. Only the more Mitch thought about it, the more mixed up it got. So he stopped thinking, which is supposed to rest the brain and let it come up with the solution. Except it didn't.

And to top things off, there was some kind of trouble about the window shades. The mail order place called up and said he should come down and straighten things out.

What with all the complications in the Freehan case, fixing up the window shade business sounded pretty simple and shaped up like a nice change of pace. Mitch went there the first chance he got. He walked back to the catalogue desk, and the female there who had probably been hired to take Natalie's place made this Brenda Blake look like a kid sister tagging along and nobody wanted her.

Her name was Lucy Pierce, and she had real class. While he was talking to her, Mitch could see Brenda mooching around in and out of the offices in the back, and it was pretty clear she was staying away from him. What he found out from Lucy was that this big good-looking guy, name of Andrews, was manager of the catalogue department and he'd hired her. Before Mitch got around to window shades, he knew that Lucy didn't like Andrews and expected trouble from him and was sorry she'd taken the job. She said Andrews was a chaser, he'd hired her for her looks, and Brenda Blake was jealous and giving her a hard time.

That was a lot of information, and Mitch digested it while this Lucy went to check up on the order sheet that Natalie had made out. What was wrong with it was, Natalie had either made a bunch of mistakes or else forgotten how to write, and probably both. Which added up to showing she'd been nervous, and something must have scared her so hard that her hand got to trembling. Since Mitch had been there when it happened, he ought to know whatever it was that had suddenly given her the jitters.

He tried to remember back. A bunch of people had showed up more or less at the same time, but they'd all been behind Mitch instead of in front of him. So—are you supposed to have eyes in the back of your head?

He asked this Lucy if he could have the order sheet, he might need it, and she said sure. He thanked her for getting it and he was starting out when he saw Jake Stubbins, Bureau of Frauds, come in and head for the offices in the rear. Jake was a tall, stringy guy, almost as old as the Lieutenant only a lot balder, and he was a whiz at figures. Mitch said hello and asked him what he was doing here.

Jake lowered his voice when he answered. "They think somebody's been playing fancy with the books," Jake said. "Sounds like a racket I ran into once before—they fake the orders, then return the merchandise for cash and pocket the refunds."

"Who?" Mitch said.

"It's got to be somebody behind the mail order desk," Jake said. "I got a warrant for Andrews, he's the manager—he's either doing it or else he knows who."

"Maybe I better stick around and give you a hand," Mitch said.

Jake had to go and crack wise on that. "You gonna help *me?*" he said. "Did they finally get around to teaching you how to add?"

"You'd be surprised," Mitch said, "but you may have a little trouble bringing the guy in."

Jake shrugged. "He's just an embezzler, they don't make trouble."

"He may be mixed up in something else," Mitch said.

The whole thing had come clear to him, just like that. Andrews had been embezzling, and Natalie had caught on and could give him away, so Andrews had killed her to shut her up. Andrews was the threat she'd been talking about, and what had scared her into making those mistakes on Mitch's order form was Andrews coming out of his office just when she was ready to accuse him. She'd panicked not at what was behind Mitch, but what was in front of him.

He didn't think it all out in detail; he just knew. And he knew that Amy wouldn't blame him now—not after he showed that Natalie was mixed up in this mail order racket. So he decided that when Jake walked in to arrest Andrews, the manager would think he was getting pinched for the homicide and he might go haywire—which he did. He threw a punch at Jake and kind of pushed him across the room and then came bulling out as if he was going to commit mayhem. Mitch pulled his gun.

"Just take it easy," Mitch said. "We got some things to straighten out."

The Lieutenant, who always handled the main interrogation, straightened them out fine. He had the motive—Jake Stubbins had supplied that—and Mitch had supplied just about everything else. In fact, he'd guessed pretty much how everything had happened, so the Lieutenant had an easy time of it and ended up getting a confession from Andrews, made voluntarily and as legal as you could want it.

What the Lieutenant always did after he'd wrapped up a case was, he stepped out of his office and gave the Homicide Squad the lowdown, and after that he saw the reporters. Whoever had done most of the work or come up with a particularly smart idea, the Lieutenant usually took them along into the press room and gave them full credit.

So Mitch, who'd done a smart piece of detection any way you sliced it, kind of rehearsed what he'd tell the reporters.

The way it turned out, though, he could have saved himself the trouble. The Lieutenant marched out of his office real businesslike and rattled off the main elements of the case, and then all of a sudden he was talking about Natalie and how she'd hurt her finger just before she'd seen Mitch. It seemed that was why she could hardly write, so Mitch had the wrong reason, and he'd never found out that she'd gone down to the infirmary right after he'd left. There they fixed up her finger and told her to see Andrews and tell him she was going home, which she did. After that, it was a cinch for Andrews to take a few minutes off and sneak over to her apartment and kill her, and then come right back to the mail order place.

It just happened that Mitch hadn't checked up on where Andrews was that afternoon, or where Natalie was, either, and the Lieutenant had the idea that Mitch had pulled a first-class boner. Mitch was ready to admit that maybe he'd been a little sloppy—the Lieutenant did have a point there. But what of it? The important thing was, Mitch was off the hook with Amy.

Hugh Pentecost

The Long Cry for Help

Over the years we have brought you many series characters cre-
ated by Hugh Pentecost—for example, Uncle George Crowder, the
lawyer-recluse; John Jericho, the crusading painter; and Pierre
Chambrun, the fabulous hotel manager. Now we give you the
first short story about Julian Quist, a PR man who wears mod
clothes, who is an Adonis in looks, whose girl Friday is "the most
beautiful chick around," and who has "a sharp and witty tongue
that delights his friends and skewers his enemies." In a phrase,
a hip guy—or whatever the newest term may be . . .

Detective: JULIAN QUIST

The offices of Julian Quist Associates are located in a steel-and-
glass finger that points to the sky high above Grand Central
Station in New York. Walking in the main door is somewhat like
stepping onto a brightly lighted stage set. The walls are a pale
pastel. The furniture, eccentrically modern, augurs discomfort until
you sit down in or on something and discover that it was designed
exactly to fit you.

After a moment or two you ignore the colors, the modern paintings
by artists like Roy Lichtenstein and Larry Bell and Don Eddy, and
focus on the receptionist, Miss Gloria Chard, wearing a simple little
$400 Rudi Gernreich black dress, sitting in the center of a circular
desk, juggling telephones, and looking as if she had been designed
and put together by some genius in the art of female allure. Mailmen
deliberately bring letters to the wrong office just to get a look at
Miss Chard; delivery boys bring milkshakes and sandwiches to the
wrong place on purpose. Miss Chard smiles and smiles and says "no"
more often in one day than most girls do in a month.

But Miss Chard is just window dressing compared to what lies
beyond in the private offices.

There is, to begin with, Julian Quist himself. He is tall, slender, with carefully styled golden hair that sets off a face and head that might have been carved on an old Greek coin. Public relations is his business—he is an image maker, and he had evidently begun by creating an image of himself. A profile writer for a magazine once described him: "Successful and therefore rich, indecently handsome, with a wardrobe of very mod clothes unsurpassed in any closets in America, and always with the most beautiful chick around who shares both his business and his private life." What the writer left out was a sharp and witty tongue that delighted his friends and skewered his enemies.

The "most beautiful chick around" is Lydia Morton, dark, sultry, who looks more like a high-fashion model than a brilliant researcher and feature writer for Julian Quist Associates. It is no secret to their friends that Quist and Lydia are more tightly bound together than marriage vows could have made them. Men envied Quist for Lydia more than for his success, his good looks, and his clothes. A man who could corner Lydia Morton for himself must be very special, because Lydia could have chosen anyone on earth who interested her.

On the morning of the day that "the long cry for help" was to begin, Quist was in his private office with Lydia and Dan Garvey. After Lydia, Garvey was the most valued of Quist's "Associates." He was the complete opposite of Quist in appearance—dark, weighing perhaps 20 pounds more than Quist, lean and hard. He had been an outstanding athlete ten years ago, with the promise of becoming the best running back in professional football until a knee injury cut short his career. He could have become a movie star but instead he had chosen to go to work for Quist. Dan Garvey was a very good man to have on your side if the going got physical. The fact that he had a Phi Beta Kappa key in his top bureau drawer was something he kept secret from most people.

"So is there anything not done that must be done?" Quist asked his friends.

He was sitting at his desk, holding a very long thin cigar between his tapering fingers. His pale blue eyes were narrowed against the smoke.

"All set at my end," Garvey said. "Pete and his boy have settled into Jack Jason's apartment. I think we've managed to keep it a complete secret. Jack's son Paul is staying there too, you know, but that will work out well because he's quite willing to keep an eye on Pete's boy."

"The boy's name is Tommy, isn't it?" Quist said. "Tell me about him."

A nerve twitched at the corner of Garvey's mouth. "He gets you where you live," he said, sounding as if it angered him to be moved by something. "What is he, nineteen? Beautiful is the word for him, I guess, with the frightened eyes of a spaniel puppy. He says, 'How do you do, sir,' when you meet him, and 'Goodbye, sir' when you go. In between, if you ask him anything, he turns away, frightened.

"He looks to Pete for help, but he isn't quite sure yet that Pete can or will help him. I asked him how he liked the apartment, and, so help me, it was as if he didn't understand the question. We were standing by the windows, and Pete jumped right in. 'He likes Central Park,' he said. 'Don't you, Tommy?' And the boy nodded. 'And the flowers,' Tommy said. He is a very nice, very well-mannered four-year-old child."

"How terribly tragic," Lydia said.

"Oh, there's nothing about him to turn you off," Garvey said. "Quite the reverse. You want to help him. You *ache* to help him. Trouble is, you don't know how."

"Maybe just with love," Lydia said.

"He seems to have made a complete change in Pete," Quist said.

Quist wouldn't soon forget the night Pete Williams had come charging into his hotel room in Hollywood, where he'd gone on business for a few days. No announcement, just a banging on the door with a clenched fist. Quist had been shocked by Pete's appearance. Some said that Pete Williams was the top song stylist in the world. He had made millions of records, on appearances at Vegas, on television.

Pete Williams had married six glamorous women and left them all drowning in his wake, along with the other women he hadn't married. He had insulted two presidents of the United States at White House parties and been loved for it, even by the presidents. He was like a tornado, devastating the areas through which he passed, but somehow loved for his irreverence, his cruel gaiety.

But that night a month ago in Hollywood, when Quist opened his hotel room door to a pounding fist, he found himself confronting a Pete Williams who had tears streaming down his face, his body wracked by strangling sobs.

It was a while before Pete could talk, a while after he'd had a generous slug of bourbon. Quist knew him well enough to wait for an explanation. Pete had been a client at one time whom Quist had eventually dropped because Pete managed to destroy every campaign planned for him with his unpredictable behavior. Quist still had a secret affection for him. There was something irresistible about Pete's outrageousness.

The dam broke finally and it all came pouring out of Pete that night. His first wife, Linda, 20 years divorced and long forgotten, had been killed in a plane crash. Linda and Pete had had a son, but Pete had deserted ship when the boy was six months old. He paid his alimony and went his way. He never asked about the boy or knew anything about him—or cared.

"Would you believe, Julian, yesterday some creep called me to ask what I wanted done about Tommy. I'd even forgotten that was the boy's name. What I wanted done? Hell, he was nearly twenty years old. Let him organize his own life. If he needed money—? That's when they told me. The boy is retarded. He's like four-five years old, they tell me. My kid!

"So I go to find out what the hell they're talking about. I figure somebody's trying to put the screws to me. And there he is, Julian —this kid, this beautiful boy. He's scared almost into a state of shock. Linda was all he'd had all these years. Now he's alone and nobody understands him, or how to make him feel safe. And I—I—his father—"

And Pete went off into uncontrollable weeping again.

It was a new Pete. He took the boy into his home. He pushed out his friends and cronies and he made an unbelievable effort to provide the unfortunate Tommy with a new security.

A few weeks ago Quist, back in New York, got a call from Pete. There was some kind of national fund drive on for retarded children.

"We'll top it off with the biggest thing ever!" Pete said. "A twenty-four-hour telethon. All the biggest people in show business and sports. I'll stay on it round the clock, sing a number every hour—something like that—the number that people ask for who give the most money each hour. Build it up any way you like, Julian, because you're going to stage it. Money no object. We'll call it 'The Long Cry for Help.'"

A network went for it. The Long Cry for Help would go on at midnight on a Friday and run through till midnight Saturday. Actors, singers, dancers, musicians, football players, tennis stars, race-car drivers—people from every conceivable entertainment medium agreed to man the telephones, and once an hour the incomparable

Pete Williams would sing the song that had rung up the most money on the cash register in the preceding hour.

It was the kind of generous outpouring of time and talent that show-business people so often give to charitable causes. Some cynics suggest that they do it for the free publicity involved, a libel on the great majority of them. Julian Quist Associates had no difficulty in lining up an All Star cast.

But there was one thing Quist had not dreamed of as he prepared for the twenty-four-hour call for help. He had not dreamed that at the very core of it they would come upon a cruel violence that threatened to blacken the occasion for generous performers and public alike. It was a violence that turned Quist, for a space of time, from a languid sophisticate into a cold avenger.

There had been details to arrange. Pete Williams would have to be in New York for two or three days. He was bringing his boy with him and he didn't want to stay at a hotel. He would be swarmed under by autograph seekers and fans, and Tommy would be subjected to the scrutiny of the morbidly curious. One thing Pete insisted on was that there should be no mention of Tommy.

Tommy would not be allowed to go to the theater where the telethon was to be held. Some kind of very private living quarters had to be arranged for, and it was Dan Garvey who found what seemed to be the ideal place. An old friend of Garvey's named Jack Jason had an apartment on Central Park West overlooking the park. Jason, a sports promoter and agent for athletes, was in Las Vegas lining up a heavyweight fight. He was glad to let Pete have his place provided his own son, Paul, could stay there. Actually that worked out very well: Paul was Tommy's age, but very bright, very brash, very mod. The two boys couldn't have been more different, but Paul Jason seemed to feel an instinctive sympathy for Tommy and was quite willing to act as a companion during the three days Tommy would be in the apartment.

The night the telethon was to begin Quist had Pete and Tommy and Paul Jason come to his apartment on Beekman Place for a buffet supper, along with Lydia and Garvey. Lydia seemed to hit it off with Tommy from the start. It was as if he had missed female attention since his mother's death. He reached out to her, actually touched her, and couldn't be persuaded to leave her side. At one point she took him out on the terrace which looked down over the East River, where the lights of boats twinkled in the darkness. Tommy didn't seem too impressed.

"I like the park—and the flowers," he said.

"Tomorrow, after your father's show begins, I'll go to the park with you," Lydia said. "Would you like that?"

"I would like that—so very much," the boy said.

Young Tommy Williams was not the only person present who was obviously fascinated by Lydia. Paul Jason, supercharged with energy in comparison with the unfortunate Tommy, was almost comic in his efforts to impress the beautiful older woman. He jumped to his feet to light cigarettes for her, he insisted on serving her from the buffet, he told her brash jokes, he almost elbowed Tommy aside from time to time to get her attention.

"You'd better watch out for your woman," Pete Williams said as he was preparing to leave for the telethon. "Those kids may steal her away from you."

"I spend half of my life fighting off the competition," Quist said. "I wonder if I was so insufferably egotistical when I was nineteen?"

"I was chasing my father's mistress at that age," Pete said.

"Success?"

Pete's face clouded. "Unfortunately. She became my first wife and Tommy's mother."

"I have a strange feeling you can bring that boy a long way up the hill—if you want to," Quist said.

It was time to go and Pete interrupted one of Paul Jason's displays of histrionics. "You're sure you don't mind staying at home with Tommy, Paul?"

"Of course not, Mr. Williams," the boy said. "We'll be watching you on TV."

And so, after an elaborate farewell to Lydia, Paul took Tommy back to Central Park West and the rest of them headed for the theater where the telethon would begin.

It was a success from the start. Quist had arranged for dozens of people to call in the minute it began so that contributions would begin at once. Pledges poured in, ranging from one dollar to thousands of dollars. At the end of the first hour Pete Williams sang the song that had been most asked for. He was beaming with delight. That first hour had amassed a sum for retarded children that approached six figures, more than they had dared hope for.

About three in the morning Quist and Lydia said goodnight to Pete. It was time, Quist told himself, that he had Lydia to himself for a while.

"It's going just great!" Pete said.

"See you about noon," Quist said. "Garvey will stand by till then."

"Thanks for everything," Pete said. "It's all working like a Swiss watch."

"Because, of course, I'm a genius," Quist said.

It was about eleven o'clock on Saturday morning, while Quist and Lydia were having coffee on the Beekman Place terrace, that the phone rang. It was Garvey and his voice sounded strained

"You'd better get over here."

"What's wrong? Pete started drinking?"

"Someone has kidnaped the boy," Garvey said.

"What?"

"Call came in over Pete's open line here. They have the boy—two hundred and fifty grand and the usual 'no cops or else.' "

"Some kind of bad joke?"

"We've tried to call Paul Jason. No answer. They let the boy talk to Pete. He's safe but scared. Pete needs your help, chum."

"Fifteen minutes," Quist said.

One of the things guests couldn't be asked to do while working on the telethon was to keep accurate records of the calls they got—names, addresses, amounts. Calls came one right after another, and the vital information was inevitably fouled up by the performers. Quist had arranged for all incoming calls to be monitored by tape recorders, the tapes to be transcribed by a paid staff of stenographers. This left the guests free to be charming without having to worry about details. So it was that there was a tape of the conversation Pete Williams had had with the kidnaper. And there was a tape of the conversation Tommy had had with his father.

Pete seemed to have shrunk inside his dark tropical worsted suit by the time Quist and Lydia arrived. The makeup he was wearing for the television cameras hid a grayish pallor. His hands shook as he tried to light a cigarette. What he had to say was unprintable, a long steady string of profanity.

"You'd better listen to the conversation," Garvey said to Quist.

They went into the office of the house manager, off the theater lobby. A tape recorder was set up on the desk and Garvey switched it on. There was the background sound of the voices of people manning telephones. Then Pete's voice, bright and cheerful.

"Pete Williams here. Thanks for calling."

"Listen carefully, Mr. Williams," a muffled voice said. Quist guessed the speaker was holding a handkerchief or towel over his mouthpiece. "We have your boy, and if you want to see him again you will follow instructions to the letter."

"What the hell are you talking about?" Pete almost shouted.

"We have taken your boy and it will cost you two hundred and fifty thousand dollars to get him back. Listen carefully because I won't repeat the instructions. You will be singing a song in exactly forty minutes—at ten o'clock. We will give you one more hour—until your next number at eleven—to arrange for the money in small denominations and unmarked bills. When you have sung your eleven o'clock song you will get instructions on how to deliver the ransom.

"Do not call the police. Do not leave the theater. We'll know if you have because we'll be watching on television. There will be no additional time given you. You will have the money ready to deliver after your song at eleven o'clock. It is then or never."

"How do I know Tommy is safe?" Pete's voice on the tape.

"Listen." There were a few moments of silence and then another voice, also muffled. "They haven't hurt me, Dad. I'm really all right. But please do what they say. I'm awfully scared, Dad." Again a few moments of silence and then the first voice came back. "Satisfied, Mr. Williams? You'd better get moving. You have a little over an hour." The tape switched off.

Quist glanced at his watch. Twenty-two minutes to go.

"The money's arranged for," Garvey said. "Whoever they designate can pick it up at the bank."

Two large tears rolled down Pete Williams' face. "He never called me 'Dad' before. When he found himself in trouble he must have come to believe in me. So help me God, if they hurt him—"

"What did he call you before, Pete?" Quist asked. His pale blue eyes had turned very cold.

"He called me 'Father,' " Pete said. "So polite, so formal, in spite of all I did to win him over, to make him feel safe. Now, finally, when he's in trouble—"

"You've called the Jason apartment?" Quist asked Garvey.

"Of course," Garvey said. "No answer."

"Play that tape again and listen to it carefully, all of you," Quist said.

Garvey switched on the tape.

"The boy's voice is all I care about," Quist said. "Just Tommy's voice."

It came through, quick and clear. "They haven't hurt me, Dad. I'm really all right. But please do what they say. I'm awfully scared, Dad."

Quist brought his fist down hard on the edge of the desk. "That's not Tommy. Never in this world," he said.

"The voice is muffled. They had something over the mouthpiece of the phone," Garvey said.

"It's not the voice that gives it away," Quist said. "Tommy hunts for words. He's slow, deliberate. They got the wrong boy."

"What are you talking about?" Pete said.

"Paul Jason." Quist turned to Lydia. "He talked to you enough last night, luv. Is that Paul Jason on the tape?"

"It could be," Lydia said. She reached out to touch Quist's hand and her fingers were cold.

"But why would they—?" Pete began.

"Julian's right. They got the wrong boy," Garvey said. "Paul was trying to let you know that, Pete, by being too glib and by calling you 'Dad.' "

"Why wouldn't Paul tell the kidnapers he wasn't Tommy?" Pete asked.

"If he could identify them he might have been smart enough to realize it would be safer for him not to tell them. Or maybe he just wants to be a hero," Quist said.

"But where in God's name is Tommy?" Pete asked.

"It's crazy," Lydia said, "but it's just possible he's in the park. I had a date with him, remember? He may have decided to wait for me out there."

"So let's go!" Pete said.

Quist stopped him, his hand on his arm. "You're going to have to play it out, Pete. Sing your next number, wait for instructions. Dan will stay here with you."

"But if Tommy's out there—?"

"You owe something to Paul Jason for not telling them where Tommy could be found. Lydia and I will look for Tommy. If we find him we'll call in at once. Play it straight when you get your instructions. You want Garvey to deliver the money—you want an on-the-spot exchange—Tommy for the money."

"And if they don't buy it?"

"You deliver the money the way they tell you—and pray."

"A quarter of a million bucks for another guy's kid?"

"A kid who is trying to save your kid," Quist said quietly.

"Sorry, Julian. I guess I'm not thinking very straight," Pete said. "I'd better get out there. It's almost time for my next number."

"Keep your cool," Quist said.

The fact that Pete and Tommy were to occupy Jack Jason's apartment had been kept secret so that they wouldn't be mobbed by reporters and fans. But "national security" wasn't involved; someone in Quist's office might, inadvertently, have been responsible for a "leak." More likely the kidnaper or kidnapers had made their plans well in advance. Pete and his boy could have been under surveillance all the way from the west coast and been followed right to the door of Jason's apartment.

"There's only one thing wrong with that," Quist said, frowning, as he and Lydia rode uptown in a taxi. "If Pete and the boy were being watched they'd never have assumed that Paul Jason was Tommy. Tommy's dark, Paul's ash-blond."

"That *wasn't* Tommy's voice on the tape," Lydia said. "The more I think about it the surer I am it was Paul's."

"Paul is a little too brash for my liking," Quist said, "but it took real guts to let them think he's the kid they want."

"What will you do if we find Tommy, Julian? Because I have a kind of bone-certainty we'll find him in the park."

"I'll go to the apartment," Quist said. "Paul is bright enough to have left us some kind of clue."

"You don't think the kidnapers may be there with Paul?"

"No. If Pete didn't choose to play along, that would be the first place the police would go—the starting point."

They got out of the taxi on the park side of Central Park West, opposite the apartment building where the Jasons lived. It was a gently warm summer day. They walked down a few stone steps into the park itself, Lydia almost running ahead of Quist.

The first person they encountered was a park policeman. Before Lydia could finish her question the man interrupted with an answer.

"I'm sure glad you showed up, ma'am," he said. "That boy's been sitting over there on a bench by the bridle path since almost seven this morning. He said he was waiting for someone, but I was just about to do something about him."

Lydia was literally flying across the grass toward the lone figure on the park bench.

"Something odd about that boy," the policeman said to Quist. "I couldn't get out of him who he is or where he lives. When I pressed him, all he would say was that someone was coming for him."

"He's retarded—and scared," Quist said. "Thanks for keeping an eye on him. I think his father may want to thank you personally. Your name?"

"Moran, Park Police. It was just my job."

Lydia was sitting on the park bench with Tommy, an arm around his shoulders. The boy's face was buried against her shoulder.

"He thought I wasn't coming," Lydia said.

"Does he know where Paul is?" Quist asked.

The boy lifted tear-filled eyes. "Asleep," he said.

"He was asleep when you left the apartment?"

Tommy nodded.

"But that was a long time ago, Tommy."

"Long, long time," the boy said, and turned worshipfully to Lydia.

"Do you have a key to the apartment, Tommy?"

The boy's face lit up with pride. He had been trusted with a key and he now produced it.

"Let me borrow it," Quist said. "And you go with Lydia to our place, Tommy. It's time you had breakfast, or lunch, or whatever. Call Pete, Lydia."

"Of course. And be careful, Julian."

"Nothing to worry about. Jason's apartment is the safest place in town at the moment," Quist said. He turned and headed back toward the street and the apartment building.

There was a self-service elevator in the apartment house, but no attendant was visible. From behind a closed door next to the elevator Quist could hear a television set going, actually hear Pete's voice talking on the phone. On a call board was Jason's name and apartment number, 4B.

Quist took the elevator to the fourth floor and let himself into 4B. He didn't expect to find anyone, and there was no one there. The apartment was what he might have expected from Jack Jason, sports promoter. The walls were covered with autographed photographs of famous fighters, baseball players, golfers, football stars. His eye was caught for a moment by a picture of a young Dan Garvey in the days when Dan had been running wild in the National Football League.

Aside from the kind of casual disorder you might have expected in an apartment occupied by two men, there was no sign that any kind of violence had taken place. Quist tried to put it together. Tommy had gone out into the park as early as seven o'clock. The kidnapers had come after that. Paul had probably let them in, not expecting trouble. They, in turn, had jumped to the conclusion that Paul was the boy they wanted.

Paul had chosen not to enlighten them, either because they didn't give him a chance, or because he thought it was safer, or because he wanted to be a hero. He might have thought of the impression that heroism would make on Lydia. They had taken Paul somewhere, forced him to talk to Pete, and Paul had, cleverly, made it apparent that it wasn't Tommy's voice Pete heard.

A boy that alert, that clever, might have left something behind that would be a lead, Quist thought. He was standing by the telephone on a side table and his eyes fell on a memo pad beside the phone. A number was written on the pad, and the number rang a bell with Quist. He had heard that number mentioned dozens of times in the last twelve hours. It was the number given out to call Pete at the telethon.

Quist turned away, scowling. Had the boys thought of calling Pete sometime at the telethon? If the kidnapers had wanted the number they would have taken it away with them. Maybe the boys had thought it would be fun to talk to Pete.

It was then that he saw the tape recorder on the table in the center of the room. Nearly everyone owns a tape recorder in this day and age, he thought. He walked over to the machine and idly pressed the PLAY button. A kid like Paul would probably have a collection of rock music on tapes.

"They haven't hurt me, Dad. I'm really all right. But please do what they say. I'm awfully scared, Dad."

Quist felt the small hairs rising on the back of his neck. The tape continued in silence for a few seconds—and then somebody giggled! It was a crazy sound, a self-satisfied sound.

Quist snapped off the machine, and at the same moment he heard a key in the front door. The door opened and Paul Jason walked in briskly, carrying a black attaché case under his arm. He stopped dead in his tracks when he saw Quist.

"What are you doing here, Mr. Quist?" he asked.

"Looking for you and Tommy," Quist said. "Nobody answered the phone."

"Tommy was gone when I got up this morning," Paul said. "I guess he went to the park. But when he didn't come back I—I went out to look for him a little while ago."

"But you didn't find him?"

"No. It's a big park, Mr. Quist."

"What are you carrying in that attaché case, Paul?" Quist asked, in a very quiet voice.

"Just some stuff of mine," Paul said. His eyes widened and there was something like fear in them.

"I'd like to look," Quist said, "because I have a hunch it contains two hundred and fifty thousand dollars in ransom money."

"Money! You better get your head together, Mr. Quist."

"I did—just before you walked in," Quist said. "I found Pete's number on your telephone pad and then I played a bit on your tape recorder. Incidentally, Tommy is safe, so no one has been hurt. But the ball game is over, boy. Just hand over that case."

What happened was a sudden and rather terrifying transformation from a bright eager kid to a dangerous and cornered animal. The boy pulled a handgun out of his jacket pocket and leveled it unsteadily at Quist. There is nothing quite so scary as a gun in the hands of a hysteric who doesn't know how to use it.

"This money is going to my father, Mr. Quist. He owes the Syndicate, and they'll kill him if he doesn't pay. Mr. Williams can afford it. You could afford it. You're all so rich and successful—you and your fancy office and your fancy apartment and that fancy girl you keep!"

"Remind me to wash out your mouth with soap when the appropriate time comes," Quist said.

"I'm going out of here, Mr. Quist. And if you make a move to stop me I swear I'll kill you. My father needs this money and he's going to get it."

"Does he know what you're doing?"

"No. He'd let himself be killed rather than do something like this. But I'm different. I'm going to get him off the hook."

"And after that?"

"What happens after that doesn't matter. Now stay just where you are, Mr. Quist." The boy began to back toward the door.

Dead heroes don't do anybody any good, Quist thought, and he stood quite still. Paul reached behind him for the door and opened it. He took a step backward into the hall.

And then, suddenly, he came hurtling back into the room, the gun flying in one direction and the attaché case in another. Then he was face down on the floor with Dan Garvey on top of him. Garvey looked up at Quist and grinned.

"I once tackled Gale Sayers like that in an open field," he said.

Quist bent down and picked up the gun. It was fully loaded, lethal.

"I may say I'm rather glad to see you, Dan," he said. "But how—"

"Instructions. Leave the money in a phone booth outside the bank. Sounded amateurish. One of the network girls picked up the money and left it in the booth. I watched. You can imagine my surprise when I saw this little jerk come and get it."

Garvey stood up and brushed off the front of his dark suit. The boy lay still.

"I had him figured ten seconds too late," Quist said.

"The other boy?"

"He's with Lydia."

"Well, I figured this kid might take me to where he had Tommy," Garvey said. "So I followed him. I was just trying to figure out how to get into this apartment when he backed out and I heard him talking to you. I saw the gun, so I hit him low and hard."

"He was risking his neck for his father," Quist said. "A kind of twisted loyalty. I think both the Jasons need help, Dan."

"Don't we all, at one time or another?" Garvey said. "But what the hell do we do with him now?"

"We have a choice," Quist said. "Throw him to the wolves or help him get his head together." He looked down at the unconscious boy. "I think I'll go for the second choice. Dan, let's help this kid."

Ellery Queen

The Adventure of the Three R's

Ellery Queen's CALENDAR OF CRIME, *published in 1952, is a series of twelve stories, each story dealing with an important aspect of a different month of the year. For example, January offers a New Year's mystery, February a tale of George Washington's Birthday, and so on through December, which is a Christmas detective story. Here is the return-to-school month, the September story, about Mr. Chipp, a member of the faculty of Barlowe College, Barlowe, Missouri, and the strange events that preceded his summer vacation . . .*

Detective: ELLERY QUEEN

Hail Missouri! which is North and also South, upland and riverbottom, mountain, plain, factory, and farm. Hail Missouri! for MacArthur's corncob and Pershing's noble mule. Hail! for Hannibal and Mark Twain, for Excelsior Springs and James, for Barlowe and . . . Barlowe? Barlowe is the site of Barlowe College.

Barlowe College is the last place in Missouri you would go to (Missouri, which yields to no State in the historic redness of its soil) if you yearned for a lesson in the fine art of murder. In fact, the subject being introduced, it is the rare Show Me Stater who will not say, with an informative wink, that Barlowe is the last place in Missouri, and leave all the rest unsaid. But this is a smokeroom witticism, whose origin is as murky as the waters of the Big Muddy. It may well first have been uttered by the alumnus of some Missouri university whose attitude toward learning is steeped in the traditional embalming fluid—whereas, at little Barlowe, learning leaps: Jove and jive thunder in duet, profound sociological lessons are drawn from *Li'l Abner* and *Terry and the Pirates*, and in the seminars of the Philosophy Department you are almost certain to find Faith, as a matter of pedagogic policy, paired with Hope.

Scratch a great work and find a great workman.

Dr. Isaiah St. Joseph A. Barlowe, pressed for vital statistics, once remarked that while he was old enough to have been a Founder, still he was not so old as to have calcified over a mound of English ivy. But the good dean jested; he is as perennial as a sundial. And the truth is, in the garden where he labors, there is no death and a great deal of healthy laughter.

One might string his academic honors after him, like dutiful beads; one might recount the extraordinary tale of how, in the manner of Uther Pendragon, Dr. Barlowe bewitched some dumfounded Missourians and took a whole series of substantial buildings out of their pockets; one might produce a volume on the subject of his acolytes alone, who have sped his humanistic gospel into the far corners of the land. Alas, this far more rewarding reportage must await the service of one who has, at the very least, a thousand pages at his disposal. Here there is space merely to record that the liveliness of Barlowe's alarming approach to scholarship is totally the inspiration of Dr. Isaiah St. Joseph A. Barlowe.

Those who would instruct at Barlowe must pass a rather unusual entrance examination. The examination is conducted *in camera*, and its nature is as sacredly undisclosable as the Thirty-Third Rite; nevertheless, leaks have occurred, and it may be significant that in its course Dr. Barlowe employs a 16-millimeter motion-picture projector, a radio, a portable phonograph, one copy each of The Bible, *The Old Farmer's Almanac*, and *The Complete Sherlock Holmes*; and the latest issue of *The Congressional Record*—among others. During examinations the voices of Donald Duck and Young Widder Brown have been reported; and so on. It is all very puzzling, but perhaps not unconnected with the fact that visitors often cannot distinguish who are Barlowe students and who are Barlowe professors. Certainly a beard at Barlowe is no index of dignity; even the elderly among the faculty exude a zest more commonly associated with the fuzzy-chinned undergraduate.

So laughter and not harumphery is rampant upon the Gold and the Puce; and, if corpses dance macabre, it is only upon the dissection tables of Bio III, where the attitude toward extinction is roguishly empirical.

Then imagine—if you can—the impact upon Barlowe, not of epic murder as sung by the master troubadours of Classics I; not of romantic murder (Abbot, Anthony to Zangwill, Israel) beckoning from the rental shelves of The Campus Book Shop; but of murder loud and harsh.

Murder, as young Professor Bacon of the Biochemistry Department might say, with a stink.

The letter from Dr. Barlowe struck Ellery as remarkably woeful.

"One of my faculty has disappeared," wrote the President of Barlowe College, "and I cannot express to you, Mr. Queen, the extent of my apprehension. In short, I fear the worst.

"I am aware of your busy itinerary, but if you are at all informed regarding the institution to which I have devoted my life, you will grasp the full horror of our dilemma. We feel we have erected something here too precious to be befouled by the nastiness of the age; on the other hand, there are humane—not to mention legal— considerations. If, as I suspect, Professor Chipp has met with foul play, it occurred to me that we might investigate *sub rosa* and at least present the not altogether friendly world with *un mystère accompli*. In this way, much anguish may be spared us all.

"Can I prevail upon you to come to Barlowe quietly, and at once? I feel confident I speak for our Trustees when I say we shall have no difficulty about the coarser aspects of the association."

The letter was handwritten, in a hasty and nervous script which seemed to suggest guilty glances over the presidential shoulder.

It was all so at variance with what Ellery had heard about Dr. Isaiah St. Joseph A. Barlowe and his learned vaudeville show that he scribbled a note to Inspector Queen and ran. Nikki, clutching her invaluable notebook, ran with him.

Barlowe, Missouri lay torpid in the warm September sunshine. And the distant Ozarks seemed to be peering at Barlowe inquisitively.

"Do you suppose it's got out, Ellery?" asked Nikki *sotto voce* as a sluggish hack trundled them through the slumbering town. "It's all so still. Not like a college town at all."

"The fall term doesn't begin for another ten days," Ellery remarked.

They were whisked into Dr. Barlowe's sanctum.

"You'll forgive my not meeting you at the station," muttered the dean as he quickly shut the door. He was a lean and gray-thatched man with an Italianate face and lively black eyes whose present preoccupation did not altogether extinguish the lurking twinkle. Missouri's Petrarch, thought Ellery with a chuckle. As for Nikki, it was love at first sight. "Softly, softly—that must be our watchword."

"Just who is Professor Chipp, Dr. Barlowe?"

"American Lit. You haven't heard of Chipp's seminar on Poe? He's an authority—it's one of our more popular items."

"Poe," exclaimed Nikki. "Ellery, that should give you a personal interest in the case."

"Leverett Chisholm Chipp," nodded Ellery, remembering. "Monographs in *The Review* on the Poe prose. Enthusiasm and scholarship. That Chipp."

"He's been a Barlowe appendage for thirty years," said the dean. "We really couldn't go on without him."

"When was Professor Chipp last seen?"

Dr. Barlowe snatched his telephone. "Millie, send Ma Blinker in now. Ma runs the boarding house on the campus where old Chipp's had rooms ever since he came to Barlowe to teach, Mr. Queen. Ah, Ma! Come in. And shut the door."

Ma Blinker was a brawny old Missourian who looked as if she had been summoned to the council chamber from her Friday's batch of apple pies. But it was a landlady's eye she turned on the visitors from New York—an eye which did not surrender until Dr. Barlowe uttered a cryptic reassurance, whereupon it softened and became moist.

"He's an old love, the Professor is," she said brokenly. "Regular? Ye could set your watch by that man."

"I take it," murmured Ellery, "Chipp's regularity is relevant?"

Dr. Barlowe nodded. "Now, Ma, you're carrying on. And you with the blood of pioneers! Tell Mr. Queen all about it."

"The Professor," gulped Ma Blinker, "he owns a log cabin up in the Ozarks, 'cross the Arkansas line. Every year he leaves Barlowe first of July to spend his summer vacation in the cabin. First of July, like clockwork."

"Alone, Mrs. Blinker?"

"Yes, sir. Does all his writin' up there, he does."

"Literary textbooks," explained the dean. "Although summer before last, to my astonishment, Chipp informed me he was beginning a novel."

"First of July he leaves for the cabin, and one day after Labor Day he's back in Barlowe gettin' ready for the fall term."

"One day after Labor Day, Mr. Queen. Year in, year out. Unfailingly."

"And here 'tis the thirteenth of September and he ain't showed up in town!"

"Day after Labor Day. Ten days overdue."

"All this fuss," asked Nikki, "over a measly ten days?"

"Miss Porter, Chipp's being ten days late is as unlikely as—as my being Mrs. Hudson in disguise! Unlikelier. I was so concerned, Mr. Queen, I telephoned the Slater, Arkansas, authorities to send someone up to Chipp's cabin."

"Then he didn't simply linger there past his usual date?"

"I can't impress upon you too strongly the inflexibility of Chipp's habit-pattern. He did not. The Slater man found no sign of Chipp but his trunk."

"But I gathered from your letter, Doctor, that you had a more specific reason for suspecting—"

"And don't we!" Ma Blinker broke out frankly now in bosomy sobs. "I'd never have gone into the Professor's rooms—it was another of his rules—but Dr. Barlowe said I ought to when the Professor didn't show up, so I did, and—and—"

"Yes, Mrs. Blinker?"

"There on the rug, in front of his fireplace," whispered the landlady, "was a great . . . big . . . stain."

"A stain!" gasped Nikki. "A *stain?*"

"A bloodstain."

Ellery raised his brows.

"I examined it myself, Mr. Queen," said Dr. Barlowe nervously. "It's—it's blood, I feel certain. And it's been on the rug for some time. We locked Chipp's rooms up again, and I wrote to you."

And although the September sun filled each cranny of the dean's office, it was a cold sun suddenly.

"Have you heard from Professor Chipp at all since July the first, Doctor?" asked Ellery with a frown.

Dr. Barlowe looked startled. "It's been his habit to send a few of us cards at least once during the summer recess . . ." He began to rummage excitedly through a pile of mail on his desk. "I've been away since early June myself. This has so upset me I . . . Why didn't I think of that? Ah, the trained mind . . . Mr. Queen, here it is!"

It was a picture postcard illustrating a mountain cascade of improbable blue surrounded by verdure of impossible green. The message and address were in a cramped and spidery script.

July 31.

Am rewriting my novel. It will be a huge surprise to you all.

Regards—

Chipp

"His 'novel' again," muttered Ellery. "Bears the postmark Slater, Arkansas, July thirty-first of this year. Dr. Barlowe, was this card written by Professor Chipp?"

"Unmistakably."

"Doesn't the writing seem awfully awkward to you, Ellery?" asked Nikki, in the tradition of the detectival secretary.

"Yes. As if something were wrong with his hand."

"There is," sniffled Ma Blinker. "Middle and forefinger missin' to the second joint—poor, poor old man!"

"Some accident in his youth, I believe."

Ellery rose. "May I see that stain on Chipp's rug, please?"

A man may leave more than his blood on his hearth; he may leave his soul.

The blood was there, faded brown and hard, but so was Professor Chipp, though *in absentia.*

The two small rooms overlooking the campus were as tidy as a barrack. Chairs were rigidly placed. The bed was a sculpture. The mantelpiece was a shopwindow display; each pipe in the rack had been reamed and polished and laid away with a mathematical hand. The papers in the pigeon holes of the old pine desk were ranged according to size. Even the missing professor's books were disciplined: no volume on these shelves leaned carelessly, or lolled dreaming on its back. They stood in battalions, company after company, at attention. And they were ranked by author, and arranged in alphabetical order.

"Terrifying," he said; and he turned to examine a small ledger-like volume lying in the exact center of the desk's dropleaf.

"I suppose this invasion is unavoidable," muttered the dean, "but I must say I feel as if I were the tailor of Coventry! What's in that ledger, Mr. Queen?"

"Chipp's personal accounts. His daily outlays of cash . . . Ah. This year's entries stop at the thirtieth day of June."

"The day before he left for his cabin."

"He's even noted down what one postage stamp cost him—"

"That's the old Professor," sobbed Ma Blinker. Then she raised her fat arms and shrieked, "Heavens to Bessie, Dr. Barlowe! It's Professor Bacon back!"

"Hi, Ma!"

Professor Bacon's return was in the manner of a charge from third base. Having flung himself at the dean as at home plate and pumped the dean's hand violently, with large stained fingers, the young man immediately cried, "Just got back to the shop and found your note, Doctor. What's this nonsense about old Chipp's not showing up for the fall brawl?"

"It's only too true, Bacon," said Dr. Barlowe sadly, and he introduced the young man as a full professor of chemistry and biology, another of Ma Blinker's boarders, and Chipp's closest faculty friend.

"You agree with Dr. Barlowe as to the gravity of the situation?" Ellery asked him.

"Mr. Queen, if the old idiot's not back, something's happened to him." And for a precarious moment Professor Bacon fought tears. "If I'd only known," he mumbled. "But I've been away since the middle of June—biochemical research at Johns Hopkins. Damn it!" he roared. "This is more staggering than nuclear fission!"

"Have you heard from Chipp this summer, Professor?"

"His usual postcard. I may still have it on me . . . Yes!"

"Just a greeting," said Ellery, examining it. "Dated July thirty-first and postmarked Slater, Arkansas—exactly like the card he sent Dr. Barlowe. May I keep this, Bacon?"

"By all means. Chipp not back . . ." And then the young man spied the brown crust on the hearthrug. He collapsed on the missing man's bed, gaping at it.

"Ellery!"

Nikki was standing on tiptoe before Chipp's bookshelves. Under *Q* stood a familiar phalanx.

"A complete set of *your* books!"

"Really?" But Ellery did not seem as pleased as an author making such a flattering discovery should. Rather, he eyed one of the volumes as if it were a traitor. And indeed there was a sinister air about it, for it was the only book on all the shelves—he now noted for the first time—which did not exercise the general discipline. It stood on the shelf upside-down.

"Queer . . ." He took it down and righted it. In doing so, he opened the back cover; and his lips tightened.

"Oh, yes," said the dean gloomily. "Old Chipp's quite unreasonable about your books, Mr. Queen."

"Only detective stories he'd buy," muttered Professor Bacon. "Rented the others."

"A mystery bug, eh?" murmured Ellery. "Well, here's one Queen title he didn't buy." He tapped the book in his hand.

"*The Murderer Was a Fox*," read Nikki, craning. "Rental library!"

"The Campus Book Shop. And it gives us our first confirmation of that bloodstain."

"What do you mean," asked Bacon quickly, jumping off the bed.

"The last library stamp indicates that Professor Chipp rented this book from The Campus Book Shop on June twenty-eighth. A man as orderly as these rooms indicate, who moreover scrupulously records his purchase of a postage stamp, would scarcely trot off on a summer vacation and leave a book behind to accumulate eleven weeks' rental-library charges."

"Chipp? Impossible!"

"Contrary to his whole character."

"Since the last entry in that ledger bears the date June thirtieth, and since the bloodstain is on this hearthrug," said Ellery gravely, "I'm afraid, gentlemen, that your colleague was murdered in this room on the eve of his scheduled departure for the Ozarks. He never left this room alive."

No one said anything for a long time.

But finally Ellery patted Ma Blinker's frozen shoulder and said, "Did you actually see Professor Chipp leave your boardinghouse on July first, Mrs. Blinker?"

"No, sir," said the landlady. "The expressman came for his trunk that mornin', but the Professor wasn't here. I . . . thought he'd already left."

"Tell me this, Mrs. Blinker: did Chipp have a visitor on the preceding night—the night of June thirtieth?"

A slow change came over the woman's blotchy features.

"He surely did," she said. "He surely did. That Weems."

"Weems?" Dr. Barlowe said quickly. "Oh, no! I mean . . ."

"Weems," said Nikki. "Ellery, didn't you notice that name on The Campus Book Shop as we drove by?"

Ellery said nothing.

Young Bacon muttered: "Revolting idea. But then . . . Weems and old Chipp were always at each other's throats."

"Weems is the only other one I've discussed Chipp's nonappearance with," said the dean. "He seemed so concerned!"

"A common interest in Poe," said Professor Bacon fiercely.

"Indeed," smiled Ellery. "We begin to see a certain unity of plot elements, don't we? If you'll excuse us for a little while, gentlemen, Miss Porter and I will have a chat with Mr. Weems."

But Mr. Weems turned out to be a bustly, bald little Missouri countryman, with shrewdly humored eyes and the prevailing jocular manner, the most unmurderous-looking character imaginable. And he presided over a shop so satisfyingly full of books, so aromatic with the odors of printery and bindery, and he did so with such a naked bibliophilic tenderness, that Nikki—for one—instantly dismissed him as a suspect.

Yep, Mr. Queen'd been given to understand correctly that he, Claude Weems, had visited old Chipp's rooms at Ma Blinker's on the night of June thirty last; and, yep, he'd left the old chucklehead in the best of health; and, no, he hadn't laid eyes on him since that evenin'.

He'd shut up shop for the summer and left Barlowe on July fifteenth for his annual walking tour cross-country; didn't get back till a couple of days ago to open up for fall.

"Doc Barlowe's fussin' too much about old Chipp's not turnin' up," said little Mr. Weems, beaming. "Now I grant you he's never done it before, and all that, but he's gettin' old, Chipp is. Never can tell what a man'll do when he passes a certain age."

Nikki looked relieved, but Ellery did not.

"May I ask what you dropped in to see Chipp about on the evening of June thirtieth, Mr. Weems?"

"To say goodbye. And then I'd heard tell the old varmint'd just made a great book find—"

"Book find! Chipp had 'found' a book?"

Mr. Weems looked around and lowered his voice. "I heard he'd picked up a first edition of Poe's *Tamerlane* for a few dollars from some fool who didn't know its worth. You a collector, Mr. Queen?"

"A *Tamerlane* first!" exclaimed Ellery.

"Is that good, Ellery?" asked Nikki with the candor of ignorance.

"Good! A *Tamerlane* first, Nikki, is worth a fortune!"

Weems chuckled. "Know the market, I see. Yes, sir, bein' the biggest booster old Edgar Allan ever had west of the Missip', I wanted to see that copy bad, awful bad. Chipp showed it to me, crowin' like a cock in a roostful. Lucky dog," he said without audible rancor. " 'Twas the real article, all right."

Nikki could see Ellery tucking this fact into one of the innumerable cubbyholes of his mind—the one marked *For Future Consideration.* So she was not surprised when he changed the subject abruptly.

"Did Professor Chipp ever mention to you, Weems, that he was engaged in writing a novel?"

"Sure did. I told ye he was gettin' old."

"I suppose he also told you the *kind* of novel it was?"

"Dunno as he did."

"Seems likely, seems likely," mumbled Ellery, staring at the rental-library section where murder frolicked.

"*What* seems likely, Ellery?" demanded Nikki.

"Considering that Chipp was a mystery fan, and the fact that he wrote Dr. Barlowe his novel would be a 'huge surprise,' it's my conclusion, Nikki, the old fellow was writing a whodunit."

"Say," exclaimed Mr. Weems. "I think you're right."

"Oh?"

"Prof Chipp asked me—in April, it was—to find out if a certain title's ever been used on a detective story!"

"Ah. And what was the title he mentioned, Weems?"

"*The Mystery of the Three R's.*"

"Three R's . . . Three R's?" cried Ellery. "But that's incredible! Nikki—back to the Administration Building!"

"Suppose he was," said Professor Bacon. "Readin', 'Rithmetic! Abracadabra and Rubadubdub. What of it?"

"Perhaps nothing, Bacon," scowled Ellery, hugging his pipe. "And yet . . . see here. We found a clue pointing to the strong probability that Chipp never left his rooms at Ma Blinker's alive last June thirtieth. What was that clue? The fact that Chipp failed to return his rented copy of my novel to Weems' lending library. Novel . . . book . . . *reading*, gentlemen. The first of the traditional Three R's."

"Rot!" bellowed the professor, and he began to bite his fingernails.

"I don't blame you," shrugged Ellery. "But has it occurred to you that there is also a *writing clue?*"

At this Nikki went over to the enemy.

"Ellery, are you sure the sun . . .?"

"Those postcards Chipp wrote, Nikki."

Three glances crossed stealthily.

"But I fail to see the connection, Mr. Queen," said Dr. Barlowe soothingly. "How are those ordinary postcards a clue?"

"And besides," snorted Bacon, "how could Chipp have been bumped off on June thirtieth and have mailed the cards a full month later, on July thirty-first?"

"If you'll examine the date Chipp wrote on the cards," said Ellery evenly, "you'll find that the *3* of *July 31* is crowded between the *y* of *July* and the *1* of *31*. If that isn't a clue, I never saw one."

And Ellery, who was as thin-skinned as the next artist, went on rather tartly to reconstruct the events of the fateful evening of June the thirtieth.

"Chipp wrote those cards in his rooms that night, dating them a day ahead—July first—probably intending to mail them from Slater, Arkansas, the next day on his way to the log cabin—"

"It's true Chipp loathed correspondence," muttered the dean.

"Got his duty cards out of the way before his vacation even began—the old sinner!" mumbled young Bacon.

"Someone then murdered him in his rooms, appropriated the cards, stuffed the body into Chipp's trunk—"

"Which was picked up by the expressman next morning and shipped to the cabin?" cried Nikki.

And again the little chill wind cut through the dean's office.

"But the postmarks, Mr. Queen," said the dean stiffly. "The postmarks also say July *thirty*-first."

"The murderer merely waited a month before mailing them at the Slater, Arkansas, post office."

"But *why?*" growled Bacon. "You weave beautiful rugs, man—but what do they mean?"

"Obviously it was all done, Professor Bacon," said Ellery, "to leave the impression that on July thirty-first Professor Chipp was *still alive* . . . to keep the world from learning that he was really murdered on the night of June thirtieth. And that, of course, is significant." He sprang to his feet. "We must examine the Professor's cabin—most particularly, his trunk."

It was a little trunk—but then, as Dr. Barlowe pointed out in a very queer voice, Professor Chipp had been a little man.

Outdoors, the Ozarks were shutting up shop for the summer, stripping the fainter-hearted trees and busily daubing hillsides; but in the cabin there was no beauty—only dust, and an odor of dampness—and something else.

The little steamer trunk stood just inside the cabin doorway.

They stared at it.

"Well, well," said Bacon finally. "Miss Porter's outside—what are we waiting for?"

And so they knocked off the rusted lock and raised the lid—and found the trunk quite empty.

Perhaps not quite empty; the interior held a pale, dead-looking mass of crumbly stuff.

Ellery glanced up at Professor Bacon.

"Quicklime," muttered the chemistry teacher.

"Quicklime!" choked the dean. "But the body. Where's the body?"

Nikki's scream, augmented a dozen times by the encircling hills, answered Dr. Barlowe's question most unpleasantly.

She had been wandering about the clearing, dreading to catch the first cry of discovery from the cabin, when she came upon a little cairn of stones. And she had sat down on it.

But the loose rocks gave way, and Miss Porter found herself sitting on Professor Chipp—or, rather, on what was left of Professor Chipp. For Professor Chipp had gone the way of all flesh—which is to say, he was merely bones, and very dry bones, at that.

But that it was the skeleton of Leverett Chisholm Chipp could not be questioned: the medius and index finger of the right skeletal hand were missing to the second joint. And that Leverett Chisholm Chipp had been most foully used was also evident: the top of the skull revealed a deep and ragged chasm, the result of what could only have been a tremendous blow.

Whereupon the old pedagogue and the young took flight, joining Miss Porter, who was quietly being ill on the other side of the cabin; and Mr. Queen found himself alone with Professor Chipp.

Later Ellery went over the log cabin with a disagreeable sense of anticipation. There was no sensible reason for believing that the cabin held further secrets; but sense is not all, and the already chilling air held a whiff of fatality.

He found it in a cupboard, in a green steel box, beside a rusty can of moldering tobacco.

It was a stapled pile of neat papers, curled by damp, but otherwise intact.

The top sheet, in a cramped, spidery hand, read:

The Mystery of the Three R's

by

L. C. Chipp

The discovery of Professor Chipp's detective story may be said to mark the climax of the case. That the old man had been battered to death in his rooms on the night of June thirtieth; that his corpse had been shipped from Barlowe, Missouri, to the Arkansas cabin in his own trunk, packed in quicklime to avert detection en route; that the murderer had then at his leisure made his way to the cabin, removed the body from the trunk, and buried it under a heap of stones—these were mere facts, dry as the professor's bones. They did not possess the aroma of the grotesque—the *bouffe*—which rose like a delicious mist from the pages of that incredible manuscript.

Not that Professor Chipp's venture into detective fiction revealed a new master, to tower above the busy little figures of his fellow toilers in this curious vineyard and vie for cloud space only with Poe and Doyle and Chesterton. To the contrary. *The Mystery of the Three R's*, by L. C. Chipp, was a labored exercise in familiar elements, distinguished chiefly for its enthusiasm.

No, it was not the murdered professor's manuscript which was remarkable; the remarkable thing was the manner in which life had imitated it.

It was a shaken group that gathered in Chipp's rooms the morning after the return from the Arkansas cabin. Ellery had called the meeting, and he had invited Mr. Weems of The Campus Book Shop to participate—who, on hearing the ghastly news, stopped beaming, clamped his Missouri jaws shut, and began to gaze furtively at the door.

Ellery's own jaws were unshaven, and his eyes were red.

"I've passed the better part of the night," he began abruptly, "reading through Chipp's manuscript. And I must report an amazing—an almost unbelievable—thing.

"The crime in Chipp's detective story takes place in and about a small Missouri college called . . . Barleigh College."

"Barleigh," muttered the dean of Barlowe.

"Moreover, the victim in Chipp's yarn is a methodical old professor of American Literature."

Nikki looked puzzled. "You mean that Professor Chipp—?"

"Took off on himself, Nikki—exactly."

"What's so incredible about that?" demanded young Bacon. "Art imitating life—"

"Considering the fact that Chipp plotted his story long before the events of this summer, Professor Bacon, it's rather a case of life imitating art. Suppose I tell you that the methodical old professor of American Literature in Chipp's story owns a cabin in the Ozarks where his body is found?"

"Even *that?*" squeaked Mr. Weems.

"And more, Weems. The suspects in the story are the President of Barleigh College, whose name is given as Dr. Isaac St. Anthony E. Barleigh; a local bookshop owner named Claudius Deems; a young professor of chemistry known as Macon; and, most extraordinary of all, the three main clues in Chipp's detective story revolve about—are called—Readin', 'Ritin', and 'Rithmetic!"

And the icy little wind blew once more.

"You mean," exclaimed Dr. Barlowe, "the crime we're investigating—Chipp's own death—is *an exact counterpart of the fictional crime Chipp invented in his manuscript?*"

"Down to the last character, Doctor."

"But Ellery," said Nikki, "how can that possibly be?"

"Obviously, Chipp's killer managed to get hold of the old fellow's manuscript, read it, and with hellish humor proceeded to copy in real life—actually to duplicate—the crime Chipp had created in fiction." Ellery began to lunge about the little room, his usually neat hair disordered and a rather wild look on his face. "Everything's the same: the book that wasn't returned to the lending library—the readin' clue; the picture postcards bearing forged dates—the 'ritin' clue—"

"And the 'rithmetic clue, Mr. Queen?" asked the dean in a quavering voice.

"In the story, Doctor, the victim has found a first edition of Poe's *Tamerlane*, worth many thousands of dollars."

Little Weems cried, "That's 'rithmetic, all right!" and then bit his lip.

"And how," asked Professor Bacon thickly, "how is the book integrated into Chipp's yarn, Mr. Queen?"

"It furnishes the motive for the crime. The killer steals the victim's authentic *Tamerlane*, substituting for it a facsimile copy which is worth only a few dollars."

"But if everything else is duplicated—" began Dr. Barlowe in a mutter.

"Then that must be the motive for Professor Chipp's own murder!" cried Nikki.

"It would seem so, wouldn't it?" Ellery glanced sharply at the proprietor of The Campus Book Shop. "Weems, where is the first edition of *Tamerlane* you told me Chipp showed you on the night of June thirtieth?"

"Why—why—why, reckon it's on his shelves here somewheres, Mr. Queen. Under *P*, for Poe."

And there it was. Under *P*, for Poe.

And when Ellery took it down and turned its pages, he smiled. For the first time since they had found the skeleton under the cairn, he smiled.

"Well, Weems," he said affably, "you're a Poe expert. Is this an authentic *Tamerlane* first?"

"Why—why—why, must be. 'Twas when old Chipp showed it to me that night—"

"Really? Suppose you re-examine it—now."

But they all knew the answer before Weems spoke.

"It ain't," he said feebly. "It's a facsim'le copy."

"The *Tamerlane*—stolen," whispered Dr. Barlowe.

"So once again," murmured Ellery, "we find duplication. I think that's all. Or should I say, it's too much?"

And he lit his pipe and seated himself in one of Professor Chipp's chairs, puffing contentedly.

"All!" exclaimed Dr. Barlowe. "I confess, Mr. Queen, you've—you've baffled me no end in this investigation. All? It's barely begun! *Who* has done all this?"

"Wait," said Bacon slowly. "It may be, Doctor, we don't need Queen's eminent services at that. If the rest has followed Chipp's plot so faithfully, why not the most important plot element of all?"

"That's true, Ellery," said Nikki with shining eyes. "*Who is the murderer in Professor Chipp's detective story?*"

Ellery glanced at the cowering little figure of Claude Weems.

"The character," he replied cheerfully, "whom Chipp had named Claudius Deems."

The muscular young professor snarled, and he sprang.

"In your enthusiasm, Bacon," murmured Ellery, without stirring from his chair, "don't throttle him. After all, he's such a little fellow, and you're so large."

"Kill old Chipp, would you!" growled Professor Bacon; but his grip relaxed a little.

"Mr. Weems," said Nikki, looking displeased. "Of course! The murderer forged the dates on the postcards so we wouldn't know the crime had been committed on June thirtieth. And who'd have reason to falsify the true date of the crime? The one man who'd visited Professor Chipp that night!"

"The damned beast could easily have got quicklime," said Bacon, shaking Weems like a rabbit, "by stealing it from the Chemistry Department after everyone'd left the college for the summer."

"Yes!" said Nikki. "Remember Weems himself told us he didn't leave Barlowe until July fifteenth?"

"I do, indeed. And Weems's motive, Nikki?"

"Why, to steal Chipp's *Tamerlane*."

"I'm afraid that's so," groaned the dean. "Weems as a bookseller could easily have got hold of a cheap facsimile to substitute for the authentic first edition."

"And he said he'd gone on a walking tour, didn't he?" Nikki added, warming to her own logic. "Well, I'll bet he 'walked' into that Arkansas post office, Ellery, on July thirty-first, to mail those postcards!"

Weems found his voice.

"Why, now, listen here, little lady, I didn't kill old Chipp—" he began in the most unconvincing tones imaginable.

They all eyed him with scorn—all, that is, but Ellery.

"Very true, Weems," said Ellery, nodding. "You most certainly did not."

"He didn't—" began Dr. Barlowe, blinking.

"I .. didn't?" gasped Weems, which seemed to Nikki a remarkable thing for him to have said.

"No, although I'm afraid I've been led very cleverly to *believe* that you did, Weems."

"See here, Mr. Queen," said the dean of Barlowe in a terrible voice. "Precisely what *do* you mean?"

"And how do you know he didn't?" shouted Bacon. "I told you, Doctor—this fellow's grossly overrated. The next thing you'll tell us is that Chipp hasn't been murdered at all!"

"Exactly," said Ellery. "Therefore Weems couldn't have murdered him."

"Ellery—" moaned Nikki.

"Your syllogism seems a bit perverted, Mr. Queen," said Dr. Barlowe severely.

"Yes!" snarled Bacon. "What about the evidence—?"

"Very well," said Ellery briskly, "let's consider the evidence. Let's consider the evidence of the skeleton we found near Chipp's cabin."

"Those dry bones? What about 'em?"

"Just that, Professor—they're so very dry. Bacon, you're a biologist as well as a chemist. Under normal conditions, how long does it take for the soft parts of a body to decompose completely?"

"How long . . .?" The young man moistened his lips. "Muscles, stomach, liver—from three to four years. But—"

"And for decomposition of the fibrous tissues, the ligaments?"

"Oh, five years or so more. But—"

"And yet," sighed Ellery, "that desiccated skeleton was supposed to be the remains of a man who'd been alive *a mere eleven weeks before.* And not only that—I now appeal to your chemical knowledge, Professor. Just what is the effect of quicklime on human flesh and bones?"

"Why, it's pulverulent. Would dry out a body—"

"Would quicklime destroy the tissues?"

"Er, no."

"It would tend to preserve them?"

"Er, yes."

"Therefore the skeleton we found couldn't possibly have been the mortal remains of Professor Chipp."

"But the right hand, Ellery," cried Nikki. "The missing fingers—just like Professor Chipp's—"

"I shouldn't think," said Ellery dryly, "snapping a couple of dry bones off a man dead eight or ten years would present much of a problem."

"Eight or ten years—"

"Surely, Nikki, it suggests the tenant of some outraged grave . . . or, considering the facts at our disposal, the far likelier theory that it came from a laboratory closet in the Biology Department of Barlowe College." And Professor Bacon cringed before Ellery's accusing glance, which softened suddenly in laughter. "Now, really, gentlemen. Hasn't this hoax gone far enough?"

"Hoax, Mr. Queen?" choked the dean of Barlowe with feeble indignation.

"Come, come, Doctor," chuckled Ellery, "the game's up. Let me review the fantastic facts. What is this case? A detective story come to life. Bizarre—fascinating—to be sure. But really, Doctor, so utterly unconvincing!

"How conveniently all the clues in Chipp's manuscript found reflections in reality! The lending-library book, so long overdue—in the story, in the crime. The postcards written in advance—in the story, in the crime. The *Tamerlane* facsimile right here on Chipp's shelf—exactly as the manuscript has it. It would seem as if Chipp collaborated in his own murder."

"Collab—I can't make hide nor hair of this, Mr. Queen," said little Mr. Weems.

"Now, now, Weems, as the bookseller-Poe-crony you were the key figure in the plot! Although I must confess, Dr. Barlowe, *you* played your role magnificently, too—and, Professor Bacon, you missed a career in the theater; you really did. The only innocent, I daresay, is Ma Blinker—and to you, gentlemen, I gladly leave the trial of facing that doughty lady when she finds out how her honest grief has been exploited in the interest of commerce."

"Commerce?" whimpered Nikki, who by now was holding her pretty head to keep it from flying off.

"Of course, Nikki. I was invited to Barlowe to follow an elaborate trail of carefully placed 'clues' in order to reach the conclusion that Claude Weems had 'murdered' Professor Chipp. When I announced Weems's 'guilt,' the hoax was supposed to blow up in my face. *Old Chipp would pop out of his hiding place grinning from ear to ear.*"

"Pop out . . . You mean," gasped Nikki, "you mean Professor Chipp is *alive?*"

"Only conclusion that makes sense, Nikki. And then," Ellery went on, glaring at the three men, "imagine the headlines. 'Famous Sleuth Tricked by Hoax—Pins Whodunit on Harmless Prof.' Commerce? I'll say! Chipp's *Mystery of the Three R's*, launched by such splendid publicity, would be swallowed by a publisher as the whale swallowed Jonah—and there we'd have—presumably—a sensational best-seller.

"The whole thing, Nikki, was a conspiracy hatched by the dean of Barlowe College, his two favorite professors, and their good friend the campus bookseller—a conspiracy to put old Chipp's first detective story over with a bang!"

And now the little wind blew warm, bringing the blood of embarrassment to six male cheeks.

"Mr. Queen—" began the dean hoarsely.

"Mr. Queen—" began the bio-chemistry professor hoarsely.

"Mr. Queen—" began the bookseller hoarsely.

"Come, come, gentlemen!" cried Ellery. "All is not lost! We'll go through with the plot! I make only one condition. Where the devil is Chipp? I want to shake the old scoundrel's hand."

Barlowe is an unusual college.

MacLean O'Spelin

The Tiger of the Mekong

Tai Shan had the requisite training for his present position of authority. In the past he had been a gambler, smuggler, mercenary, and river pirate. Now he was a mandarin, wealthy in land and lucre, but even wealthier in wives and concubines—for Tai Shan collected women from nearly every country in Southeast Asia . . .

The author tells us that this story is "set in the Far East and based on places, including the divan de fumée, *and people" he has known. And surely he has "caught the unique atmosphere of Laos" and its conflicting forces—the Royalist Lao Police and the Pathet Lao Police—and of the plots and spies and counterplots against "the man from Hanoi" . . .*

The fifth wife of Tai Shan, the one he had long ago brought to Laos from far in the south, bowed her head timorously. "I pray you, respected husband, tonight pass the *divan de fumée* by."

With affection that he kept carefully hidden, Tai Shan looked down at the shining black hair arranged in the style of Fifth Wife's native Cochinchina. So feminine, this small woman whose face bore no line or wrinkle, whose slim body still wore the cai ao and cai quan with grace and allure.

Conscious grace and allure, of course. Just as the timorous curve of head and neck was deliberate. "Fifth Wife, my nights as well as my days are mine to order as I choose. It is impertinent of you to presume otherwise."

She raised her head, concern darkening her great eyes. "The pipe has brought ruin to many another mandarin, venerated Tai Shan."

Despite himself, he drew his tall body even taller to settle his long robe in more elegantly austere lines. But, also unconsciously, a lean forefinger touched the gray mustache where its scholarly droop concealed the ragged scar that ran from lower lip to jawline. "Such men were soft," he said, his tone final. "Summon Ah Fong."

She hesitated, then crossed the polished teak veranda of the vast

house, built Lao-style on heavy stilts, and, leaning over the rail,
called to a servant hovering below.

Tai Shan smiled with inward irony; though not born a mandarin,
he assuredly had become one. For, along with the wealth and the
property amassed in his 70 years, had come almost inexorably a
mandarin's share of wives and concubines, children and grandchil-
dren, servants and hangers-on.

To oversee such a complex clutter of interrelated humanity, a
mandarin, whether born or self-made, must have a grand vizier, a
high chamberlain—or a loyal, adroit chatelaine. And in the 20 years
Fifth Wife had been in his household, the small tough-fibered woman
had grown into that role.

An indispensable woman. But utterly wrong about the danger to
him of the pipe.

She returned. "Honored husband, during your midday repose,
Kham Xai was here. I refused to awaken you."

His eyes, strangely light in an otherwise Chinese face, glittered
like yellow citrine. "The domain of Tai Shan, here beside the mighty
Mekong, must be as gall to such a one as Colonel Kham Xai."

"Colonel Weasel Face came alone, came secretly to thrust his rat's
nose where it does not belong."

"A strange mixture, your countryman."

"No countryman of mine!" Her eyes blazed. "An animal from the
north!"

But Tai Shan was descending the stairway, at the foot of which
the burly Yunnanese, Ah Fong, stood holding the door of the gleaming Mercedes. "To the boun, Fong-ah."

At the boun he would see and perhaps deal with Kham Xai of the
Pathet Lao Police. Better, he would also see Mademoiselle Brown.

Being 70 might have slowed down his appetites but it had not
dulled his appreciation. For him, to be a *collectionneur des femmes*
was preferable to being a collector of jade or porcelain or classic
calligraphy with which, in other days, born mandarins amused
themselves. To be sure, his fine house, standing nobly amid his
twenty hectares of prime land, held man-made works of art. But it
also held women from nearly every country in Southeast Asia. Some
he'd married. Some he'd acquired by other means. All were human
works of art.

The Mercedes lurched as Ah Fong swerved sharply to avoid a
buffalo cart.

The heavy car slewed violently sideways on the muddy, rutted road. "Fong-ah, have care! Break these bones and your father's ghost and his father's will curse you through eternity."

Big hands skillfully straightening the car, Ah Fong spilled words over his shoulder. "Master, both died willingly in your service. And so would your humble Fong-ah, Master."

A courteous exaggeration. No man died willingly. But Ah Fong was a fine driver and Tai Shan eased back into the soft seat and began to think almost wistfully of the fierce days on the Mekong when Ah Fong's grandfather had been young and full of fight. And he, Tai Shan, had been full of ambitious visions of wealth wrested from an ungiving world.

Then, through his reverie, he heard the drums from the pagoda where tonight's boun was being celebrated. Vientiane was a city of pagodas and each had its boun, its festival, and all were enthusiastically attended. And now there were colored streamers and ringing bells and the clash of cymbals and, everywhere, cheerful smiling faces—except those of the Pathet Lao Police, glum in baggy trousers, sneakers, and Chinese AK-47 machine pistols, on joint patrol with smartly uniformed Royalist Police.

When Ah Fong stopped the gleaming car at the courtyard of the many-spired pagoda, two young bonzes in orange robes escorted Tai Shan to the wrinkled, shaven-headed Chief Bonze sitting cross-legged under a crimson ceremonial canopy.

Tai Shan bowed, exchanged a few words in Lao with the old priest, and dropped several taels of gold into the convenient alms bowl. Amid appreciative murmurs from the crowd he bowed again and turned away.

An ostentatious gift, admittedly. But ostentation was expected of him, the legendary Tai Shan of the Mekong.

Musicians began to stroke their lutes and to coax thin, strangely seductive notes from the silver reeds of their khens. Slowly couples of all ages formed lines and began to dance the languid lam-vong.

Tai Shan made his stately way to the sidelines where a chair was immediately produced by a deferential Royalist member of the Joint Council that, more or less, governed Laos. Kings and Communists, he thought wryly, there was an ironic combination. But, while neighboring countries suffered in anguish, the Council managed to preserve a peaceful, if uneasy, status quo.

Status quo. The two words summed up his own politics. Status quo—for the domain of Tai Shan.

The lines of couples dancing the lam-vong had grown longer and he picked out Mademoiselle Brown and settled back to watch. Trim and not too tall, she kept getting ahead of the music's slow rhythm, which amused him. Nervous energy was the antithesis of the drowsy lam-vong of Laos.

Indeed, he himself had needed years of retirement before he could slow down to anything approaching the Lao pace. And that despite blood in his veins from a mother who had been a Lao-French *métisse*. Of course, the vigorous blood from his Hakka father had countered the Lao tranquility—and who knew what spice the French blood had added?

Mademoiselle Brown saw him and catching the hand of her partner, a handsome young Lao in Royalist Police uniform, she quickly moved his way. "Greetings, honored Tai Shan," she said in American-accented French. "A lovely evening, is it not?"

As a mandarin, Tai Shan did not rise for women. But a smile warmed his austere face as he looked at her. "Not half so lovely as you."

It was untrue. She was not lovely. Or conventionally pretty. But she had youth and vitality and a controlled intensity that often kindled a blaze in her blue gaze. And she had a slim, neatly proportioned figure, not overblown like that of so many of her race. Otherwise, Tai Shan would not have looked at her twice.

"You know Lieutenant Vang of the Police, of course," she went on, and Vang, in the Lao way, bowed low and smiled but said nothing.

"*Bon soir,* Mademoiselle Brown . . . Tai Shan . . . Vang." It was Colonel Kham Xai and Tai Shan examined him, looking for traces of weasel and rat. There were none—Fifth Wife had exaggerated. But the skin tone was lighter and the bone structure more angular than in most Lao faces. And naturally so. As Tai Shan had long ago learned, the man was Hanoi born, a DRV commissar illegally in Pathet Lao uniform.

"Find chairs, Vang." The Colonel's French rang metallically.

Tai Shan kept his own tone mild. "My wife regrets her abruptness this afternoon, *mon colonel,* and hopes you will honor us with another visit soon."

"I shall. A feudal establishment is always a fine study in ancient history."

Tai Shan's eyes glinted like many-faceted topazes, but his voice was level. "We will hide nothing—for we have nothing to hide."

"Yes, I have heard the tale that your years as the fierce and hungry Tiger of the Mekong are behind you." Kham Xai smiled mockingly. "Now you are a man of peace, playing at being a mandarin." He leaned close to Tai Shan. "River pirates are sometimes useful. Mandarins never."

Lieutenant Vang's quiet voice broke in. "The Honorable Tai Shan is a Lao citizen. Your words, Colonel, are insulting."

Kham Xai eyed him with contempt. "Mandarins and kings and Royalist lieutenants are vestiges—vestiges doomed to wither and rot."

Mademoiselle Brown, seated now and leaning forward attentively, said, "Do you hope to hurry the rotting process, Colonel?"

Before the Colonel could respond, Vang cut in again. "Beware, Kham Xai. Your uniform deceives no one. Perhaps it will be you who will wither and rot."

"Well spoken," said Tai Shan, pleased with the vigor of the young Lao's words. Within the Kingdom of Laos was the mandarinate of Tai Shan. And, like pit vipers, commissars can be lethal to mandarins as well as to kings.

A flush burned in Kham Xai's bony face and his mouth worked, but no words came from his thin lips. Abruptly he swung away and strode off.

"Damn," said Mademoiselle Brown. "Just when things were livening up."

"Disappointing for you," said Tai Shan drily. She was, he knew, an intelligence operative who reported to some mysterious headquarters in the city of Washington. In fact, she had once tried energetically to recruit him to spy for her.

With amused courtesy he had declined. As a practical matter of survival he, himself, used spies. But, although he had been many things—gambler, smuggler, mercenary, river pirate and, now, mandarin—he had never been a spy. And even for a young woman whose spirit he admired, he would never be.

Disappointment flickered, but she had said, "In a way I'm glad. But you will go on advising me? I so want to succeed on this assignment."

He had agreed. He approved of this practical and attractive and tough-fibered woman. A few years ago he would have tried persuasion or purchase or abduction to add her to his personal collection. Now it seemed best to view and enjoy her on display, so to speak, in a gallery that was not his responsibility.

The lam-vong music stopped. Immediately the drums filled the void and Tai Shan suggested that she and Lieutenant Vang take tea with him somewhere more quiet. She thought the idea charming, she said, but Vang, his handsome face still animated from the clash with Kham Xai, explained that he was on patrol and, regrettably, must resume his duties . . .

Perched on tall stilts, the Bo Pen Nyan Teahouse was close to the Mekong. It was too dark to see the river itself, but bobbing yellow lights on fishing pirogues told them that, as always, it was there. Inside, Mademoiselle Brown suggested a table in an alcove where they could watch the lights, adding that if she might she would have cognac and soda although she knew that he took nothing stronger than tea.

A thrust worthy of one of his wives, thought Tai Shan with amusement. And true, insofar as his not caring for the taste of alcohol.

The proprietor, round and brown and anxious, hovered over his important guests until they were served. Then Tai Shan dismissed him with instructions to give Ah Fong one, and only one, shoum-shoum. Rice beer, in quantity, did not mix with driving the rudimentary roads of Laos.

Bowing low, the proprietor withdrew, backing away as if from an audience with royalty. "All Vientiane respects you, Tai Shan," said Mademoiselle Brown, her blue eyes large above her glass.

"It is your gracious person he honors."

"Nonsense." Her sharp tone raised his gray eyebrows. Quickly she said, "Forgive me. You never talk nonsense. But I wish to talk of something important. May I?"

He nodded gravely, noticing that under the surface she was tense with excitement. There was a plot, she began—or at least she had a report of a plot. And she believed it. And she had immediately cabled it to her headquarters. A plot to assassinate Colonel Kham Xai!

"One can always hear rumors of plots," murmured Tai Shan.

"My source is the man who will do the killing!" The triumphant note in her voice pleased Tai Shan. Here was a woman who enjoyed the work she did.

He smiled indulgently. "One can always hear foolish boasting."

"I know, most respected Tai Shan. But my source is Vang!"

"Impossible!" For once, Tai Shan's composure was shaken.

"No, Tai Shan, not impossible."

"Mademoiselle, I know Vang. In a rage he would fight, perhaps kill. But never could he *plan* an assassination."

"But he has!" Finding himself under Colonel Kham Xai's command, she explained, Vang had grown to detest the foreign commissar who so obviously considered the Lao an inferior race. And in time Vang had grown convinced that Kham Xai's true mission was the disruption of the Joint Council. To create chaos. So that the DRV could move into the vacuum. And once again Laos would be dominated by foreigners. "Like most Lao, Vang is a peaceful man. But he loves his country, Tai Shan. And he serves it."

Reflectively Tai Shan stroked his jade sash buckle, an intricately carved Fifteenth Century piece he'd removed from a Chinese trading junk many years before. Handling ancient jade stimulates thought, the great philosopher K'ung Fu-tze had written.

"Your information that Kham Xai is from Hanoi is accurate, Mademoiselle. But why has Vang been so indiscreet as to reveal the plot to you?"

Her gaze was level. "He is very much attracted to me."

"I see." He nodded approvingly. "One uses the weapons one has."

Her laugh, charmingly, was unabashed. "I'd never thought of my body as a weapon—but, yes, Tai Shan, one does." She sobered. "Kham Xai is a very important man. So I gambled. I cabled the report immediately. In my profession the report of an assassination after the fact is worthless. Before the fact it is a major achievement."

"A bright jewel for your professional record."

"Exactly."

"Mademoiselle Brown, in my view Vang was boasting to a valued female friend of a deed he only dreams of." Rising, he looked down at her gravely. "For you, a kindred spirit, I shall discover whether a plot actually exists. Perhaps others more iron-minded than the good Vang are involved. But now I shall exercise a mandarin's prerogative and end this delightful interlude."

"You are a good friend." Then concern darkened her eyes. "Please take care. And . . . give up the *divan de fumée*." Concern gave way to a dancing blue imp. "That was brash. But I am a brash American, after all. And you, dear Tiger of the Mekong, are the only real pirate I've ever known."

He smiled drily. "Retired pirate, my dear Mademoiselle Brown."

Tai Shan had known La Mère Pavotte, proprietress of the *divan de fumée*, for 40 years. A *métisse* of a racial mixture unknown even to her, she had the singleness of purpose he admired. Never a beauty,

always a shrewd businesswoman, she had battled her way to a prosperity evident in the opulent décor of her opium-smoking *divan*.

She greeted him as equal addressing equal. As such, mandarins
did not impress her. What impressed this woman with the dark face
of a withered poppy was, first, a man's ability to pay her stiff prices
and, second, his ability to exchange useful favors.

"What news this night, sister Pavotte?"

"The usual. Squabbling in the Joint Council. No decisions, just
squabbling." She escorted him to a richly appointed private cubicle.
Somewhat stiffly, he stretched out on the velvet floor mat that out
of deference to his years was slightly padded. His favorite attendant,
a wrinkled wiry Cantonese, entered and began his preparations.

The old man was expert, never spoke, and, according to La Mère
Pavotte, understood no French. Tai Shan spoke in that language.
"No rumors of an assassination plot, Pavotte? Against the foreigner
from across our eastern border?"

"None I have heard, brother Tai Shan." Her black eyes were
thoughtful. "Assassinating him would be a disastrous error."

"Because it would provide Hanoi an excuse for open aggression
against Laos—thus writing the end for you and me, eh, my sister?"

She drew up a carved stool and sat. In her own way La Mère
Pavotte was a good companion. She said, "With the Royalists we can
always live. And, for Communists, the Pathet Lao are satisfactorily
congenial." She made a rude gesture. "But the Communists from
the east!"

Tai Shan's head rested on a tile neck support close to the now
burning opium lamp, which was a beautiful antique. Near it the old
Cantonese lay propped on his elbows on the bare floor, body extended
the opposite way from Tai Shan's. He had laid out the cloisonné
vessel of dark shandu paste, the slender ebony-handled heating
skewers, and Tai Shan's personal pipes. Patiently he awaited Tai
Shan's signal to begin.

"As ever, Pavotte, your reasoning is correct. When the joint patrol
arrives, my sister, have them entertained with food and drink. And
by ivory-skinned Shanghai girls, if you think necessary. Send the
senior Royalist officer to me."

Rising, she nodded to indicate that whatever he and the police
officer discussed would be their affair alone. Then, as Tai Shan
signaled the attendant to prepare the first pipe, she bowed formally
and left.

Smoking shandu can be a one-man operation, but a two-man operation is far better.

Opium is not tobacco and an opium pipe is not a tobacco pipe. It takes perhaps 15 minutes to smoke a pipe of tobacco; 15 seconds will do for a pipe of shandu.

Positioning himself carefully, the attendant handed Tai Shan a pipe that was a work of art. Then he dipped out a dark globule from the shandu pot with a needlelike skewer and held it over the lamp. Delicately he spun the skewer in his sinewy fingers as the opium began to glow.

When it burned evenly, like a dark red pearl, he glanced at Tai Shan to see if he were ready. Then, swiftly, he transferred the glowing red pearl to the small hole in the flat bowl of the pipe.

With the skill of 50 years of practice Tai Shan drew in a long even breath, timed to consume the red pearl completely while allowing no wisp of smoke to escape anywhere but deep into his lungs.

The old Cantonese took the pipe from him and laid it with the others on an oblong of silk. Tai Shan relaxed against the neck support. He felt nothing, but he seldom did before the third or fourth pipe—and he never permitted himself more than four.

Like La Mère Pavotte, he abhorred addiction and addicts. In a *divan de grande luxe* such as hers, addicts were disruptive. Often they became criminals, and criminals draw unwelcome attention from the police. The amiably routine attention Pavotte's quiet *divan* presently drew was welcome protection, and she meant to keep it that way.

To Tai Shan's mind the pure Meo-grown shandu she dispensed was to the virulent alkaloids of refined opium as shoum-shoum was to fiery straight-grain alcohol. The one a friendly relaxant, the other a deadly poison.

Not that one couldn't smoke too much shandu or drink too much rice beer. Easily done—but only by fools.

When Lieutenant Vang entered, Tai Shan was just finishing his third pipe. He sent the attendant away. Not that he objected to smoking his fourth pipe in front of the young Lao—smoking can be social or private as the smoker prefers. But he had begun to feel the effects and when he reached his limit of four the world would be more rose-tinted, more misty, more dreamlike than was appropriate for what he had in mind.

It was comfortable on the velvet mat. But even a ruthless pirate turned benign, all-wise mandarin loses force when he is supine at another's feet. So, rising, he waved Vang to a stool but remained standing himself. "Vang, these ears have heard whispers that you plan a foolish act."

Startled, the young officer stammered that he could not imagine what the most revered Tai Shan meant. But the handsome boyish policeman was no match for the tall lean man in the elegant robe. Yes, Vang finally blurted, he and three other young officers intended to rid Laos of the man from Hanoi. Yes, they had a plan, not just a dream.

Tai Shan locked their eyes, his own gleaming darkly yellow in the murky light. "It is a plan for fools. Abandon it."

Anger flared. "I am no fool, Tai Shan."

"Think. Your act would be a golden boon for your enemies. A disaster for your cause. Think!"

Vang's gaze faltered. He stared at his hands.

"You are no assassin. You are a Lao. A Lao Royalist. A Royalist officer sworn to preserve Laos, not destroy it."

Shaking his head as if to clear it, Vang avoided Tai Shan's grim and glittering gaze. A long moment passed. Then the younger man rose slowly, flexing his shoulders as if shrugging off a burden. "You are right, honored Tai Shan. Where you are wise, I was foolish."

"What, then, of the other three?"

Smiling now, Vang moved to the door. "Fear not, O wise Tai Shan. They will laugh with joy to be released from such a terrible duty."

When Vang had gone, Tai Shan grasped the silken bell pull on the wall and summoned the attendant. He had been confident he could dominate the young officer but all the same it was agreeable to have prevailed. Perhaps this night he had earned a fifth pipe—even a sixth.

The old Cantonese padded in on his soft slippers, and much less stiffly than before Tai Shan arranged himself on the velvet mat, smiling to himself. No, not tonight. The rule of four was a sound rule. And it had been unbroken for 50 years. No, not tonight . . .

When Pavotte saw him to the door, he told her that he had learned from Vang that the rumors of an assassination were completely false. She nodded with satisfaction. "Fine news to hear. Good night, brother, sleep deeply."

And he would. His mind was clear, yet he was happy he need make no further demands on it. All he need do was sink into his car's soft seat and be driven home, home to his castle, to his realm.

"Fong-ah, as you go in fear of your grandfather's ghost, drive well. Let nothing disturb my peaceful thoughts."

A soft rain was falling now and the film of droplets on the windows closed him in, made him drowsy. Yes, it had been a good night's work—even Vang would benefit. For he and his friends would have bungled the assassination. And been summarily shot for their plans. So he, the retired Tiger of the Mekong, had done well for all concerned.

Or almost all. Now, instead of a bright jewel, there would be a black stain on Mademoiselle Brown's record. Most unfortunate. But not the ultimate disaster. Merely a temporary setback to a promising career.

Still, he certainly must tender her an apology. A handsome apology. He owed his attractive young friend at least that much. But there would be time for that later . . . He stifled a yawn.

It had been a long evening. He yawned again. Ah, yes, sister Pavotte, sleep would be deep tonight.

The next morning the rain had stopped. But beyond the flowering frangipani outside his window he could see gray sky. A cool day, ideal for a leisurely tour of his domain.

He breakfasted on the veranda where he could look across the Mekong to Thailand on the far shore. Most of the many motorized sampans and pirogues on the river were his. Ferrying goods and people between the two nations was a profitable business. And, for him these days, legitimate. A mandarin does not indulge in smuggling—particularly when the need exists no longer.

He sent for Sixth Wife. And, brown and still shapely and with languorous eyes, she sang him soft songs of love in her native Malay tongue while he ate juicy, orange-fleshed mangoes and drank tea.

Fifth Wife was staying out of sight. Last night she had seen the signs of his visit to the *divan* and her chiding finally went that one centimeter too far. Instantly he had ordered her from his room.

He appreciated her concern for his health, just as he appreciated Mademoiselle Brown's. And he was fully aware that Fifth Wife and his other women, when they dared, manipulated and maneuvered him. Well and good. He enjoyed it. But he, Tai Shan, was the final authority. And final authorities have bounds beyond which no one must trespass.

He finished the mangoes, dipped his fingers into the water bowl in which a lotus floated, dabbed his lips with a square of Swatow lace, and told Sixth Wife to summon Ah Fong and the Land Rover. When they arrived, Tai Shan proceeded to tour his domain.

He inspected the rice paddies and the rice mill. He strolled through the flower gardens. From the seat of the Land Rover he viewed the rows on rows of vegetables and the fenced fields of livestock. When finally they pulled up alongside the jetties, he said sharply, "Fong, do our boatmen engage in illicit trade?"

The Yunnanese stirred uneasily. "It is in their blood, Master."

Tai Shan's tone grew wintry. "I command that it cease."

Ah Fong understood. He climbed out and walked the length of each jetty, speaking to every man there and to every woman and every child.

The petty smuggling would now stop for two weeks, possibly three. It could never be eradicated, Tai Shan knew, but it could be controlled and that was what was important.

When they returned to the house, he summoned Fifth Wife, and waving away her efforts at conciliation he gave her a series of instructions—Final Authority exerting its authority, he told himself drily. But he knew he could rely on his chatelaine to obey him not only explicitly but efficiently, a comforting thought when one is responsible for a domain.

Then he ate a light meal of rice with nam pa and retired for his siesta. And when he arose, rather later than usual, he found that Fifth Wife was following instructions and making amends to Colonel/Commissar Kham Xai by serving him citronade on the veranda.

Tai Shan greeted him, adding mildly, "I had not expected you so soon, *mon colonel*. But there is an hour or more of daylight left. Grant me the honor of escorting you around my poor and barren lands."

If Kham Xai were surprised by the cordial reception, his bony face gave no sign. What did he hope to find, Ta Shan wondered. Evidence of something illegal, no doubt. Or, failing that, first-hand knowledge on which to base trumped-up charges. Commissars were experts in trumped-up charges, with landholders their plumpest targets.

An ironic situation. For had he not saved this Colonel/Commissar from the folly of Lieutenant Vang? Even bungled assassinations can prove fatal. However—

Tai Shan would have preferred the sturdy Land Rover but he deferred to Kham Xai's insistence on making the tour in the staff car, a mud-spattered Skoda he'd driven out from the city. Probably his idea was to retain control of where they went and what they saw. Or was it simply that he did not trust the old Tiger of the Mekong?

To Tai Shan's amusement Kham Xai examined the poppies in the flowerbeds minutely. But all were of innocent varieties. Then he lingered long over his inspection of the jetties. And found nothing, of course. All signs of smuggling had disappeared immediately after Tai Shan's earlier visit.

When dusk began to fall, Kham Xai decided he had seen enough. But despite having uncovered no evidence of criminal activity, he was in good spirits. So, mused Tai Shan, the man from Hanoi thought he had seen something useful.

No matter. So long as the Lao ruled their own nation this foreigner was a nuisance, nothing more. For he, the respected Tai Shan, had Lao blood in his veins, was a Lao citizen.

But a nuisance can grow into an aggravation and a different approach from Fifth Wife's rudeness of the day before was surely prudent.

So it was with approval that he saw her standing at the top of the stairway politely awaiting their return. "*Mon colonel,* my wife is guilt-ridden by her discourtesy. Allow her to serve you a refreshing drink."

A fine rain had begun to fall and, a model of meekness, Fifth Wife ushered them inside the house and saw them comfortably seated. From a satiny rosewood table she served them hot tea and cold Danish beer, then retired into the background. Tai Shan watched Kham Xai gulp noisily at his beer and he wondered what this uncouth nuisance of a man was planning.

Then, looking past his guest, he saw Ah Fong in the doorway. Eyes glinting yellow, Tai Shan nodded slightly. Ah Fong slipped into the room.

The Colonel Commissar struggled feebly, but it was over in moments. And when the powerful Yunnanese let Kham Xai's body slide lifeless to the floor, Tai Shan nodded again. Approvingly. The man from Hanoi was a nuisance no longer.

He signed to Fifth Wife and at once she began issuing instructions to Ah Fong. Even though gentle, the rain would have deepened the treacherous mud on the narrow rutted road to Vientiane, and the spot where Ah Fong had slewed the Mercedes around last evening would be ideal for the accident.

And the fact that the lighter, less responsive Skoda would be more susceptible to a fatal skid would add an air of authenticity.

In her efficient way Fifth Wife would continue supervising. But he, Tai Shan, the Final Authority, would also be present. For it was he who had the vast fund of experience needed to see to it that there would be no mistakes made in this, his apology to his friend Mademoiselle Brown.

The news of a fatal accident to Kham Xai would mesh perfectly with her secret report of a plot to kill him. Her headquarters would commend her, not dispense the black marks she so dreaded. Truly, Tai Shan felt, it was a handsome apology.

It crossed his mind that, oh so very delicately, she might have implanted the idea in his mind, might have maneuvered him toward the action he had taken. It did not matter. He enjoyed being maneuvered by his collection of women.

Just so long as he remained the Final Authority.

Lika Van Ness

Night Fear

*Julia and Charles had passed each other several times in the hall
of the apartment house, but their first real meeting was at two
o'clock in the morning . . .*

The rapping on the door was firm and insistent. Julia turned on
the light by the daybed, rubbed hard at her eyes, and went to
the door. "Who is it?" she whispered fearfully.

"It's your neighbor across the hall, Charles Slaughter. Are you all
right?"

Julia methodically undid each of the three locks and, keeping the
chain on the guard, opened the door a few inches. The man facing
her, serious and concerned, was the one she had seen entering and
leaving the opposite apartment several times since she and her
mother had moved in the previous month.

"I'm all right," she said. "What's the matter? Is there a fire?"

"I heard screaming."

"Screaming!" she said. "Oh, not from here."

"Yes, absolutely from here. When I first heard it I came out into
the hallway—it definitely came from behind this door."

"Oh." Julia bit her lip.

"There *is* something wrong. Can I be of help?"

Julia blinked and looked back toward the living room for a tissue.
"It's nothing," she said. "No. I don't know."

"Let me come in and talk with you for a few minutes. I'm harmless,
I promise you, and maybe I can be of help."

Julia paused to reflect for a few seconds, then drew the head of
the chain across and off the guard. She stepped back and her neighbor, a sturdy man in a neat dressing gown and slippers, stepped
inside and appraised the dimly lit room, the mussed daybed in the
corner, the heavy, overstuffed, oppressive furniture.

Julia shut the door behind him and refastened all three locks with
metallic-sounding efficiency. "Everything is all right, you see?" she
said, turning to him. She walked to the kitchen to the left and turned

on the light. Taking a tissue from a box on the counter, she blew her nose. "Excuse me," she said.

"But don't you live here with an older woman? I assumed she was your mother. Perhaps she—"

"If she screamed I would have heard her. She sleeps in this bedroom here off the kitchen. Just across from me. She's deaf and might not hear me if I screamed, but I would hear her."

He hesitated. "Don't you want to check and see if she's all right? There might have been an intruder."

"The only way an intruder could enter this apartment is from the fire escape back there by the living-room window. He'd have to pass me to get to her." She turned on the gas under the kettle on a back burner. "You don't believe me that I would have heard her if she'd screamed."

"I'm just concerned. I didn't imagine the screaming and if it wasn't you, then it had to be her."

"Then it must have been me." She sighed. "If I go in and check on my mother, it will wake her. She is deaf, but she's a very light sleeper." Julia opened a cabinet door and reached toward the cups and saucers. "I'm making a cup of tea. Will you have one?"

"I will," he said. "Thank you."

They sat in the worn chairs by the small bricked-up fireplace. "I must actually call out when I have the dream then," she said. "No one has ever told me so."

"But you did dream you were screaming?"

"Yes. Funny, I haven't had the nightmare for months but here it is again."

"Is it always the same dream?"

"Yes. It's not a dream in the usual sense. It's a classic nightmare, I discovered. I was so frantic when I started having it I read every book I could find on sleep and dreaming—which was easy for me being a librarian." She smiled and he returned the smile. "It was kind of you to come over," she said.

"Not at all. Go on, what did you discover about this nightmare?"

"It's called *pavor nocturnus*—"

"Translation?"

"Night fear. It isn't uncommon—it's been traced back for centuries. You feel a heavy presence, a real and evil presence, weighing on you. You can't move. You try to move and you try to call out for help, but you can't."

"Apparently you can."

She studied the tea in her cup. "It's a dreadful feeling. I've read that you are in a state of shock and that if you don't pull yourself out of the dream you die."

"That sounds like a myth—like the one about if you dream you're falling and don't wake up before you land you die."

"The books say it's a fact."

He shifted uncomfortably in the chair. "Do the books say how the nightmare can be avoided?"

"As a matter of fact, one of them suggested that the circulation of air is important, and I think that's why I haven't had the dream for so long, until tonight. Back home I kept the window open even on the coldest nights."

"If you'll forgive my saying so, it's a bit stuffy in here right now," he said and nodded to the windows at the far end of the room. "Are they open at the top at least?"

"No, they're locked shut because of the fire escape." She searched his face. "Intruders, you know."

"I'm sorry about this nightmare of yours. It must be horrible."

"It is. I take it you've never had one."

"No. I've dreamed I can't walk, but it's nothing like what you describe. Should you—do you think you should—?"

"See a psychiatrist? No, it's physical, not mental." She smiled at him again and once more he returned it. "It has to do with coming awake too swiftly from a deep sleep. The lighter in-between sleep, the dreaming phase, is bypassed and for some reason it results in a state of shock."

"Julia?" It was a thin voice from beyond the kitchen. It came closer and sounded more peevish. "Julia? Why are these lights on?"

"Oh, dear, we've awakened her." Julia placed her cup and saucer on the end table. Charles turned and recognized the frail old woman he'd seen several times in the hall. She shuffled a few feet into the room, fitting a hearing aid to her ear with a fumbling hand. She peered toward them, her eyes adjusting to the light. Charles stood up. When she saw him, her mouth dropped open and her hands clutched the collar of her robe, pulling it closer to her emaciated neck.

"Who are you?" she cried. "Julia, who is this man?"

"He lives across the hall, Mother—there's no need to be alarmed. I apparently called out in my sleep and he thoughtfully came over to investigate."

The old woman stared at Charles with bravado. "I don't recognize you, young man. *You* don't live here!" She faced Julia. "I told you we should never have come here where we don't know anyone. We should have stayed where we were."

"We didn't know anyone there either, Mother." Julia turned weary eyes to Charles. "I'm sorry. You'd better leave. She isn't well."

"Of course," he said, putting his half-empty cup by hers on the table. "I'm relieved to know that you're both all right."

"Thank you very much," she said, following him to the door and freeing it with a clatter. She smiled up at him. "It's good to know we have a neighbor who cares." He stepped out into the hall. "Thank you again," Julia said, "Mr. Slaughter."

He hesitated. "You're courageous, you know—letting an unknown man into your apartment at two in the morning, especially one named Slaughter."

Julia's smile stayed. "I'd trust you with my life, Mr. Slaughter."

It's done, she thought, climbing under the covers, her mother safely back in her own bed and the apartment in darkness again. "How could you put us in danger like this?" her mother had complained when Julia led her back to bed. "I won't let you forget this in a hurry." Of course she wouldn't. She had never let Julia forget anything.

Her course was clear. Her mother would be a dead weight only a few months longer. She and Julia's father had kept Julia from pursuing a career in medicine, agreeing only to support her through the library school they thought the safest training for her future. They had never allowed her to date or to stay out late and, once she was out of college and working, she had had to account for every cent of her wages. They had made it clear she was never to encourage any friendship with a man, no matter how "innocent." All her life they had preached to her about the importance of preparing oneself against life's worst possibilities.

Her father had died after a long tedious illness five years earlier. All that was left after the medical bills were paid was their big old house. And when Julia lost her job at the time the branch of the public library closed and she was unable to find another job, not even in one of the hospitals or universities, she had had to look into the opportunities elsewhere. It had taken eight months, but she finally found a position in this middle-sized community miles from their home.

They had sold the house and moved, with the best of the furniture, to this apartment, which Julia hated every bit as much as her mother did. She hated the suburbs and she hated library work. She was almost 40 years old and every day her face in the bathroom mirror looked older. Life was passing her by because her parents had trained her to prepare for life's worst possibilities, not its best. And life would continue to pass her by so long as the selfish woman in the one bedroom across the kitchen refused to die.

She had many ailments, any one of which might carry her off, doctors told Julia—always adding that then again she might live to be 100; it was impossible to predict. Julia's maternal grandmother had lived to 94. One hundred! By then Julia herself would be the age her mother was now! She had to act out of self-preservation.

A nursing home for her mother was out of the question. It would eat up what money was left from the sale of the house, and her mother would behave so badly Julia doubted if any nursing home would keep her. No, instead, one night, she would firmly press a pillow over her sleeping mother's face and end the old woman's misery—and her own. And although no jury in their souls would convict her, they would have to if they learned the truth. But they wouldn't learn the truth because the dead woman's heart had been weak for years—her doctors would testify to that. They had told Julia she might slip away in her sleep anytime.

And if Julia botched it somehow and her mother did scream—now there was Mr. Slaughter to give evidence that Julia occasionally cried out in her sleep. It was only remotely possible it would come to that, but Julia felt better knowing that she had prepared for the worst possibility. They had trained her well, her single-minded parents, and for that she was finally grateful.

Before returning to bed, Charles Slaughter lit a cigarette and thought about the women across the hall. Why had the younger one opened that solidly locked door to him, a virtual stranger? Lord, how he hated the harsh sound of those locks they had had installed!

Then too there had been a play-acting quality about it all that just didn't ring true. He didn't know if mother and daughter were both acting toward the same purpose, but acting they were. The daughter especially disturbed him. She aroused his sympathy and his fear. He would, without a doubt, be hearing from her again. He knew it with a sureness he'd developed in his 16 years as a detective working out of the county district attorney's office.

Ernest Bramah

The Tragedy at Brookbend Cottage

To refresh your memory: the first blind detective in modern fiction made his appearance in 1914—"wise, witty, gentle" Max Carrados, born Max Wynn. In compensation for his blindness, Max Carrados can run his fingertips along the surface of a newspaper, find the infinitesimal height of printers' ink, and "read" any type larger than long primer. There was one amazing moment in his career when a stranger sauntered past Max Carrados and in that fleeting moment the blind detective deduced with impeccable logic that the stranger was wearing a false mustache ...

Detective: MAX CARRADOS

"Max," said Mr. Carlyle, when Parkinson had closed the door behind him, "this is Lieutenant Hollyer, whom you consented to see."

"To hear," corrected Carrados, smiling straight into the healthy and rather embarrassed face of the stranger before him. "Mr. Hollyer knows of my disability?"

"Mr. Carlyle told me," said the young man, "but, as a matter of fact, I had heard of you before, Mr. Carrados, in connection with the foundering of the *Ivan Saratov*."

Carrados wagged his head in good-humored resignation.

"And the owners were sworn to inviolable secrecy!" he exclaimed. "Well, it is inevitable, I suppose. Not another scuttling case, Mr. Hollyer?"

"No, mine is quite a private matter," replied the lieutenant. "My sister, Mrs. Creake—but Mr. Carlyle would tell you better than I can."

"No, no; Carlyle is a professional. Let me have it in the rough, Mr. Hollyer. My ears are my eyes."

"Very well, sir. I can tell you what there is to tell, right enough, but I feel that when all's said and done it must sound very little to another, although it seems important to me."

"We have occasionally found trifles of significance ourselves," said Carrados encouragingly.

Lieutenant Hollyer began: "I have a sister, Millicent, who is married to a man called Creake. She is about twenty-eight now and he is at least fifteen years older. Neither my mother (who has since died) nor I cared very much about Creake. We had nothing particular against him, except, perhaps, the disparity of age, but none of us appeared to have anything in common. He was a dark, taciturn man, and his moody silence froze up conversation. As a result, of course, we didn't see much of each other."

"This, you must understand, was four or five years ago, Max," interposed Mr. Carlyle officiously.

Lieutenant Hollyer continued: "Millicent married Creake after a very short engagement. It was a frightfully subdued wedding—more like a funeral to me. The man professed to have no relations and apparently he had scarcely any friends or business acquaintances. He was an agent for something or other and had an office off Holborn. I suppose he made a living out of it then, although we knew practically nothing of his private affairs, but I gather that it has been going down since, and I suspect that for the past few years they have been getting along almost entirely on Millicent's little income. You would like the particulars?"

"Please," assented Carrados.

"When our father died about seven years ago, he left six thousand pounds. It was invested in Canadian stock and brought in a little over two hundred a year. By his will my mother was to have the income of that for life and on her death it was to pass to Millicent, subject to the payment of a lump sum of five hundred pounds to me. But my father privately suggested to me that if I should have no particular use for the money at the time, he would propose my letting Millicent have the income of it until I did want it, as she would not be particularly well off. You see, Mr. Carrados, a great deal more had been spent on my education and advancement than on her; I had my pay, and, of course, I could look out for myself better than a girl could."

"Quite so," agreed Carrados.

"Therefore I did nothing about that," continued the lieutenant. "Three years ago I was over again but I did not see much of them.

They were living in lodgings. That was the only time since the marriage that I have seen them until last week. In the meanwhile our mother had died and Millicent had been receiving her income. She wrote me several letters at the time. Otherwise we did not correspond much, but about a year ago she sent me their new address—Brookbend Cottage, Mulling Common—a house that they had taken. When I got two months' leave I invited myself there as a matter of course, fully expecting to stay most of my time with them, but I made an excuse to get away after a week. The place was dismal and unendurable, the whole life and atmosphere indescribably depressing." He looked round with an instinct of caution, leaned forward earnestly, and dropped his voice. "Mr. Carrados, it is my absolute conviction that Creake is only waiting for a favorable opportunity to murder Millicent."

"Go on," said Carrados quietly. "A week of the depressing surroundings of Brookbend Cottage would not alone convince you of that, Mr. Hollyer."

"I am not so sure," declared Hollyer doubtfully. "There was a feeling of suspicion and—before me—polite hatred that would have gone a good way towards it. All the same there *was* something more definite. Millicent told me this the day after I went there. There is no doubt that a few months ago Creake deliberately planned to poison her with some weed-killer. She told me the circumstances in a rather distressed moment, but afterwards she refused to speak of it again—even weakly denied it—and, as a matter of fact, it was with the greatest difficulty that I could get her at any time to talk about her husband or his affairs. The gist of it was that she had the strongest suspicion that Creake doctored a bottle of stout which he expected she would drink for her supper when she was alone. The weed-killer, properly labeled, but also in a beer bottle, was kept with other miscellaneous liquids in the same cupboard as the beer, but on a high shelf. When he found that it had miscarried he poured away the mixture, washed out the bottle, and put in the dregs from another. There is no doubt in my mind that if he had come back and found Millicent dead or dying he would have contrived it to appear that she had made a mistake in the dark."

"Yes," assented Carrados. "The open way, the safe way."

"You must understand that they live in a very small style, Mr. Carrados, and Millicent is almost entirely in the man's power. The only servant they have is a woman who comes in for a few hours every day. The house is lonely and secluded. Creake is sometimes away for days and nights at a time, and Millicent, either through pride or indifference, seems to have dropped off all her old friends and to have made no others. He might poison her, bury the body in the garden, and be a thousand miles away before anyone began even to inquire about her. What am I to do?"

"He is less likely to try poison than some other means now," pondered Carrados. "That having failed, his wife will always be on her guard. He may know, or at least suspect, that others know. No. . . . The common-sense precaution would be for your sister to leave the man, Mr. Hollyer. She will not?"

"No," admitted Hollyer, "she will not. I at once urged that." The young man struggled with some hesitation for a moment and then blurted out: "The fact is, Mr. Carrados, I don't understand Millicent. She is not the girl she was. She hates Creake and treats him with a silent contempt that eats into their lives like acid, and yet she is so jealous of him that she will let nothing short of death part them. It is a horrible life they lead. I stood it for a week and I must say, much as I dislike my brother-in-law, that he has something to put up with. If only he got into a passion like a man and killed her it wouldn't be altogether incomprehensible."

"That does not concern us," said Carrados. "In a game of this kind one has to take sides and we have taken ours. It remains for us to see that our side wins. You mentioned jealousy, Mr. Hollyer. Have you any idea whether Mrs. Creake has real ground for it?"

"I should have told you that," replied Lieutenant Hollyer. "I happened to strike up with a newspaperman whose office is in the same block as Creake's. When I mentioned the name he grinned. 'Creake,' he said, 'oh, he's the man with the romantic typist, isn't he?' 'Well, he's my brother-in-law,' I replied. 'What about the typist?' Then the chap shut up like a knife. 'No, no,' he said, 'I didn't know he was married. I don't want to get mixed up in anything of that sort.' "

Carrados turned to his friend.

"I suppose you know all about the typist by now, Louis?"

"We have had her under efficient observation, Max."

"Is she unmarried?"

"Yes; so far as ordinary repute goes."

"That is all that is essential for the moment. Mr. Hollyer opens up three excellent reasons why this man might wish to dispose of his wife. Well, we will go forward on that. Have you got a photograph of Mr. Creake?"

The lieutenant took out his pocketbook.

"Mr. Carlyle asked me for one. Here is the best I could get."

Carrados rang the bell.

"This, Parkinson," he said, when the man appeared, "is a photograph of a Mr.—What first name, by the way?"

"Austin," said Hollyer.

"—of a Mr. Austin Creake. I may require you to recognize him."

Parkinson glanced at the print and returned it to his master's hand.

"May I inquire if it is a recent photograph of the gentleman, sir?" he asked.

"About six years ago," said the lieutenant. "But he is very little changed."

"Thank you, sir. I will endeavor to remember Mr. Creake, sir."

Lieutenant Hollyer stood up as Parkinson left the room. The interview seemed to be at an end.

"Oh, there's one other matter," he remarked. "I am afraid that I did rather an unfortunate thing while I was at Brookbend. It seemed to me that as all Millicent's money would probably pass into Creake's hands sooner or later I might as well have my five hundred pounds, if only to help her with afterwards. So I broached the subject and said that I should like to have it now as I had an opportunity for investing."

"And you think?"

"It may possibly influence Creake to act sooner than he otherwise might have done. He may even have got possession of the principal and find it very awkward to replace it."

"So much the better. If your sister is going to be murdered it may as well be done next week or two Excuse my brutality, Mr. Hollyer, but this is simply a case to me and I regard it strategically. Now Mr. Carlyle's organization can look after Mrs. Creake for a few weeks, but it cannot look after her forever. By increasing the immediate risk we diminish the permanent risk."

"I see," agreed Hollyer. "I'm awfully uneasy but I'm entirely in your hands."

"Then we will give Mr. Creake every inducement and every opportunity to get to work. Where are you staying now?"

"Just now at St. Albans."

"That is too far." The inscrutable eyes retained their tranquil depth but a new quality of quickening interest in the voice made Mr. Carlyle sit up. "Give me a few minutes, please. The cigarettes are behind you, Mr. Hollyer." The blind man walked to the window and seemed to look out over the cypress-shaded lawn. The lieutenant lit a cigarette and Mr. Carlyle picked up *Punch*. Then Carrados turned round again.

"You are prepared to put your own arrangements aside?" he demanded of his visitor.

"Certainly."

"Very well. I want you to go down now—straight from here—to Brookbend Cottage. Tell your sister that your leave is unexpectedly cut short and that you sail tomorrow."

"The *Martian?*"

"No, no; the *Martian* doesn't sail. Look up the movements on your way there and pick out a boat that does. Say you are transferred. Add that you expect to be away only two or three months and that you really want the five hundred pounds by the time of your return. Don't stay in the house long, please."

"I understand, sir."

"St. Albans is too far. Make your excuse and get away from there today. Put up somewhere in town, where you will be in reach of the telephone. Let Mr. Carlyle and myself know where you are. Keep out of Creake's way. I don't want actually to tie you down to the house, but we may require your services. We will let you know at the first sign of anything doing. . . ."

"Is there nothing more that I can do now?"

"Nothing. In going to Mr. Carlyle you have done the best thing possible; you have put your sister into the care of the shrewdest man in London."

"Well, Max?" remarked Mr. Carlyle tentatively when they were alone.

"Well, Louis?"

"Of course, it wasn't worth while rubbing it in before young Hollyer, but, as a matter of fact, every single man carries the life of any other man—only one, mind you—in his hands, do what you will."

"Provided he doesn't bungle," acquiesced Carrados.

"Quite so."

"And also that he is absolutely reckless of the consequences."

"Of course."

"Two rather large provisos. Creake is obviously susceptible to both. Have you seen him?"

"No. As I told you, I put a man on to report his habits in town. Then, two days ago, as the case seemed to promise some interest—for he certainly is deeply involved with the typist, Max, and the thing might take a sensational turn at any time—I went down to Mulling Common myself. Although the house is lonely it is on the electric tram route—you know the sort of market-garden rurality about a dozen miles out of London—alternate bricks and cabbages. It was easy enough to get to know about Creake locally. He mixes with no one there, goes into town at irregular times but generally every day, and is reputed to be devilish hard to get money out of. Finally, I made the acquaintance of an old fellow who used to do a day's gardening at Brookbend occasionally. He has a cottage and a garden of his own with a greenhouse, and the business cost me the price of a pound of tomatoes."

"Was it a profitable investment?"

"As tomatoes, yes; as information, no. The old fellow had the fatal disadvantage from our point of view of laboring under a grievance. A few weeks ago Creake told him that he would not require him again as he was going to do his own gardening."

"That is something, Louis."

"However, the chatty old soul had a simple explanation for everything that Creake did. Creake was mad. He had even seen him flying a kite in his garden where it was bound to get wrecked among the trees. A lad of ten would have known better, he declared."

"A good many men have been flying kites of various kinds lately," said Carrados. "Is he interested in aviation?"

"I daresay. He appears to have some knowledge of scientific subjects. Now what do you want me to do, Max?"

"Will you do it?"

"Implicitly."

"Keep your man on Creake in town and let me have his reports after you have seen them. Lunch with me here now. Phone your office that you are detained on unpleasant business and then give the deserving Parkinson an afternoon off by looking after me while we take a motor run round Mulling Common. If we have time we might go on to Brighton, feed at the 'Ship,' and come back in the cool."

"Amiable and thrice lucky mortal," sighed Mr. Carlyle.

But, as it happened, Brighton did not figure in that day's itinerary. It had been Carrados' intention merely to pass Brookbend Cottage on this occasion, relying on his highly developed faculties, aided by Mr. Carlyle's description, to inform him of the surroundings. A hundred yards before they reached the house he had given an order to his chauffeur to drop into the lowest speed and they were leisurely drawing past when a discovery by Mr. Carlyle modified their plans.

"By Jupiter!" that gentleman suddenly exclaimed, "there's a board up, Max. The place is to be let."

Carrados picked up the tube again. A couple of sentences passed and the car stopped by the roadside, a score of paces past the limit of the garden. Mr. Carlyle took out his notebook and wrote down the address of a firm of house agents.

"You might raise the hood and have a look at the engine, Harris," said Carrados. "We want to be occupied here for a few minutes."

"This is sudden; Hollyer knew nothing of their leaving," remarked Mr. Carlyle.

"All the same, Louis, we will go on to the agents and get a card to view whether we use it today or not."

A thick hedge, in its summer dress effectively screening the house beyond from public view, lay between the garden and the road. Above the hedge showed an occasional shrub; at the corner nearest to the car a chestnut flourished. The wooden gate, once white, which they had passed, was grimed and rickety. The road itself was still the unpretentious country lane that the advent of the electric tram had found it. When Carrados had taken in these details there seemed little else to notice. He was on the point of giving Harris the order to go on when his ear caught a trivial sound.

"Someone is coming out of the house, Louis," he warned his friend. "It may be Hollyer."

"I don't hear anyone," replied the other, but as he spoke a door banged noisily and Mr. Carlyle slipped into another seat and ensconced himself behind a copy of *The Globe*.

"Creake himself," he whispered across the car, as a man appeared at the gate. "Hollyer was right; he is hardly changed. Waiting for the tram, I suppose."

But the tram very soon swung past them from the direction in which Mr. Creake was looking and it did not interest him. For a minute or two longer he continued to look expectantly along the road. Then he walked slowly up the drive to the house.

"We will give him five or ten minutes," decided Carrados. "Harris is behaving very naturally."

Before even the shorter period had run out they were repaid. A telegraph boy cycled leisurely along the road, and, leaving his machine at the gate, went up to the cottage. Evidently there was no reply, for in less than a minute he was trundling past them back again. Round the bend an approaching tram clanged its bell noisily, and quickened by the warning sound, Mr. Creake again appeared, this time with a small portmanteau in his hand. With a backward glance he hurried on towards the next stopping-place, and boarded the car as it slackened down.

"Very convenient of Mr. Creake," remarked Carrados, with quiet satisfaction. "We will now get the order and go over the house in his absence. It might be useful to have a look at the telegram as well."

"It might, Max," acquiesced Mr. Carlyle. "But if it is, as it probably is, in Creake's pocket, how do you propose to get it?"

"By going to the telegraph office."

"Quite so. Have you ever tried to see a copy of a telegram addressed to someone else?"

"I don't think I have had occasion yet," admitted Carrados. "Have you?"

"In one or two cases I have perhaps been an accessory to the act. It is generally a matter either of extreme delicacy or considerable expenditure."

"Then for Hollyer's sake we will hope for the former."

A little later, having left the car at the beginning of the straggling High Street, the two men called at the village telegraph office. They had already visited the house agent and obtained an order to view Brookbend Cottage, declining with some difficulty the clerk's persistent offer to accompany them. The reason was soon forthcoming. "As a matter of fact," explained the young man, "the present tenant is under *our* notice to leave."

"Unsatisfactory, eh?" said Carrados, encouragingly.

"He's a corker," admitted the clerk, responding to the friendly tone. "Fifteen months and not a bit of rent have we had. That's why I should have liked—"

"We will make every allowance," replied Carrados.

The telegraph office occupied one side of a stationer's shop. It was not without some inward trepidation that Mr. Carlyle found himself committed to the adventure. Carrados, on the other hand, was the personification of bland unconcern.

"You have just sent a telegram to Brookbend Cottage," he said to the young lady behind the brass-work lattice. "We think it may have come inaccurately and should like a repeat." He took out his purse. "What is the fee?"

The request was evidently not a common one. "Oh," said the girl uncertainly, "wait a minute, please." She turned to a pile of telegram duplicates behind the desk and ran a doubtful finger along the upper sheets. "I think this is all right. You want it repeated?"

"Please."

"It will be fourpence. If there is an error the amount will be refunded."

Carrados put down his coins.

"Will it take long?" he inquired.

"You will most likely get it within a quarter of an hour," she replied.

"Now you've done it," commented Mr. Carlyle, as they walked back to their car. "How do you propose to get that telegram, Max?"

"Ask for it."

And stripping the artifice of any elaboration, he simply asked for it and got it. The car, posted at a convenient bend in the road, gave him a warning note as the telegraph-boy approached. Then Carrados took up a convincing attitude with his hand on the gate while Mr. Carlyle lent himself to the semblance of a departing friend. That was the inevitable impression when the boy rode up.

"Creake, Brookbend Cottage?" inquired Carrados, holding out his hand, and without a second thought the boy gave him the envelope.

"Some day, my friend," remarked Mr. Carlyle, looking nervously towards the unseen house, "your ingenuity will get you into a tight corner."

"Then my ingenuity must get me out again," was the retort. "Let us have our 'view' now. The telegram can wait."

An untidy workwoman took their order and left them standing at the door. Presently a lady whom they both knew to be Mrs. Creake appeared.

"You wish to see the house?" she said, in a voice that was utterly devoid of any interest. Then, without waiting for a reply, she turned to the nearest door and threw it open.

"This is the drawing-room."

They walked into a sparsely furnished, damp-smelling room and made a pretense of looking round.

"The dining-room," she continued, crossing the narrow hall.

Mr. Carlyle ventured a genial commonplace in the hope of inducing conversation. The result was not encouraging. Doubtless they would have gone through the house under the same frigid guidance had not Carrados been at fault in a way that Mr. Carlyle had never known him fail before. In crossing the hall he stumbled over a mat and almost fell.

"Pardon my clumsiness," he said to the lady. "I am, unfortunately, quite blind."

"Blind!" she exclaimed. "Oh, I beg your pardon. Why did you not tell me? You might have fallen."

"I generally manage fairly well," he replied. "But, of course, in a strange house—"

She put her hand on his arm very lightly.

"You must let me guide you," she said.

The house, without being large, was full of passages and inconvenient turnings. Carrados asked an occasional question and found Mrs. Creake quite amiable without effusion. Mr. Carlyle followed them from room to room in the hope, though scarcely the expectation, of learning something that might be useful.

"This is the last one. It is the largest bedroom," said their guide. Only two of the upper rooms were fully furnished and Mr. Carlyle at once saw, as Carrados knew without seeing, that this was the one which the Creakes occupied.

"A very pleasant outlook," declared Mr. Carlyle.

"Oh, I suppose so," admitted the lady vaguely. The room, in fact, looked over the leafy garden and the road beyond. It had a French door opening onto a small balcony, and to this, under the strange influence that always attracted him to light, Carrados walked.

"I expect that there is a certain amount of repair needed?" he said, after standing there a moment.

"I am afraid there would be," she confessed.

"I ask because there is a sheet of metal on the floor here," he continued. "Now that, in an old house, spells dry-rot to the wary observer."

"My husband said that the rain, which comes in a little under the window, was rotting the boards there," she replied. "He put that down recently. I had not noticed anything myself."

It was the first time she had mentioned her husband; Mr. Carlyle pricked up his ears.

"Ah, that is a less serious matter," said Carrados. "May I step out onto the balcony?"

"Oh, yes, if you like to." Then, as he appeared to be fumbling at the catch, "Let me open it for you."

But the window was already open, and Carrados, facing the various points of the compass, took in the bearings.

"A sunny, sheltered corner," he remarked. "An ideal spot for a deckchair and a book."

"I daresay," she replied, "but I never use it."

"Sometimes, surely," he persisted mildly. "It would be my favorite retreat. But then—"

"I was going to say that I had never even been out on it, but that would not be quite true. It has only two uses for me: occasionally I shake a duster from it, and when my husband returns late without his latchkey he wakes me up and I come out here and drop him mine."

Further revelation of Mr. Creake's nocturnal habits was cut off, greatly to Mr. Carlyle's annoyance, by a cough of unmistakable significance from the foot of the stairs. They had heard a trade cart drive up to the gate, a knock at the door, and the heavyfooted woman tramp along the hall.

"Excuse me a minute, please," said Mrs. Creake.

"Louis," said Carrados, in a sharp whisper, the moment they were alone, "stand against the door."

With extreme plausibility Mr. Carlyle began to admire a picture so situated that while he was there it was impossible to open the door more than a few inches. From that position he observed his confederate go through the curious procedure of kneeling down on the bedroom floor and for a full minute pressing his ear to the sheet of metal that had already engaged his attention. Then he rose to his feet, nodded, dusted his trousers, and Mr. Carlyle moved to a less equivocal position.

"What a beautiful rose-tree grows up your balcony," remarked Carrados, stepping into the room as Mrs. Creake returned. "I suppose you are very fond of gardening?"

"I detest it," she replied.

"But this *Gloire,* so carefully trained—?"

"Is it?" she replied. "I think my husband was nailing it up recently." By some strange fatality Carrados' most aimless remarks seemed to involve the absent Mr. Creake. "Do you care to see the garden?"

The garden proved to be extensive and neglected. Behind the house was chiefly orchard. In front, some semblance of order had been kept up; here it was lawn and shrubbery, and the drive they had walked along. Two things interested Carrados: the soil at the foot of the balcony, which he declared on examination to be particularly suitable for roses, and the fine chestnut-tree in the corner by the road.

As they walked back to the car Mr. Carlyle lamented that they had learned so little of Creake's movements.

"Perhaps the telegram will tell us something," suggested Carrados.

Mr. Carlyle cut open the envelope, glanced at the enclosure, and in spite of his disappointment could not restrain a chuckle.

"My poor Max," he explained, "you have put yourself to an amount of ingenious trouble for nothing. Creake is evidently taking a few days' holiday and prudently availed himself of the Meteorological Office forecast before going. Listen: *Immediate prospect for London warm and settled. Further outlook cooler but fine.* Well, well; I did get a pound of tomatoes for *my* fourpence."

"You certainly scored there, Louis," admitted Carrados. "I wonder," he added speculatively, "whether it is Creake's peculiar taste usually to spend his week-end holiday in London."

"Eh?" exclaimed Mr. Carlyle, looking at the words again. "By gad, that's rum, Max. They usually go to Weston-super-Mare. Why on earth should he want to know about London?"

"I can make a guess, but before we are satisfied I must come here again. Take another look at that kite, Louis. Are there a few yards of string hanging loose from it?"

"Yes, there are."

"Rather thick string—unusually thick for the purpose?"

"Yes; but how do you know?"

As they drove home again Carrados explained, and Mr. Carlyle sat aghast, saying incredulously: "Good God, Max, is it possible?"

An hour later he was satisfied that it was possible. In reply to his inquiry someone in his office telephoned him the information that "they" had left Paddington by the four thirty for Weston.

It was more than a week after his introduction to Carrados that Lieutenant Hollyer had a summons to present himself at the Carrados home again. He found Mr. Carlyle already there and the two friends awaiting his arrival.

"I hope everything is all right?" he said, shaking hands.

"Excellent," replied Carrados. "You'd better eat something before we start. We have a long and perhaps an exciting night before us."

"And certainly a wet one," assented the lieutenant. "It was thundering over Mulling way as I came along."

"That is why you are here," said his host. "We are waiting for a certain message before we start, and in the meantime you may as well understand what we expect to happen. As you saw, there is a thunderstorm coming on. The Meteorological Office forecast predicted it for the whole of London if the conditions remained. Within an hour it is now inevitable that we shall experience a deluge. Here and there damage will be done to trees and buildings; here and there a person will probably be struck and killed."

"Yes."

"It is Mr. Creake's intention that his wife should be among the victims."

"I don't exactly follow," said Hollyer, looking from one man to the other. "I quite admit that Creake would be immensely relieved if such a thing did happen, but the chance is surely an absurdly remote one."

"Yet unless we intervene it is precisely what a coroner's jury will decide has happened. Do you know whether your brother-in-law has any practical knowledge of electricity, Mr. Hollyer?"

"I cannot say. He was so reserved, and we really knew so little of him—"

"Yet in 1896 an Austin Creake contributed an article on 'Alternating Currents' to the American *Scientific World.*"

"But do you mean that he is going to direct a flash of lightning?"

"Only into the minds of the doctor who conducts the post-mortem, and the coroner. This storm, the opportunity for which he has been waiting for weeks, is merely the cloak to his act. The weapon which he has planned to use—scarcely less powerful than lightning but much more tractable—is the high-voltage current of electricity that flows along the tram wire at his gate."

"Oh!" exclaimed Lieutenant Hollyer.

"Some time between eleven o'clock tonight—about the hour when your sister goes to bed—and one thirty in the morning—the time up to which he can rely on the current—Creake will throw a stone up at the balcony window. Most of his preparation has long been made; it only remains for him to connect up a short length to the window handle and a longer one at the other end to tap the live wire. That done, he will wake his wife in the way I have said. The moment she moves the catch of the window—and he has carefully filed its parts to ensure perfect contact—she will be electrocuted as effectually as if she sat in the executioner's chair in Sing Sing prison."

"But what are we doing here!" exclaimed Hollyer, starting to his feet, pale and horrified. "It is past ten now and anything may happen."

"Quite natural, Mr. Hollyer," said Carrados, reassuringly, "but you need have no anxiety. Creake is being watched, the house is being watched, and your sister is as safe as if she slept tonight in Windsor Castle. Be assured that whatever happens he will not be allowed to complete his scheme; but it is desirable to let him implicate himself to the fullest limit. Your brother-in-law, Mr. Hollyer, is a man with a peculiar capacity for taking pains."

"He is a damned cold-blooded scoundrel!" exclaimed the young officer fiercely. "When I think of Millicent five years ago—"

"Well, for that matter, an enlightened nation has decided that electrocution is the most humane way of removing its superfluous citizens," suggested Carrados, mildly. "He is certainly an ingenious-minded gentleman. It is his misfortune that in Mr. Carlyle he was fated to be opposed by an even subtler brain—"

"No, no! Really, Max!" protested the embarrassed gentleman.

"Mr. Hollyer will be able to judge for himself when I tell him that it was Mr. Carlyle who first drew attention to the significance of the abandoned kite," insisted Carrados, firmly. "Then, of course, its object became plain to me—as indeed to anyone. For ten minutes, perhaps, a wire must be carried from the overhead line to the chestnut-tree. Creake has everything in his favor, but it is just within possibility that the driver of an inopportune tram might notice the appendage. What of that? Why, for more than a week he has seen a derelict kite with its yards of trailing string hanging in the tree. A very calculating mind, Mr. Hollyer. It would be interesting to know what line of action Mr. Creake has mapped out for himself afterwards. I expect he has half a dozen artistic little touches up his sleeve. Possibly he would merely singe his wife's hair, burn her feet with a red-hot poker, shiver the glass of the French door, and be content with that to let well alone. You see, lightning is so varied in its effects that whatever he did or did not do would be right. He is in the impregnable position of the body showing all the symptoms of death by lightning shock and nothing else but lightning to account for it—a dilated eye, heart contracted in systole, bloodless lungs shrunk to a third the normal weight, and all the rest of it. When he has removed a few outward traces of his work Creake might quite safely 'discover' his dead wife and rush off for the nearest doctor. Or he may have decided to arrange a convincing alibi, and creep away,

leaving the discovery to another. We shall never know; he will make
no confession."

"I wish it was over," admitted Hollyer.

"Three more hours at the worst, Lieutenant," said Carrados, cheerfully. "Ah-ha, something is coming through now."

He went to the telephone and received a message from one quarter;
then made another connection and talked a few minutes.

"Everything working smoothly," he remarked between times over
his shoulder. "Your sister has gone to bed, Mr. Hollyer."

Then he turned to the house telephone and distributed his orders.

"So we," he concluded, "must get going."

By the time they were ready a large closed motor-car was waiting.
The lieutenant thought he recognized Parkinson in the well-swathed
form beside the driver, but there was no temptation to linger on the
steps. Already the stinging rain had lashed the drive into the semblance of a frothy estuary; all around the lightning jagged its course
through the incessant tremulous glow of more distant lightning,
while the thunder only ceased its muttering to turn at close quarters
and crackle viciously.

"One of the few things I regret missing," remarked Carrados,
tranquilly; "but I hear a good deal of color in it."

"We are not going direct?" suddenly inquired Hollyer, after they
had traveled perhaps half a dozen miles.

"No; through Hunscott Green and then by a field path to the
orchard at the back," replied Carrados. "Keep a sharp lookout for
the man with the lantern about here, Harris," he called through the
tube.

"Something flashing just ahead, sir," came the reply, and the car
slowed down and stopped.

Carrados dropped the near window as a man in glistening water-
proof stepped from the shelter of a lich-gate and approached.

"Inspector Beedel, sir," said the stranger, looking into the car.

"Quite right, Inspector," said Carrados. "Get in."

"I have a man with me, sir."

"We can find room for him."

"We are very wet."

"So shall we all be soon."

The lieutenant changed his seat and the two burly forms took
places side by side. In less than five minutes the car stopped again,
this time in a grassy country lane.

"Now we have to face it," announced Carrados. "The inspector will show us the way."

The car slid round and disappeared into the night, while Beedel led the party to a stile in the hedge. A couple of fields brought them to the Brookbend boundary. There a figure stood out of the black foliage, exchanged a few words with their guide and piloted them along the shadows of the orchard to the back door.

"You will find a broken pane near the catch of the scullery window," said the blind man.

"Right, sir," replied the inspector. "I have it. Now, who goes through?"

"Mr. Hollyer will open the door for us. I'm afraid you must take off your boots and all wet things, Lieutenant. We cannot risk a single spot inside."

They waited until the back door opened, then each one divested himself in a similar manner and passed into the kitchen, where the remains of a fire still burned. The man from the orchard gathered together the discarded garments and disappeared.

Carrados turned to the lieutenant.

"A rather delicate job for you now, Mr. Hollyer. I want you to go up to your sister, wake her, and get her into another room with as little fuss as possible. Tell her as much as you think fit and let her understand that her very life depends on absolute stillness when she is alone. Don't be unduly hurried, but not a glimmer of a light."

Ten minutes passed by the measure of the battered old alarm on the dresser shelf before he returned.

"I've had rather a time of it," he reported, with a nervous laugh, "but I think it will be all right now. She is in the spare room."

"Then we will take our places. You and Parkinson come with me to the bedroom. Inspector, you have your own arrangements. Mr. Carlyle will be with you."

They dispersed silently about the house. Hollyer glanced apprehensively at the door of the spare room as they passed it, but within was as quiet as the grave. Their room lay at the other end of the passage.

"You may as well take your place in the bed now, Hollyer," directed Carrados when they were inside and the door closed. "Keep well down among the clothes. Creake has to get up on the balcony, you know, and he will probably peep through the window, but he dare come no farther. Then when he begins to throw up stones slip on this dressing-gown of your sister's. I'll tell you what to do."

The next sixty minutes drew out into the longest hour that the lieutenant had ever known. Occasionally he heard a whisper pass between the two men who stood behind the window curtains, but he could see nothing. Then Carrados threw a guarded remark in his direction.

"He is in the garden now."

Something scraped slightly against the outer wall. But the night was full of wilder sounds, and in the house the boards creaked and sprang between the yowling of the wind among the chimneys, the rattle of the thunder and the pelting of the rain. It was a time to quicken the steadiest pulse, and when the crucial moment came, when a pebble suddenly rang against the pane with a sound that the tense waiting magnified into a shivering crash, Hollyer leaped from the bed on the instant.

"Easy, easy," warned Carrados; feelingly. "We will wait for another knock." He passed something across. "Here is a rubber glove. I have cut the wire but you had better put it on. Stand just for a moment at the window, move the catch so that it can blow open a little, and drop immediately. *Now.*"

Another stone had rattled against the glass. For Hollyer to go through his part was the work merely of seconds. But an unforeseen and in the circumstances rather horrible interval followed, for Creake, in accordance with some detail of his never-revealed plan, continued to shower missile after missile against the panes until even the unimpressionable Parkinson shivered.

"The last act," whispered Carrados, a moment after the throwing had ceased. "He has gone round to the back. Keep as you are. We take cover now."

From half a dozen places of concealment ears were straining to catch the first guiding sound. Creake moved very stealthily, burdened, perhaps, by some strange scruple in the presence of the tragedy that he had not feared to contrive, paused for a moment at the bedroom door, then opened it very quietly, and in the fickle light read the consummation of his hopes.

"At last!" they heard the sharp whisper drawn from his relief. "At last!"

He took another step and two shadows seemed to fall upon him from behind, one on either side. With primitive instinct a cry of terror and surprise escaped him as he made a desperate movement to wrench himself free, and for a short second he almost succeeded in dragging one hand into a pocket. Then his wrists slowly came together and the handcuffs closed.

"I am Inspector Beedel," said the man on his right side. "You are charged with the attempted murder of your wife, Millicent Creake."

"You are mad," retorted Creake, falling into a desperate calmness. "She has been struck by lightning."

"No, you blackguard, she hasn't," wrathfully exclaimed his brother-in-law, jumping up. "Would you like to see her?"

"I also have to warn you," continued the inspector impassively, "that anything you say may be used as evidence against you."

A startled cry from the farther end of the passage arrested their attention.

"Mr. Carrados," called Hollyer, "oh, come at once."

At the open door of the other bedroom stood the lieutenant, his eyes still turned towards something in the room beyond, a little bottle in his hand.

"Dead!" he exclaimed tragically, with a sob, "with this beside her. Dead just when she would have been free of the brute."

The blind man passed into the room, sniffed the air, and laid a gentle hand on the pulseless heart.

"Yes," he replied. "That, Hollyer, does not always appeal to the woman, strange to say."

"Q"

Roy Vickers

Blind Man's Bluff

Roy Vickers was our most gifted practitioner of the "inverted" storytelling method invented by R. Austin Freeman. Vickers raised this detective-story method to new heights. His Department of Dead Ends stories relate the full case histories of unusual murders—"a minute and detailed description of the crime, setting forth the antecedents, motives, and all attendant circumstances." Readers "see the crime committed, know all about the criminal."

In the novelet, "Blind Man's Bluff," Robert Swilbey is compelled by circumstances to change from a promising young lawyer to a successful playwright. In the process Swilbey teaches himself how to create a new personality—rather how to split his personality—to meet each new condition in his life . . .

Detectives: DEPARTMENT OF DEAD ENDS

Until he committed murder, Robert Swilbey was a model citizen. Everyone admired him for one or another of his qualities, including the go-getters who admired only his business abilities. The example of his courage under a devastating affliction helped other sufferers. Many who knew him well would speak of him almost reverently.

Yet he was, in vulgar parlance, a tough guy, with a toughness that would have frightened any gangster who had brain enough to understand it—a toughness with which even Scotland Yard was impressed.

"That man," said Chief Inspector Karslake, "practises all the virtues as if they were vices." All that, from Karslake, after a single murder!

His father was a country solicitor who, perceiving Robert to be something exceptional, scraped and saved and sent him to the Bar. He died when Robert was twenty-three, leaving him about a thousand pounds. Having no influence, Robert at first secured only dock briefs in defense of impecunious criminals. Through these he soon attracted favorable attention. But as his income remained perilously low, he occupied his spare time in writing sketches for West End revues—cheeky little seven-minute playlets—with enough success to enable him to carry on at the Bar without dipping into his small reserve.

His knowledge of law was but little above the average, but his advocacy was of a high order, and he had the adroitness of an old hand in humoring his Judges. His early success was helped, in some measure, by his magnificent physique, his full-toned voice, and his handsome face. Win or lose, he always made the most of his case. As generally happens to young defenders who show consistent ability, the Crown gave him a chance to function as prosecutor.

In his fourth year at the Bar, when he was twenty-six, he earned nearly a thousand pounds—six hundred in practice—the balance deriving from a minute share in the royalties of a revue to which he had contributed three playlets. He was already crawling along the road to success—a road along which he intended to gallop.

He had surprised himself by falling in love with Mildred Keltson, the daughter of a doctor who had attended him for a trifling ailment. Women tended to favor him: he had had his share of adventures and believed himself free from the danger of a serious entanglement. But Mildred did not appear to him as an entanglement. Tall and exquisitely shaped, with grey-green eyes and chestnut hair, intelligent and perceptive but temperamentally docile, she attracted him as he had not been attracted before. Considered impartially, he told himself, she was an ideal wife for a man such as himself. He proposed and was accepted in February: they were to be married in the Easter vacation.

In this phase he is seen only as a successful young man obviously destined for a brilliant career. He was bumptious, but no more so than any other rising barrister, and certainly no tougher. The toughness was, as it were, flashed into being, a few days before the Easter vacation by a wretched woman called May Dinton, the associate of a burglar whom Swilbey was prosecuting.

It required no great ingenuity on Swilbey's part to destroy the alibi the girl was trying to create for her man. But he carried on for another hour and with some subtlety, extracted from her additional facts which aggravated the prisoner's guilt.

At dusk, when Swilbey was returning to his lodgings, May Dinton appeared from behind a pillar box.

"You got my boy seven years when the cops said the judge 'ud only give 'im three," she accused.

"My dear girl, what the cops say means nothing to me. I am sorry if you have been made unhappy, but you know that sort of thing is my job."

"You did more than you had to do for your pay. Twistin' my words round like that! You've made Ted think I ratted on him. But he won't think it any more—*now!*"

He had seen her draw a broad-stoppered bottle from under her coat: he supposed indifferently that she was about to swallow poison. He put up no guard—with the result that some three fluid ounces of vitriol splashed into his face.

On regaining consciousness after the operation, he asked when he would be likely to recover the use of his eyes. The doctor stalled, but broke down under Swilbey's expert questioning.

"Very well! Perhaps you'd better take the full shock while you are under our care. I am very sorry, Mr. Swilbey—there is no hope at all. Moreover—well, bluntly, old man, for appearance's sake, you'll have to wear two glass eyes."

"Thank you," said Swilbey. In the time it took to utter those two words he re-planned his career.

Inspector Karslake himself had come to the hospital. They were personally acquainted, and respected each other's work.

"D'you feel strong enough now, Mr. Swilbey, to tell us what happened?"

"I haven't the least idea."

It was not the smallest of Swilbey's achievements that he was able to think clearly while his body was racked with pain.

"We know it was May Dinton," prompted Karslake.

"But you can't prove it or we shouldn't be talking about it—you'd charge her. Sorry, Karslake! I can't afford vengeance. Got to be very economical. Got to avoid law courts. Got to forget I was once a lawyer."

The bumptious young barrister had been drowned in three ounces of vitriol, and Swilbey's unquenchable vitality was already creating a new personality, which had to be coddled during its infancy. He must forget May Dinton as well as the Law. The new personality must have no grievance against life, or it would not make the grade.

Through a nurse, he wrote to Mildred: *Please don't come to see me until the pain has passed. Pain in your presence would confuse me.*

These words show he was aware that, no matter how much his personality might change, he would still have a normal nervous system, would still be sensitive to the charm of women, with all its disturbances. Mildred, of course, would be in charge of that side of his life. So there need be no disturbances.

Mildred's father visited him every day. Swilbey found the visits tedious, except when they were talking about Mildred.

"You'll very soon feel well enough to let her come, won't you?"

"Practically ready now. Say the day after tomorrow."

"I'll tell her." Dr. Keltson cleared his throat. "There's one thing I want to mention before then. I can safely say that Mildred will keep her promise to marry you, if she sees that you wish to—er—hold her to it."

"There's no means by which a man can 'hold' a woman to such a promise."

"Oh, yes, there is, my friend!" The father was fighting for his daughter's happiness and dared not soften his words. "When Mildred accepted you, you were on the threshold of a brilliant career. She must have looked forward—quite properly—to sharing fame and prosperity with you. By a tragic accident you can now offer her only poverty and a treadmill of small services to yourself. Show that you expect her to stick to you, and she will. As would any woman of character."

Dr. Keltson had done his painful duty. The answer brought him but cold comfort.

"You want me to humbug her with a wistful little speech about my not having the right to blight her life. Wistfulness is not in my program. You needn't worry. I shall not blight her life. I shall give her a square deal."

He meant what he said. Indeed, Swilbey never lied to himself nor anyone else—except, eventually, to the police. But he failed to see that in the matter of Mildred he had appointed himself judge to his own cause—to his own ultimate ruin.

When she came to the hospital, he was still bandaged—was in a chair on a terrace overlooking the river. A motor launch was passing and he did not hear her approach.

"I'm here, Robert," she said and thrust her hand in his. The significance of having to announce herself to him upset her self-control. A tear dropped on his wrist.

"Darling, you've got the wrong slant on this!" he exclaimed eagerly. "To us it won't make any essential difference. I've adapted my thoughts to it and know I can manage it. Listen! Believe I'm telling the truth and not just trying to cheer you up. These last few seconds—while I've been holding your hand—I've taken a great leap forward. You've touched some nerve or other. I can *visualize!*"

"I'm glad, dear, but I don't understand. Go on talking about it—it'll make it easier."

"Darkness!" he exclaimed. "At first you're always waiting, waiting for the light. Having breakfast in total darkness! It muddles your other senses, produces a sort of animal fear. I found difficulty in thinking of things by their shape and color. But now—holding your hand—I can see the sun shining on your hair, making the wavy bit in front look like copper wire. I can get the angle of the sun, too. It doesn't matter a damn if the sun isn't actually shining at the moment. The important thing is that I can visualize the effect of light under the stimulus of an emotional urge—meaning you. That guarantees I shall be able to visualize stage lighting."

Fascinated by the mechanism of his own brain, he pursued his thoughts in silence, which she broke.

"While you're here, could I come every day to teach you Braille?"

"I'm not going to learn Braille—nor anything else the blind learn. I'm not going to be a blind man. I'm an ordinary man, who can't see."

That which she believed to be his pathetic courage, his gallant faith in the wreck of himself, destroyed her judgment—though it is easy to see, even at this stage, that there was no pathos in his courage, and that he had not been wrecked by his blindness.

"This is the program. I've got one toe in the theatre with those sketches. I intend to plant both feet. Now, when I've paid up here I shall have about fourteen hundred pounds, all told. I shall want five hundred for my working expenses, which will include the purchase of a dictaphone."

He proceeded to detail a practical plan of domestic finance. "Allow a hundred and fifty for our honeymoon and unforeseen expenses after we move in, and we shall have a reserve of eighteen months at the rate of five hundred a year. I shall be well in the swim within six months. Have you made notes of all this?"

"Yes, Robert." Prudence was awakening. Suppose he were not "well in the swim"—ever?

"If you'll see my bank manager we'll fix a power of attorney so

that you can deal with the checks and the contracts. Remember, I
can't sign my name. By the way, you'll have to do a lot of reading
for me at first. Shall you mind?"

She answered that she would not mind. Her tone made him ask:
"I say, darling! The program as a whole? Including me? I've been
rushing on, building a new life on your shoulders. Feel like it—or
not?"

She was, in the words of her father, a woman of character. To
leave him in the lurch would be utterly impossible. She bent and
kissed him.

"It will be wonderful—building together," she said, which was
exactly what he had expected her to say. He visualized the expression on her face as she said it. But the visualized expression was
quite different from her actual expression of honest doubt of herself
and him.

"I shall have these bandages off in a fortnight," he told her—and
altogether failed to visualize the shudder that followed his words.

For the next few years we see Robert Swilbey as the embodiment
of the virtues extolled in the literature of success. In him character
really did triumph against enormous odds. He did laugh at his set-
backs. He did believe that failure was impossible. Also, of course,
"luck came to him who earned it." His stage plays happened to be
adaptable to a certain comedian in whom Hollywood had sunk a
good deal of capital, and Swilbey's rates rose with each success.

In the first year he climbed on Mildred's shoulders more than he
realized. Indeed, Mildred herself did not know that it was she who
put him so quickly into the West End. His first full-length farcical
comedy was tried out in the provinces, seven months after their
wedding. It was undercapitalized and badly mounted and was in
some danger of collapse, when Turley Wain saw it in Liverpool.

Wain was a company promoter, mainly in the cotton market, with
no expert knowledge of the theatre, who had the amateur's belief
that he could spot a winner. He was impressed by Swilbey's dynamic
drive, but he was more impressed, in a different way, by Mildred's
courage and devoted care. He could see that he was in a position to
dictate terms, but in Mildred's presence he held his hand and let
Swilbey drive him. True that he eventually made money out of the
play. But Swilbey made so much that he was able to finance his
next play himself. Before the run had ended, Wain came to live in

London and thereafter saw much of Midred, without suspecting danger.

At the end of six years, living in affluence and with strong financial reserves, Swilbey believed that his marriage was as successful as his career. He was unaware that after the first eighteen months of struggle Mildred had been extremely unhappy. Even on their honeymoon, he had refused to perceive that her feeling for him had become exclusively maternal and protective. This feeling had been steadily thwarted by his progressive efficiency.

While they were still comparatively poor she had the arduous task of keeping him abreast of events and ideas by reading to him for long stretches every day. Then she had to take him for walks and in the intervals run the home with inadequate assistance. But the comradeship of it sustained her, gave her a sense of fulfillment.

Yet even in this first phase of their marriage, she had what one may call the first premonition of the ultimate disaster. She took her fear to her father.

"He drives himself so hard, Daddy. And although in a way it's all so splendid, I'm a little worried as to whether it's quite—healthy. I know you'll think I'm a fool—I think so myself—but this happens. When we're discussing plans for the week, he speaks as if he and I were making arrangements about someone else. He even says: '*he* must go to that rehearsal, and if we can get *him* back in good time we'll let *him* try a re-write of that last scene before *he* goes to bed.' The frightening part is that it's not meant to be funny. He only speaks like that when he is very concentrated."

"There's nothing in that," said Dr. Keltson. "I suspect you've been reading some stuff about split personality without, my dear, quite understanding what you read. I'm no psychiatrist, but I can tell you that, though it does attack exceptionally clever people sometimes, there's no fear at all with a balanced, mentally disciplined man like Robert. I've never met any man I admire more—for mental discipline, I mean."

Six years later she again approached her father on the same subject.

"He's begun to 'split' me now," she told him. "Yesterday, I read a contract to him. He said: "Ah! *There's* something for him to tell his wife!" And he did tell me, last night. He always does tell me how wonderful he is. This time he spoke as if I knew nothing about the contract."

Dr. Keltson was still unimpressed. He asked: "Anything else? Has he any morbid habits?"

"Not that I know of. But I see so little of him except for business, or when others are there. He won't go for walks any more. He 'goes for a row' in that rowing contraption in the gym that makes a noise like a real boat on real water. And a bicycle-thing that can make him feel he's going up and down hills. And he has a journalist to read to him. If anything gets in his way he invents an expensive gadget so that he need not ask me to help him. He has so built things round him—things and persons—that I don't believe he any longer wishes he could see. Perhaps that's morbid."

"You aren't happy with him, Mildred, are you?"

"No!" She added: "What makes it uncanny is that he *is* happy with me. I suppose I'm beastly to him pretty often. It never hurts his feelings. He never retaliates—just cleverly makes me feel ashamed of myself. And then"—she shuddered—"we make up!"

"Well, at least he is loyal to you. At the back of my mind—"

"Loyal?" It was as if she asked herself a question. "Women run after him. He's so big and strong—and handsome, if you can ignore his poor, staring eyes. But I think he's afraid they might put him out of his stride. He's positively Victorian with them. When he's going to rehearse a new actress he sends for me. He says to the girl: 'It's essential that I should be able to visualize you. May I touch you?' And then I have to chip in and say something pleasant."

"At the back of my mind—"

" '*May I touch you!*' " she repeated bitterly. "With me standing by to make it impersonal and uncompromising. That's what I'm for. I'm not his wife. I'm just—*women!*"

"At the back of my mind, my dear girl, there has been for some time the feeling that I ought to warn you that there are whispers about your friendship with Mr. Wain. I know there can be nothing in it—but there it is!"

About the same time the whisper reached Swilbey.

Every Tuesday night Swilbey gave a party in his house in St. John's Wood, a couple of miles from theatreland. For the rest of the week he was strictly not-at-home to anybody to whom he had not given a definite appointment.

In the lofty L-shaped drawing-room that was also his working room he would hold an inner court round his gadget-laden armchair. Now and again he would rise and walk among his guests, who were required merely to avoid impeding his progress. His system enabled him always to know where he was standing in his house or in the theatre. On first nights he could walk unaided to the proper spot from which to take his author's call—for which purpose he wore spectacles and a careful makeup; for he did not wish his public to know that he "could not see."

It was by the bend of the "L" that he overheard the whisper; and for the first time since he lost his sight he found himself shirking a reality.

For some days he vacillated. Mildred's behavior to himself was the same as it had been for years. He worked out ways of asking her for details—a frank approach. But in his heart he was afraid of receiving a frank answer that would break the smooth routine of his career. On the fourth day he wrote to Wain, under a thin pretense of being able to offer him another flutter in the theatre.

He received him, as he received everybody, alone in the drawing-room.

"I say, old man! Some infernal scandalmongers have been coupling your name and Mildred's. I thought you and I had better get together about it. Cards on the table and all that!"

He was alarmed by the length of the pause before Wain answered.

"Before I say anything else, Swilbey, I have nothing to confess to you. I've never so much as touched her hand. I can't imagine what is being said. We have always taken care not to give the talkers a chance."

That killed the last hope that there might be nothing in it. Wain seemed to think that Mildred had already discussed it.

"I'd better go on." Wain's voice sounded unctuous and sentimental. "I've been in love with her for years, and shall be all my life. But I doubt whether she knows it's any more than friendship. Anyhow, if circumstances were normal I would speak to her—then ask you for a divorce. I've told you all there is to tell, Swilbey."

"I appreciate that." The fellow, thought Swilbey, was a mere sentimentalist, who would run from a challenge. "But I don't follow that bit about 'normal circumstances.' Why not speak to her? I have never regarded women as property. I stake no prior claim. How do we know she wouldn't be happier with you?"

Sentimentalist or not, Wain shook the edifice of six years with his answer.

"Swilbey, you asked for cards on the table. So you'll let me say that we both know she would be happier with me—if I could retain my self-respect. But how could I? Knowing I had taken his wife from a blind man?"

In the recesses of Swilbey's brain, a voice was speaking about Swilbey: *That'll upset him—calling him a blind man! Mind he doesn't do anything rash.*

Through darkness the other voice, that of Wain, penetrated.

"To Mildred, your well-being is a sacred mission, Swilbey. Her power of attorney has more than legal significance. She stands between you and the outside world with which you could not cope, even with all your assistants and servants. You would be the first to acknowledge that you owe your career not only to your own qualities but also to hers."

Again came the illusion of an inner voice speaking: *Look out! That'll make him worse. Wain is telling him that he's a blind man living on the charity of his wife's eyes.*

"I quite agree." Swilbey's voice was calm as ever. "By the way, years ago—when I was starting—did you finance my play because of Mildred?"

"N-no. At least, I don't think so. Not altogether. Does it matter, now?"

The personality had been thumped into numbness. Only the mannerisms remained active—and some resolution he did not yet understand. Swilbey rose from his chair.

"I'm glad we've had this talk. One way and another, Wain, you've been a factor in my life. I would like to be able to visualize you. May I touch you?"

"Of course! I'm a shrimp compared with you."

"Yes, you're shorter. And you've kept slim." The hands crept lightly to the head, crept over the features, outlining the heavy, prominent chin with a dimple in it, crept below the chin to the throat—

Don't let him do anything rash!

But how would it be possible to keep "him" quiet? For the first time for six years consciousness of the perpetual darkness returned, and with it the animal fear.

At six o'clock, Menceman, the journalist, came as usual with a digest of the day's papers. Swilbey barely heard a word throughout the hour's reading. At seven-thirty, when he was going upstairs to prepare for dinner, he crashed into the balustrade.

The parlormaid, who had been with him for years, gasped with astonishment. Never before had she seen him miss his direction.

"Have you hurt yourself, sir?"

"No, thanks. My foot slipped," he lied.

That evening, alone with Mildred in her little sitting-room upstairs, he got up to go to bed, faltered, and then: "Will you take me to my room, please?"

Sheer astonishment made her ask: "Why, Robert?"

"Because I'm blind!" he cried, and broke down like a child.

The next day Mildred beat down his protests and took him for a holiday up the river where he could scull for hours while she steered. The first nervous crisis passed. She made no mention of Wain.

He evolved, during that holiday, an interim personality—an understudy to sustain the role of Robert Swilbey. All the mannerisms were faithfully copied, but the inspiration was lacking. The interim personality could not write dialogue that sparkled with clever nonsense. He was working then on *Playgirl Wanted*, but had to abandon it before he had completed the first act.

"Menceman, I'm going to try my hand at straight drama. I shall have a background of police work, treated realistically. You might begin by going through the verbatim reports of trials, picking out the small points overlooked by intelligent murderers."

Now and again, the inner voice would register a half-hearted warning. *He's planning to kill Wain. Better humor him.*

"David Durham advised me to have a model theatre on the table beside me, as he does," he told Mildred. "Of course, my sense of touch isn't developed enough for that sort of thing. But I could rig up a model stage at the other end of the drawing-room." He meant at the short end of the "L." "Scale about one to four I should think. I could use it, too, for rehearsing special scenes."

He spent sixteen hundred pounds on what became not a model but a miniature stage, with many of the fitments of a full-sized stage. Unable to concentrate enough for original work, he rehearsed revivals on the miniature stage.

At rehearsals he necessarily worked through a subordinate stage manager.

"I want to be able to handle the rigging myself—get the feel of the controls," said Swilbey, because he now knew that he intended to hang Wain, thereby giving the murder the outward semblance of an execution.

There is no doubt that Swilbey planned the murder of Wain in minute detail. But there is considerable doubt whether he meant to carry it out. Remember that daydreams and fancies and castles-in-the-air possess a special kind of reality to a playwright—they become as real to him as a parcel of speculative shares is to a business man.

In a sense, Swilbey soothed his wounded ego by murdering Wain every night. The taunt of being a blind man, who could only hold his woman by invoking her pity, was nightly avenged by the fatal blow that was not actually struck. Nightly, too, the heads of Scotland Yard were made to confess themselves beaten by the dazzling brilliance of Robert Swilbey—a man who, as it happened, could not see.

Certain it is that for two years he made no attempt to use the "engine of death," as counsel called it—more simply, the essential parts of a gallows, disguised as rigging for shifting scenes and the heavier stage properties. Nor did he take any step to lure Wain to the house. Ironically, Wain was, as it were, put on the spot by Mildred herself.

"I want to ask something of you, Robert," she began. "About Turley Wain. It's two years now since he gave you an explanation. He told me at the time that you had been very kind to him."

"He was very kind to me. I told him I'd fix a divorce, if you wanted it."

He hoped she would say she had never, and would never, want a divorce. But she did not. The darkness came down on him again.

"We exchanged parting gifts. I have only seen him once since then. Today. He is very changed. I drew from him that things have gone very badly with him, and he expects to be made bankrupt. Will you help him?"

"Of course, I will! Apart from your friendship with him, he did me a good turn when he financed *Brenda Gets Married.*"

He felt her approaching. The darkness vanished as he visualized her physical beauty against the background of a sun-lit flower garden. She thanked him warmly—because he had said he would help Turley Wain.

"When shall I tell him to come and see you about it?"

In the nightly murder Wain always arrived at five-thirty on a winter afternoon. And Mildred was always out of the house. He reminded himself now that, on Fridays, Mildred always visited her parents, who were in retirement in Canterbury.

"Next Friday at five-thirty," he answered, and added: "February fifteenth—my birthday—good omen for Wain!"

It was about five-thirty when he came, Inspector. I was in the rehearsal theatre. I showed him the tackle for shifting the heavier pieces.

That was part of the scene in which the police, every night, were "hopelessly baffled."

On Friday Mildred left for Canterbury after lunch; she would stay for dinner, returning on the last train.

At five-thirty precisely, the parlormaid announced Wain. Speaking from the miniature stage, Swilbey greeted him with the opening lines composed two years ago.

"Hullo, Wain! I've just finished here. You haven't seen this little rigout before, have you?" Swilbey could hear the parlormaid drawing the curtains. He spoke loudly enough for her to hear. "It's the engineering I'm proud of. Have to haul everything up to the flies when we want a change. With the double reduction on these pulleys, a child could manage it—designed the whole thing myself. How's that for a blind man, eh! Have a cigarette?"

He felt for his cigarette case in one pocket and another. Like many a sighted man, he was never sure of his pockets.

"You dropped it on that bench, sir." The parlormaid left the curtains, hurried to the stage, recovered the cigarette case, and handed it to Swilbey.

Wain, who did not know that the very word "blind" was a danger signal, made polite murmurs. When Swilbey heard the parlormaid draw the last curtain, he said:

"Let's go and sit down. I won't bother to put the tackle away."

Back together down the short arm of the "L," a left turn into the long arm, to his armchair and the group of chairs round it. Swilbey felt the hands of his watch. Five thirty-four. Not a minute to waste.

"Mildred told me you might go bankrupt. How much do you want?"

"Bankruptcy is one thing. There's another!" Judging by his voice, Wain had gone to pieces—he was almost cringing. "To leave out technicalities, I got caught in a landslide, Swilbey. I swear to you I didn't try to save myself at the expense of others. I threw in all my own resources, including even my furniture, when I need not have done so. It wasn't nearly enough. In trying to save the investments of others I committed a technical breach of the criminal law. At this moment I am actually wanted by the police."

"Better give me the figures!" Thirty-eight minutes past five. The babble must not last more than another four minutes. And he mustn't forget Wain's cigarette. It might set the house on fire—which would disarrange the plan.

Wain seemed to shrink from coming to the point.

"Last week a detective came to see me. Very decent fellow. Kars-lake. He knew you when you were at the Bar. I drew wool over his eyes because I didn't want to be arrested there and then. And now I'm keeping out of his way."

"Wain, old man, how much do you want?"

"The technical breach—well, five thousand pounds would cover that. But look here, Swilbey, I've no excuse for asking you."

"Yes, you have. You and Mildred together made it possible for a blind man to make a living. My career pivots on you two. She hinted that you might want a wad of ready cash. Come with me."

Swilbey felt some squeamishness in promising money that would never be given. But there is no gentlemanly method of committing murder.

"D'you mind putting your cigarette out, old man? Have to be careful of fire where we're going."

On the way back round the turn of the "L," to the rehearsal the-atre, he asked:

"And what about the bankruptcy?"

"Astronomical! Fifty thousand pounds, if a penny!"

"Hm! We'll have to talk about that later. We're going over the stage. That door at the back is still in use. All right! I can manage. In their own place, the blind can manage as if they were not blind. Mind that pulley!"

Wain, as he had himself said, was a shrimp beside Swilbey. More-over, he did not know how to use what little weight and strength he had. So the "compensatory fantasy" was translated into reality without muscular strain.

When Wain was dead, Swilbey turned on the main switch which flooded the stage with light. The room lights of the short arm of the "L" had been turned on by the parlormaid.

The parlormaid! Halfway to the corner he stopped. He had had a sudden mental picture of the parlormaid handing him his cigarette case after he had dropped it on the bench.

"If I've dropped anything this time—"

He went back to the stage and groped on the bench: he was leaving when his foot touched something on the floor which ought not to have been there. He bent down.

"That damned case again!" Like frightened snakes, his fingers slid over the tessellated pattern of the slim gold case. "Phew! I had a sort of intuition. Subconscious memory. Good! It means 'he' won't make any mistakes!"

He thrust the case into his breast pocket and hurried away.

At four mintues to six Swilbey, back in his gadget-laden armchair, switched on the radio. Luck again came to him who had earned it. A drama critic was talking.

At six punctually, just as the radio critic was finishing, Menceman, the journalist, came in.

Swilbey turned off the radio and spoke as if Wain were sitting near him.

"Wain," he said, "let me introduce Mr. Menceman who—"

"There's no one in the room but ourselves, Mr. Swilbey."

"Oh, then Wain must have slipped out—I had to listen to that critique! My fairy godfather. Backed my first play. Badly hit in the Slump. Let's have the Slump news first."

There was no fear of Menceman strolling about the room, turning the bend of the "L" and seeing the corpse.

Swilbey gave his full attention. The plan was fulfilling itself. Menceman would leave at seven. By domestic routine a housemaid would discover the body of Turley Wain at seven-thirty, by which time he would be in his room dressing for dinner.

But at nine minutes to seven the sequence of the plan was broken by the house telephone.

"An officer from Scotland Yard, sir. Chief Inspector Karslake. He wants to speak to Mr. Wain."

For a second only Swilbey hesitated.

"Mr. Wain left a long time ago. But tell Mr. Karslake I would like to see him if he can spare the time."

With a nod he dismissed Menceman and concentrated on the problem of the detective.

Swilbey held out his hand and waited, as the blind do, for Karslake to grip it.

"It's good to see you after all these years, Mr. Swilbey. I always take the wife to one of your plays when I get the chance."

"And it's good to hear your voice!" echoed Swilbey. "We must have a chat sometime. At present you've got something on your mind, and Wain has told me what it is. You may take it that will be settled at once—in full."

"Well, I'm glad to hear it, since he's a friend of yours. All the same, I can't stop the machinery at this stage, as you know. Can I see him, please?"

"He's not here," said Swilbey. "Left about six."

There was a short, strained silence.

"Mr. Swilbey, his coat and hat are in your vestibule."

"Surely not! Wait a minute." On the house telephone he spoke to the parlormaid.

"What time did Mr. Wain leave?"

"He hasn't left, sir. I thought he was in the drawing room with you."

Swilbey repeated the girl's words.

"Then d'you mean to say he sneaked out of the room without saying goodbye or anything?" asked Karslake.

"Apparently, he did. I'd told him what I could do for him, and we'd really finished. I asked him to excuse me for a few minutes as I wanted to hear the end of a dramatic critique on the radio. At six, when Menceman came in—you saw him just now—I began to introduce them, when Menceman told me Wain wasn't here."

Karslake noted a half-smoked cigarette on the ashtray by his side: nothing in the tray within Swilbey's reach. That tallied with what Swilbey was saying.

"He left the room, then, but not the house," said Karslake.

"He wouldn't wander about my house without permission," asserted Swilbey. "It's much more likely that he heard Menceman arrive and thought it was you coming to collect him. He was in a very nervy state."

"If he left the house—without his hat and coat—which way did he go?" pressed Karslake.

Swilbey had seen that question coming—had seen, too, that he was in no danger, provided he did not shirk the logic of his position.

"He could have got into the garden by going through the door at the back of my rehearsal stage, and along the corridor. That door was locked on this side. If he slipped out that way, it must be unlocked now."

"Can I have a look at that door?"

Swilbey stood up.

"Come with me," he invited. "The stage is in this room—round the corner."

Karslake followed Swilbey round the corner of the "L." A corpse, as such, could not shake Karslake's nerve. But his nerve was shaken this time, partly because he thought, for a second or two, that the corpse was a stage property.

Looking some thirty feet down the short arm of the "L," he saw a well-lit stage-set of a saloon bar. Left back, at an angle, was the bar, with shining pump handles; left, a pin-table; right, a bench in green plush; and centre, a human form suspended by its neck in what appeared to be a noose attached to the hook of a pulley block.

Two paces nearer he recognized the features of Turley Wain.

"What?" Swilbey stopped in his stride. "Did you speak?"

"No. It's all right." Karslake was thinking quickly. "Carry on, please, Mr. Swilbey."

Swilbey, a couple of feet ahead, walked on. With the steadiness of a sighted man, he stepped on to the stage. He passed within a dozen inches of the man who was obviously dead. So to the back of the miniature stage.

"Nothing doing!" exclaimed Swilbey. "The door is still locked on this side."

Fascinated, Karslake watched Swilbey return, wondering whether, this time, he would collide with the dangling corpse. Again there were a dozen inches to spare. Perhaps, he reflected, the blind always walked in the same track in familiar surroundings.

"Surely it isn't worth investigating, Karslake! The charge against him is pretty certain to be dropped, after restitution. Forget it for a few minutes and have a drink."

"That sounds like a good idea," said Karslake, who had meantime satisfied himself that there was no hope of saving life.

Back, with the blind man, round the corner of the "L" to his chair. Swilbey sat down. Sitting gave him the range of all the gadgets. He leaned forward and opened the door of a cabinet.

"Whiskey, gin or—"

"Whiskey, please." Karslake glanced uneasily at a row of decanters. "Allow me!"

"It's all right, thanks. You sit down." Swilbey's voice had a slight edge to it. He passed his guest the whiskey decanter, a tumbler and a siphon, then held out his hand for the return of the decanter.

"Can I pour yours for you, Mr. Swilbey?"

"No, thanks!" Swilbey's tone barely escaped rudeness.

Karslake watched Swilbey pour his own drink with a deftness that made his hands seem like independent agents, able to think and act for themselves. Meantime, he was groping for a line of action. That corpse, actually in the same room with them, presented a tricky problem in presence of mind.

"Cigarette, Karslake?"

"Oh—er—thanks!"

Swilbey thrust his hand into his breast pocket for his cigarette case—kept it there for seconds as if his arm were paralyzed. Then he tried his side pockets.

Karslake saw a thin, tessellated gold cigarette case on the ledge, flush with the dictaphone. But he had observed that Swilbey was very touchy about being helped. So Karslake said nothing.

"Dammit, I thought I had my case on me!"

Karslake was glad of the respite. His mind on the corpse, he watched Swilbey's hand creeping, spiderlike, along the ledge by the dictaphone.

"Ah, here it is!"

For an instant the hand hovered, quivering over the case as if it were puzzled. Karslake dismissed this eerie fancy, took the offered cigarette, and made his decision.

"To come back to Wain for a moment," said Karslake, "you might tell me exactly what happened while he was here."

This was the cue for the scene in which the police were "hopelessly baffled."

He had but to repeat the oft-repeated words.

"It was about five-thirty when he came. I was in the rehearsal theatre. I showed him the tackle for shifting the heavier pieces. Then we came back here and talked. He told me he had committed a technical breach of the criminal law and that he was playing tag with you. Mentioned you by name and said you remembered me. I said I'd let him have the five thousand in the morning. Then he explained that he would be in for a civil bankruptcy to the tune of fifty thousand pounds. I said bluntly I couldn't manage that much—after which things became mildly unpleasant."

"What sort of unpleasantness?"

"After I'd turned down the fifty thousand idea, he said something about the five thousand being wasted—that it would be cheaper for all if he jumped off Waterloo Bridge on a dark night—the usual suicide threat that is never implemented. Between ourselves, Karslake, I don't like that man. He financed my first play. I admit he was thundering useful to me at the time, and I'm glad to let him have the five thousand. Fifty thousand is another pair o' shoes. So I made the excuse that I had to listen to the radio critique. And I suppose he buzzed off in a huff as well as a panic.

"He's coming here tomorrow morning for the five thousand, and he's sure to surrender to you as soon as he's got it, so you don't have to worry. Have another drink?"

"No thanks. May I use your telephone?"

Karslake dialed the Yard, asked for an internal number, then gave Swilbey's address.

"Homicide!" said Karslake. "I'll be here when the team arrives." He hung up. "Wain is on that stage of yours, Mr. Swilbey—with his neck in that scene-shifting tackle."

"My God! Doing it in my house!" exclaimed Swilbey. "That's a dirty, malicious trick, Karslake! The publicity will do me no good—no darned good at all."

It was near the truth to say that Robert Swilbey was disappointed when it appeared that the police were not "baffled"—that they hadn't the wit to see that there was anything to be baffled about. On the other hand, he received, in the Coroner's court, a severe shock which put him momentarily in fear of his life. For the Coroner described exactly how Wain had been murdered—which Swilbey had thought no one could ever guess.

"Accident," said the Coroner to his jury, when all the evidence had been heard, "may be ruled out. If you are to return a positive verdict, therefore, you must decide between murder and suicide. Let us consider what evidence, if any, supports the theory of murder."

He dwelt on the virtual impossibility of anyone entering the drawing-room without the servants or Swilbey being aware of it—he elaborated obvious absurdities.

"Apart from such absurdities, you have to postulate—to sustain the hypothesis of murder—a very powerful man who suddenly attacked the deceased, constricting his victim's throat so that he could not cry out—or the servants, to say nothing of Mr. Swilbey, would have heard him. For this purpose he used a curtain cord, an item in the fittings of the stage set. This hypothetical murderer then proceeded, in the clumsiest possible manner, to attach his victim to the hook on the pulley block.

"As you have been told, the device of a noose, or slip-knot, was not employed. A curtain cord, itself a stage property securing a curtain on the stage set, was wound round the throat of the deceased in such a manner as to make four complete coils. This cord was tied at the back of deceased's neck with three knots—the kind of simple knot which one uses for one's shoe laces, the difference being that this simple knot was tied three times instead of once. Through three of the coils, the hook beneath the pulley block was inserted, greatly increasing the pressure of the coils round the neck. The hands were unbound. Medical evidence as to the condition of the hands—and microscopic examination of the ropes above the pulley block—make it clear that the unhappy man attempted to free himself by reaching above his head and pulling on the ropes.

"Why did our hypothetical murderer permit this attempt to frustrate his purpose? Add that this eccentric murderer must have swung the dead, or unconscious, body in such a way that the shoes could be pressed into the upholstery of the bench—and you may come to the conclusion that no such person as the murderer existed."

The Coroner had reconstructed the murder in order to ridicule the theory of murder. As a dramatist, Swilbey knew the danger of playing tricks like that on an audience, who would sometimes pick up an unexpected angle. But the fact of his blindness—above all, Karslake's evidence of his behavior in the presence of the corpse—headed off suspicion.

Swilbey's dread was dispelled when the Coroner went on to say what Swilbey had intended him to say.

"On the hypothesis of suicide the deceased slipped silently away when Mr. Swilbey turned on the radio. After adjusting the pulley to the height he required, he wound the curtain cord round his throat, as one might wind a narrow scarf, and tied it, as described, at the back. He stood on the bench, worked the hook under the coils, then swung himself off the bench. Police measurements, on the chart before you, show that the ropes would then swing, pendulum-wise, to the centre of the stage, bringing the feet of the deceased within three and a half inches of the floor.

"Like many a suicide and would-be suicide before him, he repented of his act before it had been completed, and tried to interrupt it. Had he secured himself with a noose, he would in all probability have succeeded. To free the hook from the coils of curtain cord was a great deal more difficult than loosening a slip-knot—doubly so, through the fact that his jaw was large and prominent."

The jury, ever ready to believe that a simple explanation must be the true one, accepted the Coroner's interpretation. Only Chief Inspector Karslake was heard to mumble that the suicide had been clear-headed enough to measure the pendulum swing, correct to three and a half inches. After a verdict of suicide while of unsound mind, public interest in the case evaporated.

On the evening following the inquest, Robert Swilbey resumed work on the first act of *Playgirl Wanted*, abandoned two years previously. The play was put on the following autumn. It ran all through the following year.

Eighteen months later he was at work on another play—when the end came.

A junior detective from another department flung open the door of the Department of Dead Ends and ushered in a seedy individual with patched trousers but a very decent sports coat.

"This is Mr. Joe Byker, sir," said the detective facetiously. "Hensons', the pawnbrokers, 'phoned us. Mr. Byker was trying to pawn this." He laid on the table a slim gold cigarette case with a tessellated design. "Mr. Byker says the case is his and he bought it with his own money."

Among the burglaries, petty thefts and whatnot in Detective-Inspector Rason's file were eleven missing gold cigarette cases, five with tessellated design. He opened the case in the hope of finding some identifying mark.

For Remembrance he read. No name. No initials.

"You bought it, eh, Byker! From a man in a pub whose name you don't know?"

"No, sir. I bought it right enough, a matter o' six weeks ago, off a respectable dealer name o' Clawson's, Theobalds Road."

"They're second-hand clothes dealers, Byker."

"That's right, sir. Matter o' six weeks ago I bought this 'ere sports coat as I'm wearin' this very minute, sir, and I didn't know till this morning when I was havin' me breakfast that I'd bought that cigarette-case with it. In here it was, sir." He took the coat off. "In between these two bits o' stiffening—that's where I had to cut the lining to get it out. And me walking about with it for a matter of six weeks."

Clawson, the dealer, was able to supply the name and address of the man from whom he had bought the sports coat. Interviewed by Rason, the vendor of the coat was inclined to be indignant.

"Yes, I sold it to Clawson's—and what's the matter with that? The missis gave it to me to do what I liked with."

"And who is the missis?"

"Mrs. Swilbey—wife of the gentleman who writes all them plays. I'm his gardener."

Swilbey, a writer of plays! In a few minutes Rason remembered the freak suicide of eighteen months ago. Byker would drop in for "stealing by finding" if Mrs. Swilbey would consent to prosecute, he reflected on his way to the house in St. John's Wood.

"Perhaps you could tell me, Mrs. Swilbey whether this is your husband's cigarette case?"

"It looks like it. I wonder where he dropped it!"

Mildred took the case, opened it, and caught her breath.

"No," she said. "It is not my husband's."

"But you do know whose it is, Mrs. Swilbey!" It was a statement, not a question.

"It belonged to a friend of ours who—is dead. A Mr. Wain. I gave it to him myself. It is exactly like the one I gave to my husband—bought at the same place. That's why I thought at first it was his."

"Mr. Wain," repeated Rason. "I remember. Very sad. You're sure this is the case you gave Mr. Wain?"

"Quite!" She added the name of the jeweler where she had bought both cases. "How did it come into your hands, Mr. Rason?"

"It has been stolen," answered Rason, and bowed himself out.

He checked up at the jeweler's, then decided reluctantly that he must bring Chief Inspector Karslake into it.

"He was a lawyer once," warned Karslake, as it was Rason's case. "You won't get him to admit anything. But I'll stooge you all I can."

At five-thirty that afternoon they were being shown into the "L" shaped drawing-room. Karslake introduced Rason with a somewhat elaborate heartiness.

"I've got to worry you about the estate in bankruptcy of the late Turley Wain, Mr. Swilbey," said Rason.

"Before we start, Mr. Swilbey," cut in Karslake, "d'you mind if we smoke?"

"Do! Here, have a cigarette!" Swilbey felt ın one pocket and then another, then found his cigarette case on the ledge that was flush with the dictaphone. "I don't know anything about Wain's affairs."

Rason observed the cigarette case. It looked exactly like Wain's—the same tessellated design. It would feel the same to a blind man—and that was all Rason wanted to know.

"What an extraordinary thing!" exclaimed Rason. "That case is exactly like Turley Wain's." He added carefully. "You may remember—it dropped out of Wain's pocket—onto the floor of your stage—during the poor chap's struggles."

There was a tiny perceptible stiffening of the large frame. But it was the long pause that made Rason sure of his ground.

"I don't remember, because I was never told," said Swilbey.

"You didn't need telling! You picked the cigarette case up after you had killed him. You thought it was yours, put it in your pocket.

It was in your pocket when you were sitting in here, offering Mr. Karslake a cigarette."

"Any ass can make wild assertions!" snapped Swilbey. "Are you in this foolery, Karslake?"

"Well, Mr. Swilbey, I must say I do remember your offering me a cigarette out of a gold case."

"Then I wonder, my dear Karslake—" Swilbey had pounced as, years ago, he would pounce on a witness "—I wonder whether you also remember that the case was *not* in my pocket, as I thought it was, but on this ledge here?"

"Y-yes, I do remember, now you mention it, Mr. Swilbey." Karslake spoke as one making a reluctant admission. "Rason, I think you'll have to apologize."

"Wait a minute!" said Rason. "*Suppose* the case on the ledge there, out of which he offered you a cigarette, was his own case? And *suppose* Wain's case, which Swilbey had put in his pocket, had slipped down the lining. And *suppose*—"

"Suppose my grandmother's foot!" Swilbey emitted a roar of laughter. "Karslake, haven't you taught this man any evidence?" Swilbey leaned forward in the direction of Rason. "My good man! If you could prove that I put Wain's cigarette case in my pocket—eighteen months ago, mark you!—we would not be talking about it. Mr. Karslake would charge me with murder—wouldn't you, Karslake?"

"Yes," said Chief Inspector Karslake. In sudden silence, the distant rumble of traffic seemed to fill the vast drawing-room. Presently Karslake added: "Perhaps you'd like to ring the bell, Swilbey, and tell them to pack you a suitcase?"

"Q"